RED
WINTER
JOURNEY

Printed in Australia

First Printing: April 2022

Shawline Publishing Group Pty Ltd
www.shawlinepublishing.com.au

Paperback ISBN- 9781922701510

Ebook ISBN- 9781922701565

A catalogue record for this
book is available from the
National Library of Australia

Paul Rushworth-Brown

About the Author:

Paul Rushworth-Brown was born in the United Kingdom in 1962. He was educated at Charles Sturt University in New South Wales, Australia. Paul became a writer in 2015 when he embarked on a six-month project to produce a written family history for his children, Rachael, Christopher and Hayley. Through this research, he developed a passion for writing, and 'Red Winter Journey' is the sequel to his first novel 'Skulduggery', a written portrait of the way his ancestors lived.

Come along on this historic fictional, adventurous and mysterious journey that twists, turns and surprises until the very end. If you like history, adventure and intrigue with a dash of spirited love, then you will be engrossed by this tale of a peasant family getting caught up in the ravages of the English Civil War in 1642.

The story keeps readers on edge, surprising them with twists, turns and mystery, all the while painting a vivid picture that places you in the time and in the place. The comical, crudeness of the writing mirrors times when peasants were a lowly, uneducated, rough lot, but this only adds to this realistic and vibrant tale.

Reading this novel, one can immerse themselves within this factually accurate tale and discover the more colourful, candid details of what it may have been like to live in this rebellious time.

ANOTHER NOVEL BY PAUL RUSHWORTH-BROWN

SKULLDUGGERY

A historical fictional story set on the West Yorkshire Moors follows wee Thomas and his family shortly after losing his father to consumption.

Times were hard in 1590, and there were shenanigans and skulduggery committed by locals and outsiders alike. Good Queen Bess has died, and King James sits on the throne of England and Scotland.

Thomas is now the man of the house, being the older of the two boys. He is set to marry Agnes in an arranged marriage, but a love story develops between them. This rollicking adventure paints a descriptive picture of the characters, the hardships and the landscape they fill. The writer keeps us in suspense till the final pages, where one hopes good will triumph over evil.

Contents

PLAN, VI.

LANDS in HAWORTH.

Glossary:

Aye up: Hi

Bairn: Child

Beggar-maker: Publican

Breeches: an article of clothing covering the body from the waist down, with separate coverings for each leg, usually stopping just below the knee.

Cavalier: a term of abuse for the wealthier Royalist supporters of King Charles I and his son Charles II of England during the English Civil War

Copyholder: a form of customary tenure of land common in England

Curate: a member of the clergy engaged as assistant to a vicar, rector, or parish priest.

Demesne: a piece of land attached to a manor and retained by the owner for their own use.

Dog lock pistol: a type of lock for firearms that preceded the 'true' flintlock in rifles, muskets, and pistols in the 17th century.

Footpads: a highwayman operating on foot rather than riding a horse.

Freeman: status in feudal society, but in England, it later came to mean a man possessing the full privileges and immunities.

Haworth manufacture: Ale brewed in Haworth

Kersey: a kind of coarse, ribbed cloth with a short nap, woven from short-stapled wool.

Kirtle: a woman's gown or outer petticoat.

Lotterel: rascal, scoundrel

Market wallet: an all-purpose carrying bag that was used by civilians and military personnel from the 16th century.

Millers: Most manors had windmills or watermills. The right to mill was in the gift of the Lord of The Manor.

Morion helmet: in England, this helmet (also known as the pikeman's pot) is associated with the New Model Army, one of the first professional militaries. It was worn by pikemen, together with a breastplate and buff coat as they stood in phalanx-like pike and shot formations, protecting the flanks of the unarmored musketeers.

Nob: came from the term 'nawab' (a governor of the Mogul Empire), from which came the 17th-century term 'nabob' (a person who came back to Britain after becoming wealthy in India).

Nowt: Nothing

Pay eur call: Urinate

Pike: a pole weapon, a very long thrusting spear formerly used extensively by infantry.

Puritan: English Protestants in the 16th and 17th centuries who sought to purify the Church of England of Roman Catholic practices, maintaining that the Church of England had not been fully reformed and should become more Protestant.

Reeve: a manor official appointed by the lord or elected by the peasants.

Roundhead: the name given to the supporters of the Parliament during the English Civil War. Also known as Parliamentarians.

Shilling: a coin worth one-twentieth of a pound sterling, or twelve pence. It was first minted in the reign of Henry VII as the testoon and became known as the shilling from the Old English schilling.

Shoffe-grote: played predominantly in the United Kingdom. Two players compete against one another using coins on a tabletop board.

Shuttle and warp: a tool designed to neatly and compactly store a holder that carries the thread of the weft yarn while weaving with a loom.

Spartle: kitchen tool

Steward lord's deputy: it was his job to defend his lord's rights and to look after his property. Legal knowledge was an important qualification since he had to represent his lord in court.

Swallowed a hair: an alcoholic drink taken to cure a hangover.

Swill-belly: a drunkard

Tarreur: goodbye

Willeying: pull apart and mix the fibres of the wool before they are carded.

Wimple: a cloth headdress covering the head, neck, and the sides of the face

Wood in the hole: Close the door

Wooden horse: torture device, of which there exist two variations; both inflict pain by using the subject's own weight by keeping the legs open, tied with ropes from above, while lowering down the subject.

Wool Brogger: 17th Century, a thief, an immoral troublemaker who raised the prices of wool and played a part in the misfortunes of many who tried to make a living in the early Yorkshire wool industry.

Margery's End

The story of the English War is one of political machinations, one of religious freedoms and, of course, the right of divine rule ostracised by the strength of a growing democratic political system. Much has been spoken about the power of government at this time and the fine line between autocratic rule and people's choice, but what about the common people, those that lived day to day. How might this hostility, this brazen battle for change, have affected their lives? One cannot envisage these changes without first coming to terms with the day-to-day lives of these people.

At this time, most of the English wool was exported abroad to Flanders, Bruges, Ghent and Ypres, and they would pay highly for it. Those working with it lived reasonably well. As time went by, the wool trade was to become significantly affected by the coming war and with its decreasing popularity and shortage. Thomas Rushworth and his family tried to earn what coin they could from their spinning and weaving of any wool they could obtain. This, along with seven acres of barley and a small vegetable garden, kept the wolves of famine away.

William's twin children, John and Robert, were now twelve and old enough to work and spent their days combing and carding wool. Each week Tommy and his father Thomas would make the mile journey to Stanbury and retrieve the mushy wool which had weathered and worn tips from the farmers who sheered and sold it. They would bring it home, and Isabel would spend the day stomping the grease and oil out of it in a barrel of stale urine, then the family would turn it into broadcloth for sale at market. This was a tedious process that required Agnes and Lucy to spend many hours at the spinning wheel and with the shuttle and warp of the handloom.

The political upheaval at the time made good wool hard to find as often it was bought in bulk by unscrupulous broggers who hid it away and waited for prices to go up. The Rushworth family struggled to get the same coin they had in the past and desperate times called for desperate measures. For the last eight months, the family had also been spinning and weaving wool for the manor steward on *put out*. Thomas knew that he wasn't paying them the correct coin for their labours, but there wasn't much he could do, and the fivepence per day they earned was better than nothing.

Thomas' son Tommy felt sad for his father, who wasn't getting any younger and worked from dawn until dark to provide for the family and afford them with basic nourishment to sustain them. It was all they could do to keep the pangs of hunger away in the trying times brought on by the coming war.

The manor steward's power and fortune continued to grow. It was said that his sheep herds and lands in Stanbury had grown significantly, built up over time by the misfortunes of others, some would say. Thomas had thought about complaining about the steward's indiscretions with his payments to the Justice of the Peace. He thought better of it as he knew it would make no difference. He was on the side of the rich and powerful and was well paid by them to keep the peace and dispense with any trivial complaints whether they had foundation or not.

Thomas sat there on the hard-backed wooden chair beside the hearth. He smoked his white clay, long-stemmed, barrel-shaped pipe and stared silently into the flames, watching them silently dance among the wood and dried peat. Tommy sat there with him in silence, relishing the safety and comfort of their hearth. He liked the feeling of the radiant warmth of the fire while hearing the wind howl and blast the snow around outside. Their current circumstances did little to brighten his feelings of destitution. This feeling grew within him like the root of a large tree. He thought long and hard about how he could lessen his families' burdens but coming from simple means made this difficult.

When his father had given up the copyholder tenancy, they had all thought that becoming freemen would allow the family more rights and freedoms, as they were no longer required to work the demesne of the Lord of the Manor, well unless he paid them. They cherished their newfound freedoms for a short time and thought things would improve; however, this was soon interrupted by the war. They still had to pay rent to the Lord, tithe to the church, and taxes became higher and higher under the new government. Food was scarce, and often grain was unavailable, but they made do as best they could in the circumstances.

Due to the labour shortage from the sickness of the plague, Tommy knew that he and his father could move the family elsewhere. Still, *better the devil you know than the devil you don't,* he thought to himself.

Tommy, like his father, had the respect and admiration of the locals as a man with a sensible head on his shoulders and one that didn't make decisions lightly, especially when it came to his family. The villagers knew him as the strong silent type who only spoke when he had something important to say, preferring to think on the subject before deciding. For this reason, they respected his decision and paid him no ill thoughts about remaining at home in these troubling times. His mother and father were starting to get older now, and the sixteen-hour workdays were beginning to take their toll. *Even more reason to stay and look after them as a good son should* he thought.

He looked at his father, who sat on his chair opposite, indisposed to his presence, whittling a piece of pinewood, making a toy for the next addition to the family. He held the wood in his left hand and braced his thumb against the timber, drawing the blade towards him as if peeling an apple. He made short and controlled strokes and was deep in thought, rarely venturing to look up except when the wind blew so loudly it sounded as if the shutters would be punched in. He was always very protective and looked as if he would spring into action if they did.

Thomas was a confident, kind man with an adventurous spirit and an amiable personality. He was always the first to help if a family had fallen on difficult times, well as much as circumstances would allow. In the summer, he would be the first to offer his assistance to families left poverty-stricken, harvesting their grain and shearing their sheep if the husband or sons were ill or had been taken by the sickness.

Thomas and his family had lived at Hall Green as far back as he could remember, and he liked to tell tales of what it was like in days past under the reign of the King. He spoke of his father and mother,

Margery, and he would tell stories of how he and Agnes had met. She would look up from the spinning wheel occasionally and correct him if his story went too far from the truth, then smile and blush if the story entailed specifics of their courting days.

Agnes, his mother, sat on a stool spinning yarn at the wheel, humming a pretty tune. Her nimble fingers and calloused hands worked methodologically with the teased fleece, and the wheel spun with a slow, mesmerising whirring sound. Stopping intermittently to untangle a piece of yarn, she often looked up contentedly and smiled if she caught her son looking at her. She was proud of her Tommy and the man that he had become. He was strong and sensible and never strayed from the things that he held most dear.

Their cottage, built some years ago, needed some repair. Some of the mortar between the stones had started to crack, and rags had been pushed into the gaps between the shutters. There was plaster on the walls, and long branches supported the sides of the roof. When a strong wintery wind rushed over the moors, the cottage shook, and the roof vibrated.

A ladder at the side of the chimney led to the loft where they kept the straw and hay for the animals. It was also where twins John and Robert slept, preferring the soft hay to the hard stone floor below. The slanting thatch roof leaked in places, but John and Robert had learned to strategically place their mattresses on the edge, in areas closer to the fire that were not subject to the annoying drip. On occasion, a leak would find another outlet through the thatch, and one of them would climb under their blanket only to find their straw pillow soggy and wet. Fixing the roof with new thatch was a job for summer, so their nightly complaints would continue until the snow melted and new thatch could be cut.

Isabel sat at the loom; she smiled when she noticed Tommy take a glance in her direction. She was a good wife and tended to his needs. They never fought or disagreed, for she knew her place, especially in front of the others. In spring and summer, she only saw Tommy for a couple of hours in the evening, usually because he and his father were always out in the fields tending to their barley crop. She was always busy spinning the wheel, which was like a cog in the engine which kept the family going. In winter, after the wood was chopped, peat cut, and animals tended to, they could spend more time in each other's company.

The adults preferred to sleep on a rolled out straw mattress by the low glow of the fire at night-time. Tommy never showed much affection towards Isabel in front of the others, but she knew he loved her. She always looked forward to the whispers that they shared at night as they slept close for warmth under the woollen blanket. It was often the only time they could be together away from the eyes of the others, and it was here that Tommy showed his affection kissing her gently on the neck and shoulders.

Often, in the middle of the night, the dark silence would be disturbed, and Thomas and Agnes would be awoken to grunting and quiet love sounds. Once finished, all knew that it was time for sleep and the end of another day until the cock crowed to start the next.

The Rushworths lived a simple life; they had little choice in their one-room stone cottage. There was extraordinarily little room with the loom and even less when the animals had to be brought in out of the weather. Winter on the moors was a time of rest, and they worked hard throughout the year, working the hide and spinning and weaving the wool to ensure this. There was always a fear of famine in the village. Still, they were luckier than some and usually managed to put enough grain and vegetables away to last them.

A spark flew out of the fire but was quickly extinguished by the dampness of the smashed gravel floor and trodden straw, which at times, with no drainage, flooded with the melting snow and ice.

Agnes watched as Thomas knocked the barrel of his pipe on the stones at the hearth of the fire and proceeded to refill it from the pouch which sat on the small wooden table beside him. He looked up at Agnes as she slowly stirred the pottage under the tottering chimney and chunky oak mantelpiece, stained black from the smoke from the continually lit fire.

The back of the fireplace was covered in soot, and an iron chimney crane with hooks allowed Isabel to swing the earthenware cauldron into a more easily accessible position. Split logs and dried peat and manure sat in the corner of the fireplace, and all manner of wooden skillets hung from the inside wall. On top of the mantlepiece sat the earthenware jugs and bowls, including the wooden stand for his father's pipe, which he had handcrafted himself out of a small fallen oak tree branch. Leaning beside the front wall of the chimney, there was an iron poker, ash shovel and tongs, along with a wooden water bucket from which Agnes took water she used to thin the pottage.

Isabel stood from the loom and hyper flexed her back to counter the added weight from the rather large baby bump extending from her lower abdomen. She was a good woman and knew her place among the other women in the household. Younger than the others, she lacked their experience but more than made up for it in effort. It wasn't comfortable moving into your husband's cottage with his family, and it had taken her some time to get used to it.

Agnes welcomed her when she arrived from Stanbury, and she liked her. Isabel had worked as a servant girl prior and was well versed in the running of a household. She knew how to bake bread and brew ale and was proficient in making pickles, preserves, and the jellies that they all loved so much. She also spun wool and linen and sold the extra garments at Haworth markets to earn extra coin. She was very timid and shy to start with but started to feel more at ease with Agnes after a period, and they had become good friends.

The smoke from the sweet aroma of Thomas' pipe tobacco filled the room, a respite from the smell of freshly released animal faeces at the back of the cottage. He felt the mark that his father had engraved, with his knife, in the top of the wooden table beside him. He remembered watching him do it, a reminder of times past, but not forgotten.

Like his father, family was important to Tommy. Even though he didn't know much about his father's folk before he was born, he felt a kinship, a belonging to the moors and dales and didn't want to leave. He had met Isabel in Stanbury when he and his father had travelled there. They purchased the cheaper wool that nobody else wanted from the local farmers.

Tommy remembered, as a young lad growing up in the old cruck house with Nan Margery and later the stone-walled cottage that uncle William and his father had built for her and his mother, Agnes. Labour was in short supply at the time, so they tended more land. The lord permitted improvements to the cottage, paying them five shillings a week to work his demesne. It was more significant than the old cruck house he remembered as a child. The walls were made of limestone rubble and rendered with lime and sand mortar which kept the weather out, and there was finally a chimney.

Sadly, Nan Margery was gone now. She had made her peace with God before she went, confessing and repenting her sins for all to hear. She was such an important part of all their lives, and Tommy started to recollect the days before she died.

He recalled as a youngster how she called him over to her while she lay in her bed and quietly whispered to him.

"Wee Tommy, you're a good lad, and you have the look of yer father about you," She placed her hand on his lovingly.

"I luv you, Tommy, and you make me so proud; look after thy mother and thy father and let no harm come to them when I'm gone."

He didn't know what to say, so he leaned over and rested his head on her hand softly and sadly, "Don't go, Nan Margery, please don't go."

"Ooy there Tommy, tis me time, an' I'm going to a better place and, besides, I'm tired." Her breathing was raspy and laboured.

She coughed and took a deep breath, "So very tired," she closed her eyes and drifted back to sleep.

He turned, going back to sit on the stool silently beside his father and Uncle William, who lovingly placed his hand on his shoulder to comfort him.

Tommy heard the heavy breathing that night, sitting quietly beside her. She rested with her deep-set, darkened eyes closed, cheekbones lying beneath the loose, saggy skin on her face, her hands clasped together on top of the blanket. The shadow from the small candle flickered on the stone wall, the smoke from the flame rose to be absorbed by the stained thatch ceiling. Cousin Mary, mother and Mrs Hargreaves knelt at the side of the bed with their hands clasped together, saying quiet prayers. Father and Uncle William sat on wooden stools, not saying much but consoling each other by their presence. Then the breathing stopped, and all was quiet. Father stood and placed two coins on Nan Margery's eyes to ward off a haunting. Mother wept, and Mrs Hargreaves whispered the Lord's Prayer.

Tommy's eyes quietly filled with tears that dripped like the first drops of rain then ran slowly down his face. He turned away and quickly wiped them with his sleeve before his father or uncle could notice. He didn't know how to deal with this feeling of sadness, this grey shadow of grief, so he climbed the loft ladder and slept it away.

The next morning, wee Tommy awoke to the noise of movement and prayers downstairs. He sat up and picked the sleep from the corners of his eyes. John and Robert were absent from the loft. He remembered the events of the previous evening and looked over to see Nan Margery's mattress empty. He quickly dressed into his brown, cut hand-me-down knickerbockers and frayed undershirt and climbed down the ladder. The cottage walls, shutters and mirror had been cloaked in black linen, and a curtain hung on a piece of rope separated the room.

He peeked behind the curtain and saw Nan Margery's body; it had been wrapped in a winding sheet and placed on planks sitting on wooden stools on the other side of the curtain. Friends, family and neighbours arrived at the cottage. Two members of the parish, accompanied by the curate, placed her in a black wooden coffin on loan from St Michael and All Angels. The rest of the family walked outside to wait for the vicar; when he arrived, the procession made its way across the farrowed field, up to Sun Street, past the manor, onto Main Street. The residents from the cottages along the road stopped what they were doing and came outside to the road and ducked their heads solemnly, the men removing their woollen hats in respect.

The curate led with his bell, followed by the vicar, holding his King James Bible piously in front of him. His father, Uncle William, John Hargreaves and the reeve of the manor followed, carrying the coffin on two long wooden poles; their heads lowered with respect and with sorrow. It wasn't heavy, for the sickness had reduced Margery's body to a skeleton. The rest followed slowly behind, including wee Tommy and his mother, who held his hand tightly for comfort beside her.

At St Michael and All Angels cemetery, the coffin was placed on two stools beside the gravesite of her husband, her feet facing east. Each of the men took off their hats, and the curate rang the bell six times, then one ring for each of the years of Margery's life.

The vicar stood in front of the coffin, his black cassock, white gown, and dark tippet draped over his shoulders.

He cleared his throat. and raised his hand and with an unemotionally deep voice began,

> "I am the resurrection and the life,"
> says the Lord. "Those who believe
> in me, even though they die, will live,
> and everyone who lives and believes
> in me will never die."

The vicar sprinkled holy water on the coffin,

> "God of all consolation, your son
> Jesus Christ was moved to tears at
> the grave of Lazarus, his friend.
> Look with compassion on your
> children in their loss; give to troubled

hearts the light of hope and strengthen
in us the gift of faith, in Jesus Christ
our Lord. Amen"

They all repeated, *"Amen"*,

After prayers, her body was carefully lifted from the coffin and placed by the members of the burial guild into the pre-dug hole.

The vicar said one more prayer,

"O God, whose son Jesus Christ was
laid in a tomb: bless, we pray, this grave
as the place where the body of Margery
Rushworth, your servant, may rest in
peace, through your son, who is the
resurrection and the life; who died
and is alive and reigns with you now
and forever. Amen."

"Amen," they all repeated.

Those who were present walked to the mound of dirt beside the shallow grave, picked up a handful of rocky soil and carefully dropped it onto Nan Margery's body. It was a quiet, solemn moment, then the heavens opened with a crack of thunder, and the rain started to fall as if signalling the end of her days.

After the burial, all the men who were at the funeral retired to the Kings Arms, the women and children to the Rushworth Cottage for black bread, biscuits and ale. Agnes and Tommy started walking back around the horizontally placed tombstones. Tommy turned back around to see his father soaking wet and unperturbed by the rain. He just stood there soaking wet, standing over the mound of her grave. He saw him holding his grandmother's wimple but then clutched it tightly to his face and fought hard to hold back his emotions. This disturbed him as he had never seen such emotion from his father before. His uncle William, standing beside, put his arm on his shoulder to comfort him. He held his black woollen, felt hat in his other hand and solemnly looked downwards at the grave, quietly whispering his prayers and goodbyes.

His mother, still holding his hand tightly, said, "Come, Tommy, let thy father and uncle say tarreur to Nan Margery in their own way."

She knew that the two men would not like to be seen expressing their emotions in public and certainly not in front of wee Tommy, for in Yorkshire, that's not what men did.

It continued to drizzle as they walked out of the graveyard, past the pillory holding the now subdued and forlorn drunkard from the previous night, down Main street, which was muddied and wet. They continued downhill past the manor onto Sun Street, past Woodlands Rise, then uphill toward home.

A wave of sadness overcame Agnes, and she reminisced. *The first time she had met Margery was when her parents had met with her to discuss the dowry for their betrothal. It seemed like a lifetime ago now. The passing of Margery made her think of her own mortality, and it made her feel lonesome and afraid of the future. It dawned on her that she was the mistress of the house now. The feeling that came with it was one of responsibility and obligation. She would call on the wisdom and shrewdness that she had learned from her to safeguard her family.*

A farmer, pulling an ox and cart full of fleece, brought her out of her thoughts, and as he passed them on the road, he doffed his hat, "Condolences Missis," and continued up Sun Street.

The ox having some difficulty getting tread on the muddy road grunted and groaned in frustration until the farmer gave him a nudge with his shepherd's hook. He found his tread and moved forward.

Agnes sadly nodded her acceptance and approval, the drizzle continued, and their woollen cloaks became saturated and cold. Wee Tommy began to shiver, his feet frozen from the mud which clung to his thin leather shoes. The recent events were all new to him, and he didn't quite know how to act or what to say to his mother in her state of melancholy, so he said nothing.

The sky was low, grey and bleak, and the weather had set in. They climbed over the stone wall and walked uphill through the hide to the cottage. He clung tightly to his mother's hand and tried to keep up with her as she hurried up the hill to get out of the weather. Beyond the cottage, wee Tommy could see their white sheep grazing in the hills, contrasted by the brown heather of the moors. Agnes shivered, there was a chill in the air, and she knew winter was on its way.

☙ CHAPTER TWO ❧

She Will Never be Forgotten

The villagers had come to accept the sickness and death of its inhabitants as forty years of life was the normal age of longevity. The thing is, Margery was not normal, and she had far outlived this, although nobody really knew how old she was, and it was believed she didn't either. What they did know was that she was a wise, kind and caring woman that, in one way or another, had touched all their lives.

After the funeral, Thomas and William went to the Kings Arms, a tavern across the square from St Michael and All Angels. Most of the men had known the family for many years, and most were good friends of Margery's husband, who had passed away from consumption sometime before her. As the local matchmaker, Margery was well known to all and had played a major part in most of their banns and handfastings. Often, marriages were arranged, and she was always the one to do it.

Thomas and William ducked their heads as they went through the doorway of the tavern. It seemed darker and quieter than usual, and they really didn't feel like socialising. Still, they had been persuaded by the men inside.

The reeve noticed them and called out to the publican to pour two more jacks of ale, "Come lads, let us drink to Margery and the life she lived. Never one to shy away from life's burdens and always cheerful in the face of adversity. She will never die, for those that die are only dead when we have forgotten them, and she will never be forgotten, I assure you."

They all lifted their drinks in unison and skulled them. William tried to cough away the lump in his throat, slapping his chest blaming it on some ale that had gone down the wrong way. He didn't fool his brother, who smiled and felt the same knot in his throat.

To distract himself, Thomas looked beyond the reeve's shoulder and looked toward the back of the room. An old tinker leaned against the wall, allowing a stream of urine to flow into a bucket in the back corner. He tried to put the day's events out of his mind and listened to a farmer argue with a wool brogger over the price for his fleece.

The farmer held his hand up with the coin he had been given, "Ya don't understand, tis not enough ta feed me, I dunno about me family!"

The brogger knew that by the time he distributed the raw fleece to the clothiers and stored some away to increase demand, he would still be left with a tidy profit once sold. "Aye, and what you don't understand is I'm not getting as much as what I was fer fleece with the clothiers."

"Come on now, be honest with me ya cheatin' bastard, I know how much you get in York fer the fleece!" The farmer exclaimed angrily.

The brogger put his hands up defensively, "Aye, but there's a shortage of fleece now, ya know that! This war is interrupting trade, and then there's the King's levy on exports."

The farmer became more agitated, "A shortage of fleece, they're getting way more in York than what you pay us here."

"Well then, take yer wool ta York and sell it yerself!" The brogger was starting to become impatient and became uncomfortable with other farmers looking at him.

The farmer shook his head with frustration, "Ya know I can't do that, I've got a herd ta run!"

Thomas and William made a point of not getting involved in the dealings of others but knew that generally, the brogger's played a part in the misfortunes of many. They turned to the bar and ordered another ale but watched on as the voices of the farmer and brogger got louder and louder. Other farmers who had had their fair share of ale started heckling the brogger. He sensed the deteriorating mood in the tavern and made a quick exit.

Thomas whispered, "Tis right what he says, the clothiers and broggers get richer while the poor folk and farmers scratch out a living."

William looked at him worriedly, "Aye, but what are we ta do about it."

Thomas took a sip of his ale and thought for a moment, "Nothing we can do really; it is what it is."

The shutters were open and allowed some of the smokiness from the fire and pipe smoking to escape. Three-legged stools and wooden tables were used for the card games. Wide, rough planks made up the bar which separated the barkeep from the tenants, freemen and yeomen that frequented the place after dark.

A handful of men stood at the bar playing shoffe-grote on a rectangular wooden board. The shelves behind housed leather jacks, wooden bowls and tankards. Most of the light came from the fire in the hearth. Still, the odd tallow candle provided enough light for the card games and arguments about the dissolution of Parliament and King Charles' right of divine rule. The serving maid walked one way, then the next refilling tankards of ale and chastising the occasional patron that couldn't keep his hands to himself.

An old woman, her left eye whitened by the cataract that had slowly tunnelled her vision then completely erased it, limped from table to table the old stick she held supporting her cracked and painful hip. She wore a dirty, ochre, frayed kirtle and moth-eaten wimple that had lost its true colour years ago.

The old woman held out the wrinkled, worn palm of her hand, begging for a penny from the patrons, "Spare a penny, sir, spare a penny to feed the bairns. Spare a penny, sir?"

One of the patrons lifted his eyes from his cards, "Be off with you foul old woman before ya feel the pointy end of me foot up yer arse."

She rolled her eyes, grunted in frustration and walked up to the men standing at the bar, "Spare a penny, sir, spare a penny to feed the bairns, spare a penny, sir?"

The barkeep looked at the poor wretched soul, "Be off with ya, old woman!"

Thomas placed a penny on the bar, "Ales barkeep".

He turned around, shocked by the wrinkled face that was bent over before him, her whispery white hair poking through the sides of her wimple. Deep wrinkles in her face spread like a roadmap, her left eye, almost moonlike with its colour and sadness, a reminder of the poor wretches in the world.

He didn't have much, but he had felt the pangs of hunger and would not wish it on any other, "Here, take this and be off with you, feed yer bairns or more likely yer husband that has no more work left in him." Thomas placed two pennies in her hand.

She lifted her trembling hand, which was wrapped in a dirty, small woollen mitten with the fingers cut at the knuckles, "Thank you, sir, God bless ya."

She knew the weight of a penny and raised it steadily to her one eye for a closer look to ensure she hadn't been tricked like times before. She paused then focused her one good eye on Thomas' face to remember it for the future, "God bless ya, son."

She hobbled through the door, no doubt back to her husband, that waited for the homebrew that she would collect from one of the cottages on the way home.

William looked puzzled, "Why'd ya do that, Thomas?"

Thomas smiled, "There's some in the world far worse off than we, brother, and one good turn deserves another."

Some men came up to shake the hands of the two brothers and pay their condolences. There was the baker from the manor with his stained, floppy white hat, the reeve, who smoked his pipe and all manner of patrons, free tenants and yeomen that had heard of Margery's passing. They had come to pay their respects and to tell and hear stories of Margery.

Thomas spoke of the time that he and William arrived home to find a dead man flat on his back, in the old cruck house, his nose hanging to the side of his face after the English Mastiff had attacked him, protecting their mother. This brought back memories of the footpads and coney-catchers that had terrorised the village and surrounds all those years ago.

The reeve reminded them of times gone by. "Aye, they were strange times, they were, who'd have thought it was the steward's men takin' advantage of the good folk of Haworth. Seems like just yesterday," said the reeve.

"Anyway, they got their just deserves, probably still chained to a wall in Castle Prison, I'd say," replied William.

"She was a cunning old girl," said Thomas. "I was just a boy. If it weren't for her, Agnes and I wouldn't be together. She arranged the banns and the hand-tying with the vicar, even settled the dowry after me father passed."

"She was always up ta some sort of shenanigans," replied William, "What about the time she dragged you off to see the steward about the tenure for the hide."

Reminiscing, Thomas tried to pep himself up in front of the others, "Aye, seems like a lifetime ago now, plenty of water under the bridge since then, brother."

"And you William, you have another on the way?" The baker from the manor asked, sensing the sad demeanour amongst the others.

William was reminded of his pregnant wife at home, "All I have ta do is wave me breeches over the bed, and it brings the bairn."

The men laughed, all except the reeve who was always up on the latest news in the town, "You should be so lucky mate, there's many young ones with the sickness here bouts, tis gonna be a long hard winter for some. John Pigshells missus lost another to the consumption last week, only four years old. Only one of four of his have made it to their sixth year, bloody sad it is."

Children in the village were subject to many diseases and physical hardships. They had all encountered the black death, smallpox and illnesses such as measles and influenza. The infant mortality rate was extremely high.

Thomas looked at his brother William and watched as he looked down gloomily, "Aye, there's more worse off than we. That bastard steward, he's been the cause of hardship for many in the village."

William, the younger, more outspoken of the two brothers, had a likeable, spirited personality. Unlike Thomas, who thought before he spoke, William was the opposite. He spoke his mind whenever and wherever often getting himself into some sort of strife that his brother had to bail him out of.

The reeve trying to change the subject, "Aye, old Margery wasn't backwards in coming forwards that's for sure always kept me on my toes. Came to the manor to borrow a hoe once, refused to pay for it said she was doing me a favour stopping the seeds from weeds spreading onto the lord's demesne. Just walked off, never saw the hoe again!"

They all smiled, including Thomas, who knew he still had the hoe back at the cottage. "Treasure she was, hated the old lord with a passion because of the way he mistreated Father when he was sick and coughing blood."

"Aye, I remember, still cursing him, I'd say," William declared.

Thomas getting a little tipsy preferred to change the subject and stall his feelings of sadness. He raised his tankard, "Oh here's to other meetings, and merry greetings then; and here's to those we've drunk with, but never can again!"

All the others followed suit; they all lifted their tankards and skulled their ale, slamming them down on the bar and, in unison, called out, "To Margery!"

"Barkeep, more ale," yelled John Hargreaves,

"May as well, if we don't drink it, some other bastard will," said the reeve.

All who heard smiled a little. Thomas reached inside his tunic and felt Margery's wimple that he carried there. He knew that it would still smell of her, and back at home when nobody was looking, he would take it out and reminisce. He would think about the life lessons he had learned and the wisdom she had taught.

The Kings Arms started to empty. The barmaid went around busily wiping the spilled ale from the tables; and waking up the drunk who had momentarily fallen asleep at a table in the corner. His head on his forearms, still holding tightly to his half-finished pewter tankard. The barkeep went around with a bucket collecting any dregs from the jacks left half-empty on the tables to be poured back into the other barrel for the more destitute.

The barkeep was a large rotund man. His red waistcoat stretched tightly across his protruding abdomen, revealing the dirty grey undershirt beneath. His brown tunic was stained and covered in wet patches from the ale that he slopped from noon till night. His dirty white, ragged apron rested below his waistline, which he continually pulled up and tightened. He wasn't an overly joyous man and kept the locals coming back by knowing their names and pouring ale quickly with no slops.

After too many ales, Thomas and William started on their way home, made harder by the constant drizzle. They walked through the fields, a dog barked in the distance, past the manor house at the foot of Main Street with its deeply recessed candlelit mullioned windows, down Sun Street, muddied and slippery underfoot. The cottage merchants quietened their trade and shut up shop to get out of the drizzle. The vastness of open Pennine countryside and moorlands lost their expanse with the encroaching fog and low cloud as if the Lord himself was wiping them out to start colouring in again. The upper part of the church steeple of St. Michael and All Angels mostly lost to the weather. They walked in silence for a while, contemplating what it would be like without her. Their only solace was the thought that they had to be strong for the rest of the family.

The drizzle turned to rain, and then it started to pour, soaking their felt wide-brimmed hats, cloaks and tunics and drenching them through and through. They continued to trudge home, then Thomas stopped, taking off his hat, which had lost part of its shape, to push his slick hair back and wipe the droplets of wet from his eyelashes. William was staggering and finding it quite challenging to keep his balance. Both were not quite as nimble as they once were, especially Thomas, who laboured more during the uphill journey while trying to balance his brother.

"Do ya think she's with Father?" asked William.

"Aye, I think she's with Father, William. God rest her soul."

Tommy and the English Mastiff heard the ramblings of Thomas and William coming up the hill. The dog stood quickly and went to the door sniffing underneath it to try and get a scent of who approached. It was familiar, so he waited for the latch to lift and the door to open. The two men staggered in, disregarding the dog, who sniffed and looked up at them. With no affection directed his way, he turned and walked back to the hearth, slumping down with a groan and a grumble.

It was pitch black outside, and the rain was relentless beating down with anger and no respite. Tommy looked up at his uncle William who was loud, drunk and filthy, from where he had fallen over in the mud. He rarely saw his father and uncle like this. It disturbed him as he knew that with this came anger and chastisement from his mother, who had no patience for men who couldn't handle their drink.

"Look at you two," exclaimed Agnes, while shepherding them in quickly through the door to keep the downpour at bay.

Father and Uncle William were soaking wet and chilled through to the bone, shivering. Their tunics and hose were caked in mud. A distinct aroma of fresh manure wafted through the cottage, joining with the animal smells already present.

Father had one hand around Uncle William's waist, and he had his arm around Father's shoulder. Still, he found it difficult to stand upright. Father lowered him down carefully on the form by the wall, where he closed his eyes and leaned his head back, mumbling something that nobody could understand. Father sat down beside him, taking off his muddied tunic, giving it to Ma. His thin leather and woollen shoes were saturated and muddy, so he took them off and put them under the form.

Suddenly, Uncle William opened his eyes and bolted upright; he stood there swaying and trying to focus, "More ale," he hollered. William was always a bit more confident in the household when he had a belly full of ale.

"I think you've had quite enough, William," said Agnes trying to take off his tunic.

She was the only woman in the household who had the courage and the tenacity to scold the men. She knew Thomas wouldn't retort, lest he sleep with the animals in the cold and consume cold pottage in the morning. When he carried on like this, she knew he was only trying to reassert himself in front of his watching son and the others, who had enough sense to ignore his rantings and ravings.

Agnes had a stern look on her face, "Come on, husband get yer gear off and don't embarrass yerself in front of wee Tommy."

She was a wise woman, and the years of hard work, sacrifice and lost young ones had taken their toll. She had a tough, unemotional demeanour, but all could sense her quiet, sensitive side that she tried so hard to hide unless she was dealing with the young ones. Tommy was the love of her life, and she doted on him, often protecting him from the wrath of his father if he dropped the eggs or forgot to put the wood in the hole on a cold night.

Agnes lifted Thomas' arm up and pulled his sleeve to get his tunic off, "Come on you two off with those mucky clothes before ya get the chill a' death into ya!"

Lucy walked over to help William, she lifted his arm to take off his unbuttoned tunic, but he wouldn't have it and shakily stood to his feet, "More ale, woman! Bring more ale,"

Lucy rolled her eyes and put her hands on her hips impatiently, "Da ya think you've not had enough? You'll feel like a dog's breakfast in the morn' if ya don't sleep it off,"

She tried to lift his arm, but he shook away her grasp, stood and put his arms around to embrace her.

Unaccustomed to such displays of affection, Lucy pushed him away, "What's got in ta ya William?"

William tried to keep a hold of her but lost his balance and plonked himself back down on the form.

William stood again and staggered and almost lost his balance until Thomas grabbed and steadied him, "William, what's got into ya,' behave!"

Father rose slowly and steadily walked over to the clay jug, covered with a linen cloth, and poured two tankards of ale. He walked back and gave one to Uncle William and downed the other.

Uncle William taking his, took an awkward step to steady himself, recovered, spilled some of it while taking it to his lips and then skulled the rest.

"William, I've got work ta do; this wool isn't gonna spin itself!" Lucy declared with impatience.

"More!" William yelled as he lifted his empty tankard into the air as if an offering to the Gods.

Father once again filled their tankards, and Uncle took a step forward; still unsteady on his feet, Lucy and Ma held him upright. He took the tankard and brought it to his lips, taking a large gulp.

"William yer need ta' get ta bed, it's late, and there's work ta be done in the morning," Lucy proclaimed with increasing impatience.

"We'll never get him up that ladder," remarked Agnes, so they walked him over to the animal enclosure.

They dropped Uncle William down on a mound of clean straw, used for the animal's bedding, fully dressed. He leaned backwards, his eyes rolling upwards so that you could see the whites of his eyes until they closed. He took one deep breath and went limp, passing out mumbling something incoherently. They took his muddy leg warmers, strappings and hose off and left the wet undershirt.

Agnes placed a blanket over him as the cow mooed with dissatisfaction having him occupying her corner of the room. The ox continued to chew its cud and unceremoniously watched what was going on in his peripheral vision. The sheep scattered to the other side of the enclosure, and the chickens squawked and flapped their wings. The pig grunted, and the sow stood, neglecting the piglets that had not finished feeding and started to squeal being unfastened from the teat.

Tommy watched his father as he tentatively walked back to his high-backed wooden chair near the fire. He took out his clay pipe and lit it with a piece of straw, puffing on it efficiently until he was happy with the state of the ember in the barrel.

Tommy had never seen his uncle in such a state, and his father had a quiet solemness that filled the room like a dense fog. Not much was said after that, and the women continued their evening chores. Lucy stayed with her spinning wheel, and Agnes pounded the bread dough for the morning.

When the cock crowed the following day, William started to stir. Father, having not slept, had already left to visit Nan Margery's grave, so Tommy was spared helping his father pluck rocks and stones from the earth to prepare for the Spring sowing.

William started to come around, he felt the heavy tiredness and pain behind his eyes, and he tried hard to fall back to sleep but couldn't. He slowly tried to open his eyes and then, squinting at the light from the open shutters, immediately closed them again and groaned. He tried to swallow away the bad taste in his mouth, but it was too dry, and the surface of his tongue had a woolly feel to it. He squinted, trying to let his eyes adjust to the light slowly, then rolled over, kneeling on all fours in the mound of straw. Pieces of straw protruded from his hair and stuck to his undershirt, and he groaned when he smelt the fresh manure and droppings plop on the ground beside him.

"You better get those animals over to the common green William, the day tis half over," said Agnes shaking her head.

He pulled himself up from the straw pile and crawled over to the animal's half water barrel. He dunked his head in it and blue bubbles trying to rid himself of the pain behind his eyes. He splashed his face pushing his wet hands through his hair, grimacing from the shock of the cold water, his head feeling heavy and uncooperative. He cupped his hands and splashed his face a few more times, and then tried slowly to open his eyes fully. He looked around, trying to get his bearings and make sense of the previous night.

Agnes ignored him and did not pay him any attention whatsoever while she was tending to the vegetables that she had collected from the patch. Now she collected eggs from the chickens who squawked their disapproval.

William, still on all fours, looked around and saw wee Tommy looking at him suspiciously, scrutinising his every move with interest.

William raised his head, "What're ya looking at, boy? Be off with ya help yer mother," he bellowed.

Then realising his mistake, he held onto the side of his head, coughing up the phlegm that had collected through the night. He felt the pain and frowned with each cough and continued to moan and grumble.

Tommy ran across the room and stood behind his mother as she placed the eggs on the table; he peeked out from behind her kirtle and continued to watch his uncle with fascination.

Agnes smiled, "There, there Tommy, pay no mind to yer uncle swill-belly. He swallowed a hair and will have barrel fever fer the rest a' the day. You go outside an' play now."

Tommy watched his uncle as he tried to stand too quickly and lost his balance, dropping to his knees back to the stone floor, head down in shame. He then slowly looked up, squinting. His eyes were red; he blinked, trying to focus in the light.

William reached out with his hand, "Help me, boy."

William's head was muddled and his memory of the previous evening cloudy like the beck after a good rain.

Tommy hesitantly walked over to him and slowly tried to lift him like he had seen his father do the night before, but he was heavy and couldn't quite reach around his waist. William put his open hand on the top of Tommy's head and used it for balance to steady himself and walk to the door. He opened the door and was taken aback by the cold wind. He staggered outside into the chill to try and revive himself with the wind in his face, but it was too much, and he staggered back inside to take up a place in his brother's chair beside the fire.

Lucy said nothing but watched his every movement while the spinning wheel whirred in front of her. She frowned, then smiled at his uncovered knobbly knees. She provided no sympathy as she slowly teased the thread and pushed the peddle to spin the wheel. She loved the whirring of the wheel; it was almost mesmerising, and it took her to another place away from the hardships of her own simple life. She missed her father and her sister but was still very hurt by his wrongdoings. Putting it out of her mind, she glanced over at William and shook her head.

Agnes bent down and scooped some steaming pottage into a wooden bowl from the cauldron under the chimney and passed it to him with a jack of ale. He accepted it without gesture and then, feeling a queasy feeling starting to rise in his stomach, ran to the door, lifted the latch and dropped to his knees outside. Tommy watched on as he saw his uncle's back arch followed by a steady stream of liquid which poured from his gaping mouth. He coughed, then arched his back again, and a further stream of clear liquid splashed to the ground. His back arched again, but there was no more, so he dryly coughed, trying to rid his throat of the distasteful acidic phlegm that now presided there.

When he eventually stood, he staggered back inside, holding onto the door jamb for balance; none of the women looked at him but continued their spinning and weaving. He stopped for a moment expecting some comment to be made, but the women knew that silence was their best insult. William staggered back over to the fire and sat down again. He stirred his pottage and sipped it from the bowl, hoping it would help silence the pounding of the blacksmith working behind his eyes.

ᵒ₰ CHAPTER THREE ₰ᵒ
Coming of Age

The King had introduced 'unfair taxes', and the anti-Crown sentiment was beginning to grow all around the country. In the west, they hoped that they were protected from the threat of coming hostilities due to their remoteness.

Tommy had watched as many of the young men of the village packed up and left to join the army. At least fighting for Cromwell, they were guaranteed an income to send home to their families and put some food in their bellies. Tommy once considered joining them but wouldn't contemplate leaving his mother and father alone and destitute to the ravages of winter on the moors.

"Here ya are, Tommy," said Isabel as she brought a much older Tommy Rushworth out of his thoughts by placing a bowl of pottage and dark bread on the table.

Now a grown man, Tommy had the look of his father, thick dark brown eyebrows and heavily recessed blue eyes. Whispers of dark brown hair peeked from under his brown felt cap. His reddish, windburned face gave him the rugged look of a Yorkshire man. In the spring and summer, he worked the field from early morning to night, and his hands were rough and calloused like roughly shorn timber. His skin had been aged slightly by hardship and the Pennine wind and summer sun. He wore a loose dark brown, sleeveless jerkin over an open grey dirty tunic with dark brown hose and woollen foot coverings strapped with leather that had spent far too much time in the mud. The sleeveless jerkin kept the draft and coldness from his back, and a cloth hood dangled loosely, which, when required, shielded part of his face from the punishing icy wind.

"What were ya in such deep thought about, husband?" Isabel enquired as she sat down on the stool next to the fire. Isabel knew when her man was out of sorts and knew to leave him be when something was troubling him.

He had a quiet strength like his father, and the nut didn't fall far from the tree, she thought. *He wasn't openly affectionate, but he was honest and good to her. He could always be trusted and didn't spend coin on whores or the dogfighting at the tavern like some in the village.*

It was only underneath the blanket at night that his whisperings became quiet and loving.

"Just thinking about times gone by." Tommy put his head closer to the bowl. He spooned some pottage into his mouth, wiping the excess with the sleeve of his greyed linen shirt, which poked out of his tunic.

The wind howled outside like a wild beast, and a small line of snow blew under the door and started to gather into a small mound. The shutters vibrated stubbornly, keeping the wind and snow outside. Still, a steady drip of water melted by the warmth of the fire dripped from the ledge beneath the shutter.

"What made ya think of the past?" Isabel asked as she turned to stoke the fire, knowing not to press him too hard on the subject.

"Just thinking about Father and William and how they were when Nan Margery passed."

The cottage was poorly ventilated except for the shutters, which they couldn't open at night, and the two slits in the wall in front of the animal stalls. Steam from the body heat of the cow and ox rose and dissipated amongst the thatched ceiling. The pigs squealed as they contested the rotting vegetables, and the boar grunted as it sifted through the old peelings and rotten cabbage leaves from the collection of autumn leftovers.

Agnes heard her son's melancholy words as she eavesdropped from the animal quarters at the back corner of the cottage. She shovelled manure through the hole in the wall designed for the purpose and closed the hatch to keep the weather outside. Putting her hands together, she blew on them, then rubbed them together to get the circulation back, "This draft will be the end of me," she grumbled to herself.

"I wonder when yer father will be back." Said Agnes as she walked toward the fire to warm herself, lifting her kirtle a little to warm her feet.

"Where's he gone, Mother?" Tommy asked curiously.

"Gone into the village with John Hargreaves to talk to the reeve about something."

"About what?"

"Tommy, ya know he tells me nowt about his plans and goings-on, have ya not learnt that yet?"

"Aye, I have," knowing that he kept specific details from Isabel in the same way.

Isabel walked over to the spinning wheel and sat down on the stool in front of it. She took some waste yarn around the bobbin, fed it through the flyer and tied it to a six-inch roving. She pumped the treadle and, at the same time, gently fed out the fibres by pulling lightly to keep it taught. In the winter, there wasn't much to do on the hide, so their days were spent spinning yarn and the never-ending weaving of cloth. It was a tedious process, and it took them almost a week to make one kersey which was then sold back to the clothier.

Isabel turned to her husband curiously before walking to the hearth to stir the pottage, "And you, husband, is there any secrets that you should be telling me?"

Tommy stayed quiet as he didn't want to scare her with stories of what he had heard at the Kings Arms about what was coming and took another spoonful of pottage. Isabel knew not to push the subject as she teased more of the fleece.

Agnes smiled at his restraint, *just like his father,* she thought to herself as she climbed up the steps of the ladder, being careful not to trip on the bottom of her kirtle. She climbed to the loft above the animal enclosure and dropped half a bale of hay down; the startled chickens squawked, dodged and fled, flapping their wings in terror, loose feathers rose and then floated slowly to the ground. Carefully climbing down, she separated the hay and threw it into the trough in front of the animals. A rickety, old worn-out structure with vertical wooden strips of timber denied full access to separate the hay so that each had their own portion.

She walked out of the animal enclosure and over to the fire, "Ere, Isabel, you take a load off, I'll do that, ya need to rest, and so does ya babby."

"Baby's fine, Agnes, kicking like a young lamb," she said as she placed her hands under the bulge and straightened, grimacing from the dull ache in her lower back.

She sat down at the table opposite Tommy while Agnes placed a bowl in front of her and Lucy, who was also six months pregnant.

"I've put some extra meat in the pottage for the babby," said Agnes.

"Oooh, there's no need, Spring is still a long way off, and we need to make it last."

"Never you mind that, if we run out, Thomas will just have ta butcher another pig, baby needs to be strong and healthy."

Isabel was pretty, dark hair dropped to just above her eyebrows with a fringe, she had kind, dark eyes which sparkled with the light from the fire. The continual rosiness of her cheeks gave her a healthy glow. Her blue kirtle and tan partlet had a plunging neckline which joined with the open-fronted gown, which was laced across her chest with a leather cord. The shapeless sleeves were attached to the dress with stringed stitches at the top of the shoulder. A fawn, linen apron dirtied and stained ballooned out from her lower abdomen and dropped to the floor.

Tommy looked at Isabel as she sat down at the table and smiled. *She was a good woman,* Tommy thought to himself and had settled into life at the cottage well. She worked hard and did her share of the cooking, mending and spinning. It had been some years since they had met in Stanbury, and even though they only saw each other for a couple of hours in the evening in Summer, he cherished her even though he would never let on.

Their courtship was short, and her father had refused Tommy's advances toward his daughter. Years earlier, Isabel's mother had died trying to give birth to her younger brother, something that her father never really got over. Now he was alone, and although Tommy knew she felt guilty leaving him, she knew it was for the best. The wedding took place in Stanbury, and when the Rushworth family left, they took Isabel back to Haworth with them.

Later that night, Isabel went into labour. Tommy was ushered out the door by Agnes and wasn't allowed back in the cottage. He waited outside in the dark and drizzle, but he could hear the screams of pain and anguish and Isabel calling on all the saints for help. He wasn't used to being in this situation and now knew why his father trekked into the village. He had done the same when Lucy had given birth, but this was different; this was his wife and his baby.

Agnes had covered the shutters with linen to keep out the humours, blown out the candles and allowed the fire to die down to just a glow. Agnes rubbed scented butter on her stomach and rubbed her back forcefully with each growing contraction.

Isabel was propped up on pillows against the wall; the straw mattress was already wet from the clear liquid that had gushed from below. She frowned with the uncomfortable back pain and cramping in her lower abdomen and closed her eyes, praying to God for the health of her baby.

Agnes felt her stomach to gauge the direction of the baby's head. It was hard, and the skin was stretched tightly over the baby mound as if it would split. Isabel tried to deal with the growing pressure. She could feel her breathing naturally increase, and she closed her eyes as if it would make the increasing pressure go away.

Agnes lifted her knees up and draped a linen cloth over them.

"Ah want ta pay eur call," said Isabel uncomfortably.

"It's alright, luv, it will pass, and besides, if ya have the need, do it where ya lie."

"Arghhh," Isabel felt the heaviness and pain in her lower back from the contraction.

"Breathe deeply, lass, 'tis very close. There, there Isabel, it won't be long now."

"Aye, but close isn't...... close enough, Arghhhhhhhh!" Isabel screamed again and heaved her head and shoulders up off the straw pillow, holding her position, then flopped back down, panting deeply, trying to catch her breath.

Lucy, sitting on the edge of the bed, wiped her sister's forehead with a wet cloth, "There, sister, it's almost done."

Agnes looked under the linen sheet, "Isabel, I can see its head; with the next pain, I want you to push with everything ya got left."

Isabel gritted her teeth as the contraction started to build. She heaved her head and shoulders forward and screamed one last time, then flopped back down, exhausted. Her chest heaved up and down, and there she stayed until she heard the first cry. Agnes cut the umbilical cord with the sharpest knife she had, the one she used to cut vegetables. She picked up the baby and placed it on Isabel's chest, which continued to heave in and out.

Agnes wiped the blood and mucous-like covering from the baby's face, tying off the cord with a piece of entwined string like her mother had shown her all those years ago. The baby continued to howl while Agnes wrapped him in a linen shawl, and then he quietened as he felt his mother's heartbeat.

"Why lass, ya have a strong lad."

"A lad, thank the Lord, Tommy will be so happy," exclaimed Isabel panting as she started to get her breath back.

Lucy continued to wipe the sweat from Isabel's forehead, "Oh sister, you have a beautiful boy; he has the most beautiful blue eyes."

"There always blue when they're firstborn," claimed Agnes.

Agnes wrapped up the linen sheet that she had placed underneath Isabel and gave it to Lucy to dispense with. Lucy walked over to the fire and put them in. The linen caught quick, and the flame danced toward the opening of the chimney, higher, higher and higher. The blaze burnt hot, so Lucy had to turn away; the fire roared.

Sensing the radiant heat, Agnes turned quickly when she heard the roar, "LUCY NOT IN THE FIRE!"

Tommy looked toward the cottage; he heard a scream. He kept looking but saw nothing except a greater brightness emanating from the closed shutters. Steam started to come off the chimney outside; then he heard the door open with a thump and Agnes and Lucy supporting Isabel through the door. Tommy began to run.

"TOMMY!" Agnes yelled.

Tommy ran as fast as he could. He could see sparks coming out the top of the chimney contrasted by the blackness of the sky.

"Ma, what is it?"

"FIRE!" she coughed, "fire."

Tommy ran up the hill, soaking wet; he ran inside to see the flame from the hearth touching the top of the mantle. He quickly took the water bucket at the bottom of the ladder and threw it on the fire. A gust of steam erupted and filled the room with a steamy, pungent smell. The cow panicked, broke its tie rope, turned and trotted out the door; the chickens flapped their wings and followed. Lucy, Isabel and Agnes huddled together under a woollen cloak trying to protect the baby. They all cowered under the eve of the thatch, trying to keep as dry as they could from the dampness and constant drizzle.

The steam from the chimney still sizzled, but the drizzle had calmed it.

The baby started to cry, and Tommy heard it. He walked outside to find them all huddled together under the thatched eve.

"Come in quickly; tis a mess, but better a mess inside than a chill out."

Agnes helped Isabel, who looked worse for wear and hobbled inside, the afterbirth running down her leg. The baby continued to cry; she passed the baby, all wrapped up, to Agnes and climbed back on the bed.

Exhausted, she breathed heavily, "Never a dull moment, husband!"

Agnes passed the baby back to Isabel, and she cradled him in her arms, now worried that the drafts would harm him. "Poor darling."

She pulled the blanket up over her legs so that Tommy couldn't see the stained sheet below. Then she pulled the bundling and held the baby close to her to warm him.

"I'm so sorry, Isabel; I don't know what I was thinking."

"It's alright, replied Isabel, "No harm done, he's warm enough."

Agnes turned to look at the mess, "Tommy, we need to get the fire started or else we'll all catch the chill of death."

"Aye, I'll get some dry peat," said Tommy as he marched out the door back into the drizzle.

"Lucy, you stay here with Isabel and the babby."

Agnes walked over to the shelf and took the tinder from the tinderbox, and placed the char cloth on the floor of the hearth. She struck the flint with the steel until the char cloth started to glow. Once it was glowing, she transferred it to a bundle of tow and slowly started to blow it into a flame. She then carefully placed dried wood shavings onto the flame, and it grew. Smaller twigs were added until the modest fire was born.

Tommy walked in and placed two more smallish pieces of cut, dried peat beside it. He knelt and blew on the flame to raise it. Both he and Agnes held their hands down toward the flame to warm them.

Agnes looked over at Lucy and Isabel, "We best clean this place up before Thomas gets home."

Tommy looked at his mother and smiled, " Don't worry about that, Ma, for I guarantee he will be delayed when he hears the news.

"Ya right there, Isabel?" whispered Lucy as she dabbed her forehead with a wet cloth.

Lucy turned to Tommy, "Well, are ya not going meet yer son," she called out.

In all the excitement Tommy had neglected to look, he walked over to Isabel and leaned over.

"Is grand it is," he whispered as he lowered the top of the bundling so he could see his little face. Tommy's frown was slowly replaced with a proud and relieved smile.

"Ya did a grand job, wife. He's a grand lad, but sa tiny."

Isabel had never seen Tommy with such a broad smile and

exhibiting so much pride, and she felt incredibly close to him, "Did ya want him full growd husband?"

Tommy, still mesmerised by the bundle, didn't answer.

Isabel looked at Agnes and rolled her eyes, "Full growd, twas hard enough getting this one out." She took a deep breath as the baby started to cry again.

Shocked, Tommy stepped back with an alarmed look on his face. "What I do?"

"Nothing, husband, he needs a feed, that's all." Isabel readjusted, brought the baby's head to her bosom and guided her large brown nipple to his lips.

The baby continued to cry, sensing the milk nearby, and became impatient, moving his mouth back and forth erratically to try to find the nipple and suckle. Finally, latching on, he quietened, and Isabel grimaced, smiled and rolled her eyes toward the heavens.

Isabel opened her eyes for a moment, then looked down at the baby with a tender, doting expression. He was suckling contentedly, and she could feel the vibrations coming from the bottom of the bundling.

"Have ya come up with a name yet, son?" asked his mother.

Tommy looked down in thought, "William, his name is William."

"That's a grand name, husband, a grand name."

Agnes Smiled, "William Rushworth, there it is then, named after his uncle, we'll call him Will."

Tommy left the women to tend to their business and walked to the Kings Arms where he knew his father, uncle and grandfather, John Hargreaves, were waiting. He walked through the door; he saw them sitting at one of the tables nervously waiting to hear any news.

Tommy, soaking wet, stepped through the door. There wasn't much in the village that went unnoticed, and all looked up worriedly. The patrons in the tavern stopped talking and looked over to eavesdrop on their conversation. There was an eerie quiet that fell over the room; even the barkeep stopped polishing the tankard he was holding and looked up inquisitively.

Thomas rose to greet him, "Well, spit it out, son!"

Tommy smiled, "A lad!"

The whole tavern cheered, "HURRAH!"

"On ya, Tommy," yelled John Pigshells.

They all stood to walk up to Tommy and his father, uncle and grandfather to shake their hands and congratulate them. Thomas was as proud as punch and tried hard to fight back the enormous gush of emotion he felt.

"Barkeep ales fer all!" Thomas bellowed while patting his son on the back.

"Isabel and the baby, they okay?" John Hargreaves asked curiously, slurring his words.

Tommy turned to him, "Couldn't be better," he said proudly as if he had accomplished the feat on his own.

"Babby is as strong as an ox, and he is named William, Will fer short," Tommy looked at his uncle proudly.

"Oh, that's grand, just grand," said Thomas, who looked down for a split second, remembering when his first son was born and then lost to the croup weeks later. A slight tear welled in the bottom of his eyelid, but he wiped it away quickly before anybody noticed and took his tankard in hand.

The patrons in the room had taken their seats again, all except three that were retrieving their penny ale from the barkeep.

John Hargreaves stood and slapped Tommy on the back, and slurring his words, he raised his tankard, "May your jack be ever full. May the roof over yer head be always strong, and may ya be in heaven half an hour before the devil knows yer dead."

The patrons in the tavern, those that were listening, cheered, laughed and raised their tankards to toast the new father.

William and the others stood and raised theirs with the rest of the other patrons. Some called out in support, others cheered, and others finished sculling their tankards, ready for a refill.

The barmaid was as excited as the rest and always loved a celebration. She was a buxom lady with a strong, likeable character. Her enchanting personality and confident smile brought a warmness to the establishment, and the men knew not to mess with her lest they receive a stiff slap like the last chap who tried his luck.

There was a feeling of merriment in the tavern, and the barmaid started to sing:

> "Bring us in no brown bread, for that is made of bran...
> Bring us in no white bread, for therein is no game...."

The rest of the patrons joined in with deep baritone voices.

"But bring us in good ale,
Bring us in good ale, for our Blessed Lady's sake,
Bring us in good ale,
Bring us in no mutton, for that is often lean,
Bring us no tripe, for they be seldom clean,
Bring us in good ale,
Bring us in good ale, for our Blessed Lady's sake,
Bring us in good ale."

The patrons cheered and started singing another song as the barmaid continued making her rounds of the tables ensuring that jacks and tankards were full.

William, John, Thomas and his son continued to sing and drink the night away. It wasn't often that they spent times like this for most of their time together was working the hide and the wool and tending to the animals. Tommy was finally starting to feel like one of the men, and even though he had the respect of all, he still felt they regarded him as a boy under the shadow of his father. However, Tommy had ambition and now, with a family of his own, felt it was his duty to make life more tolerable for them all if he could.

Slowly, the Kings Arms started to empty, the patrons once again congratulating Tommy and his father on the way out. It was well into the night by the time they walked up the hill toward the cottage. It was dark and quiet, except for the glow from the fire through the cracks in the shutters. Tommy stumbled, but his father helped him recover as he reached the door. They tiptoed inside, being sure not to wake anybody and receive a verbal flogging from Agnes.

William immediately climbed into the loft, where they now slept beside the twins John and Robert. He climbed into bed beside Lucy snuggling into her back. Lucy didn't mind the affection if it was up in the loft away from the others. Usually, William waited for the rest of the household to fall asleep before he snuggled closer to her. She would always hear the movements from below and then feel the bulge sticking into her lower back. She knew this was the time to turn so that he could position himself between her legs; well, that was if the brewer's droop didn't have other ideas. She tried to keep the rustling of the straw mattress to a minimum, and luckily, his thrusting and heavy breathing didn't last long. Once finished, he turned over and went to sleep, leaving her to stare up into the darkness.

Thomas tiptoed over to his wooden chair near the fire, sat and took out his clay pipe, stuffing the barrel full of the aromatic tobacco that he liked so much. He stared into the flame of the fire recounting the milestones of his life, now a grandfather, he thought to himself. Once again, a tear started to pool in the lower lid of his eye, which he quickly wiped away before Tommy could see.

He looked at his father's face. Worry lines creased his forehead, and whispers of hair streaked with silver fell sporadically, accentuating his receding hairline. His long bushy eyebrows were dusted with silver, and wispy white hair protruded from his nose and ears. A white shirt, greyed by frequent washing, opened at the top to show bristled chest hair, speckled with grey. His bearing was upright, and he had quiet confidence and wisdom. When he raised his pipe, you could see the veins protruding through the backs of his hands which were dotted with brown spots born of hours in the sun.

Tommy joined him at the hearth, a proud grin most pronounced on his face. "Father, tell me about yer da, what sort of man was he?" he whispered.

Thomas puffed on his pipe and paused and thought for a moment, then whispered, "A good man. Had the respect of the people hereabouts, and the heather was seeded by the blood from his hands. He spoke ill of none, and none spoke ill of him. He was the first to give and the last to take."

Tommy looked up to see a faint tear slowly flood his father's bottom eyelid as he choked back his memories of times gone by. This emotion was new to him, and he felt that the birth of his son had brought back hidden memories. Tommy could see that his father was uncomfortable talking and remembering, so he did not broach the subject any further.

Thomas looked at Tommy and reservedly started recounting stories of his father. He spoke of times and how his father would take him with him when he tended to the lord's *Demesne*. How they would fish for the lord's table and play hide and seek in the long wheat stalks and sneak apples from the manor orchards. Then his demeanour turned as he started to think about how he worked from dawn till night scratching a living out of the rocky ground. Thomas paused and swallowed, then spoke of his father's sickness and how the consumption had finally taken him.

Tommy never asked him the same question again.

ɕ CHAPTER FOUR ɞ

Words of a Tale

The church always played a role in the lives of the people of Haworth, and they went not only to escape the fine and be in God's good graces but also to hear of news from other parts of the country. As most were illiterate, this was quite often the only way they could hear the news of the political unrest and the struggle between King Charles I and his Westminster Parliament. All except John Hargreaves, who met enough travellers coming and going through the village to know before anybody else.

The following day the storm had abated and dressed in their only other set of clothes, their Sunday best; the family proceeded up Sun Street to St Michael and All Angels Church. It was a beautiful winter's day, and the curate, the vicar's assistant, rang his bell, which echoed off the surrounding hills, calling all who could hear to prayer. Thomas and Uncle William walked ahead while Tommy supported the arm of Isabel. She carried baby Will wrapped in swaddling and covered in a blanket. He bit down on Isabel's finger as she tried to calm his increasing irritability. John Hargreaves and his wife followed closely behind, breathing heavily from the extra exertion walking up the hill.

They trudged through the fresh, virgin snow, which was ankle-deep and a blinding white that hurt their eyes, causing them to squint. The land was a patchwork of white that stretched as far as the eye could see. Intermittent clouds cast their shadows on the hills of the Pennine. Dormant yellow winter grasses layered the slope down the hill at the side of the road, waiting to turn bright green again with the birth of Spring.

As they entered the church, their eyes adjusted to the dim light as they walked down the aisle and sat in two of the empty wooden pews. The large circular patterns adorning the walls displayed bible scenes, saints' apostles, angels and Christ in faded reds, ochres and yellows. Some of the white plaster had come adrift, exposing their stonemason's chip marks. The barrel-vaulted ceiling rose to the heavens, and the winter sun streamed through the new coloured window above the large stone altar. There was a wooden cross but gone were the large pewter candlesticks and ornaments because the church had been Puritanised and displays of grandeur were deemed 'ungodly'.

Agnes, Isabel and Margaret looked around to see who was arriving, who was there and who wasn't and who would be fined for their lack of attendance at the upcoming manor court. Thomas and William whispered about the news they had heard earlier from John Hargreaves about events in London and York. They wondered if it was true or not.

There was a hush over the congregation. The vicar appeared at the pulpit dressed in his regal-looking black double-breasted cassock buttoned at the neck, white gown with balloon sleeves and black square cap with four peaks.

They, following the vicar's lead, recited the Lord's Prayer,

> *"Our father who art in heaven,*
> *'allowed be thy name, thy Kingdom*
> *come thy will be done, on earth as it*
> *is in heaven. Give us this day our daily*
> *bread; 'n forgive our trespasses as*
> *we forgive them who trespass against*
> *us; lead us not into temptation, but*
> *deliver us from evil."*

After prayers, the vicar raised his hand to his mouth and coughed twice to gain the attention of the congregation, which quietened to listen to news he always provided at the end of prayers.

The church wardens walked down both sides of the aisle, passing a pewter plate along the rows of pews. Members of the congregation placed coins for the tithe to pay for the standard of living that the vicar was accustomed to. There was no set amount, but if the stewards thought it wasn't enough, then the plate would be handed back for a further contribution.

The plate was passed along the pew in front as Tommy watched each man place a coin, all except for one individual. He reached into his tunic to reveal an egg, which he carefully put on the plate and passed it to the next person, who looked down and frowned. The church warden, upon receiving the plate back, lifted the egg between his finger and thumb and looked at the man dumbfounded. The man looked back, shrugged his shoulders and smiled, hoping to achieve an empathetic judgment from him. The vicar watched on curiously as the steward walked past him with the egg standing on its end being held up by the small mound of coin.

The vicar, momentarily disturbed by the strange occurrence, turned back to the task at hand.

The congregation hushed and listened intently to what the vicar had to say, for it was, in most cases, their only way of hearing the news from outside the village.

The vicar began, "His Majesty, King Charles, has entered the House of Commons with an armed guard and issued the warrant for the arrest of five members of Parliament for high treason."

There was a hum of excitability. The parishioners looked at each other and whispered their shock and confusion. John Hargreaves turned to look back at his daughter Agnes worriedly. She looked again, confused by what was announced.

"Aye up, this means trouble," whispered Thomas.

William, not entirely sure of what Thomas meant, remained silent and continued to look at the vicar to try and grasp an understanding of what he was saying.

The vicar relished his feeling of importance that this part of the services provided. Being one of the few in the parish that could read or write, he liked how powerful it made him feel and often liked to exaggerate the news to instil fear and trepidation in his parishioners.

The vicar put his hand to his mouth and coughed to hush the crowd. He continued, "His Majesty the King has left London and has established his court at York. Last week, King Charles' army besieged the city of Hull but was turned away by a large army loyal to Parliament. As a result, the King has declared Lord Hotham, Governor of Hull, a traitor to the Kingdom and has raised his standard at Nottingham."

A low hum spread over the congregation. The parishioners were a simple people and confused; they whispered to each other, unsure of what or how this would affect them.

Feeling the air of confusion and fear in the room, the vicar raised his hands to quieten his flock. He continued, "Furthermore, the Earl of Cumberland has the command of the northern counties, including the West. Lord Birkhead, lord of the manor, will raise a troop from among the local tenants and parishioners. All men of fighting age are to band together to form a troop to defend the village against marauders and protect the lord's grain stores and property.

Agnes placed her hand on top of Thomas' and squeezed it fearfully.

"Don't worry yerself, wife." Thomas put his hand over hers discreetly, and she felt warmed by his uncharacteristic gesture.

"But Thomas, they can force you to fight," she whispered.

"I'm a freeman wife, can't force me ta do nowt."

Tommy looked at his father and then back at Isabel, who gently rocked the baby back and forth. She looked at Tommy worriedly, then back at her father and mother, who sat in the pew behind.

When they left the church, Thomas, William, John Hargreaves and Tommy bid farewell to the womenfolk and walked to the Kings Arms, the local alehouse that they frequented after church. It wasn't supposed to be open on a Sunday, but two taps and a pause before the third tap at the back door magically gained them entry.

Entering the alehouse, they ducked their head going through the door. The reeve was in the process of drumming up support for the lord's troop of clubmen. The steward's trusted advisor dealt with his lordship's demesne. He was the one that dealt with the grievances and tended to business with the tenants and copyholders. He was from a good family that had been in service to the lord for some generations, with both his father and his father before him holding the same office. Saying that he was beholden to the peasant farmers who worked the land because it was them and not the steward who voted him in each year at the manor court. He was well respected thereabouts, and even though he received his stipend from the lord, he was both fair and just with the demands of his position.

The reeve had known the Rushworth family for most of his life and always knew them to be an honest, hardworking lot. In fact, it was he that had convinced them to become freemen on his lordship's land, taking away the bindings of a feudal copyholder existence and gaining the freedoms and pure rewards that came with it.

The steward's clerk had positioned himself at a table near the back door, taking the names of volunteers and asking them to make their mark on his ledger. As none of them could read or write, there was a half-page of wobbly X s written down the middle of the page beside a smartly written pronunciation of their names.

Tommy didn't frequent the establishment at the behest of his mother but on occasion was urged to come hither by his uncle William who wanted "to make a man of him". Now that he was older and a father, he felt more confident to go against the wishes of his mother. He relished the accompanying freedom and respect awarded him by his father, uncle and grandfather John Hargreaves.

Entering the alehouse, he was always immediately stunned by its smoky, dampness. It wasn't the first time that he had been, but, in some instances, he always felt intimidated by the arguing and roughness of the place. He really preferred to be out in the moors or tending to more worthwhile pursuits on the hide with Isabel and the English Mastiff.

The rotting stale food that had been dropped satisfied the rather large rat consuming what he could until the beggar-maker, as his grandfather used to call the barman, shooed him away with his cloth. The old grey cat sitting on the top of the barrel was totally disinterested. He had had his fill earlier and had some trepidation about taking on a rat this size.

A large wooden table and two long benches were at the centre of the room, and large oak beams held up the ceiling, which was yellowed and stained from pipe smoke. A large wooden ornate mantlepiece surrounded the fire, an old jug and pewter tray sitting on top of it. Most of the hand craftsmen, workmen and labourers sat on hardback forms and the abject poor treated themselves to the slops left by others. They all insisted on discussing and arguing the politics of the day of King, country and Parliament.

"The King's starting to mobilise pike and musket at Wakefield," whispered one man.

The other turned to look at him worriedly, "That's only a day's march away,"

"Aye, but not an easy march, especially in winter, besides what would they want with the moors, it's considered a cold and desolate place for most."

"Don't be so sure. Roundheads are mobilising at Bradford and are counting on the support of the people of the west to support them in their cause."

The shutters were closed on a Sunday, and most of the light came from the fire in the hearth and the odd tallow candle. The serving maid tracked backwards and forwards, filling empty leather jacks and the odd pewter mug for the more well-off patrons. These men often disappeared upstairs for political discussions away from the eyes of others.

"Aye up, men come, sign your mark and receive five pennies and a tankard of ale, a token from his lordship." The reeve called out.

There was an initial zeal by some men of the local area, especially those who worked for his lordship. The reeve had been put in command of the local *clubmen*, a ragtag bunch of volunteers with little or no experience in military affairs.

The reeve noticed the Rushworth men come in through the door, "What about you, Thomas Rushworth, will you not fight with us?"

"Me family, that's the only thing I fight for." Thomas, now a freeman, knew that the reeve or even the steward couldn't force his hand, so he walked past the clerk and sat at one of the empty half barrel tables.

Tommy, William and John Hargreaves looking down to erase any idea of support, followed. William took a three-legged stool from an empty table nearby and joined them.

Tommy watched the young men that signed the ledger, "Maybe we should join," said Tommy naively.

Thomas glared at his son, "War's not glamorous, Tommy, I remember me da telling me about it when I was a lad. His da left one day and never came back. Left his wife and young ones to fend for themselves, and they ended up begging in the street in York."

"I agree, Thomas, and besides who will tend the hide in spring if we are gone, no idea how long this will last, we'll be worse off than we are now and what about the young bairns?" declared John Hargreaves.

Thomas leaned forward, his forearms taking over most of the table and whispered, "King or Parliament, Roundheads or Cavaliers makes no difference to me or mine, still have to pay the tax and the tithe to the church. I'll not give me bullocks as well!"

"Aye, true that Thomas," whispered William thinking of his wife Lucy and his young bairn on the way.

"I heard they been forcing them to join in York," said John alarmingly.

Thomas leaned back onto his stool, "Aye, there be dangerous times ahead."

Old John Hargreaves, the more outspoken of the men, leaned back on his stool. "Who do you have to kill ta get Haworth manufacture 'round here?" John looked around, "barmaid four jacks of ale before I die a slow, painful, thirsty death."

"Aye up, John, enough with the killing and dying there's enough of that on the way," said the barmaid who had known about the whispers of news for a time.

The back door opened, and a beam of sunshine flowed in, followed by the steward, the administrator responsible for the dealings of the manor. Many of the patrons quietened their chat and turned their eyes away in distrust and contempt, knowing that he under-priced the fleece that they sold him.

He wore a long blue coat, brown breeches with tan hose underneath, a wide-brimmed hat which he took off to expose his long dark, greying, shoulder-length, curly hair. He carefully caressed his thin greying moustache on his upper lip. At the same time, he allowed time for his eyes to adjust to the dim-lit room. His beard was neatly trimmed to a point just below his chin to give him that regal look. Keeping with the mood of the day, he kept his hand on the guard of a sword, but he was inexperienced in its use and only wore it for show.

He was used to men turning away when he entered the alehouse; he liked how powerful it made him feel. The only three that didn't were Thomas, John and William, who had dealings with him in the past. Saying that they were still not foolish enough to trust him or say too much in his presence.

"Well, who da we have here then, it's master's John and Thomas," he grumbled in a derogatory tone which was more of a put down than a greeting.

"Oh, and young Tommy, I see you follow in your father's and grandfather's footsteps; they've always been a bit too partial to the ale."

Tommy glared at the steward, but his father, seeing this put his hand on his shoulder to calm him.

"Seems you have a high-spirited lad there, Rushworth. I'd keep an eye on him; he might get himself into some trouble before too long."

Thomas took off his hat and looked down submissively, "No, Your Grace just too big fer his boots, that's all, no harm meant sir."

"So, Rushworth, the reeve tells me you haven't signed yer mark to his lordship's ledger."

Standing in respect after his son's attempt at chivalry, Thomas bowed his head respectfully, knowing the difficulties that could arise if he were to get on the wrong side of him. "I have nowt ta give sir, except as cannon fodder, and besides if I'm gone, who'll tend the hide come Spring?"

The steward sensing Thomas' ploy, responded, "Never ya mind that, there's plenty of souls ta do the lord's bidding come Spring. You wouldn't want to see ya loved one's heads on pikes because that's what'll happen if the Roundheads and Cavaliers get up here," he growled.

John and William remained nervously quiet, looking down at the table so as not to make things even more difficult than they already were. The other patrons looked the other way, hushed, lest the steward move his attention to them. Tommy watched his father's passive stance in front of the steward, and it seemed uncharacteristically foreign to him.

"Right you are Rushworth, we should let the younger ones prove their worth to his lordship. What say you, William? I remember you as a brave young lad. Will you not take up arms against the treasonous bastards that threaten us?"

Nervously William replied, "Aye, I will, but my dearest is just ready to have our babby as ya know your grace. She's full of it and will surely fall victim to the devil's curse if I'm not there to hear its cry. We've already lost one ta the croup, and another would surely cause her end. Once the babby is here, I'll make me mark."

"Aye, and what about you, Tommy Rushworth, that stubborn, boisterous spirit of yours might come in quite handy for his lordship's troop."

Thomas interjected, "Your Grace, ya don't need him in the ranks. He's a stupid lad, bit simple if you ask me, comes from his mother's side. Be more use out of the troop than in. Be more of an advantage to the enemy than to you," he said, being sure not to show loyalty to either side.

Agnes' father, John Hargreaves, was about to defend his daughter and gave Thomas the filthiest of looks but was smart enough to abandon his contempt. He then realised the game Thomas was playing and continued to look oblivious to the conversation. He took a swig of his ale then looked at Tommy with pride.

John Hargreaves was a large, heavy chested man, fully bearded with long dirty blonde, unkempt hair that fell wildly to his shoulders. His nose was perpetually red, and his eyes had a look of wisdom. Still, only those who really knew him saw past the drunken larrikin persona he portrayed. He was uncultivated, rowdy and had disregard for any social or political conventions. What he did have was a good heart, and all knew this and forgave him for his at times wild outlandish, drunken ways.

"Right then," I'll inform the reeve that he can expect you." The steward walked away to the next table and started the conversation the same way.

The steward moved onto the furthest parts of the room to have a similar conversation with others that he knew hadn't signed the roll. Others closest to the back door that he hadn't spoken to up and sheepishly left unwilling to be volunteered.

"Let that be a lesson, Tommy. There's a time when you stand up fer yerself and be recognised and a time when tis smarter to bend like the bulrush in the wind. Right, I'm off then," said Thomas, sculling the rest from the leather jack.

"Aye up, wait for me," said Tommy, who didn't quite have the confidence to remain behind on his own. William stood from the table and followed them out. John preferred to stay; he picked up his jack and joined another group of men at another table.

Thomas squinted and turned his head away as his eyes adjusted to the brightness of the day. The sky was a fresh blue with no cloud to be seen. The icy hills in the distance were a bright white speckled with the dark greys of the uncovered rocky outgrowths that lined the hills.

William ducked through the door, "Here don't let on about the goings-on of the day, Lucy as enough on her mind, last thing she needs to hear is all this."

They started walking down Main Street, Tommy and William running and picking up speed to see who was the fastest. They laughed hysterically as William fell flat on his face when his foot caught the edge of a tree root hidden beneath the snow.

They walked across the white fields to Sun Street past the broken cottages on the left and rising hills dotted with sheep grazing on what fodder they could find through the layer of snow on the right. Up the hill they went; it was tough going, and their breath curled like steam from their mouths after it was warmed.

Tommy raced ahead, and William stopped and waited for Thomas to catch up.

Thomas was deep in thought, "Barkeep told me he heard the King is starting to mobilise pike and musket at Bradford under the Earl of Newcastle."

"That's only half a day's march away," claimed William.

William's comment made Thomas think, "Aye, it is at that."

"Will we need to make plans just in case it gets any closer?" asked William.

Thomas looked at William and imagined the whole family trudging through the snow with the few provisions they could carry, "What plans might they be?"

William thought for a moment.

"No, brother, I think we are better off staying here than traipsing about the countryside with the bairns and women. At least here, if things get worse, we can disappear into the moors for a time; they'll never find us out there," asserted Thomas.

William nodded, "Maybe the trouble would be further east with the King interned at Nottingham."

Thomas replied with regret, "William, I hope you are right, but when the hostilities start, I'm sure it will affect us all. Can you imagine what damage a cannon could do? And what of trade and of course who is going to feed that army?"

Thomas, William and Tommy walked up the partly snow-covered hard muddied field that had slightly melted in the sun. The thin layer of ice crunched as they walked, and the English Mastiff sensing their approach bounded down the hill after them. Its ears flapping up and down and drool cascading out the side of its black lips. Reaching them, it jumped up onto Tommy excitedly, licking him in the process until he told it to heel.

The white fields were divided by the grey, walled, stony divides. There were sheep on the hills; you could hear them. The bare birch trees standing lonely and cold, waiting for the birth of spring. The brown grasses tried to raise their head above its white cloak, almost as if it was trying to save itself from a suffocating end. The days were shorter now, and with the evening, as the sun started its descent, came the chilled wind across the moors. They knew they had to get home to the warmth of the hearth, for they knew only mad dogs and Irishmen braved the night.

"Come on, boy," commanded Tommy as he jogged up toward the cottage. The English Mastiff followed quickly behind, tail wagging with joy that they were home.

"Brother, do you remember when we had that much vigour?" Thomas asked William, who was walking beside him.

"Aye, we had vigour, but I was always the fastest," claimed William smiling.

Thomas looked at him, "What a lot of rot, I held me own, what about the race we had at the wedding feast, left you fer dead."

"I had ta let you win besides yer a cheating bastard," claimed

William, who proceeded to nudge his brother with his elbow.

"Aye, I got you that day," said Thomas smiling, "did what I had ta do to get the garter, bloody well worth it an' all."

They reached the cottage and lifted the latch. As they opened the door, they could smell the aroma of the well-cooked pottage and were immediately greeted by Agnes.

She stood there with her hands on her waist with a look of contempt. The ties of the dark brown wimple hanging down the sides of her face which had a rosiness from the radiant heat of the fire. Her beige kirtle was dirtied from the day's labours and wet and stained with manure and sod. The dark brown bodice laced loosely across her stomach did nothing to hide her mummy tummy, which she had slowly become accustomed to.

"Where have you dirty stop-outs been?" Agnes asked, fully aware of where they had been. "Vicar will have you at the manor court if he finds out what yer up to on a Sunday after church."

She had expected them earlier for dinner and was cranky. Isabel and Lucy preferring to keep on the brighter side of their husbands.

"Give over, wife," Thomas smiled at her mock crankiness, "Working all week, are we not allowed a quiet ale when time permits?"

"You better sit down and have yer supper," she ladled pottage into three bowls and put them on the table abruptly.

Lucy walked over and touched William on the shoulder as she put mugs for the ale on the table. William, not wanting to appear sensitive in front of the others, ignored her gesture.

They sat at the table, "Been chatting business with the steward," said Tommy. Having not learned yet to say only what needed to be said to the fairer ones in the cottage.

Thomas and William gave him a stern stare as he had obviously forgotten about William's earlier request. Thomas looked at Tommy and discreetly shook his head before blowing on a wooden spoon full of the watery stew before slurping on it.

"Oh, and what business might that be, Tommy?" asked Isabel as she placed the jug of ale on the table in front of them.

Lucy walked over with the bread she had baked that morning and placed it in front of them, waiting for a response to the question. All three of them looked down at the bowl of pottage and picked up the spoon in nervous silence.

Finally, Thomas slurped from his spoon, "Pottage is grand Agnes, better than last week."

Agnes was annoyed and stood with her hands on her hips, looking at Thomas impatiently, "You can't fool me, Thomas Rushworth. I know what you men have been talking about and don't get any ideas about goin' off with the rest of 'em. His grace can fight his own battles!"

Knowing, of course, that he was not going to let on, Agnes gave him the stare then turned away, shaking her head and grumbling something under her breath that only she could hear.

Thomas ignored the gesture and took another spoonful.

Lucy thought to herself and wondered if there would ever be a day when she and William would have a falling out. Their marriage wasn't bliss, but it worked, and she felt quite content living here with William's family after they took her in. Lucy remembered what they had to go through and to think they now had two boys with another babby on the way.

The Truth of the Secret

In these days of political turmoil, Puritan dogma had taken over and affected all their lives in some way. Lucy knew the custom of courtship and marriage had been affected. Cromwell's conservative attitude was that the holy union was more a public and social event. A union was for procreation and not to be enjoyed.

Since the adoption by the church of more Puritan values, marriage and the signing of banns, especially to a man below one's station, was deemed inappropriate. Young women were expected to seek their parent's blessing beforehand, and the spousal contract did not necessarily have to take place in a church. The present time was one of confusion and religious sanctity. The church tried to impart respectability and social prestige through the signing of banns; however, sight unseen, this was not always the case.

Women were considered physically, intellectually and morally inferior to their male counterparts. It was usually the head of the household who made decisions of matrimony on their behalf. In poorer households, women had more freedom to choose a husband and, dismissing the Puritan ways, embarked on her own to find a man she loved and who loved her.

Lucy remembered their courtship; it was a difficult time for them both. Her courtship with William was seemingly doomed for failure from the very beginning. She recollected those times, and it still angered her and whether rightly or wrongly, she became estranged from her father as a result.

Lucy worked at the alehouse back then and was used to seeing William, his brother and John Hargreaves on a regular basis. Still, on this occasion, William was alone.

"Aye up, young William is here," as she placed a tankard of ale before him.

He ignored her.

"I'm sorry you're looking melancholy."

"None of yer' business," said William bluntly.

"Why the sadness, William?"

"Just thinking about me mother, that's all."

Lucy looked down with sympathy, "I'm sorry, my condolences. She was a fine woman."

"What would you know about her," William swallowed and paused, trying to swallow the sadness away. "What would a serving maid like you know about me Ma?"

Lucy became irritated by what he had said, especially because she had always had a fondness for him. "Well, first off, you don't know me from a bar of soap, so don't begin to presume you do."

William looked embarrassed about what he had said. Still, the embarrassment was overshadowed by his thoughts of his mother and their last times together, "I'm sorry for what I said, I'm just feeling down, that's all."

Lucy smiled that wide bright smile, "Apology accepted, William, you don't know me apart from what you see here in this God-forsaken place. This is just a job to help my family. No different to what your brother's wife does at the manor, really."

"Tis a bit. She doesn't make the candle chandeliers shake every evening."

"Ooooh, that, no need ta worry about that, harmless fun, that's all. His Grace has me keep an eye on the barkeep and listen out for secrets. He thinks the barkeep has been diddling the coin."

Lucy had a soft spot for William and had for some years but knew that her reputation would make it difficult to find a suitor.

Lucy leaned forward to whisper, "William, if ya can keep a secret, I'll show you this is all a ruse. I work fer His Grace, not the barkeep, although the coin he pays me fer serving is a bonus."

"What do you mean a ruse?" asked William.

"It's all put on; my real job is ta serve ale and hear secrets at the gambling tables and pass them on to His Grace."

"What about the chandelier?" William asked inquisitively.

Whispering, "Next time I go upstairs, you come up afterwards; I'll leave the door open a little, and you peek inside. You must promise

46

me that you won't let on about our little secret, though."

"Right you are then," William was confused and frowned quizzically in frustration, really wanting to be left alone with his thoughts.

Lucy refilled William's tankard with ale and turned to serve her other customers.

William watched her walk away, and she could sense that he did. As she walked to another table to fill the jacks, she looked back, smiled and flicked her blonde curly hair. She had a lovely figure; thin waist and her bosom and cleavage were accentuated by the leather drawstrings of her bodice, which were pulled together tightly.

Later that evening, the baker from the manor walked in. He didn't bother with the ale, just walked straight up the rickety stairs. Lucy looked at William and winked; she placed the empty jacks down on the bar and followed her customer up. The barkeep had his back turned, and the rest of the clientele were engrossed in their games and conversations. William sculled his ale and stood as the chandelier started to shake; he was hesitant but curious, so he quickly shot up the stairs. At the top, he noticed the door ajar just as Lucy had promised. He tiptoed over and carefully peeked through the gap between the door and the jamb. There was Lucy fully dressed, fixing her hair. The baker from the manor sat on the side of the bed and jumped up and down, making the bed and the floor creak. Shocked at what he had seen, he slipped back down the rickety stairs and sat back down. A few moments later, the baker followed and walked out the door, followed by Lucy, who pretended to fix her gown and prop her bosom.

Minutes later, smiling, Lucy returned to William's table. "Another ale, kind sir?" She lifted his tankard and refilled it from the clay jug.

Confused, William looked around to see if anybody was in proximity and was about to question her.

Lucy whispered, "No, not now, meet me by the big oak tree by the beck on Sunday after church and don't be late."

William looked down at the table in deep thought, he was about to whisper, but Lucy walked away to refill jacks on another table. William watched her go, and she could sense that he did. As she was filling the jacks, she looked over, smiled then continued as if nothing had happened.

The following Sunday, parishioners filed out of the church, and William headed south down Main Street, along Bridgehouse Lane, then walked along the bank of the beck for half a mile. He didn't expect to see her, but when he arrived at the old oak tree with its massive trunk and bulbous roots that spread out tentacle-like from the ground, he saw her. She was leaning up against the trunk smiling and humming a pretty tune. As quietly as he possibly could, he walked up behind the tree, reached around and put his hand on her shoulder.

Lucy screamed, "WILLIAM RUSHWORTH, YOU FOOL, YOU SCARED ME HALF TO DEATH!"

William took a step backwards and started to laugh, bending over and putting his hands on his knees.

Lucy bent over and picked up a thick, broken branch and flung it at him, hitting him in the shin. He hollered and rubbed his shin while Lucy looked for another.

Still rubbing his shin, his laughing had abated, "Stop, stop, can't you take a joke? You've cut me look; there's blood."

"Serves ya self-right, what are ya doing creeping up on poor unsuspecting women and scaring the be Jesus out of 'em!"

Embarrassed, William looked melancholy, trying to get some sympathy and whispered, "I'm sorry, Lucy."

"Alright then, but don't do anything like that again," she smiled at his boyish look of sadness. "Now then, let me have a look at that cut."

"It's alright, just a scratch," said William, trying to sound as manly as he could under the circumstances.

"Let me have a look," Lucy bent down and moved his hand from the cut. She looked at it and wiped the drop of blood away with her apron. He watched her with intent looking down at her long eyelashes and the big blue eyes framed by whispers of golden hair and, of course, her cleavage.

When she looked up, he looked into her eyes and planted a kiss quickly on her lips.

She pushed his face away, "William!" she yelled, "What's got into you?"

She stood up abruptly and started to walk away quickly.

William stood and chased after her, "Wait, Lucy, come back!"

He caught up to her and touched her on the arm, "I'm sorry Lucy, I thought after the Kings Arms, you wanted to...."

"I told you and showed you William all that was a ruse, do you not believe me?"

"Of course, I believe ya, Lucy, but I still thought ya wanted to," he paused...

"Not like this, William. If my father knew that we were here alone, he'd probably beat me and have your guts for garters. Come on, let's walk and talk for a while before I must get back."

"Back to the tavern?"

"No, not Sunday. Father won't allow it."

"So why weren't you in church this morning?" William asked curiously.

"I was, but at an earlier service before you arrived, vicar gives me family private prayers each Sunday morning."

"Aye up, so who is thy father?"

Ignoring the question, "William, I've got ta run before we're seen, and he gets wind that I'm out here alone without a chaperone." Lucy started running back toward the village."

William took two steps after her, "Wait, when can I see you again?"

"I'll let ya know," she yelled without turning back around.

William walked along the beck, the days were getting shorter now, and leaves had started to fall. The banks of the beck were an epitome of colour. The brown, beige and deep red were a stark contrast to the green moss which climbed the north side of trees hanging over the beck.

William picked up a stone from the bank and threw it, trying to make it skip on the surface of the water, but it was quite shallow in parts, and his attempt was cut short by the pebbly bottom. He was deep in thought about Lucy, troubled and frustrated by her mysterious ways. He picked up another stone and tried to skip it again; it bounced three times but was then halted by a large rock jutting out of the surface of the water.

The sun was starting to get low in the sky, and there was work to do in the morning. He continued to walk along the bank of the beck, on occasion needing to walk up towards Sun Street because of the density of the trees and bushes that lined the bank. The sky was a pale white, and the clouds had the shadow of rain coming from the west. When William was parallel with the hide, he started walking east out of the valley through the green fields, up to Sun Street and Hall Green.

Tommy was outside helping his father chop wood, and the chimney was chugging smoke from dried peat that Agnes had obviously just put on the fire.

As he neared the cottage, the English Mastiff, still a puppy, bounded towards him, his ears flapping beside his large head, saliva trailing behind him. He had a broad, black snout and shiny beige coat and relished the scratch behind the ears that William gave him when he reached him.

"Aye up, Thomas, you all right?"

"Where have you been, William? The animals need bringing in and tending to."

"Right you are, Thomas, I'll tend to them right now," William replied, feeling a little guilty and neglectful that he had been gone for so long.

William walked to the common green and untethered the ox and cow, leading them in by ropes attached to rings through their snout. He then returned to the common green and herded in the handful of sheep that they had, including the new lambs that had birthed in the spring. He shepherded the animals into the enclosure, put fresh hay in the crib for the cow and ox and topped up the water. The boar had been sniffing in the long grass around the outside of the cottage for scraps and other carrion. The sow stayed in the enclosure, standing up, trying to deter the piglets from engaging with her teats. She squealed with delight as Agnes threw a bucket of scraps into the enclosure, cuttings from preparing the tea. The boar, hearing this bolted inside to join her in sniffing out the more delectable pieces.

William went back outside and helped Thomas stack the wood that he had chopped under the eave at the back of the cottage before it started to rain. Normally they didn't have wood to chop, but this was a payment from the lord for work done on his demesne.

Thomas knew there was something on William's mind, "You're troubled William, anything you want to share?"

"No, brother, just thinking about something, that's all." William knew he couldn't share what had happened today with his older brother for fear of chastisement as he knew he had no time for who he called the 'bar wench'.

It started to rain, not drizzle but a downpour which beat down a thunderous angry roar followed by the zzzzzzzzzzPANG!!! of thunder and the zap of lightning which split the sky.

Agnes appeared at the door, "Come in, Tommy, quickly before you catch a chill."

Thomas picked up his son Tommy by the back of his tunic and carried him inside, much to the youngster's amusement as he started to laugh and giggle. The dog, seeing the rough handling of the young one, barked and jumped up at Thomas' leg, then licked Tommy's face as he was placed on the stone floor inside. Tommy giggled again and put his hands up to his face to protect himself from the dog's affection. He turned over with his behind up in the air, face to the floor. He put his arms around his head for cover as the dog began pushing his snout under his arms to lift them, so he could get in to lick his face. Tommy giggled with merriment and tried to push the dog away. Still, he was too strong, so he resorted to the best defensive position again by putting his face once more to the floor. The dog stood there wagging his tail, looked at Thomas, had a small whine, then continued trying to push his snout under the young one's arms.

"That's enough dog, heel," bellowed Thomas.

The dog spared the youngster, walked over and laid down at Thomas' feet near the fire but all the time watchful of the young one, lest he want to continue the game.

Agnes poured more grain, cut up potatoes and carrots and put them into the earthenware pot hanging from an iron pole supported by two upright iron stands at the sides of the fire. The large rectangular stones at the back of the hearth were darkened with soot. A small stack of branches sat in the corner of the hearth drying and situated ready for use if the fire started to dim. An assortment of wooden ladles and iron fire tools dangled from hooks on the inside wall of the fireplace. A three-legged stool with a thick base sat on the other side of the hearth, opposite Thomas' chair. Behind it was a barrel with a candle and an earthenware jug of ale. In front of the fire sat a small table with a small iron candle holder where the family had their meals.

Agnes gave the pottage under the chimney a good stir with the spartle. She put bread on the table with butter that she had churned a day ago and moved the jug of ale to the table.

Thomas stood from his chair and moved it to the head of the table. Sitting down, he waited for William and Agnes to be seated. Agnes placed the bowls of pottage on the table in front of him and William.

Thomas closed his eyes, put his hands together, and the others followed suit,

"Bless, O Father, Thy gifts to our use
and us to Thy service; for Christ"s sake. Amen."

They all replied in unison, "Amen."

Agnes picked up Tommy and sat him on her lap, blowing on the wooden spoon and feeding him as drops of the watery mix dribbled down his chin.

They ate in silence after saying grace, then Thomas returned his chair to the side of the hearth and took out his pipe. William stayed at the table fidgeting with his tankard of ale and going over the unexpected events of the day. He was confused, and Thomas could tell.

Thomas knew that there was something up with his brother, he could always tell, but he wasn't going to push the issue. He knew that when William was ready, he would confide in him. He did have a feeling it had something to do with the barmaid down at the Kings Arms. *What was her name?* he thought to himself. *Lucy? Why his brother wanted to get mixed up with the likes of her, he didn't know, but each to their own. If he didn't bring her back home, it was his business*, he thought.

The Winter of Red

There was a sombre attitude in the village. All braced for the coming hostilities as they seemed to get closer and closer to the village; some made plans, others didn't. Propaganda was rife from both King and Parliament, for both sides knew that to win this war, they needed to win the hearts of the people.

Occasionally, a traveller from York would arrive distributing prints of satirical pamphlets depicting a weak King being bewitched by his evil Catholic Queen. These pamphlets seemed to sway public opinion in favour of the Parliamentarians, and unrest grew.

Most women stayed out of the political debates, especially Lucy, who erred on the side of caution and kept quiet when Thomas, William and Tommy spoke of such things. Her father, she thought, swayed more to the side of the King and disclosing this could cause problems for her and the boys. It had been almost five years since Lucy had moved into the cottage with the Rushworths and, now estranged from her father, rarely saw him. She doted on her two children and husband, although a third was undoubtedly a treasure but tedious and tiring, to say the least.

She was an attractive lady and, since passing on her dubious position at the Kings Arms, had settled down. As Lucy didn't have the need to play her games at the Kings Arms anymore, she dressed more moderately, and William told the family about her special duties and responsibilities at the Kings Arms. She was devout and clean. Still, they didn't believe William but accepted that he was happy, and that's all that mattered.

Lucy tried to help as much as possible and would stand there for hours with the spinning wheel; she had become quite proficient. She would take the fibre in her left hand and slowly turn the wheel with her right. Overlapping a piece of fibre with the leader, she would begin to slowly turn the wheel clockwise while simultaneously pulling backwards and drawing the fibre in the left hand away from the spindle. It was a tiresome and monotonous process, but it made her feel as though she was contributing, and this pleased her.

Arriving home with news, Thomas, William, John Hargreaves and Tommy sat together at the table. "Men's business not fer the ears of womenfolk," stated Thomas grumpily as he looked up at Agnes and Lucy.

William spoke in a hushed tone, " I was speaking to John Pigshells the other day he told me that the Royalist Sir Francis Doddington, well he strung up twelve civilians all in the same tree."

"It seems all morality, compassion and the laws of war are lost," whispered Thomas shaking his head.

"Aye that," said John. " The Roundheads at Hopton castle surrendered, the prisoners were bound together and stripped naked, then under guard, they were taken to the basement and clubbed to death."

Overhearing what John had said, Lucy looked over. "That's barbaric!"

"Wife, keep ta yer spinning and keep the bairns quiet, lest they get a whipping," demanded William.

William's sons John and Robert sat on the floor, waiting for their father to finish his supper. They knew not to disturb him or their uncles while they were slurping pottage and talking grown-up business. They had been taught that children should be seen but not heard and would be threatened with the whipping stick if they didn't keep to it. It didn't get to that point as usually their father's step toward the stick in the corner was enough to quieten them.

One of William's sons, the eldest Robert, wore dirty, beige and baggy knickerbockers and long woollen winter hose splashed with faeces from mucking out the animal shelter. A dirty tan coloured shirt ripped at the front from where his brother had grabbed him while playing with the bound cloth ball in the snow. Dark brown hair framed an angelic face. His younger brother John sat on the cold floor beside his mother, a dark brown tunic buttoned at the top but spread open, showing his dirty grey shirt. A triangular collar folded over under his chin. Bare lower legs topped by brown cut hand-me-down knickerbockers, kept up by a piece of string. The quieter of the two boys but stubborn like his father and not scared to give his brother back as much as he received even though he was a good hand shorter.

It was getting late, and Thomas brought a pamphlet out of his tunic and placed it on the table in front of William. The pamphlet depicted Royalists holding children up on the end of their pikes and the King taking a baby away from its mother, begging on her knees in front of him.

"Wife, send the bairns to bed," demanded Thomas authoritatively.

Agnes spotted what was on the pamphlet and put her hand over her mouth alarmingly. She rounded up the children and shooed them up the ladder to the loft. Lucy got back to her spinning, and Isabel continued making a basket from the wattle she had collected.

William whispered, "I've heard that the local villages are recruiting men to help defend Bradford."

"They won't stand a chance. They say Sir William has cannon up there; they'll all be slaughtered," said Thomas worriedly.

John leaned in closer, "The King's Foot and Horse soldiers are there drumming up support; anybody that doesn't sign their mark gets a beating. They been smashing up the town, and two men were killed the other night walking through Bradford."

"So what are we going to do?" asked Tommy.

Thomas looked at his son worriedly, "Not much we can do at present, just hope the weather and terrain keeps them away."

"I say we should fight," said Tommy with bravado.

"Calm yourself, son. You've never seen what a matchlock musket ball can do to a man." Thomas stood and lowered his voice standing behind his son threateningly.

"Imagine a hot ball of solid lead three-quarters of an inch in diameter. At thirty yards, it pierces yer skin, breaks your bones, and splatters part of yer guts as it comes out yer back, leaving a hole you could fit yer thumb into."

Tommy smiled nervously and swallowed hard, looking ahead and saying nothing as William and John Hargreaves looked on mischievously.

His father put his hands on his son's shoulders and leaned in even closer, whispering, "And if you were lucky enough to survive," he paused,

"that musket ball would have taken a bit of material from yer tunic in with it and left it there where it would fester and rot, then you'd get the sweats, and a fever would take over. No matter how much they tried ta help you, the wound would start to smell like a dead lamb left in the sun on a hot summer's day. A day or two later, you would be delirious, probably calling out yer mother's name. They'd take you outside and leave ya because they know yer dying. If yer' shot in the leg...."

Agnes heard her husband as she came back down from the loft and knew what he was up to, "Husband, leave the lad. I think he gets the idea."

Thomas smiled and slapped his son on both shoulders with his hands, "There you have it, war in a nutshell!"

William picked up the pamphlet to have a closer look, then put it in his tunic away lest the women and children found it.

Thomas walked around the table and sat back down on his chair near the fire, taking out his pipe in the process. William and John followed, pulling up a stool near him.

"You put the fear of Jesus into him," whispered John as William chuckled anxiously.

"Aye, but war's not a game of ball, many men will die before its end, and it will be a winter of red you mark my words," grumbled Thomas.

Thomas stared into the fire, saying nothing but contemplating the consequences of war on his family and their future.

❧ CHAPTER SEVEN ☙

The Prince's Daughter

Before the fighting began, many of the nobility and aristocrats swore allegiance and had joined the King's army. Roundheads grew in numbers spurred on by the London apprentices demonstrating their support for Parliament. Others with no allegiance to either joined up with the first army that came along with the hope of pay and plunder.

John Hargreaves told Thomas that in other parts of the country, tenants were being forced by their landlords to join the army, and beggars were being conscripted by parish constables and others forced at gunpoint. This gave Thomas an uneasy feeling, and an uncertain future worried him. Still, he, John and William did everything they could to keep life as normal as possible for the family. This included collecting raw fleece from the steward.

He, Isabel, Lucy and the children would card and spin it and weave it then return it for coin. Trade was slowed because of the war, and it was getting more difficult to find wool and what they could find was of poor quality.

Any poor-quality wool leftover would be spun and sold at the market in Haworth. Lucy and Agnes would trek up the hill each Tuesday, which was market day.

Days later, William was outside with the boys, willeying fleece with long thin willow branches to separate matted fibres. Thomas was inside at the loom. The handloom consisted of four wooden uprights joined at the top and bottom to form a box-like framework which took up an enormous amount of room in the cottage. There were wooden rollers between both pair of uprights, one for the warp and one to collect the cloth. Thomas would send the shuttle containing the weft back and forth through the threads of the warp. A device operated by a treadle lifted and lowered alternate threads. A lathe hung from the top of the loom enabled him to push each thread of weft up against the cloth already woven. It was a tedious and lengthy process, and the family received little coin for their labour; however, it kept them going in the circumstances.

William, Robert and John stopped what they were doing; in the distance, they could hear horse galloping, the sound of the hooves echoing off the hills about two furlongs away. William called out to his brother, who appeared at the door just as the horses appeared at the top of the hill and then they disappeared down Brow Top Road toward the village.

"Where's Tommy and Agnes?" asked Thomas.

William stopped what he was doing and looked up excitedly. "Tommy escorted Agnes and Lucy to the village to sell the leftover spun wool."

"Right, I'm going to get them; you stay here with the bairns, get them inside," said Thomas with some urgency.

Thomas headed off earnestly toward Sun Street. As he walked up past the hillside cottages, closer to the village, people were hurriedly taking their animals inside, closing shutters and calling for their children to come home. He trudged up West Lane, it was muddy and hard to walk, and he wondered why Tommy had not had the sense to come home with soldiers in the village.

As he neared the village centre, it was deserted except for five horses which were tied up outside the Kings Arms. He started to get worried, trying to think where Agnes and Lucy had got to. As he neared the Kings Arms, he could hear talking and commotion inside. He stuck his head in the door and was terrified by what he saw.

His son and three other men were stood up against the wall by three men with swords. One other sat at a table with a tankard of ale, and the candle chandelier shook, hinting at the whereabouts of the other.

The three men were dressed in beige coloured leather buff coats. Thick heavy belts crossed against a breast plate pressed tightly against their upper torso with an orange sash that was tied at the back. They wore thigh-length boots which reached above their knee, and star-shaped spurs protruded from the bottom of the heel of their boots. Three heavy round top helmets were lined up on the bar like centurions from another age. With his back turned, the barkeep nervously poured ale from the barrel.

The soldier sitting down immediately stood up and drew back his sword in Thomas' direction as he entered the room. Thomas put his hands up submissively as the soldier took a step forward towards him.

"FATHER!" Tommy yelled, surprised to see him.

"What have we here?" said the soldier, "Another Royalist?"

"We ain't Royalists, do we look like Cavaliers?" exclaimed Thomas sarcastically.

The soldier lowered his sword and backhanded Thomas knocking him off balance. Thomas recovered and stood straight and confident.

"FATHER!" Tommy screamed. "LEAVE HIM BE!!"

"If you are not Parliamentarian soldiers, then you are Royalists," said the soldier who had already had his share of ale.

Thomas stood up straighter and looked at the soldier stubbornly, wiping the drip of blood that oozed from the corner of his mouth.

"Stand over there with the other traitors," said the sergeant as he pointed in their direction with his sword.

The barkeep walked out from behind the bar and put three tankards of ale on the table where the other soldier sat. At that point, another walked down the rickety stairs, lowering his head to duck under the opening. He had his tunic over his arm and held his sheathed sword and flintlock pistol. He began to tuck his shirt back in and gestured to the soldier sitting at the table.

The other man ducked his head and walked up the stairs. Thomas, his son, and the other two looked up at the ceiling as the candle chandelier started to rock once again.

The soldiers started to let their guard down, laughing and playing shoffe-grote at the bar, arguing and wagering on the outcome. They had placed their swords against the supporting beam beside them.

Thomas and the three others sat down on the cold floor, "Where's your mother and Lucy," he whispered.

"They went home after market," Tommy whispered.

"I didn't see them on the way," stated Thomas curiously.

"They must have gone the way of the beck. Mother left the water buckets there this morning to save a trip."

Thomas whispered, "It's starting to get dark outside; they'll be worried if we're not back soon. William has probably already told them about this lot."

"What are we going to do with them," asked the soldier as he waited for his turn on the shoffe-grote.

"We'll take the younger of the men with us to Bradford; they can join with us. The other two, we'll let go; they're too old."

After more rounds of ale and more anger and arguing over the results of shoffe-grote, one soldier moved the coins back to the bottom of the board before the other had a chance to check.

After sculling his ale, he put his tankard on the bar spilling it and angrily slammed his fist down on the board, "You are a cheating bastard, don't move the coins until I've had a look."

"You got two," said the other as he resented being called a cheat.

The bigger of the two put his hand on his knife, took a step closer and put his face directly in front of his, "You're a dirty cheating bastard!"

The sergeant stepped in and forced them apart, "We have more pressing matters to attend to. Let's make way for Bradford before we all get a whipping."

"Right, you and you stand up and turn around." He took out some rope and proceeded to bind Tommy and the other man's hands behind them.

His father also stood.

"Not you; you stay where you are," he gestured for Thomas to sit.

Thomas looked at his son worriedly, "Where are you taking them?"

"These two are going to be soldiers in Sir Thomas Fairfax's army, pikemen probably."

"Take me not my son," commanded Thomas.

"No, we only want the younger ones. They can march a distance; you'll die on the road."

"NO, I'm fit as a fiddle. Take me with you," Thomas stood up.

"Take you, then we have to feed you; best you stay by the hearth of your fire, old man."

"It's a grand thing your son is doing, fighting for Parliament, and I'm sure he will be rewarded if he makes it through and we defeat that whoring bastard who calls himself King."

The soldier tied up Thomas and the other to a vertical beam. The other two soldiers pushed Tommy and the other younger man toward the door. One of them opened the door, and they went out into the evening. The snow was just starting to gently fall again, and there was an eerie quietness in the street.

As the soldiers went outside, two of them drew their pistols quickly as the lord's troop of clubmen had assembled themselves from one side of the lane to the other. All standing shoulder to shoulder, pitchforks, sharpened branches and all manner of yard implements that could do damage were pointed forward.

"STAND BACK AND LET US THROUGH AND NOBODY WILL GET HURT," yelled the sergeant with a deep, gruff voice.

The reeve stepped forward confidently, "Why don't you lower your arms and let them go?"

One of the soldiers immediately grabbed Tommy from behind and put his knife to his throat, "MOVE AWAY, OR I SWEAR THERE WILL BE BLOOD SHED TONIGHT!"

Thomas saw this and yelled, "Nooooo! Let them through, Tommy stay still and do as your told!"

Tommy had a look of fear in his eyes and was not willing to blink; his eyes grew wide and white. He used his peripheral vision to try to look at the soldier behind, but he was terrified and shivered with more fear than chill.

"COME, MEN MOUNT YOUR HORSES," the sergeant of the soldiers, a career man, could sense the fear in the men that stood opposite. The other four soldiers took out their flintlock pistols, cocked them and pointed them at the clubmen.

Tommy and the other man were forced up onto the back of the horses, and their captors led them towards the clubmen.

One of the clubmen lowered his pitchfork and rushed the horses, "STOP!" The sergeant directed his flintlock at the man and pulled the trigger. The flintlock fired with a cloud of smoke, the lead ball hitting the man in the chest, killing him instantly. The ball hit with so much force that he was knocked backwards off his feet and landed on his back. There was a small, bloodied hole in his chest, and the ball had come out his back and pierced the hard-rocky wall behind, splattering bits of bone and innards over it.

Other men behind him were shocked as blood splattered onto their tunics. Too shocked to wipe it from their faces, they grabbed the man by the arms and pulled him away, but it was too late.

"HE'S DEAD!" One of the clubmen yelled out.

"BASTARDS!" The reeve became increasingly agitated and menacingly stepped forward with his pitchfork.

"I TOLD YOU STAND BACK! We didn't come here looking for trouble, now let us pass, lest more die this evening," bellowed the sergeant as the soldier beside him cocked his pistol and aimed.

The line of men on either side of the lane looked at each other before they succumbed to fear and parted to let the riders through. The Roundhead soldiers, still with their pistols pointed menacingly, slowly walked their horses forward. They walked their horses down Main Street and, once out of sight of the Haworth clubmen, mounted their horses and galloped down the hill and east along Brow Top Road toward Bradford.

The reeve rushed over to the dead man as one of the others rushed into the tavern. He untied the bindings, and Thomas ran to the door just in time to see the riders disappear into the night. Saddened by the fact that he couldn't do more to protect his son, he walked home in the darkness with a heavy heart capitulating about what he would say to Isabel and Agnes.

Sun Street and Main Road were deserted and dark, a ghost of a village. Thomas walked following the light of the moon, which, when not blanketed by cloud, acted as a beacon to the direction of home.

He trudged through the snow drifts and across the fallow field, disturbing the virgin snow in the process. Arriving back at the cottage, he could see the twirl of grey smoke coming from the chimney, a contrast to the dark of the night. William and the English Mastiff heard the crispy footsteps and stood to open the door. When the door opened, Agnes, Lucy and Isabel stood to greet him with a look of worry on their faces.

"Thomas!"

"Husband, you're safe, thank goodness," yelled Agnes as she walked quickly to embrace him, relieved that he had returned.

Isabel worriedly fretted, "WHERE'S TOMMY... ?" She ran past Thomas to the door and looked out to see if he was walking up the hill. She put her hand to her mouth in desperation.

"WHERE IS HE?" Isabel stood there, motionless for a moment, then brought her hand up to her mouth.

Thomas took off his hat and looked down guiltily, not knowing how to broach the subject. "They took him, he whispered. There was nothing I could do. They were armed with flintlocks. James Warren, reeve's brother, was shot."

Agnes and Lucy lifted their hands to their face fearfully, their eyes darting backwards and forwards, alarmed by the news.

Isabel fell to her knees and broke down in tears; she put her hands over her face, "NOOOO," and sobbed into them.

Lucy walked over to her and quickly put her arm around her, lifting and helping her to the form next to the hearth.

"There, there, pet, he'll be fine. I'm sure he'll be back tomorrow," exclaimed Lucy worriedly as she looked up at her husband for guidance.

"There was nothing I could do, I swear, The Roundheads, they've taken him to Bradford."

"We need to go get him!" insisted William without thinking, then remembering the conversation that Thomas had with Tommy the previous day.

Thomas tried to remain calm even though his heart was beating like a snare drum, "Not now, they're on horse and halfway to Bradford! I'll see John Hargreaves and the reeve tomorrow to see what we can do."

William became excited by his chance to prove his courage, "Well, whatever you do, I'm doing it with you," he contested.

"Steady on William, with a babby on the way, you need to be here with Lucy, somebody has ta stay behind, can't leave them alone with the soldiers around."

Agnes' face was painted with worry; she looked then walked up to Thomas. "Please, you must get him back; you have to get my boy back. I don't know what I'd do if anything were to happen to him."

Thomas embraced her. "Aye, love, but we must not panic; these are times for level-headedness. I'll see John Hargreaves in the morning."

Isabel sobbed uncontrollably as Agnes went to her and slowly guided her to the ladder. Isabel carefully guided her baby bump up into the loft. She laid down on her bed quietly sobbing into the straw pillow while Agnes, with tears in her eyes, gently removed the hair from her face.

A mile into their journey, Tommy, not used to riding, started to feel the pain in the inside of his upper thighs, and the continual jolting on the back of the horse was painful. He held onto the saddle cantle as they galloped down Brow Top Road.

The snow-covered hills were illuminated by the moon's rays. The odd cottage and snow-covered tree lined the road on both sides then cleared as they passed through the tiny township of Flappit Spring. Tommy had never ventured this far from home before, and the flatness of the fields differed from what he was used to.

The sergeant slowed to a trot and raised his hand to signal the other soldiers. They slowed as they approached the small bridge over Hewenden Beck, then picked up speed to come out the other side of the valley. They passed through the small hamlet of Herecroft and finally reached the outskirts of Bradford. Tommy could hear the horse's laboured breathing, and he could feel the wetness of the horse's sweat through his hose.

Trotting along, Tommy shouted, "ALL THIS BOUNCING, I NEED TO PAY A CALL, SIR!"

The soldier turned his head sideways so that he could hear, "If you need to go, go where you be because we are not stopping until we get to Bradford."

The clouds parted, and the moon's light shone the way. They travelled further east of Bradford then turned off the main road into the fields, heading north into the flat countryside. Tommy could see the light of fires in the distance and assumed it was where they were headed.

As they neared, the horses slowed to a walk. Men were sitting around large campfires in front of cramped rows of tents. Iced canvas and snowdrifts piled up on the windward side of the tents. Long fourteen-foot pikes were lying on the ground near them while one man sharpened the metal end of his pike slowly and purposefully with a sharpening stone. Tommy looked into his soulless eyes for a glimpse of humanity, and there was none. They were inexpressive, cold and dark as if the devil himself looked through them. Tommy looked away quickly.

The men looked over at Tommy, and his companion as their captors helped their captives from the horses. Still bound at the wrists, they marched them to a tent behind the men. The flap was parted, and Tommy was forced inside. The tent was almost twelve feet in length and six-foot-wide, but owing to the number of blankets around the inside, there wasn't much room for anybody. Pine branches had been placed over the snow-covered ground as a barrier to the earthen chill, and the sides of the tent had been pegged down. Snow was heaped around the bottom to keep out the wind. Six other men sat on blankets within, a half-burnt candle the only light which illuminated their worn, troubled faces. They looked up, unshaven and discouraged, not saying a word, the radiant heat from the fire outside the only solace from the winter night.

Tommy and the other man crouched down near the flap, frozen and exhausted from the journey but seizing the warmth of the fire like morning birds to the sun.

"Where are you from?"

"Haworth," said Tommy, "How long ya been here?"

"Robert Town is the name, we been with the army since mid-December, but they still don't trust us, think we're gonna up and run. It has crossed me mind."

"So why haven't you," whispered Tommy.

"Because I saw what happened to the last bloke that tried, only took them an hour to catch him. He was exhausted from running and dodging. They made him ride the 'wooden horse' dangled him from the top of that tree branch. No hose or tunic with his ankles tied to his wrists. They lowered him until his arse cheeks straddled that triangular-shaped wooden horse. Lower and lower he went until his arse cheeks straddled the thin, sharpened edge. Kept going until his arse was split from ear 'ole to breakfast time. Took him a full night and a day to die; I can still hear his agony as they lowered him, poor bastard. His guts splattered red against the white. You can still see part of his remains under the horse; terrible way to go."

"So, what happens to us now then?" asked Tommy.

"Well, we're up at the cock's crow, have a bit of pottage, and melted snow, then spend half the day with pikes military training, but more like a military madness because no bastard knows what they're doin'. The rest of the day, we spend sharpening sword and pike and sleeping before guard duty."

"If you ask me, it's cannon fodder training," growled another, huddled under a blanket at the back of the tent.

Robert smiled and looked back at him, "Don't mind him."

The stranger spoke again, "Lord Newcastle has double the men we have and cannon. If it comes to it, we'll be slaughtered like pigs fer Christmas."

"Don't listen to him. Lord Newcastle is in Pontefract, two days march from here, and Lord Fairfax is on his way with more than four hundred men and should be here tomorrow."

Robert whispered, "A rider brought a letter for his lordship yesterday from Sir Saville in Leeds saying he was going to burn the town to the ground. Captain gives us news every morning of the intelligence, and on most mornings, it's not good. I just bloody hope that Fairfax gets here tomorra."

Thomas heard footsteps outside, the canvas parted, and two blankets were thrown inside, one for him and one for the other recruit.

"Welcome to the army," said the stranger at the back of the tent sarcastically.

Tommy grabbed the blankets, kept one and threw the others to his co-captive from Haworth, who by now was huddled with the others together in the corner of the tent. There was a bit of a melee as two other men contested the blanket. Tommy unfolded his and wrapped it around his shoulders. He looked over, and one man in the corner of the tent didn't move, just laid there coughing and shivering, yet beads of sweat glistened on his brow.

"Is he alright?" asked Tommy.

"Hasn't eaten for three days and spends most days puking and filling the latrine behind the tent," replied Robert.

Shivering, Tommy laid down on the pine branches and tried to get some sleep; he closed his eyes. Still, sleep didn't come because he was fearful of the wretches laying alongside him and the pending days ahead. He was in a semi-conscious state, then quickly fell into a deep sleep and started to dream. He dreamt of times gone by, of Isabel and home and a great respite from the troubles of the day.

cs CHAPTER EIGHT ဆ
Men in the Mist

Tommy was woken from his sleep by the annoying yelling of the
sergeant, which quickly reminded him of his reality.

"RIGHT, YOU LOT UP, UP, UP!" the sergeant ducked his head and
walked into the tent, kicking the feet of all the sleepers.

One of the men didn't move, so he pulled the blanket off him, but
he still didn't move and curled up in a ball to delay the inevitable.
He started shivering and slowly lifted his head and squinted through
one eye. His long dirty brown hair covered his face, and he eventually
sat up. He pulled the blanket back around his shoulders and looked
around the tent, which was now empty except for the sergeant and
the frozen stiff at the back of the tent.

He walked out and spoke to his men, "Right, first order of the
day, take the stiff out the back and bury him and be quick about it if
you want to eat." The warm breath mixed with the cold air causing
steam to emanate from his mouth as he barked his orders.

"Time's a wasting we need to turn you lot into soldiers, not that
it will make much difference 'cause most of you will be dead in a
week!" He chuckled and walked back to his horse. Tommy and the
six others sat around the fire, groggy from the night of forced sleep
and sore from the ride.

His companion from Haworth stood up and walked as if there was
a miniature, invisible horse between his legs. He rubbed the inside
of his thighs and groaned, "Bloody hell, I feel like I been buggered
by Satan himself!"

"Yer, and what would the dark one want with you, when he has
all those wicked, wicked women down there with him," said one of

the other men.

The men laughed and brought a long-awaited smile to all sitting in front of the fire, including Tommy.

Tommy and Robert, the man he'd been talking to the previous night, lifted the corpse by the feet and dragged him outside and up into the trees behind the tent. He had a rash of small pink sores and, through the night, had bled through his nose, which was now dried and frozen. They took a shovel and started to dig a shallow grave in the snow beside the corpse. Rigor mortis had set in, so the man's head was raised off the ground, and his arms and knees were bent.

"Hurry up, you two," yelled out the sergeant.

Tommy and Robert pulled the corpse into the grave and started to cover it with the iced dirt and snow. Robert turned to return to the camp.

Tommy stood up and called out to Robert, "Hey, should we say something?"

Robert stopped, turned around and started walking back, taking off his woollen hat; he looked down at the ground, trying to remember something.

"I suppose we should at that, 'Whatever is true, whatever is noble, whatever is right, whatever is pure, whatever is lovely, whatever is admirable—if anything is excellent or praiseworthy—such thoughts and such deeds, Grant, O Lord."

"Amen."

"Amen, let's go!" They both walked off toward the camp.

Tommy stopped and turned back to look at the mound, wondering if soon he might be placed in an icy, shallow grave.

They continued back to the camp with Tommy following quickly behind, "Robert, so how does this all work?"

Robert stopped for a moment, "Quite simple really, we're what they call pikemen. The colonel, he's the commander of a regiment with four companies of one hundred men, you'll be in a regiment with me. In our regiment, there are pikemen and musketeers; we're supposed to protect the musketeers from the enemy cavalry. You'll have a sixteen-foot pike and be trained to form a 'schiltron'. Just keep yer head down and do as your told, and you'll be fine."

When they arrived back at the fire, the others were already up and feasting on the pottage.

A lamb, thieved from the farm just over the hill, had also been gutted and was slowly basting. Its dark eyes open in a transfixed stare, looking oblivious to the pointed stick that had been cast through its bottom end emerging from its continually smiling mouth. Fat dripped slowly from its skin and hissed on the fire blow.

Tommy and Robert spooned pottage from the cauldron into wooden bowls and sat on the tree stump purposefully placed near the fire, and began to eat. Ale had been poured from a small barrel, which had been stolen from a local cottage by the others, and the full jacks were lined up on the top of it.

Tommy looked around at the men as the sun began to rise. Steamy breath emanated from their mouths as they consumed the hot pottage and drank their ale. They all huddled together, oblivious to their surroundings, preferring to focus on the meal and on the fire. They covered themselves with their blankets, desperately trying to ward off the freezing breeze that rustled through the trees. They all sat as close to the fire as they possibly could, but still, some shivered silently. Each of them wore the clothing of poor farmers that worked the fields. Their hose was soiled, and their tunics ripped and frayed. Each of the men wore a woollen felt cap and thick woollen socks, which were wrapped with leather bindings up to the knee.

It was a cold, crisp morning, and Tommy felt groggy from the broken sleep and exhausted from the long ride. He felt the imaginary horse still standing between his legs and bruised buttock from the continual jolting of the horse's gallop. Getting closer to the fire, he warmed his hands which by now were red and frozen from digging in the snow. Holding them to his mouth, he blew on them then rubbed them to try to bring the feeling back. Looking around, he tried to get his bearings; there must have been thirty tents all set up in orderly exact rows. Each with its own inhabitants sitting outside, they all looked to be farmers and yeomen, much like him. They had probably been volunteered by the sergeant's men from the local villages, he thought. Although he had heard that the men of Bradford were supporters of the Roundheads, and many may have volunteered.

Men in uniform stood on top of the hill; he could see them through the pine trees, on guard looking east towards Leeds. They wore breastplates and helmets and an orange sash which was tied around their waist. These were seasoned soldiers, men that had already seen battle. They stood there proudly, muskets in hand, ready for battle should it eventuate.

Robert watched the sergeant from the previous night approach the tent. The men stopped talking and looked up nervously. Tommy felt intimidated by him as he was dressed for battle in his thick leather brown tunic. His thick heavy belts crossed against a shiny, metal, dented breastplate. Like the men on the hill, an orange sash was tied around his waist and knotted at the back. His back sword swung at his side, and the sixteen-inch dog lock pistol protruded from his belt. Thigh-length, thick leather boots reached to the bottom of his leather doublet, and star-shaped spurs protruded from the bottom of his heel. A lobster tailed, round, metal helmet was strapped to his chin, a thin protective bar ran vertically from the visor. He was a formidable sight, unshaven; an old scar could be seen on his cheekbone, *a close call from a previous battle*, Tommy thought to himself. His eyes were cunning and cold, and he looked as if they had seen too much death and mayhem. He had an air of power and dignity, not a lord, but one who seemed as if he had often been in the presence of such types. Tommy later found out that he was a career soldier who had fought on the continent for the Dutch against the Spanish; a seasoned veteran of many battles, it was said.

With a raspy, deep voice, the sergeant bellowed orders for all to hear, "Right you lot, you have ten minutes to ready yerself and be in that field over there. Oh, and don't get any ideas about skipping off 'cause I have men on the top of those ridges, and they'll put a musket ball in ya without a second thought. If you're lucky, you'll be dead; if not, you'll ride the wooden horse like the last fool that tried it."

By the time Robert and Tommy approached, the sun was low in the sky, the rest of the men had already started to assemble in the morning fog. They lined up in rows, their sixteen-foot pikes held beside them. They looked like black ghosts against the white of the snow; the sharpened points of their pike glistened in the early sun and rose to pierce the fog above them. Some of them had a helmet, and others had a breastplate, but it was only the sergeant and his men with the orange sash that had both.

The sergeant sat atop his horse and started to bellow orders and get the men into some semblance of order. The horse stomped and struggled with the bit; a steady stream of breath poured from his large black nostrils as its long tail thrashed from side to side. He went to rear on his back legs, but the sergeant expertly managed his steed and then patted him on the inside of the neck, trying to calm him.

He pointed to Tommy and the other new recruits from the tent, "YOU THERE, PICK UP A PIKE AND JOIN THE RANKS!"

Tommy noticed one of the other men on a horse beside the sergeant as one of the men that had ridden with them from Haworth.

The sergeant bellowed, "I HAVN'T GOT ALL BLOODY DAY, TAKE UP YOUR PIKE AND GET IN LINE BEFORE I HAVE YA WHIPPED."

Robert, more experienced in their ways, had already lifted his pike and quickly disappeared to join the rank and file.

Tommy and the other recruits bent over and picked up a pike each. They struggled with the weight and length of it, and it took them a moment to get it vertical. Trying to balance it, Tommy started running toward the line-up of soldiers. He got into the rank and file and looked sideways to see the other men trying to line themselves up straight. He followed suit, taking a step forward to ensure he was lined up evenly with the men to the left and right of him. Several men were standing in the front perfectly straight and aligned with the corporal, one of the few men with a pike that had a breastplate, helmet and orange sash.

The sergeant bellowed orders, and the other soldiers on horses split up and repeated his orders to the two corporals at the end of the rank.

Tommy's corporal, who was positioned the last man to the left of him, yelled, "RIGHT MEN, IN TIME WITH ME, FORWARD MARCH!"

The drummer who was standing in front of them started to drum a beat for the men to march to.

The file moved forward, trying to keep in step to the corporal and the drumbeat. Still, it seemed hopeless with most, if not all, out of step and finding it difficult to walk and handle the pike at the same time. Eventually, a group of two hundred pikemen were engineered into a block in the middle of the field.

There they stood, being chastised by the sergeant, "NOW LISTEN HERE YOU LOT, IF YA DON'T GET IT TOGETHER YOU CAN KISS THAT SWEETHEART OF YOURS GOODBYE BECAUSE YOU WON'T BE GOIN' HOME!"

Tommy looked at a group of about eighty musketeers in squads of forty, four deep on the left and right side of his rank and file. There were about a hundred men on the march. He noticed that one of the men on the outside was one of the men in the tent the previous night. He held his four-foot matchlock musket against his shoulder and a wooden support rest which he carried in his other hand.

Tommy looked across, and he noticed Robert, but he wasn't dressed as he was before; gone were the worn hose and ripped tunic. He wore a shirt, a pair of baggy breeches, a coat, doublet, breastplate and helmet and finally, an orange sash tied around the waist. His footings had been replaced with leather boots, and thick brown hose rose to the bottom of the breeches. Confused, he frowned and called out to him, but Robert didn't hear him and started to bellow orders much like the other corporal.

Looking sideways while shouting out orders, Robert noticed Tommy looking at him, so he cheekily smiled and winked, then looked forward to focus, listening to the commands given by the sergeant.

After further marching, the sergeant rode around the group of men and then stopped and turned and rode back the other way, then stopped in front. He hollered some obscenities and paused, "I'VE NEVER SEEN A MORE DISAPPOINTING, RAG TAG, BUNCH OF WEAK EXAMPLES OF MEN IN ME ENTIRE LIFE. I'D BE SURPRISED IF ANY OF YOU LAST THE WEEK!"

The sergeant split the pikemen up into four separate companies of a hundred men; Robert and the other corporal took charge of their company and drilled them in point and push. They showed them how to level their pikes and advance toward an enemy to get close enough to draw swords which they didn't yet have.

The corporals then split the men again, Robert taking Tommy's half of the company, "Right men, stand with your pike close to your side, hold it with your left hand now reach as high as you can with your right. Now lower your pikes together, not too low, chest height."

The men in the company lowered their pikes slowly, but one of them dropped his pike. Another allowed the tip to touch the snow; they both recovered and manoeuvred them to the level of the others.

"Right, when I tell you, you are to take a step forward and thrust, and as you do, yell FOR GOD AND COUNTRY!"

"Go!"

The men took a step forward and thrust their pike into an imaginary foe, all out of time and only a few of them nervously yelling what they had been told.

"STOP!" Robert yelled frustratedly.

"Now listen here, if you don't work together, you're gonna die, and your guts are gonna end up on the ground in front of ya."

Tommy nervously thought about Isabel and the baby and their life without him, which made him even more determined to learn what had to be done.

The men tried again and again and continued to practice until

Robert could see some improvement in their discipline and dexterity with the pike.

Each command that the corporal gave had a different meaning, and it took Tommy and the men in his rank many hours of practice to get it right. If one got it wrong, the corporal would yell and scream and threaten punishment for the whole rank and file.

The sergeant rode over and watched. There were threats of whippings, reduced rations and the threat of the 'wooden horse' for one man described as a lowly creature, "YOU DON'T KNOW THE DIFFERENCE BETWEEN THE SHARP END AND THE BLUNT END OF THE PIKE!"

All the threats of whippings and corporal punishment was a sobering thought, and this wasn't helped by the episodes of dysentery and camp fever that had spread.

ೞ CHAPTER NINE ಙ

Out of the Valley

Back in Haworth, Isabel hadn't slept. When she climbed awkwardly down the ladder from the loft, Thomas and William were already up and dressed. The storm had abated, and there was a nervous quiet over the household. Thomas had placed some food in a market wallet and rolled up a blanket. He hurriedly finished the pottage and piece of bread and cheese that Agnes had prepared for him. Isabel's eyes were swollen and puffy from crying through the night, and she held onto baby Will to comfort him.

Agnes had heard that small sieges and skirmishes were occurring further east as companies of soldiers were determined to destroy the economic basis of their opponents while preserving their own resources. Houses were being destroyed, crops and livestock were stolen to feed both armies. Soldiers forced people to provide free food and shelter to them when they turned up at their village, and disease like smallpox and measles was rampant. Isabel and Agnes were scared, and it showed on their faces especially hearing that civilians were being targeted.

Thomas could tell that Agnes and Isabel were terrified, "Don't worry, Isabel, I'll get him back."

"You be careful, husband," said Agnes while handing Thomas his cloak.

"No fear of that wife!"

"William, you look after the family until I get back and stay around home, shouldn't be gone more than a week, less if they're still held up in Bradford." Thomas threw his cloak around his shoulders and placed a knife in the middle of the rolled-up blanket.

He turned and hugged Agnes, who was forlorn and saddened about her husband's parting.

Thomas stood in front of her, put his hands on her shoulders and gave her a peck on the cheek, "Don't worry yourself, wife. I'll be back in time for church on Sunday; mark me words."

As Thomas lifted the latch and opened the door, piled up snow fell inside. It was a bright, sunny day, and the snowdrift was deep up against the outside of the cottage door. He walked out, and William followed behind while Agnes, Isabel and Lucy watched him walk off down the hill.

William called out, "If you're not back by Sunday, I'll be coming to look for ya," he walked through the door back inside in a huff.

The two boys, Robert and John, quickly jumped from the ladder and ran over to peek through the shutter, "Where's Uncle Thomas going, Mother?"

"He's going on a journey to meet up with our Tommy," Lucy claimed.

"He'll be back soon as ya know it," Lucy put her arms around her boys and smiled, trying not to let on about the gravity of the situation.

She watched Thomas trudge through the knee-deep, virgin snow, the powder kicking up behind him as they went. Eventually, when he was out of sight, all that was left was a reminder, a line of lonely, empty footsteps creating a path down the hill.

When Thomas got to the road, the snow had been turned muddy by the sheep who had been herded to a new grazing location. Small, round, shiny mounds of sheep droppings and yellow urine stained the snow giving an indication of their number and direction. He could see the farmer and his dog herding the black snouted sheep up into the moors where the grasses were taller and easier to graze on.

He walked up Sun Street onto Marsh Lane and down, turning left on Moorehouse Lane and crossed the field to the Hargreaves cottage. John was outside stacking dry peat and noticed him approach. He stopped work, shielded his eyes from the sun and waited for him to get closer; he could tell that all was not well by the look on Thomas' face.

"Aye up, Thomas, how's our Agnes? She doesn't come ta visit us much these days."

"She is well, John, but I have more pressin' business."

"Aye, and what might that be?" John inquired curiously.

Thomas looked forlorn, still feeling guilty that he couldn't do more to save his son, "They've taken Tommy, soldiers on horseback, last night, Roundheads."

John turned toward the door of the cottage, which was open, "You better come inside. MARGARET, THOMAS IS HERE."

Thomas followed John inside, stepping through the door and stamping his feet, "They got him at the Kings Arms! I went up there, but they had swords and pistols, not much I could do. They killed one of the clubmen on the way out of the village."

The cottage was a layered stone and mud structure with a thatch roof and chimney. The hay crib was at the end of the house but cordoned off by a small wooden partition for the ox, three lambs and a cow who helped themselves to the hay on offer. A large half barrel filled with water was close by for the animals to drink their fill. The chickens and the rooster were in out of the cold for the day and spent their time scratching at the fresh straw on the floor. In the centre of the room was the bed and straw mattress with the blanket turned down to keep the vermin from making it their winter place. The inner roof was a patchwork of thick wooden trellis holding the thatch and keeping out most of the weather.

Mrs Hargreaves appeared, "Aye up Thomas ya orl right?"

"Fine, Margaret, but I have bad news," Thomas reiterated.

Knowing that his wife would be worried about Agnes, John cut in, "Tis Tommy, he's been taken by Roundheads. BASTARDS, why can't they leave poor folk alone? We don't want any part of their war."

"They were going to Bradford, so I'm off to get him back," Thomas stated, hoping that John would offer some support or advice.

"Thomas, you know there's trouble brewing there; it's a dangerous thing you do! Well, ya can't go on your own, give us a minute, and I'll get me stuff, and I'll come with ya", said John.

"John Hargreaves, your too old to be trapsin' around the countryside in this weather; there's another storm coming tonight."

"Quiet woman, this is men's business, and I can't stand by and let the bastards get away with our boy. Now get me some grub and ale ta keep us going!"

Mrs Hargreaves turned toward the table in the corner of the cottage, huffed and said something under her breath that only she could hear, "Silly old fools are gonna get themselves killed!"

"It'll take us half a day to get ta Bradford in this snow and ice, maybe longer if a storm comes up," claimed John.

Thomas thought for a moment, "Aye, but at least most of it is downhill once we get to Denholme, so let's make haste, don't want to be stumbling around in a storm after dark."

Margaret walked up to John and placed a market wallet over his shoulder. It contained a blanket and some bread, dried vegetables and dried bacon.

Mrs Hargreaves had a fretfully worried look on her face, "Now you come back soon and please be careful, husband!"

"I'll be back by prayers on Sunday, wife, and If I'm not, have the vicar ring the bell nine times and a bell for each year of me life. Don't fret because I'll be in a better place than you, all right," he smiled and gave her a kiss on the cheek.

John picked up his cloak from the hook near the door, donned his red hat and walked out the open door into the day. He went around the side of the cottage and picked up his sharpened axe. Thomas looked at Margaret Hargreaves, shrugged his shoulders and followed him out.

"You look after him, Thomas, do ya here, you look after him," called out Mrs Hargreaves letting sentimentality get the better of her.

She closed the door after Thomas and turned, leaning back against it with her eyes closed. She brought her hands to her face and began to quietly sob, "Bring him back to me, Lord, please bring him back."

Thomas stepped in John's footsteps in the snow as they walked up Moorhouse Lane and continued to Denholme Road. It was a hard climb uphill and even harder on the calves with the slippery mess they called a road. The dormant, bare trees at the side of the road stood like sentinels guarding the way. Speckled patches of white sat atop of their branches; an orange-breasted Robin looked inquisitively with his beady black eyes as they trudged past.

With all the walking uphill, Thomas could feel sweat running down the middle of his back. His undershirt was drenched and now cold under his tunic and cloak. They continued up, and Thomas could see the wind starting to pick up and blow the powder-like snow off the hills. The black dry-stone walls snaked their way through the brilliant white cover. Low, grey winter storm clouds started to fill the sky, overtaking the blue to threaten the day. The odd cottage with smoke curling out of the chimney reminded him of home and the warmth of his hearth.

After a couple of hours, John looked up. He could see a group of cottages and a tavern, "We'll stop at the Old Dog Inn up the road there on the left, try and get out of this cold for a bit, besides there's a storm brewing, and we don't want to get caught in it."

"Good idea John. I've just about had it, wouldn't hurt to see if the locals know anything."

"You're right, Thomas, but let me do the talking. Start asking too many questions out here, and you'll find yourself on the blunt end of a shiv."

They continued walking up toward the tavern and sighed relief when they got to the top as they knew an ale and a warm fire beckoned. John opened the door for Thomas, who by this time was frozen through. He dispensed with manners and walked up to the fire. He took his hat from his head and his cloak from his shoulders as the melting snow fell to the ground.

It was a two-room inn with a bench before the door and a form against the wall. An old wooden table was centred in front of the fire on a plain earthen floor with scattered straw. A fat sow continued to nudge through the straw under the table, looking for scraps. Two men did not allow themselves to be distracted from their cards. The walls were a dirty rendered grey, stained from the smoke and the odd splash of dried ale left as a memory of the last debate and political yarn that turned nasty.

A stranger occupied a corner of the hearth; he set one hand on the mantle and another on a pewter mug which he drank from.

Thomas inadvertently sprayed wet snow in the direction of the stranger as he took off his cloak, "My apologies, Your Grace."

The stranger brushed the snow from his arm, "All is forgiven, it is a cold evening and no doubt going to get colder with that storm brewing; you are wise to occupy the hearth in such weather."

"Aye, it was a long uphill journey today," stated Thomas.

"You have come from the west then. What news do you bring with you?" The stranger asked.

Remembering what John had warned, Thomas replied, "Just as you said, there's a storm brewing."

"So, what brings you to Denholme?" asked the stranger.

John noticed Thomas and the stranger in conversation; he walked over and cut in, "Visiting relatives that's to the east, that's all."

"Ahh, very good. It seems that many are heading that way. I am travelling there myself, and if I was not in such a hurry, we could have travelled together. Safety in numbers in these times as you are no doubt aware!" The stranger could tell that John was on edge.

"Maybe another time," replied John abruptly.

"Thomas, the back of my throat is parched, and now that I have warmed the outside, I need ta warm inside, to the barrel we should go." John turned and walked toward an empty table.

Thomas followed, looking back around briefly at the stranger. He was quite a tall man, brown leather shoes with thick white stockings reaching to the knee and tied with a black garter that dangled loosely from the knot. Baggy blue knee-length breeches matched the blue tunic, the sleeves turned to show a clean white, ruffled undershirt. Dark blue buttons rose from his waist to his neck, and a white collar folded over below his chin. He had a black beard which was shaped to a point below his chin, and a considerable moustache met with his beard at the side of his face. Long black, shoulder-length hair was topped by a wide-brimmed hat which was lifted to show his deep-set, wise-looking eyes giving him a look of dignity and mystery.

At the table, John threw down two pennies as the barmaid approached, "Two ales missis, and make sure it's from the barrel, not the swill I know ya keep leftover from the drunkards last night."

"Who do ya think he is, John, the stranger?" Thomas looked at him with curiosity.

"Whose ta know, mate, what were ya talking about before I came over?"

"Asking about news from out west, I wouldn't trust him as far as I could throw him," whispered Thomas.

"Aye, don't trust anybody, this isn't Haworth, they could be Roundheads or men spying for the Cavaliers; sooner we're out of here, the better."

"Innkeeper, we need grub and a room for the night out of the storm, what say you?"

"Sorry gentlemen, one-room three beds, that's all we got, the gent there at the hearth already has one, and the other two have the others. You'll have to sleep out here on the floor with the woman and I."

"How much, enquired Thomas?"

"Four for the ale and grub and a shillin' for the night, two shillin' for a shag from the woman."

Thomas stood and placed the coin on the bar, "From the barrel, kind sir, and your woman can have a good night's sleep."

"Are you sure? Look at those tits. Like mountains of pleasure, even ride ya like a horse, dangle her big pink nipples in yer face."

She had a kind face, plump and round, and yes, her bosom was substantial, and she tightened the leather straps of her red bodice to accentuate them. Her wide hips, pale, thick arms and smooth skin were enticing. She was a healthy specimen of a woman, quiet and a doting woman to the old innkeeper, and although she didn't love him, he was kind and gentle to her.

"Like I said, let yer woman have a good night's sleep," Thomas reiterated.

The two men at the table continued to play cards, albeit more time was spent defending accusations of cheating than playing. The stranger was no longer there and had retired to his bed as Thomas and John sat close to the hearth, whispering their plans and concerns.

The storm raged outside, the inn shook, and the straw on the floor danced from the draft.

One of the card players, frustrated with proceedings, also went to bed, leaving the other, who promptly fell asleep at the table with his head on his folded arm. The innkeeper threw three mangy mattresses on the floor in front of the fire and gestured for Thomas and John to have them, which they did, taking out their blankets and settling for the night.

The innkeeper's woman blew out the candle and started to undress; Thomas and John could see her naked plumpness in the light of the fire.

Her ample bosom hung, her nipples erect from the cold air. Her pubic region hosted long curly, dark hairs which curled to the corners of her legs. When she turned, Thomas could see the dimpled skin of her buttocks and the thickness of her upper thighs in the glow from the fire. She had released her hair from the wimple, and it cascaded delicately down her back. She teased it with her fingers to loosen and divide the strands knowing that she was being watched. Climbing into bed, she pulled the blanket over herself, cursing at the coldness of the linen and straw mattress on her skin, hoping that either man would climb in with her.

A minute later, the door opened, and the innkeeper entered from outside. He closed the door quickly behind him to bar the wind and the snow from coming in and grumbled in the process. There was a small flurry of snow which he couldn't keep out, and it spun in the air and settled gently on the ground. He stoked the fire, put two pieces of dried peat on the renewed flame and started to undress in the darkness. He took off his floppy felt hat to reveal his bald head, sided by thicker grey hair and longish grey beard, which was unshaped and contained traces of pottage that he had consumed earlier. His skin was pale and loose, and his belly protruded beyond the dark mound of pubic hair. The head of his penis jutted from it while his testicles hung low like an old ram. He lifted the blanket and laid down on the mattress beside the woman to warm himself, grumbling in the process.

Thomas finally closed his eyes and started to doze. He turned on his side, placing his hand under the side of his face and wiggled his buttocks into the straw mattress. He could hear John's quiet, controlled breathing and the odd choke when his brain didn't remind him to breathe.

Suddenly, Thomas was shocked out of his slumber by a prolonged, mournful high-pitched cry from the mattress beside him. He turned over and resting on his elbows, he looked over to see the old innkeeper between the woman's large white legs humping away for dear life. He grunted with each thrust, and she continued to wail much to John's silent protest as he bolted upright, ready to give somebody an earful until he realised what was going on.

Thomas looked at John in the darkness, and they both turned to look at the couple who were both still thrusting and wailing. The old innkeeper could tell he was being watched, so mid-thrust, he turned to them both and smiled with his toothless, gummy smile. Both John and Thomas laid down and turned the opposite way, closing their eyes, hoping it would drown out the sounds. It didn't, he continued to hump and groan, and she continued her high-pitched cry, which was now interjected with a pause and grunt at regular intervals in time with the innkeeper's thrusts.

Thomas laid there patiently, eyes wide open and waiting for it all to stop. He rolled his eyes and started to tap the mattress with his finger slowly in time to each of the innkeeper's grunts and the woman's wails. John just laid there, eyes open, then he pulled the cover over awkwardly and tried to push some of the blanket in his ears, but it didn't help.

Eventually, the innkeeper's groans got quicker, and his woman stopped her wailing and started to pant, her groans getting faster and faster. Soon after, the innkeeper, out of breath, stopped thrusting and let loose with a mighty deep growl and his partner returned the compliment with one last mournful high-pitched cry.

Thomas stopped tapping his finger, closed his eyes and prayed to God that it was all over. John, suffocating under his blanket, pulled it down to gasp for air. There was a rustling of straw, the innkeeper or his partner or both belched, passed wind, and then there was silence.

John looked to the heavens and said a quiet thank-you; he settled in, wiggled himself into the straw mattress and started to go back to sleep. He was just about to drift off when it started, a chorus of deep glutaral sounds and long-winded whistles from the couple beside him. John and Thomas turned on their backs and looked up at the cross-work of thatched roofing in the darkness.

The following day Thomas and John woke to the stirrings of the household, the woman was up, dressed, and baking bread, and the innkeeper was tending to the deep snow outside. The storm had abated, and the other three men had already up and left, no doubt fully rested. Thomas, still clothed, stood and started to roll up his blanket. His dark hair was standing on end, and his eyes were a little puffy from lack of sleep. John sat up on the mattress, scratching his head and then trying to wipe the sleep from his stinging, tired eyes.

"Thought yer were gonna sleep the day away," said the woman while she pounded the dough on the table.

Neither Thomas nor John answered.

John stood and walked over to the chamber bucket in the corner and released a steady stream of urine, smiling with satisfaction mid-stream. He blew wind from his bottom, cleared his sinus from the night and spat into the bucket. After he had finished, he pushed his manhood back behind the codpiece and turned to allow Thomas time at the bucket. Thomas undid his codpiece, took it out and was just about to let nature take over.

"Let me empty that for ya," the woman reached down in front of him, her face inches from his manhood and grabbed the bucket.

"Don't you worry yourself; I'll be back in the blink of an eye."

She picked up the bucket, trying not to spill any of the acidic smelling urine left by the visitors that had left earlier. She took it outside and returned a few moments later with it empty. Thomas still faced the wall but had lost the urge to urinate.

"There ya go, luv," she put the bucket down in front of Thomas, her presence far too close for his liking.

"If ya need a hand with anything else, you just let me know."

Thomas tried to urinate, but all the attention from the woman had interrupted the flow. He stood there for a time, hand on the wall, then gave up. He tied up his codpiece and turned to see her continue her bread making. She rolled the dough into a phallic-looking shape then, stretched it, then pounded down on it with her fist. Thomas stood in awe, then slowly swallowed and gulped a mouthful of air. All the while, John saying nothing, watched Thomas' reaction in amusement.

The innkeeper walked in from outside, "Aye up, you're awake; the others left before the cocks crow. Did ya sleep well?"

Thomas looked at John and rolled his eyes, then spoke sarcastically, "Harsh night, the sounds from the storm kept me awake, there was a howling and a thumping, didn't ya hear it?"

"Me, noooo, slept like a log," said the innkeeper. "So, where are you off to today?"

"We'll stay on the road to Denholme, then onto Bradford and further if we have to."

The innkeeper put his hands on his hips and looked at them with dread, "I'd be careful round there; there's trouble brewing. The Kings Foot and Horse are billeted there. I've heard they been smashing up the place and harassing folks who don't support King Charles. Most have fled the trouble, and those that stayed live in fear. There's gonna be bloodshed once the Roundheads get there."

Worriedly, Thomas replied, "Aye, I had a feeling that was the case, but we have to go there because we're looking for my son Tommy. Roundheads kidnapped him for their army."

The innkeeper was up on all the troop movements, "Aye, I hear they been doing that all over the country, anybody capable of marching and carrying a pike gets taken in as cannon fodder. Well, if it's Roundheads you're looking for, I've been told they're interned at a camp east of Bradford."

The innkeeper picked some bread up off the table, "Look, take some bread and dried mutton with ya for the road and may God watch over you."

Thomas held out his hand to shake hands with the innkeeper, "I thank thee for your kindness, sir."

The innkeeper wiped his runny nose with the back of his hand and reached out to shake his hand, "Think nothing of it and good luck to you both."

Thomas and John turned to say goodbye to the woman, still busy with her dough, "Tarreur then."

She looked up, still holding a thick sausage-like piece of dough and ripped the top quarter off, "Oh tarreur then, safe travels and come back again."

Thomas and John both swallowed slowly, looked at each other, then opened the door and faced the bright, white winter morning.

CHAPTER TEN

The Truth of Danger

By this time, the war was affecting every level of society. It was said that the King had over fifteen thousand men in his army and growing. Fortunately for the Parliamentarians, they had the Royal Navy, the munitions stored in London, and were supported by most of the major cities. Some men tried to stay neutral, but it was difficult, and every day more conscripts would arrive in camp. Some volunteered, and others like Tommy didn't. They were treated much the same as Tommy had been, and it wasn't long before they picked up a pike and joined the ranks.

That morning the pikemen were once again being put through their paces marching, thrusting and practising with the pike. The men tried again and again and continued to practice until the corporal could see some improvement in their discipline and dexterity with the weapon. As the afternoon shadows got longer, a halt to the training was called by the sergeant, and the corporals were ordered to take their men back to camp.

When Tommy arrived back, he went into the tent; blankets had magically turned into mattresses. There were Morion helmets, snap sacks, beige woollen coats, leather buff coats, leather gloves, short-bladed swords, baggy breeches and leather shoes piled in the middle of the tent.

Tommy put a pair of boots on and tried a woollen coat and then a leather buff coat. He tried on the helmets until he found one which fit; it felt heavy, cold and uncomfortable, so he took it off and walked outside to join the other men at the fire. The men saw his boots and coat, stood and ran inside to get their own.

Robert slowly walked up the track in front of the long row of tents, "I see you got your gear."

Tommy felt the leather of the buff coat, "Aye, it's a bit warmer than what I was wearing, and it's good to get a good pair of boots and a warm coat."

Robert smiled, "It will do more than keep you warm; it should protect you from the slash of the sword in the melee."

After some swearing, haggling and arguing, the men returned to the fire in their new coats, one man sticking his finger through what was obviously a musket ball hole in the chest of his coat. Another complaining about the boots that were miles too big.

Robert took off his helmet. "Right you are men, drink ale, rest and be merry, for we start marching again early tomorrow."

The corporal could see Tommy scratching his chest under the coat, "Tommy, take off the coat quickly!"

Surprised by his request, Tommy looked at him curiously, "I've only just put it on."

"TAKE OFF THE COAT!"

"You other men, take off your coats and come with me." The corporal grabbed the shovel and went to the back of the tent, and began to dig a hole in the snow.

"Right, chuck your coats in here," the corporal pointed to the hole that he had just dug.

One of the men frowned and started to take off his coat. The others looked on curiously.

"Just trust me!" Robert looked serious and started helping one of the men take off his buff coat.

The other men followed suit, including Tommy and threw their coats into the hole. The corporal used the shovel to cover them with snow while the men stood back and watched.

"You can wear them tomorrow without the lice and the scratching," Robert undid his breastplate and went inside the tent.

Tommy followed, picking his blanket up and putting it back around his shoulders, "Why didn't you tell me you were a soldier?"

Robert smiled, "You never asked, and besides, the sergeant has us corporals billeted with new men, so we can get intelligence, keep an eye on them and make sure they're not Royalist sympathisers."

Tommy looked at Robert curiously, "And what if I had tried to run when we buried that dead man behind the tents?"

Robert parted the door of the tent and stepped outside, "Come outside, and I'll show you."

Tommy pulled his blanket around tighter and followed him outside. The other men sat around the fire watching.

"Do you see the musketeer up on the hill on guard there between the trees?" Robert walked over and placed a clay jug on a rock about seventy-five strides away from the musketeer, then he whistled.

Tommy watched the soldier up on the hill; he could see him take a cartridge of gunpowder, pouring it down the barrel of the musket. He blew on his piece of match cord and placed it. He then turned the gun and placed a musket ball down the barrel and, taking out his scouring stick, proceeded to scour home the charge pushing the stick down into the barrel. He replaced the scouring stick in the side of the barrel and lifted the matchlock to fire. He aimed, and Tommy could see a spark and smoke then the loud bang which echoed through the trees. Tommy turned his head toward the rock quickly and watched as the clay jug was smashed to smithereens, ale exploding and splashing all over the rock.

Tommy stood there shocked. He'd never seen a musket fired before, although he had heard the foul matchlocks when the lord from Haworth manor and his guests went hunting and the quiet of the moors was disturbed.

Robert smiled and waved to the musketeer, "Glad ya didn't try and run Tommy, it would of made a nasty mess of ya, and if you had survived, I was telling the truth about the wooden horse."

A few hours later, a troop of horsemen rode in and were heralded by the cry of one of the soldiers on the hill. William then heard the drum and trumpet of the regiment.

"It's him, Lord Fairfax," said the corporal excitedly.

The fifty horsemen and six-hundred foot soldiers were led by Fairfax, who sat atop a dirtied, grand white horse. The other men in the row of tents came out and started to cheer him and wave their hats above them as they rode by. Fairfax politely nodded to the men; his right arm bent at the elbow rested on his waist. He wore a beige, wide-brimmed hat with an orange sash tied around it. He had dark, wise eyes and long dark hair tied at the back and a straight, regal posture as he sat atop his steed.

The sound was like a low rumbling of thunder with the clatter of harness, bit and sword as they trotted by to the empty field beyond. Tommy, never seeing a force such as this, his mouth agape with wonder, watched in silence as the other men from his tent cheered and waved their hats in support.

Tommy, not as excited as the others, noticed an air of dignity and nobleness that he had not seen before. His sword hung from his waist and bounced away from his high leather boots as his horse trotted along and a dog lock pistol holstered at the side glistened in the sunlight. Like Robert, he wore an orange sash around his waist and a long beige buff coat that reached down to his boots. The red of his breeches wrinkled up the length of his lower leg to his knee. This was protected by a wider, more rigid piece of leather which was open at the back to allow him to bend his knee atop the horse. His saddle was on top of a red and gold embroidered horse blanket, a coat of arms clearly visible to enhance his majesty.

A taller, even more, imposing figure rode beside him on a brown horse who snorted a heavy breath, steaming the air in front of him. He had on a feather capped helmet, breastplate and a dark brown tunic with dull, golden piping; he scanned the area for danger and threats to his lord and master. Behind him rode another soldier, his forehead bandaged from an earlier battle, smiled and chatted to the horseman riding beside him. Then came the cavalry, centred by the flag bearer, who rode high and proud displaying Sir Thomas Fairfax's banner, raised high for all to see. The infantry followed in rows of four, each carrying a sixteen-foot pike vertically. Tommy could see that these men were battle-hardened; he could tell by their expressionless demeanour, the empty eyes and the worn, weathered look of their faces.

A large cart pulled along by two oxen were the last to arrive. It creaked and wobbled as the wooden wheels struggled under the weight of the barrels and boxes full of provisions and stores. An old, bearded servant, a young boy and two other servants walked beside it. The old servant gently tapped the oxen on the buttocks with a long thin stick and guided it to the clearing.

Tommy watched on as one of the horsemen dismounted and, taking off his helmet, started to loosen the belt and unsaddle his mount. The coat of the horse, shiny with perspiration, shook, and he waved his head as the bridal was removed, then lowered his muzzle to feed on the yellow grass poking through the snow. The horse waved its tail, signalling delight in his freedom from the burden. The horseman placed the saddle on the ground and helped the others erect their tents in rows at right angles to the ones already there.

The old servant stopped the cart in the clearing, unhitched the oxen and began to unload the cart of a large, white, four posted tent for Lord Fairfax. It wasn't like the other tents, almost triple the size and held up with solid oak posts and thick rope.

The bearded servant, his offsider and two others proceeded to fill it with all manner of furniture, including a small bed, table, chair and chest. Next came the portable writing table and what looked like a bundle of legs for it. They then began to set up an awning at the back of the tent, the boy placing large stones for the hearth and manoeuvring tied branches to hang the cauldron. While his tent was being prepared, his lordship stood with the colonel and his captains, laughing and discussing the events of the day.

Tommy was to later find out from Robert that his lordship's forces had already encountered Royalists at Tadcaster and, although inflicting some damage to their troops, had been forced to retreat due to lack of ammunition and powder. They had travelled through the night to reach Bradford.

Tommy watched as prisoners were gagged, tied and bound, then put in a tent at the bottom of the hill. A soldier was placed on guard nearby to watch them. The prisoners looked exhausted as they were forced to march all the way to Bradford tied behind a horse. They were dirty and bloodied from the journey where they had fallen over and been dragged through the snow. The next morning, they were released and allowed to wash and take food and ale.

Tommy donned his thick leather buff coat, picked up his pike and, with the other men in his tent, walked to the open field for training. On the way, he walked past the prisoners. He looked on curiously as they were in the process of being sworn in as Parliamentarian soldiers.

Tommy could hear the vicar talking to them while three guards stood by.

Robert had told him the previous night that it was often the case that prisoners were given the option to either be drafted or taken to Pontefract Castle, where they would remain for the rest of their days.

One by one, they each, in turn, placed their hands on the bible and repeated after the vicar, "By Almighty God, I do swear to never bear arms against the Parliament."

They repeated, "I swear."

They were then conscripted into the Parliament rank and file, given long beige woollen tunics, an orange sash, helmet, and allowed to march and train like the rest of the pikemen.

That morning the sergeant ordered the corporals to split the pikemen up into separate companies of one hundred men. Robert and the other corporal took their company and drilled them in more point and push. Tommy and the other men were getting much better at wielding the pike and were becoming more effective at the complex set of drills and postures.

"MOUNT YOUR PIKE," screamed the corporal.

In unison, the men reached down and grabbed the butt of the pike with their right hand and grabbed the shaft with their left, bringing it up vertically.

"ORDER YOUR PIKE," bellowed the corporal.

Tommy was getting more used to the weight of the pike and grasped it at shoulder height with his left hand, then lowered the pike so that the butt sat on the ground.

The corporal yelled, "SHOULDER PIKE."

He moved the pike out in front of him, grabbed it with his left hand and grabbed the shaft with his right hand at eye level, then leaned the pike against his shoulder. The company marched across the field to the beat of a drum.

After training, Tommy and the other conscripts sat around the fire eating a bowl of pottage with meat in it. It had been some time since they had meat, and apparently, the chicken was seized from a farmhouse. They ate with relish and discussed the events of the day between mouthfuls.

"Did ya hear one of those prisoners they swore in this mornin' has bolted, took a sword, stole a horse and took off northeast toward Undercliffe, handful of Horse have gone after him," explained one of Tommy's tent mates.

One of the men continued to wear his helmet, which was far too big and sat crooked on his head, so he took it off, "The pike is long and awkward, but I'm getting used to it, but I can't say the same for me helmet."

"Well, some pikes are longer than others," said one of the others as they all laughed.

"You've been peeking, haven't you," said a third man smiling.

They all laughed except Tommy, who had a moment of sadness. He felt it difficult to laugh, knowing that Isabel and his boy were back at home wondering what had happened to him. *If only there were some way to get word back to them*, he thought to himself.

His father would have known that they were heading to Bradford, but what could he do, on foot and without means and besides, he didn't want him travelling out and about in these times.

Fairfax's intelligence had discovered that there was a battalion of Royalists interned at Undercliffe about two miles away. They were outnumbered, so the next day, Fairfax ordered his drummer, flagman, twenty musketeers and fifty pikemen, including Tommy, to march into Bradford to enlist men for the cause.

They marched the mile to the outskirts of the town, it was a busy market town, and even though there was trouble brewing and many had fled, those who stayed stubbornly continued their day-to-day existence. Puritans, in their customary black garb, set up roadblocks on the roads into town and fortified places of defence on the main thoroughfares the best they could.

The Puritans had become a political force and religious reformers who saw the Church of England moving in a direction opposite to what they wanted. Most importantly, they supported the Parliamentarians because they objected to the King's Catholic influence both at Court and within the Church.

The troop crossed the bridge over the beck, past the ducking stool used for the obstinate women's punishment and on through the wooded valley. There was mostly poor farming land suitable for sheep and the odd enclosed field for crop cultivation. The day was cold and bleak. They marched down into the valley past the parish church. As they went on, the snow started to fall quite heavily, but that did not deter the townspeople that came out from Kirkgate to cheer and applaud the small Parliamentarian force. Tommy looked behind and saw that a large group of men, both young and old, had started to march behind them through the town.

They returned half a day later with about eight hundred militia and clubmen with all manner of different implements and farming type weapons. All supporters of the Parliamentarians and mostly Puritans rebelling against the non-purist Protestant ways of the Archbishop.

As the sun went down, the corporal commanded two of the men to take watch on the eastern side of the camp. Tommy and the other would be woken in two hours to take their turn at guard duty. They were told to take a sword and blanket but to not light a fire lest it give away the location of the camp.

It started to snow, and the wind caused a flurry, which would make the lookout difficult and dangerous. Tommy went into the tent, climbed beneath the blanket and tried to get some sleep, but it was difficult because he couldn't stop scratching, and the other men in the tent were the same. It was a challenging predicament, and for a time, he lay there looking at the shadows from the fire cast on the canvas. He wondered what Isabel was doing, probably sitting by the fire waiting for him to return. He shivered and tucked the blanket under his feet and buttocks to make it cocoon-like, and he eventually drifted off to sleep.

Bride of Spirit

Lucy hadn't spoken to her father since that fateful day all those years ago, and now, thinking back, it saddened her.

"So, who is thy father," William asked inquisitively.

"William, I've got ta run before he gets wind that I'm out alone without a chaperone," Lucy started running back toward the village.

William took two steps after her, "Wait, when can I see you again?"

She smiled, "I WILL LET YOU KNOW." Yelling without turning back around.

The wind had started to pick up, and ripples of silver squiggled along the surface of the beck with the breeze. William stopped for a while and threw pebbles into the water, trying to make them skip. He thought long and hard about Lucy and her secretive ways and wondered if he was doing the right thing getting caught up in her goings-on.

What to do, what to do, he asked himself. *I'll find out from the barkeep about her; that's what I'll do.*

The following evening after he, Thomas and Tommy had finished ploughing, they all went to the Kings Arms for ale and a respite from the women and children at home.

It was a busy evening with all manner of yeomen, tinkers and farmers clinging to tankards laughing, arguing the politics of the day and spreading gossip of what was happening in York, Leeds and London. The war was disrupting the wool trade, and there was less demand for it in the major cities. Even the tradesmen in Leeds were apparently struggling, and export had all but stopped.

The straw on the floor hadn't been changed in a while, so it was wet and sloppy from the spilt tankards and wet, muddy boots and foot coverings. Most of the men were playing cards trying to make up for the coin lost the previous night but often, spending their last coin from the selling of cloth that their wives had spun. There was a morose feeling in the room as most had heard that the price of cloth had declined, and this was not good for herdsmen or weavers.

William let his eyes adjust to the darkness then looked for Lucy. He saw her at one of the tables at the back, wiping the surface around a man who had fallen asleep with his head in a bowl of stew, his hand still clinging to the tankard that she tried to remove. Lucy shook his shoulder and tried to rouse him, but he didn't budge, so she left him where he lay. She turned to see William staring at her, which made her blush and flick her light blonde hair that framed her face.

Thomas and William sat down at a table; John Hargreaves walked in and sat next to Thomas, "Lucy bring us three tankards of your finest ale and be quick about it because the mouth of a perfectly happy man is filled with ale."

"Well, we better keep ya happy then, John Hargreaves," replied Lucy as she walked to the bar.

Thomas looked at William as he watched Lucy walk away, "Yer sweet on that wench are ya not brother?"

"William turned to Thomas, "Do you know her family, John?"

"Why do you want to know William if you're not sweet on her," asked Thomas.

"You be quiet, nothing to do with you, Thomas!"

"There now, brother only interested in yer wellbeing, don't want you getting mixed up with the likes of a tavern wench."

"You don't know anything about her," said William angrily.

"Aye, I do. She works here serving ale and providing favours for the clientele. Don't know where she's been."

They all held their silence while Lucy walked back and gave them their tankards of ale. She could tell they had been talking about her and felt saddened that William may have told them about their encounter by the beck. As she handed over the tankards, she gave William a disdainful look and turned to serve others.

William looked embarrassed about the conversation with his brother, so he walked to the bar, "Barkeep, what do ya know of Lucy, she from around here?"

The barkeeper was wiping out a tankard, "No idea, she arrives, works the night, brings in customers with her flirting ways and leaves, not a local, she never talks much, just does her bit then goes home. I asked her once; I think she lives in Stanbury."

Lucy returned to the bar; she ignored William and dropped the empty tankards, and walked away.

"Why do you ask William?"

"No mind, just asking, that's all," William returned to the table.

William watched Lucy as she plied her trade; she smiled and flirted with the men at the tables. It made him a little jealous, and he didn't like it.

"What are you looking at, brother? You haven't taken your eyes off that barmaid since ya got here!"

William, sensing that it was obvious, turned to Thomas, who had a look of worry on his face.

"Brother, you worry too much!"

Thomas reached into the leather pouch that hung from his belt and took out shillings, and held it in front of William, "Look, if you like her, take her!"

William took it quickly and walked toward Lucy at the back of the room.

She laughed and flirted with the patrons, "Robert Ferguson, ya keep losing coin like you won't have enough for the fairer things in life."

"If I keep losing like I am, I won't be able to enjoy the fairer things in life 'cause the missis will have done away with something that I need, to enjoy the fairer things in life with."

The men sitting around the table and the next who heard him laughed. Some, those that were winning, were in hysterics, leaning back on their stools. One of the men almost fell off his stool but managed to steady himself with his hand on the floor, but then realising where his hand had been, wiped it repeatedly.

William stepped in, "I'd like to enjoy the fairer things in life, Lucy."

The men went quiet; Lucy looked embarrassed, "No, not now, I have the cleaning and the ales ta pour!"

"Gew on William, don't take that; she'll make a man out of ya, give her one," claimed Robert Ferguson, one of the farmers from down the hill.

"Aye, I might at that, John," William grabbed Lucy by the hand and dragged her unwillingly toward the rickety stair.

She struggled and resisted. "No, don't you dare!"

Lucy hit him in the arm and grabbed a vertical beam to stop their forward movement. He pulled, but she had a good grip, so he stopped, stepped back, then bent down and lifted her onto his shoulder.

The tables at the back of the room cheered, "Gew on William for King and Parliament!" Robert Ferguson watched on with amusement.

The rest of the men at the back laughed and cheered as they watched William carry her up the stairs.

Thomas and John looked around to see what all the commotion was about and were shocked to see William confidently carrying the barmaid toward the stair.

"Come on, John, let's get home, leave William to it. There's fleece to be carded tomorrow."

Once upstairs, William put Lucy down gently on the bed. She reached over and grabbed the closest thing she could lay her hands on, the oil lantern, and chucked it. William ducked, and it crashed against the wall just behind him, spilling oil down the wall.

William smiled, "There, there lass, no need for violence!"

Lucy rolled over to the other side of the bed and stood, "YOU, erghh!" She looked for something else to throw; she noticed the clay washing bowl and threw that. It smashed on the door just to the right of William, spraying water everywhere.

"Come now, Lucy, let's be civil!"

"CIVIL, HOW DARE YOU MAKE A MOCKERY OF ME HERE!"

William put his hands up defensively, took a step closer, then another.

Lucy picked up the water jug and raised it above her shoulder, ready to throw it, "COME CLOSER, GO ON I DARE YA!"

William took another step closer, and Lucy flexed her arm, ready to throw the jug, but just as she was about to, William knelt. He raised his left hand to defend himself, then reached into his tunic with his right hand and brought out a small posy of flowers and lifted it toward her.

Lucy, still breathing heavily from the exertion, lowered her throwing arm and sank slowly onto the chair near the bed; she started to weep.

"Lucy, are you all right?" William stood, approached her, then knelt before her lovingly.

"NO, I'M NOT ALRIGHT, YOU! Ya have me guts twisted, and me mind tangled!"

Back downstairs, Robert Ferguson commented, "All I know is if the missis were that difficult, we'd have no kids to tend the hide and nowt to tend the flock."

The other men, Arthur Hart, James Brown and Thomas Weatherborn, cackled and laughed in delight.

Robert Ferguson, Arthur Hart, James Brown and Thomas Weatherborn were all tenant farmers that hadn't quite been bold enough to become freemen. They had known each other since childhood and spent their evenings at the alehouse insulting and blaming the lord, steward and the King for any hardships they faced. They had all been married, all except James, who preferred the life of a herdsman and spent most daylight hours up in hills with his sheep. One by one, their wives had passed, either in childbirth or with consumption. Only Robert's wife remained and nagged him at home when the others kept him out far too late.

Robert Ferguson was a tall man and the most outspoken of the four. He had small, engaging, blue-grey eyes with a long, wide nose that seemed too large for his face. When he smiled, his teeth were black and worn down close to the gum. His grey hair was long and pushed back off his face behind his ears. He had a weathered look beneath his eyes, the wrinkles making him look older than his years. A light grey moustache and beard adorned his face and met with his bushy, grey sideburns. His thigh-length, brown tunic was done up at the top and opened as it neared his thigh, revealing a mottled red wool coat. Dirty, stained hose reached to beneath his knee where homemade garters tightened them to the leg. Woolly winter socks covered his lower leg and were strapped, criss-cross with thin straps of leather to keep the dust and dirt out. Large brown leather ankle boots covered his feet, making them look longer than they were.

"Wasted shillings if you ask me," said James.

"Yer, well we all know ya likes the company of yer sheep," replied Robert, who was smiled with his quick-witted reply.

They all laughed at James' expense; he was the only one that didn't quite catch on to what they were inferring.

"Of course, I like me sheep; they're the only thing that keeps me from the begging lane."

The men found this hysterical and laughed, Arthur choking on the mouthful of ale that he had just poured into his mouth, spitting it out all over Thomas Weatherborn, who was sitting opposite. Arthur laughed so hard he lost his balance and almost fell off his stool.

They all looked up at the candle chandelier that was rocking and heard the smashing. Then there was silence.

Upstairs, William still knelt in front of Lucy as she continued to weep into her hands. He went to put his arm around her to comfort her but remembered what happened the last time he showed her affection.

William lamented, "I don't understand Lucy."

Lucy's weeping turned into a quiet sob, "William, ya fool, I'm sweet on you, do ya not understand?"

William smiled, "Then why are ya crying and carrying on like this?"

Lucy's sobs stopped, and there was anger in her voice, "Cause yer family think I'm a whore and I'm not."

"All that matters is that I like ya, Lucy, don't worry about any other!"

Lucy had stopped sobbing and turned to William, "Do you, William?" she paused, "Like me?"

William looked up into her eyes, "Course I do, couldn't wait ta see you again, I want to court you, Lucy."

Lucy wiped her eyes, "You do?"

"Course I do," whispered William.

"You'll have to ask me father," she said with a tone worried tone.

"Whenever you are ready," William replied.

Lucy smiled, "Tomorrow?"

"Of course, when and where?" asked William.

"Meet me in the square tomorrow afternoon as the sun reaches its highest point."

"Right you are then, tomorrow afternoon," William smiled confidently.

Lucy started jumping up and down on the bed to make the chandelier swing downstairs. William followed suit and bounced up and down on the bed, laughing and giggling as they followed through with the ruse. After a while, they stopped, and William walked down the stairs; the men sitting at the back of the room stood, clapped and cheered as he appeared. Blushing, he continued walking and left through the door. Lucy appeared moments later and fixed her bosom as she went to the bar to continue her service.

Legacy of Wind

Continuing their journey from the Old Dog Inn, Thomas thought about what the innkeeper had told him. *Well, if it's Roundheads you're looking for, they are camped east of Bradford, but where?*

Thomas wondered how they would recognise the company that Tommy was in. He knew that he would be with the Roundheads somewhere. He thought, *but how did one tell Roundhead from Cavalier?* They all wore the same; buff coats and pot helmets were worn by both sides. John had heard that officers wore a different coloured sash or coloured rag tied around the arm, but what about pikemen?

The snow was deep and untouched except for the snow-covered footsteps from the other lodgers that pointed the way to Bradford. The storm had passed, but it was icy cold, and still, they could hear the crunch of the snow at each step as they made their way up to the top of the hill. The road then sloped downhill, a restful respite from the hard march they had the day before. They passed a few cottages; a farmer was letting his sheep out of the keep into the light of day.

"Aye up, the top of the morning to you," he called out.

"Mornin'" yelled John.

"I'd be turning round and heading back where ya come from," shouted the farmer.

Thomas waved, "Yes, we've heard, but we're looking for my son."

"Well, find him and get out as best you can, for there's a storm brewing, and it won't be in the heavens. It's gonna be worse than last night, so good luck to ya."

"Yer and thank ya muchly," called out John.

The road continued through a small, wooded area. The road was lined by ash, alder, beech and silver birch trees, their leaves gone for the winter. As the trees cleared, Thomas could see the snow-covered, thatched roofs of the tiny hamlet of Denholme. They passed the turnoff at Main Road that led into the hamlet and continued uphill along Halifax Road, past the hamlet of Thornton and turned east along Thornton Road. They could see the township of Bradford and walked along Westgate. It was starting to get late; the sun was going down, and they didn't want to get stuck without lodging for the night. As they turned into Ivegate, they could see that the road was blocked with barrels and carts.

John squinted and could see men standing, with muskets at the ready, behind a roadblock in the distance, "Aye up, look at this, here's trouble!"

"All those men with muskets make me nervous. Are they Cavaliers or Roundheads?" whispered Thomas.

"Doesn't matter, come on, we got nowt to hide," said John as they meandered down the road.

As they got closer to the roadblock, they lifted their hands high and slowed their walk. It was starting to get colder and darker now, and many of the men had taken cover on the other side of the barricade.

"STOP WHERE YOU ARE, THAT'S CLOSE ENOUGH," yelled a man from behind the upturned cart.

"WHAT BUSINESS DO YOU HAVE IN BRADFORD," called out the stranger as several muskets poked through the barricade.

"WE'RE HERE TO FIND SOMEBODY," yelled Thomas nervously, trying to look between the gaps in the barricade.

John could see a floppy hat moving just behind the barricade and thought, *must be Cavaliers, but all men of means wear that type of hat, so who knows?*

"WELL, MOST HAVE LEFT, SO THEY ARE PROBABLY NOT HERE, BEST YOU TURN AROUND AND GO BACK WHERE YOU COME FROM," called out the stranger who started to get closer to the front of the barricade.

"IT'S GETTING LATE; WE NEED FOOD, ALE AND LODGING FOR THE NIGHT," yelled John.

"STAND AND BE RECOGNISED," shouted the stranger, as four others jumped over the barricade armed with pistols and swords pointed.

Startled, John and Thomas took a step backwards, "What are ya doing? We're no threat to ya, just let us be, and we'll be on our way."

"THROW YOUR BELONGINGS ON THE GROUND AND TAKE A STEP BACKWARDS," called out the man behind the barricade.

John and Thomas did what he said. Two men kept their pistols pointed at them, and the other two rummaged through their market wallets and blankets. They found Thomas' knife and John's axe and held them up for all to see.

"They're for the footpads," called out Thomas.

"And why should we trust the likes of you? Are you not Royalist spies? Come ta see our plans and make off to Undercliffe," said the man behind the barricade, getting closer.

"NO, NO, I SWEAR, we have no allegiance to King Charles or Parliament, just need food, ale and lodging for the night," yelled Thomas.

"And that you shall have!"

Thomas and John looked at each other confused.

A man in a wide-brimmed hat rose from behind the barricade. He had on a wide-brimmed hat, a black beard which was shaped to a point below his chin and a considerable moustache that met with it at the side of his face.

"It's the stranger from the inn," whispered Thomas nervously.

John looked at Thomas then looked at the man that approached them smiling. The four men lowered their pistols and swords, one of them rolled up their blankets and gave them back, another handed back the knife and axe.

"You can never be too careful," the gentleman smiled as he put his pistol back in his belt and sword back in its sheath, then walked slowly toward them.

"Come, the Sun Inn is a short walk down Ivegate; you will be my guests this evening. Please allow me to apologise for your harsh treatment before, for there are spies in our midst. It seems our destinies may be entwined, my friends," said the stranger that they had met from the Old Dog Inn a day earlier.

Bradford was a small market town in a valley that was built on cloth manufacture and farming. It had a population of about 2,500, but most had left, all except 300 Puritan men and others who had family that couldn't travel. The Puritan men stayed because they were in dispute with Archbishop Laud and the Royalist acceptance of his religious ways, that in their minds, were far too close to Catholicism.

As John, William and the stranger walked along Ivegate, there was an eerie quiet and a darkness that fell quickly over the town.

Houses were dark and empty, and dogs barked and howled in the distance. There were Puritan men stationed every two hundred yards armed with a lantern, musket and sword, and they all doffed their cap for the stranger as he walked by.

As they neared the inn, Thomas could hear the beck as it transcended the bleak quietness of the night. They walked to the rear of the inn, which was a dim looking, run-down establishment. The front door and windows were all boarded up and nailed shut. There was a pale glow emanating from the broken window down the side; the flame from one small candle on the inside ledge danced in the breeze.

The stranger led them round the back. A face appeared out of nowhere, its toothless and wrinkled ugliness illuminated by the lantern he held.

"Who goes there, say your name and standing, for if ya don't, me *chive* don't care and will cut ya in the guts no matter what."

"It's alright, Henry, it is I John Hodgson with friends from the west, sheath your blade my friend and rest it for the days ahead."

"Apologies, Captain Hodgson," he took off his hat and dropped his chin with respect allowing all to pass.

The captain approached the door and lifted the latch allowing John and Thomas to enter, "Please come in. Innkeeper, I have two guests for you."

The captain spoke as they walked toward a table, "Since the Cavaliers came to town and started harassing folk, most have left, a couple of men were killed, so you are guaranteed a bed this night."

The innkeeper brought a candle and placed it on the table in front of them. He then left and returned with three tankards of ale, placing them on the table.

John and Thomas greedily sculled their ale and put the tankards back down on the table for the innkeeper to refill. He did so then returned to the hearth to spoon pottage into earthenware bowls for them.

"I should introduce myself. I am Captain John Hodgson of the Parliamentary Guard sent here by his Lordship Thomas Fairfax to organise reinforcements and defend the town until help arrives."

"I am John Hargreaves, and this here is Thomas Rushworth. We are here to find his boy Tommy Rushworth who is also my grandson. He was taken from us two nights ago by the Parliamentary army from Haworth."

"I'm afraid so, Thomas." The captain had heard about the misdeeds that were being forced on the local people by the army, and it disgusted him.

Thomas looked at the captain worriedly, "Do you know where my son would be?"

"I would say that he was probably recruited into Lord Fairfax's army. They were encamped on the eastern side of town but have since left after the Cavaliers departed and now march east toward Tadcaster."

"Left?" Thomas looked across at John quizzically.

Captain Hodgson frowned, "These are dangerous times. My spies tell me that there is a Royalist army less than half a day's march from here at Undercliffe, and as you can see, we prepare for battle."

"I would suggest you stay for a day or two, for if you are seen travelling east from Bradford, you will surely be captured by the Cavaliers and interned or shot as Parliamentarian sympathisers or worse, spies," lamented the captain.

"This is not our battle; we just want to find my son Tommy," exclaimed John angrily.

With sympathy in his voice, the captain regretted what he had said, "I am saddened by your predicament and understand your worry, but please eat and rest, for tomorrow is another day. Innkeeper, give these men what they want and place it in my debt."

The captain whispered, "Sleep well, my friends, as the time for sleep and rest will soon be in short supply." He bid his farewell, stood and walked toward the door and out into the cold night to check the watch and earthworks being built.

All in the tavern, including John and Thomas, rose from their seats as the captain left. After he left, they all sat back down as the innkeeper placed more tankards of ale in front of them.

Thomas and John didn't talk for a while, preferring to drink silently and consider their options.

Thomas thought of his son and the man he had become. He remembered him as a lad and the joy that he brought to both he and Agnes. The laughter he brought and the cheekiness he displayed. He was tough, though, and Thomas thought that if anybody could get through this, it would be Tommy.

"What are you thinking, John?" Thomas whispered.

"We'll rest here tonight and travel further east in the morning," John stated.

Thomas had a concerned look on his face but agreed, "Aye, I agree, but we'll have to stay off the main road, cut through the fields until we find his camp."

CHAPTER THIRTEEN

White Silence

East of Bradford, Tommy shivered and tucked the blanket under his feet and buttocks to make it cocoon-like. He eventually drifted off into a deep sleep.

He was tired as he and several of the others had spent most of the afternoon collecting faggots, bundles of branches and twigs bound together to be used as fuel or as gabions that could be filled with earth and used as cover for battles. It was hard work for eightpence a day.

What seemed like moments later, he was woken with a shove in the darkness.

"Aye up, it's your watch!"

Tommy lifted his head and still felt groggy from lack of sleep. He opened his eyes fully and allowed his eyes to adjust to the candlelight.

The soldier who woke him jumped straight onto the mattress, pulled the blanket over his head, and went to sleep.

Tommy yawned, stretched his arms and put on his boots, wool coat and his leather buff coat. He picked up the backsword which Robert had provided to him the previous day and, with his blanket around his shoulders, stepped outside the tent.

The wind had picked up and continued to blow the snow around, making visibility poor. He stood there by the fire, waiting for the other soldier to come out of the tent. They both walked up the hill, into the woods and east through the trees to the edge of the wooded area. The man already on lookout heard their steps, startled, and turned and raised his flintlock toward them.

"Courage or die," Tommy whispered the field words the corporal had given him.

The soldier on watch uncocked his pistol and pulled his blanket back around his shoulders. Without saying a word, he walked past Tommy back toward camp and the warmth of the fire.

Tommy and the other soldier he knew as James stood beside a tree looking out. Still, it was dark and almost impossible to see more than twenty feet away. Tommy could see the curling hotness of his breath in the light of the moon. He shivered and put his hands under his armpits to warm them. James stomped his feet, trying to bring circulation back to his toes.

Worriedly, James whispered, "You know for all we know there could be armed Cavaliers ten foot away, and we'd never see them. They could put a blade between your ribs before ya knew it."

Tommy whispered back, "Aye, but I slept better knowing that somebody was up here keeping an eye out while we slept, and I think we owe the same to the other men in the camp."

James stomped his feet again, "It's so bloody cold, and I've heard we're moving out tomorrow; his lordship is taking the army further east."

"Christ, what about Bradford," asked Tommy disappointed that he was being forced to travel even further east away from home.

"I just don't know; I just go and do what they tell me to. They tell me where to go, and I do me best to stay alive," said James apprehensively.

Tommy was saddened as he came to terms with his situation and the finality of his possible mortality. He looked off into the darkness and was mesmerised by the small snowflakes which flew around lit by the moon like fireflies.

Two hours later, Tommy heard rustling in the trees. He took out his back sword and pistol. He pointed it in the direction of the noise until he heard the field words from the approaching corporal, " Everything quiet, no noises or movement?"

"No Corporal, no noises or movement," Tommy replied.

The corporal gesticulated for them to leave, "You two, go and get some rest. Two others are on their way up here. We're leaving today, so get some sleep and then help the others break camp."

James turned and left immediately, and Tommy whispered, "Corporal, what about me family, me bairn, is there any way to get word to them?"

The corporal whispered apologetically, "I'm so sorry, Tommy. Any messages are to be for military intelligence only, his lordship's orders."

Perturbed, Tommy followed James walking through the trees then down the hill toward the fire outside the tent. Tommy took off his boots and belt, snuck back onto his mattress and pulled the blanket up. He said a quiet prayer for Isabel and wee Will and prayed to God to keep them safe and out of harm's way.

A couple of hours later, he awoke to the sounds of rummaging and packing. He felt groggy and still tired from lack of sleep. James, who he had been on guard duty with, was still asleep, so he put on his boots and went outside. His lordship's tent had already been disassembled, and his servants were busily putting his belongings on the cart.

Tommy started to help the other men pack up, then he felt an uncomfortable pain in his stomach, so he immediately ran to the latrine at the back of the tent, a pit four-foot-deep half full of all kinds of unmentionables.

He quickly undid his hose and squatted over the pit, just in time, as a steady stream of fluid streamed from his rectum. He looked down into the pit, which was half full of mucus, bloodied mess. He stayed there for a while until he felt there was nothing else to release, then used one of the re-usable rags that hung on a stick. He pulled up his hose, tied his codpiece and returned to packing up the tent.

Tommy felt another wave of nausea, and he started to sweat as the pain in his stomach returned, so he ran back to the latrine. He undid his codpiece once more, dropped his hose and squatted again. Another long stream of watery mucus and blood was expelled from his rectum. His anus stung from overuse, and he felt warm and sickly as he walked slowly back around to the front of the tent. He had his hand on his stomach and grimaced as the abdominal pains started to take hold again. *There's nothing else to come out,* he thought to himself, so he continued to unpeg the tent with the other soldiers.

The canvas from the tents were folded and placed on pack horses that had been brought over. The fire had been extinguished, the latrine filled in, and the stand of the cauldron packed away. The sergeant on horseback rode up and down the row of tents shouting orders and rousing the men as James wondered out bleary-eyed and still half asleep. Once everything had been loaded onto the pack horses, they were ordered to get ready to march. The men put on their helmets and were marshalled in the field. Tommy had never seen so many men in one place, over eight hundred of them.

Tommy stood in line, his pike laying on the ground at his feet; he looked ahead, waiting for the corporal's orders.

"MOUNT YER PIKE!" the corporal seemed to be just as sluggish as the other men until the sergeant gave him a verbal dose of obscenities.

The men reached down in sync and lifted the pike holding it at the side with their left hand and resting the butt on the ground.

With a little more enthusiasm, the corporal screamed again, "ORDER YOUR PIKE!"

"SHOULDER PIKE!"

The men grabbed their pike and moved it to the front, then leaned the pike on their right shoulder.

"TURN TO THE RIGHT."

They turned so that there was an even line of four and a long file of men ready to march.

Lord Fairfax, mounted on his white horse, left the ground first with his captains and Regiment of Horse, followed by the flag bearer. A small troop of musket followed as most of them had left earlier. The sergeant stood beside the column and nodded at the drummer, who proceeded to pound a slow beat.

"CORPORAL GET THEM MOVING, MARCH," bellowed the sergeant.

The soldiers in the rank took their first steps to the beat of the drum, followed by another company of pike. Up the rear followed the clubmen, a ragtag group of farmers and peasants who had been commandeered from the local villages around Bradford. They all held pitchforks and other farming implements and tried to imitate and keep in time to the beat of the drum but didn't and looked awkward in their attempt.

They marched east along Leeds Road; it was tough going holding the pike and marching in the snow. Still, they had to just in case the royalists had prepared an ambush coming south from Undercliffe. His lordship had sent two horsemen north of the town, along Leeds Road, to keep a watch out and ensure this didn't occur.

They passed over the river Aire and stopped at Headingly just north of Leeds. Tommy had never been so far from home, and he felt homesick and apprehensive about the coming days.

Headingly was a small village with a chapel arranged around a triangle of land where roads met from the north, west and south. The lay of the land was vastly different, flat and featureless, with empty and abandoned cottages, farmsteads and enclosed white fields.

They were in a valley, so his lordship sent horseman south to the top of a rise to watch for signs of Cavaliers coming from Leeds. They parked themselves in a clearing at the east end of the village. The men were tired, hungry and sore from the four-hour march and Tommy's stomach was still not right. He was sweating and cold, and his shoulder ached from carrying the pike for so long. He dropped his pike in the snow, took off his helmet to reveal his sweaty wet hair and sat on it beside James.

"Lookin' a bit grey around the gills, Tommy," remarked James.

Tommy grimaced as he felt a sharp pain in his stomach, "I'm so hungry and thirsty."

James agreed, "Aye, me too, but they won't feed us until we get to Tadcaster."

"How much further do you think?" Tommy grabbed his stomach and groaned.

"Dunno, I'm not from around here, but I heard the sergeant say that we were about halfway, should get there before nightfall."

The sergeant rode over and yelled to Robert, who was sitting on his helmet not too far away. "Corporal, take three men and search that cottage, bring back any supplies, animals and ale you can find."

Robert stood and looked behind him. There was a small farmhouse and barn about a half-mile away across the snow-covered field. Smoke rose from the chimney, but nobody could be seen.

The corporal looked at Tommy, James and the two men sitting closest to him, "You four come with me, leave yer helmets."

Tommy and the two other men slowly stood and followed the corporal. With little supplies, Tommy realised they had to rely on the theft of the local people to feed the army, but it didn't make it any easier. This was even more difficult in winter when poor harvests and lack of trade reduced food supplies.

They walked across the field, stepping in the corporal's footprints in the knee-high snow. As they neared the cottage, their pace slowed, and the corporal unsheathed his hanger. The others did the same, although Tommy was not comfortable doing so. They crept around to the front of the cottage; the corporal peeked through the shutter to see if he could see anything. The corporal lifted the latch quietly and pushed the door open as it made a drawn-out squeal.

"IS ANYBODY HOME?" Robert shouted with a nervous but clear voice. "If there's anybody there, come out; we will not hurt thee. We just need food and drink, and then we'll be on our way."

The four soldiers crept into the cottage, there was nobody there, so they all walked quickly to the fire hearth and warmed their hands and feet. One of the men grabbed a ladle and scooped some soup out of the cauldron, and swallowed it greedily. Tommy went to the table and ripped some bread, giving half of it to James. The corporal, still worried about a possible ambush, approached the shelf fashioned out of the stone in the corner and lifted the earthenware jug of ale. He poured some into a tankard, lifting it to his mouth and chugging it greedily, part of it spilling down the front of his leather buff coat.

Robert turned, "Check the barn, I can hear a cow; we're taking it with us,"

Tommy went out to the barn and led the cow outside, tying it to the small fence which surrounded the farmhouse. He went back inside as the others were filling sacks full of vegetables and dried meat that hung over the fireplace.

The corporal was just about to take one of the sacks outside when he heard a noise from upstairs in the loft, "WAIT, did you hear that?"

The men stopped what they were doing and listened, quietly taking their swords out of the sheath.

Robert cocked his pistol and pointed it at the loft, "We can hear ya, and we're armed, come down and be recognised, or else we'll come up!"

They could hear footsteps from the loft.

A moment later, a stranger appeared at the top of the ladder, "Please leave me be, take the food, but leave the cow."

The corporal pointed his hanger at the man, "Come down here. Is there anybody else up there with you?"

The man started climbing down the ladder, "No, just me, my family has fled."

"Tommy, go have a look and be careful; there's Royalist sympathisers here abouts," whispered the corporal.

Robert kept his pistol pointed at the stranger, "What's your name?"

"My name is Oliver, Oliver Cook. My people have lived in these parts for generations. I own me own lands and have nowt to do with Cavaliers or Roundheads."

As the man reached the floor, he stepped aside to allow Tommy to climb the ladder. He could sense the fear coming from the stranger and smiled, "Don't be afraid we won't harm thee."

Tommy slowly climbed the ladder and peeked his head over the top of the floor of the loft. There, he saw a woman and two children with terrified looks on their faces, cowering in the corner beside a bale of straw. The woman had her hand clasped tightly over a little girl's mouth.

"WELL, TOMMY?"

Tommy winked at the little girl who looked terrified, "Nowt up here, Corporal!" He looked away and slowly descended the ladder.

Just as he reached the bottom of the ladder, he turned to see Robert raise his hanger to the man's throat. He pushed the tip of the blade into the fleshy part of the throat beside the Adam's apple.

"WHERE IS IT? Yer stash, coin, gold, silver where is it? Tell us, and ya might live to see yer family again!"

The man raised his hands in his defence and took a backward step to relieve some of the pressure of the tip of the sword on his skin, which had been slightly nicked and dripped a small droplet of blood onto his ruffled collar.

Oliver trembled with fear, "There is no stash, just what you see. Do you think you are the first lot that has come scrounging for food and money?" He tried hard not to look in the direction of the entrance to the hidden underground root cellar.

"Tie his hands behind him," ordered the corporal as one of the other men started to ransack the kitchen area.

Robert raised his pistol and gestured for Oliver to sit on the chair, "I can smell a Royalist when I see one!"

While the other soldier tied his hands, Robert asked him again, "Where is it damn ya!"

Robert back handed him around the face bloodying his nose.

With a look of empathy on his face, Tommy stepped forward, "Robert, ya don't know he's a Royalist, let him be!"

The corporal looked at Tommy, realising that he may have gone too far, "Right, we're commandeering any food and livestock on behalf of the Parliamentary army. Here's a signed letter from Lord Fairfax himself."

Blood started to drip down his face from his nose, "I can't read," said Oliver. He could read but didn't want to let on for fear they may deduce his former services to the court.

The corporal couldn't read either, but the sergeant had told him what it said. "It says that we have full entitlement to take any food or belongings for the benefit of the Parliamentary army."

"What am I supposed to live on now, snow?" said Oliver stubbornly.

Robert put the tip of his backsword at his chest, "That is not our concern, we are just following orders, and I'd keep me trap shut if I were you before I remove yer tongue."

The soldiers continued to fill another sack, and another picked up a small barrel containing ale and heaved it onto his shoulder.

Tommy was a little saddened as both the family and the farmhouse reminded him of home. However, it was obvious they were a bit more well off, "We have to leave them something, Robert!"

"Don't you worry, they'd have a stash or root cellar hidden somewhere to tide them over, don't ya, old man?" The corporal smiled.

Oliver looked down, saying nothing.

Robert frowned, "Yea, that's what I thought!"

"We're not going to get it out of him, come on men, let's go, we have enough," exclaimed the corporal discouraged, as he picked up a hessian bag full of potatoes.

The soldier with the barrel on his shoulder walked out next carrying two full bags of dried vegetables. Tommy followed with two more bags, but just as he was about to reach the door, he dropped one of them and closed the door behind him before any of the other soldiers noticed. On the way, he unhitched the cow and urged it forward with him.

Oliver struggled to loosen the rope around his wrists, and they eventually became loose, and he freed his hands. He walked quickly to the spilt vegetables and peeked out the gap in the shutter watching the soldiers walk back across the field with his cow.

"It's alright, they're gone, you can come down now," the two children and their mother climbed carefully down the ladder.

"Oh Oliver, I was so scared, the soldier, he saw us and said nothing!" His wife put her arms around him and put her head on his shoulder.

The children ran to the shutter to peek out.

Oliver looked over. "Children, what do you see?"

The boy looked around, "Nothing, Father, they've gone, but there must be a whole army on that road. There's horses and many, many men with pike and muskets."

Oliver paused for a moment, "Son, I want you to keep an eye out and tell me if they so much as look this way again."

"Aye, Father!" The boy felt proud of his new responsibility and didn't want to let his father down. He looked eagle-eyed through the shutter as the soldiers got back to the road.

Oliver moved the table and kicked away the cracked stone

and straw to reveal a linen cover; he picked it up, shook it off, then opened a wooden trap door in the floor. Inside were several hessian bags filled with a portion of last summer's garden harvest. He pulled them out and placed them beside the table. He then moved some dirt and another hessian bag in the hole to reveal a lower trap door. He knocked on it three times and lifted it with the leather strap, pulling it out and placing it on the floor beside him. He looked down at the barrels of two pistols, pointed at him, and two faces staring up at him, one of which was his nephew, the steward. Oliver helped them up, closed the door, replaced the linen cover, kicked the cracked stone and the straw back over it and moved the table back.

The reeve silently walked toward the shutter, put his hands on the shoulders of Oliver's son, and peeped through, watching the pikemen readying themselves to march again.

"That was a close one, Oliver," claimed the steward.

The reeve still staring through the shutter, "Aye, it was, but now they have what they want; bastards probably won't be back."

The reeve continued to watch as the soldiers stood and got ready to march as the drum started its slow rhythmic beat.

"Bastard Roundheads have taken my cow," said Oliver disappointedly.

"Better your cow than your guts, and at least we still have the horses. If they had seen them behind the trees, they would have taken them as well," claimed the steward. "The hideaway came in very handy!"

Oliver smiled, "Yes, it has come in handy over the years. Apparently, Father used to hide Catholic Priests down there many years ago."

The reeve continued to look through the gap in the shutters.

The steward had a pensive look on his face, "We'll stay here for now and make way by the light of the moon."

"Where will you go, brother?" asked Oliver.

"To Tadcaster, then back to Bolling Hall to give news and intelligence to the Earl of Newcastle," muttered the steward.

"You know if they catch you, they'll kill you," declared Oliver.

"Don't intend to stay long, just long enough to scout their earthworks and then be gone, besides, I owe it to me brother," exclaimed the reeve who had taken up arms after the death of his brother at the hands of the Roundheads in Haworth. He had sworn revenge and would do anything he could for the Royalist cause.

The steward turned to the reeve, "How many men do ya see?"

"Mmmm, I'd say about six hundred pikemen, fifty horsemen, but no musketeers."

"Musketeers are already in Tadcaster guarding the bridge," claimed Oliver. "I saw them there last time I went into town, treasonous bastards!"

"Did you see ordinance?" asked the steward.

"No, there was no ordinance, but the musketeers, they looked ready for a fight," claimed Oliver.

The steward smiled, "They'll be outnumbered and outgunned when Newcastle gets there with his cannon."

The reeve continued to look through the shutter, and he heard the slow beat of the drum, "They're on the move!"

The steward called out to the reeve, "Come and eat something. We'll wait until it gets dark and follow them into Tadcaster."

"I'll come with thee," said Oliver. "I'll try and get my cow back!"

His wife, who was usually quiet and agreeable, disagreed, "No husband tis too dangerous!"

"Quiet woman, I'll not lose our cow to the Roundheads, besides if they been pilfering, there will be clubmen that I know out and about, and they may be able to assist."

"It's alright. Roundheads will be too busy digging in ta worry about him," claimed the steward.

The steward and his brother sat by the fire eating dried lamb, cheese and bread while the reeve chewed on a piece of mutton while still looking through the shutter, watching the last of the Roundheads disappear down the road.

"What have you heard of the King?" inquired the steward.

The steward's brother took another bite of the cheeses and stared into the fire. "Charles has set up his court at York, and Queen Henrietta Maria has fled to Europe to raise money and munitions from the French."

Oliver's wife shooed the children upstairs and poured the men a tankard of ale from the new barrel that she hid in the underground stash. She gave one to each of them and went about her business cleaning up the mess that the soldiers had made when they ransacked the room.

An hour later, the sun had set, and a quiet fell upon the countryside.

The reeve opened the door looked over the countryside, "It's so quiet, you wouldn't think there was a war on! We should go; I'll get the horses." He walked out the door and around the back towards the trees on the edge of the property.

"We'll go into town via the road to Wetherby, leave the horses and have a look about."

"Goodbye, Oliver." The steward extended his hand out for him to shake it.

"Be careful, Stuart, and God be with you."

The reeve arrived back with the horses, they climbed up on their horses, "God save the King!" declared the steward in a bold tone.

"Aye and God be with thee, and God save the King," answered Oliver.

"Stuart, there'll be clubmen about. If you are harassed, just say my name, and they'll let thee pass. I'll walk into town via the backroads and rouse some men. They'll be less likely to pilfer if they know clubmen are about."

The reeve doffed his hat, and they both turned their horses and trotted down the lane to the main road. They made their way to the outskirts of Tadcaster and hid their horses tied to a tree in a glen. They then walked the half-mile to the outskirts of town.

The Forgotten Man

Back in Haworth, Lucy watched William cutting wood outside. She remembered when they had first started courting. It was a difficult time all those years ago. She felt saddened as she remembered when he had first met her stubborn father.

That fateful night when they had discussed William's courtship, and he asked if he could call on her. She had said yes but thought it best to ask her father first, as was the custom. As they were not nobles, she knew she had more freedom to choose the man she wanted to marry, so she was not overly concerned.

William had discovered that she was from Stanbury, a small village one mile west of Haworth. Lucy told William where she lived on the freehold farm owned by her father. She requested him to call on her so that they could meet and ask for permission to see each other.

Back at home, Lucy told her father of the courtship, "FATHER PLEASE!!"

Lucy's father was shocked and dismayed by the news, "What do you know of this man and his family?"

"THEY ARE A GOOD, HONEST..."

"Lucy, you do not need to shout," Lucy's father walked into the sitting room and sat down on the high-backed wooden chair near the fire.

Lucy followed him in and quietened her tone respectfully stood in front of him.... "Family... Father."

Her father looked into the fire. He was upset and afraid that he would lose her sooner than he wanted to, for he knew that marrying the right man was important to her future and their families. He thought about the importance of this union... *Lucy would be labelled according to the status of her husband. Yes, she did have a dubious reputation locally from working at the Kings Arms, but that was all a ruse that her future husband would never need to know about. No, he wanted her to have a better life than what he had, so it was paramount that she married a man of higher station. A man with lands and means.*

Her father looked at her curiously, "Yes, and does he own lands?"

Lucy paused, "I'm not sure, Father; I know he's a freeman."

This comment angered him, "A freeman, that's all you know, and how do you know this man? Please don't say the Kings Arms! What's his name?"

Lucy paused again and lowered her voice expecting the worst, "William Rushworth."

"William Rushworth? Absolutely not Lucy; I've known the family for years," declared her father.

Suddenly there was a knock at the door; Lucy ran to the window. "It's him, Father; please be civil."

"What already? This is absurd, Lucy!"

"For me, Father, for me!"

William had arrived early, dressed in his Sunday best; he'd washed the grit from his nails and wet down his hair. He had a small posy of autumn flowers in his hand. He nervously knocked on the door, and he could hear stomping on the wooden floor and some heated exchange. He knocked on the door again and nervously waited for someone to open it. He looked at the posy and then down at the gravel, moving it with the side of his thin leather boot.

The door opened; William looked down at a shiny pair of black leather shoes with a grand silver buckle. He nervously raised his head a little and took note of the beige hose and blue garter, tied at the knee. He raised his head even further to notice the tan breeches, then further examined the white fabric of his shirt. Finally, he looked up to look Lucy's father in the face. The steward stood there, carefully caressing his thin grey moustache on his upper lip, then ran his hand down to his neatly trimmed beard. He had the look of sheer evil in his eyes.

"Steward... Your Grace," William was completely taken by surprise and took a step backwards on the gravel.

The steward paused and looked William up and down, then grumbled, "What do ya want, boy?"

William held out the posy in front of him, "I...I've bought these for Lucy, sir."

The steward looked at the flowers; they had wilted somewhat since he had picked them.

The steward just stood there holding the edge of the door as if he was about to slam it shut. William stood, for what seemed like an eternity, watching the steward look him up and down with a look of disdain, waiting for acknowledgement, but it didn't come.

Lucy appeared at the door, "William!"

She stepped forward and grabbed William's hand, and pulled him inside the house, much to the steward's annoyance.

She led him into the farmhouse. It had two rooms, a grand set of stairs and another two rooms upstairs. Lucy led him into the first door, the sitting room; it had a large window that faced the front of the house. It wasn't a large room, but it was comfortable with a solid oak chair, table and clean stone pavers for the floor. There was a simple, high backed wooden form decorated with a set of red cushions. In the middle of the room, there were two high backed wooden chairs that faced the fireplace. A small oak table sat underneath the window with an iron candle holder; the candle half-melted, drips of wax had dried as it flowed down the side. Lucy nervously waited for her father to enter the room.

The steward entered, "Lucy, wait for us in the kitchen, please."

"Father, please don't!" Lucy looked at him with a feeling of trepidation.

The steward looked at Lucy sternly and repeated, "Lucy, wait for us in the kitchen."

She didn't want to make it any worse, so she let go of William's hand and walked toward the door. Looking back, William stood there still holding the posy of flowers that had wilted even further. She walked out of the room, but not without giving her father a despicable look.

Lucy stopped, a sadness in her eyes; she took one more look at William before closing the door slowly to prolong their parting.

"Sit down, Rushworth," the steward gestured for William to sit at the high back form in the middle of the room.

"I'm okay, Your Grace, I would rather stand," said William bravely, having some idea about the coming conversation.

The steward stood facing him with a serious, expressionless look on his face, "What are you doing here, William?"

William stood there bravely, not forcing himself not to be intimidated by the man who all in the village feared, "I'd like to court ya daughter, sir."

The steward looked down at William's muddy shoes, "William, you know that's not going to happen. I don't know what you've said or done to attract her, but you know, she's not for you."

William took a breath to steady himself, "Sir, I'd like ta court yer daughter Lucy."

The steward smiled with repugnance, "William, yer a good lad, I like you, I like your family, but you know this isn't right. William, what do you have to offer her? You have no land; your family pays dues to the lord, which you can't afford. You have no stock; little means and no future."

William stood there looking downtrodden and dejected, "Sir, I'd like to court ya daughter, Lucy. I'll work hard...."

The steward cut him off, "William, you know you don't want this. I'll give you ten shillings to turn and walk the other way; look what you could do for your family with that."

"Sir, I don't want yer coin. I want ta' court Lucy."

The steward started to get angry, "GODDAMIT boy, will you not see sense?"

The steward walked off toward the door, opened it and walked down toward the kitchen. As he did, Lucy came running past him to the sitting room. She slowed as she got to the door looked in to see William standing there holding the flowers that dangled toward the ground, limp and lifeless; the petals had fallen like his heart.

The steward walked back into the room, "Lucy, I forbid it, now ask your guest to leave."

William dropped the flowers on the floor, "I'm so sorry, Lucy." William walked to the front door, opened it and left, walking down the path in shame.

Lucy ran up the wooden stairs sobbing.

The steward sat at the table in the kitchen, pondering his decision and confirming his decision was correct for his daughter's sake. *Lower grain prices, higher land taxes and now this,* he thought to himself. *If it wasn't for the skimming, the stipend he received from Lord Birkhead, the rat baiting and of course Lucy's duties at the Kings Arms, they would have lost the farm years ago. Imagine that, going back to be a tenant for his lordship as his grandfather had done years before. His father would turn in his grave!*

Lucy was lying on her wooden frame bed when the steward walked in. He sat on the edge listening to his daughter cry. "Lucy, listen to me. My father and his father before him worked themselves to the grave to purchase this farm and send my brother and me away to become gentlemen."

Still sobbing and red-faced with anger, Lucy turned to her father, "HAS NOTHING TO DO WITH ME!" she yelled, then turned back around and continued to sob into her pillow.

Her father stood, "Do you not see, if I let William court you, we'd be taking the family right back to where we started, in the fields!"

Lucy had stopped sobbing and sat up, then stood up in front of her father, looking at him with disgust. "You know the only reason we're not still in the fields is that yer grandfather was a thief," she said angrily.

The steward felt hurt and wanted to leave the room. "Quieten yourself, Lucy. You have my decision!"

Lucy walked toward the door, "At least the Rushworth family are honest."

She walked down the stairs and out the front door looking for William. He was long gone by now. She ran down Hob Lane then turned into Main Street; she could see William slowly walking down West Lane in front of her, so she called out to him. He didn't hear her, so she called again. William stopped and turned to see Lucy running full pelt after him.

He started to run toward her, "Lucy, what are ya doin'?"

Lucy was out of breath but clenched onto William. He put his hands out, not knowing what to do, then relented and returned the affection.

An older couple walked by and shook their head in disapproval, "Did you see that she touched him and a chaperone nowhere to be seen!"

Lucy still clutched William as he saw the older couple's look of disapproval as they walked past.

Lucy pulled her head back and looked into his eyes, "I don't care about my father; William, I love you!"

William took a step back, looked into her eyes and put his hands on her arms. He was going to argue and explain why it wasn't a good idea but thought better of it and pulled her close to him, "I love ya, Lucy, always have," he whispered.

They turned and started walking down West Lane together, both deep in thought. William turned to look at her, "What are we going to do? Wouldn't be right courting you without yer father's permission, especially now I know who he is."

Lucy's eyes grew large with excitement, "We'll see each other in secret until I can convince my father otherwise."

All those years ago, Lucy thought to herself, *and now to think that there are two children and another one on the way.* She felt sad whenever she thought about her father but knew it was for the best as she knew he would never accept the life that she had chosen.

The Sword's Nothing

Meanwhile, in another time and place in the West of Yorkshire, two men continued to seek their long-lost son Tommy, "Tis, not our battle, we just want to find my son, exclaimed Thomas!"

"I understand your predicament, but please eat and rest, for tomorrow is another day. Innkeeper, give these men what they want and place it in my debt." The Captain stood and walked toward the door.

"Sleep well, my friends, as the time for sleep and rest will soon be in short supply."

John and Thomas rose from their seats as the captain left.

The innkeeper showed them to the room, there were four beds, and each was occupied with men sleeping in them, one with two. It was not uncommon for strangers to share a bed while travelling. Bedtime etiquette demanded that to ensure a good night's sleep, your bedmate was to lie still, not hog the blankets, and generally keep to one's self. However, this was not always the case.

Thomas looked at the innkeeper, "Have you nothing else?" he whispered.

"Pardon the circumstances, but these men have been on guard most of the day and night; it's either share or sleep on the floor," The innkeeper closed the door after him as he departed.

Thomas looked at John and shrugged his shoulders. They walked in and stood in the middle of two beds occupied by strangers. They dropped their belongings, took off their tunics and stripped to their undershirts. John placed his blanket on the bed, lifted it and climbed underneath. The man beside him grunted and rolled over, taking half the blanket with him. John tugged part of it back in haste and watched Thomas get into the bed alongside. The man beside Thomas was lying on his back, snoring; Thomas turned over and closed his eyes, weary from the exertions of the day.

Suddenly John's bed mate passed wind with a long reverberating rumble. Both Thomas and John opened their eyes, each hoping that the noise came from one of the other beds. Thomas knew the answer to that mystery when John jumped up from the bed and pulled the blanket off with him. Thomas smiled and watched John creep over to the other bed and climb in beside the other stranger.

In the morning, they woke early and sat at one of the unoccupied tables. "Sleep well?" asked Thomas.

John looked at Thomas, lifting his one eyebrow questioningly, "Did ya not hear him through the night? He had more wind than a winter's gust over Haworth Moor!"

Both looked weary and haggard and sat there quietly contemplating the past days. Thomas smiled as he took another spoonful of the pottage that the innkeeper had put in front of him, "Where do ya think they've taken Tommy?"

John shook his head frustratedly, "No idea. I think we need ta speak to the captain as soon as we can." He called out, "Innkeeper, where will we find Captain Hodgson this morning?"

"I hear there's been Royalist movement east of the city; I'd say he'd be over there. Just go back to the old prison, then go east along Kirk Gate over the bridge, then walk southeast to Leeds Road. Follow the church steeple; you'll find him. If anybody stops ya, just say Spirit a' Hodgson, and they'll let ya pass."

John and Thomas finished their pottage, rolled up their possessions and started walking toward the door.

John stopped, "Wait a minute, the bloke there at the table, that's him!"

Thomas rolled his eyes, "What's wrong?"

John had a mischievous look on his face; he smiled and winked, "Wait outside."

"John, don't!" Thomas rolled his eyes and looked up, swaying his head with impatience.

Thomas walked toward the door and, lifting the latch, took one more look back as Hargreaves approached the table.

He stood at the table looking down at his former bed partner, "Morning, have a good night's sleep, did ya?"

The man looked at his mate sitting beside then back, frowned and looked up at John, confused, "Why do ya ask?"

"Nothing, just asking," John turned, grunted, then let out a huge reverberation that made the dogs look and the man opposite lean back and almost fall off his stool. His bed partner, still confused, stood and stared at John as he walked out the door.

John's bed partner had a quizzical look on his face; he looked at his mate, "What was all that about?"

His mate shrugged his shoulders, a moment later, they both screwed up their nose, and both stood and walked away to find another table.

Thomas waited outside, "Y' orl, right?"

John smiled and winked at Thomas, "Never better, now let's find the Captain."

They walked to the old prison, then went east along Kirk Gate, over the bridge, walked southeast to Leeds Road, then kept walking until they could see the church steeple. When they got to the church, there was all manner of activity. Men were pushing old carts and rolling barrels into place on the road; others were creating mounds on either side. They buried sharpened wooden poles which stuck out menacingly toward the east. Others had carts full of sacks of wool which were being taken toward the church.

"Looks like they're getting ready to do battle, no way we're going to get out of town with all this going on; let's make ourselves scarce," said Thomas nervously.

They ran toward a house and ducked down behind the wall. There was a loud whistle from the steeple of the church that all could hear, and all behind the barricade sprang into action. Some had flintlock pistols, others swords and muskets and others armed themselves with pitchforks and other farming implements.

"RIDER APPROACHES," called a man from the church steeple.

Thomas saw Captain Hodgson exit the church and come running toward the barricade, "AT THE READY!" He yelled.

A Cavalier on horseback slowly approached the barricade. He had long brown curly hair which bounced on his shoulder as he rode; his moustache and beard gave him a regal look. He wore a fanciful grey wide-brimmed hat, complete with a plume of red feathers protruding from the back of it. He was unarmed, a red sash sat diagonally sat across his chest, and he wore a brightly coloured tunic with elaborate trimmings and puffed lace collars and cuffs. He held the reins in one hand and a rolled piece of parchment in the other.

As he got closer to the barricade, the men on this side nervously cocked their muskets; others ducked below the barricade out of sight, swords drawn.

"THAT'S CLOSE ENOUGH," yelled Captain Hodgson.

The Cavalier reined in his horse about twenty feet from the barricade, "I have a message from my Lord Saville," he said with a posh southern accent.

The Cavalier unrolled the paper and called out boldly, "his lordship demands, in the name of King Charles, that the people of Bradford stop this resistance at once and lay down their arms. You are hereby ordered to contribute stores, supplies and coin to the Royalist army. Any men of fighting age are to be recruited into the King's Regiment. If these terms are accepted, no one will be hurt; if not, the town will be burnt to the ground. You have one day to accept these terms, remove the barricades, and lay down your arms."

The rider waited for an answer, but as none came, he turned his horse and began to trot away back down Barkerend Road.

As the rider trotted away, the men behind the barricade started to yell insults in defiance, "GEW ON BACK TA YA CASTLE YA LOTTEREL!"

Another man laughed, "YER GEW ON YA ARESWORM, BACK WHERE YA COME FROM, OUT YER MOTHER'S ARSE!"

Most of the men behind the barricade laughed and then cheered as the Cavalier looked back, astonished by the disgusting insults not used to such language directed at him.

Well, that went well, Captain Hodgson thought to himself. "Right, you men there with muskets, position yourself up in the church steeple as they advance aim at any officer you see. The rest of you men come with me."

Thomas and John watched the captain scurry off with a handful of men who held rusty swords and the odd fowling matchlock. The captain sent them off to the villages around Bradford.

As John and Thomas walked around from the wall, Captain Hodgson approached, "Are you still here? Good, we need all the men we can get. I've just dispatched five men to the villages around Bradford to get as many men as they could to fight and defend the town."

Thomas had a look of appreciation and respect on his face, "Captain, we appreciate yer kindness, but as I said last night, we're not here ta fight; we're here to find me son."

Captain Hodgson frowned, "LOOK! When those Cavaliers get here, they're not going to care who's for Parliament or King. All I know is if we don't defend the town, they'll kill every mother and son on this side of the earthworks, then possibly march further west."

Thomas and John looked at each other, "Further west?" Thomas asked.

"Yes, further west, the way I see it, you have three choices, take your chances going east where you will probably be picked up by Royalists and shot, stay here and help or go back where you came from."

Thomas swallowed, then looked down pondering a decision, then looked up at John for his thoughts. John just shrugged his shoulders, "Damned if we do and damned if we don't, may as well stay 'ere and help. Besides, never liked those nabobs much, what with their airs and graces."

The captain looked and smiled at John, "I tell you what, once this is all over, I'll send word to Lord Fairfax and see if he knows the whereabouts of your Tommy."

Thomas shook his head in frustration, "Captain Hodgson, we're farmers, not soldiers. What can we do?"

"Go up to the church steeple. My best marksmen are there; just reload their muskets after they've fired them, that's all."

The Captain walked quickly back to the barricade and started giving orders to his men. Some were sent over the barricade to occupy houses east of the church; another on horse was sent down Barkerend Road to see if he could see any sign of the enemy.

The horseman came back twenty minutes later; he was out of breath. "CAPTAIN HODGSON, CAPTAIN..."

"WHAT IS IT, MAN? Well, speak up," called out the captain apprehensively.

The horseman breathing heavily took a couple of breaths, "They got about a thousand men about a mile out of town, and they got cannon!"

The captain turned his head and thought for a moment, "Cannon, how are we to defend the town against cannon?"

He looked up and turned to the men standing behind him, "You men there get sacks of wool from the shed, tie them to ropes and hang them from the roof of the church. We must protect the church and the musketeers in it!"

"Aye, Captain," said one of them as he turned; the men ran off to get the sacks of wool and carried out the captain's orders.

Thomas and John walked to the church then up the fifteen flight of stairs to the base of the steeple. There were ten men just sitting around on the area surrounding the steeple and two keeping a good watch east. When Thomas and John walked out from the landing, they went quiet, turned and held their stare, looking them up and down.

Thomas and John looked at each other, wondering what they were looking at, then glancing down at their appearance, they realised. Their clothes had succumbed to the rigours of the journey frayed, dirty and worn and their faces were painted with hardship and worry.

Thomas looked over the balustrade and watched a horseman gallop towards the barricade, "Wonder what all that urgency's about?"

John and two of the other men looked over; they kept looking and watched the captain give orders to the men, who then ran off westerly.

Thomas looked at the men who defended the balustrade. Puritans, all of them, dressed in black with tall, round wide-brimmed hats, heavy black cloaks and clean, large angular collars. Not a marksman amongst them, Thomas thought to himself. They all had their muskets at the ready and another leaning against the steeple wall behind them.

One of them, an elderly man with a long grey beard, turned to Thomas, "Have you ever fired a musket, son?"

"No sir, haven't much use for them where I come from."

"Well, now, we might have to remedy that situation, won't we."

cg CHAPTER SIXTEEN 80

The Frozen Time

On the road to Tadcaster, Robert, Tommy, and James shared the bread and ale with the others in the rank and watched other men arrive back with food and animals from the cottages that they had visited.

"I'm not sure about this pilfering," said Tommy, "that family was much like me own. Doesn't seem right takin' all their food and livestock and leaving them nowt."

Robert looked at him, "Well, it's them or us. If we don't get provisions, we die, and besides, the normal crimes and laws don't apply to us. Crimes perpetrated against civilians are excusable in times of war."

Tommy disagreed, "Just because there's a war on doesn't make it right!"

Tommy felt another pain in his stomach and felt the urge. He raced over to the middle of the field and quickly undid his hose, and squatted just in time to release a steady stream of watery undigested vegetables and blood from his rectum. He wiped his behind with some snow, which eased the burning sensation, pulled up his hose and returned to the road with a distraught look on his face, still holding his stomach.

"Ya orl right lad?" James could see that Tommy was losing weight, and his face was starting to become drawn and emaciated.

"Here, lad have some more bread," James reached into his buff coat and brought out a large lump of dark bread.

"No, I can't; you have it."

"Gew on, I had enough back at the cottage," James handed over the bread to an appreciative recipient.

Tommy lamented, "Don't know why I bother. Anything I eat ends up coming out me arse in a stream."

"Aye, I know how ya feel. I had the runins for a month, even shite meself twice."

Tommy tried to change the subject, "What about you, James? Do you have family back home?"

"Yer got family in Stanbury, wife and two bairns but haven't seen them for a while. They got me out of jail in Bradford, just walked in and opened all the cells, told us we were soldiers in the Parliamentary army. What about you?"

"What were ya in jail fer, if ya don't mind me asking."

James smiled, "Petty theft from a shop in Bradford stole three shillings, got a whippin' and fourteen days. I hadn't eaten in a week; it was either that or starve to death."

"Got me in Haworth, held a blade to me throat and brought me to Bradford. Got a wife and bairn back home probably wonderin' where I am. No way to get word to them," lamented Tommy.

"Aye, difficult times," James thought of his own family. "We were spinning and weaving just like everybody else, then soon as all the trouble started, everything slowed then stopped. Clothiers stopped comin' 'round with wool, no putouts, no money. We had a few pence stashed away, but that soon went, kids were hungry, wife was always on me back, so I left for Bradford to find work. I carded wool for a day or two, then that dried up as well. I was sleeping under a bridge at night and started thieving, just to eat like."

"At least I've got Thomas, me father, and William, me uncle, to look after them should anything happen to me."

The sergeant rode up on his horse and interrupted, "RIGHT, MEN READY YOURSELF!"

"You heard him, ON YER FEET, READY YER PIKE," shouted the corporal.

The men in the brigade gingerly rose, putting their helmets back on.

"Right, you know the drill, MOUNT YER PIKE," the corporal screamed.

The men reached down in sync and lifted the pike holding it at the side with their left hand, the butt resting on the ground.

"ORDER YER PIKE, SHOULDER PIKE!" screamed the corporal.

The men grabbed their pike and moved it to the front, then leaned the pike on their left shoulder with precision.

"TURN TO THE RIGHT!"

The men turned so that there were eight in a row and four men deep ready to march. They continued marching down Shadwell Lane, north on Wike Ridge Lane, then turned off onto Tarn Lane and headed for Scarcroft.

There were several cottages along the route, but as soon as they approached, the people barricaded themselves inside, apparently scared off by the looting and pilfering that had been going on.

Lord Fairfax had sent a rider on ahead towards Scarcroft, and he returned twenty minutes later, "My Lord, clubmen, they're organising just outside the village."

He sent the horseman back to give them a message, "Tell them we mean no harm, just passing through on the way to Tadcaster. Tell them if they allow us to pass, we will be gone within the hour."

Lord Fairfax knew how important it was for the general populace to support the Parliamentarians. He did not want to lose this opportunity. *The war would be won in the hearts of the people, not on the moors. It wouldn't hurt to try and pick up some more of the local clubmen for his militia, he thought to himself.*

As they approached, James could see the clubmen massing. They were armed with rusty old swords, pitchforks and the odd fowling matchlock, "They look like they're up for a fight."

Tommy disagreed, "No, what against this lot? It'll be over before it starts once those musketeers start shooting."

The sergeant halted the army, and the corporal ordered them to down their pikes.

"I can't feel me toes said Tommy," as he started to stomp on the ground to get some feeling back.

James laughed, "Aye, I know how yer feel, I havn't felt mine since Bradford, I could have left "em back there for all I know."

The other two men in Tommy's rank laughed and slapped their upper arms and stomped their feet, "It's getting colder," said one of them.

"I wish they'd bloody well hurry up, sooner we get ta Tadcaster, sooner we can start a fire," said another.

Tommy called out, "What do you think they're doing, Robert?"

The corporal turned, "Probably asking for permission to pass through the town without it turning into a battle."

The horseman returned and spoke to Lord Fairfax. The sergeant rode down toward rank and file and ordered his corporals to get them moving.

"Right you are men, READY YER PIKE!"

The drummer started a slow rhythmic beat, and off they went marching down Tarn Lane toward the fifty or so clubmen that were stretched from one side of the road to the other. As his lordship's horse got closer, the clubmen opened their ranks to allow them to pass. Tommy and James kept looking forward and marched slowly and purposefully toward the clubmen. Tommy used his peripheral vision, and there standing at the front of the men on the right side was the man whose cottage they had raided. He had an angry look on his face and was holding an axe across his chest.

"Ohhh Christ, James look who's standing over there, the man from the cottage."

"Ohh bloody hell, da ya think he'll recognise us?"

"SHUT UP, YOU TWO," barked the corporal who had apparently also noticed him.

As they marched by, Oliver's fingers started to twitch on the handle of his axe. He didn't take his eyes off Robert, who, of course, was the closest to him being on the outside. Then he noticed Tommy and James and, with a scowling look, spat at the ground. They all looked ahead, refusing to give credence to his insult. They continued on, then did a left wheel and turned into Wetherby Road. They continued through a wooded area, then over a small bridge at Bardsey Beck.

The land was so flat, Tommy thought to himself, probably good rich farming land down here. There was a cow in the field beside them that hadn't been pilfered yet. Then he remembered Oliver's cow that was tied to the back of Fairfax's cart, and he felt guilty about what they had done.

They diverted around the village of Bramham and continued along Toulston Lane eastwards, then marched off the road and cut into Bramham moor.

"Come on, lads, let's get these tents up," Fairfax's servant brought over the pack horses.

The tents and the cauldron were unloaded and spread out once again in tidy, straight rows.

The corporal noticed Tommy frowning and holding his stomach, "Tommy, seeing as you been so busy at the pit, go dig another behind the tents, not too close we don't wanna be hearing yer grumbles and yer moaning."

"Aye, Corporal," just the thought of the latrine made Tommy's sphincter sting and his stomach growl. He took the shovel which had been unloaded and followed the corporal's orders. He chose a spot about twenty paces behind the tents and started to dig; the ground was hard, dark and rich, not like the soil around Haworth.

Tommy kept digging until the hole was about four feet in depth and one foot in diameter. He piled the dirt between the latrine and the tents to offer some privacy. Just as he finished digging and flattening the top of the frozen soil mound, so you could see over it, he saw James Fewtrall come running over from the tents.

"THAT PIT BETTER BE DUG!" He looked comical while he yelled, running and undoing the front of his hose at the same time."

James got to the pit and awkwardly pulled down his hose just as Tommy was walking away. He squatted quickly, and Tommy heard his grunt and liquid-like release, which he had come to know so well.

"Sard!" When James arrived back at the tent, his complexion had changed from a fresh pink to a pale white, and a frown had become fixed to his face.

"Ya know how I been feeling now," said Tommy empathetically.

"Aye, I do at that, feel like me guts is coming out me arsehole," groaned James.

"Oh, it gets worse ya get sick in the guts, at times I dunno whether ta shit or spew. Sometimes it feels like ya need ta do both," exclaimed Tommy.

James smiled, "Yer well thanks fer sharin'."

Once the camp had been set up, they were ordered into rank and file for the march into town. They marched down High Street toward the river, and as they got closer, people came out of their cottages and began to cheer and wave their hats.

Tommy called out to Robert, "What's all that about?"

"Got no bloody idea, but I'd rather them cheering than spitting at us," he replied.

As they marched, they passed a grand house, timber and limestone walls with bow windows and whitewashed nogging. Two musketeers stood outside and stood to order as the regiment marched by. Lord Fairfax's horse, among others, were tied up outside.

James looked to the left, "Ooy, that must be where his lordship and his captains are billeted, bloody hell look at the place. Ahhh, what I would give for a dry mattress, some warm pottage, a tankard of ale and a good woman to keep me warm through the night,"

Tommy laughed, "Yer, well ya got nowt chance of that old son and don't get any ideas."

They arrived at Tadcaster Bridge, which had five segmental arches made of stone. The arches spanned the River Wharfe. The river intersected the town, a shiny blue mirror of slow running water, running east to west, creating an asymmetry between earth and sky as Tommy tried to remember the fairer things in life.

The soldiers of the Horse brigade had set up a temporary camp there, a lookout to monitor the traffic coming and going. They allowed their horses to graze on the shafts of grass that peaked up above the whiteness.

The pikemen and musketeers set up a temporary camp built a fire, and brought a felled tree that was cut up over to the fire for somewhere to sit.

The men sitting around the fire looked up as they heard the distant stomping of hooves coming closer. Suddenly, three horsemen galloped past them and then across the bridge at full speed, an urgency to their riding.

"What do ya think all that's about?" Tommy whispered.

James paused, "No bloody idea, but somthin's amiss."

The corporal walked over to the fire and called out, "RIGHT YOU LOT GATHER ROUND, sergeants just told me, there's Royalists in York about half a day's march away."

"How many, Corporal?" James asked quickly.

Robert looked at him impatiently, "Don't you worry 'bout that! We've been ordered to dig in at the crossroads over the bridge. Bring shovels from the pack horses with ya."

Tommy looked, "Christ James, this is it!" Tommy and the other men knew that this could mean trouble, and they were terrified of meeting the enemy in battle.

"Corporal, we been marching all day," James remarked in a sombre tone.

The corporal turned to him, "Look, I don't make the orders, I just give 'em, so grab a shovel," he said with earnestness.

They all grabbed shovels and walked across the bridge. Some other soldiers were chipping away at the stones in the road over the bridge and removing them.

Tommy watched on curiously, "What are they doing? How we supposed to get back across if they destroy the bridge."

"Who knows, God knows," replied Robert as even he became fearful of the coming Royalist tide.

The corporal pointed, "Right, start digging a trench on both sides of that cottage from there to there, pile the dirt up in front, from that cottage to that one and let's be quick about it."

With a grumble, the men walked over and started digging; the ground was hard and frosted over. It took several attempts before they cracked it, and the soil became not soft but easier to dig out.

It was chilly, but they started to sweat from their labour, so they took off their buff coats. They faced the bridge and started mounding dirt on the other side of the ditch, which by then was three feet deep.

Other soldiers were sent into the woods to cut branches and tie them together in large faggots; these were stood on end on the closest side of the dirt mound and filled with dirt as cover.

It was getting dark, so the corporal organised some oil lanterns to be lit. They were sporadically placed on the lower side of the ditch, so the men could see what they were digging.

"Right, now keep digging out from the bottom of the pit out to about here." The corporal stuck a sharpened branch into the ground. He walked backwards and forwards behind the men digging, berating those who stopped and taking over for those who looked totally exhausted.

After about four hours, the ditch had become a trench about five feet deep, more than double that if you added the height of the dirt mound and four feet wide. The trench spanned the road stopping at a house east of the High Street and another twenty paces west. A lone cottage sat at its centre, acting as a lookout east towards York. Its shutters and door were barricaded up except for small holes which had been punched through for the muskets.

Tommy, James and the rest of the men, exhausted, tired and hungry, walked around the earthworks and up on top to have a look at their handy work.

Twenty musketeers had been ordered to stand watch spanning the earthworks, their muskets placed at the ready on top of each faggot. One of the musketeers was an older man, long grey hair and a beard with wise-looking eyes that could barely be seen because of the shadow created by the candle that he held. He wore a dirty beige broad-brimmed hat and a red woollen tunic underneath his sleeveless leather buff coat. A pair of full and baggy faded green breeches tightened to the knee, and red hose were folded down over his garter. Leather gun powder pouches dangled from a belt that sat diagonally across his chest.

The other left to go back to the makeshift camp, but Tommy stayed for a moment.

The musketeer noticed that Tommy couldn't take his eyes off his musket, "What's wrong lad never seen a musket before, gew on pick it up if ya wish."

The other musketeers noticed and looked over.

Tommy was embarrassed and felt like he had been put on the spot, "No sir, but thanks fer offering."

"Gew on lad," the musketeer picked up his musket and offered it to him.

Tommy took it in his hands uncomfortably, "What if it goes off?"

"No chance of that lad, the pan's empty, and I'm holding the match cord. See here?" The musketeer blew on the match cord, and the tip became red.

Tommy took the matchlock, it was heavy, solid wood and metal, and he remembered how the soldier had held and fired back in Bradford. He stood at the edge of the faggot and pointed the barrel down the road towards York.

The old man pushed the barrel higher with his finger, "Gew on lift the barrel higher, one foot back, that's it."

Tommy felt its weight, "It's so heavy, heavier than I imagined!"

Henry smiled, "Aye, has ta be lad, to bust through that breastplate."

By this time, the other musketeers were watching intently and smiling, "Got another recruit, Henry?"

Those that heard laughed.

"He's probably got a better shot than you old son," he replied cleverly.

"Well, that wouldn't be hard," called out another.

All the other musketeers jeered and laughed, appreciating the old musketeer's wit.

The old musketeer looked at Tommy, "Don't mind them, where ya from, lad?"

Tommy smiled, "Haworth sir, up in the moors to the west."

"Aye, I know where Haworth is, cold desolate, windy place, and that's in summer!" The musketeer smiled.

Tommy was feeling embarrassed; all the musketeers went quiet, looking and listening, watching intently, smiling cheekily.

Tommy put the matchlock down on the faggot and started to walk away, "Thank you, sir."

"Here lad, take this," old Henry took a musket ball out of his leather snap sack and held it out.

Tommy thought back to when the reeve's brother had been shot in front of him outside the Kings Arms and remembered the carnage and mayhem it had caused.

Henry tapped the musket, "Come back tomorrow, and I'll let ya shoot it, all right?"

Tommy smiled, "Thank you, sir," feeling just a little special, then turned to catch up to James, who was lining up with the rest of the rank and file to march back to the camp. It was cold; they were dirty, sweaty, tired and hungry; the wind started to pick up.

James heard Tommy come running up, "Where ya been, I didn't want you ta get a whipping for being out of rank, sergeants on the prowl."

Tommy smiled, "I been learning the ways of the musket."

"Oh aye, suppose you want to run off and join them, leave us poor pikemen bastards as cannon fodder!"

Tommy paused, smiled cheekily, "Maybe, beats carrying the pike all day with you!"

James paused, looked at Tommy sarcastically and smiled, "Now that hurts."

Morning of Destiny

Back in Bradford, John and Thomas entered the church. They walked past the wooden alter holding the unornamental wooden cross. They followed two men going through a door at the back and climbed a ladder ascending to the steeple. At the top, Thomas helped John up onto the floor; it was dusty and a little cramped. At the top, they looked out, it was high, and you see the beck snake to the west through the white fields. Thomas could see men stationed through the town with muskets and others overturning carts and barrels to hide behind. It was a hive of activity, and there was a fear of dread in the air.

He could see men going into the church below, and others brought out pews and stacked them on top of each other to make a wooden wall in front of the church door.

Thomas had heard about the growing Puritan political force in the major cities. He knew they saw the Church of England and the Archbishop of Canterbury as traitors to their way of Christendom. They viewed the King's marriage to the Catholic, Henrietta Maria of France, as hypocritical and labelled Charles and his advisor Archbishop Laud as defectors of the faith.

The eldest, an older Puritan with a long grey beard, called them over and started to show them how to load the musket. "Hold the musket like so, take the powder and pour some in the pan, close the cover and make sure you blow off any loose powder; pour some down the barrel, followed by the wad and the ball. Take the scouring stick and scour home the charge. Replace the stick."

"Now blow on the match cord to get a light and put it in the jaws atop, making sure that the match cord aligns with the powder in the pan. When you are ready open the pan, present and pull the trigger, keeping hold of the end of the match cord. Now you try it. Just don't fire and scare the wits out of the men at the barricade."

Thomas and John took a musket from the wall and fumblingly loaded the musket, although John left the scouring stick in the barrel.

The old Puritan smiled at him, "Make sure ya replace the scouring stick, wanna be firing more than a piece a wood at them."

John smiled at his error and replaced the scouring stick along the bottom of the barrel.

"Right, load the others," said the Puritan as he walked back to the opening in the lantern, looking east.

Once Thomas and John had loaded all the muskets, they took out their blankets and sat on the floor.

"What now?" asked John.

The Puritan took off his hat to place it on the floor beside him. "Now we wait."

On the 23rd of October, Royalists broke camp in Undercliffe and advanced toward Bradford. There were eight hundred Royalist soldiers, Pikemen, Calvary and of course cannons.

The town was quiet and peaceful at the time, and most had fled earlier after a troop of Royalists, on horseback, had come to town and harassed locals, killing two men in the process. Sensing coming hostilities, most citizens got out while they could. Now houses were empty, and chimneys were absent of fire and smoke, and all that remained was a feeling of uneasiness.

Looking out, Thomas could see the men hiding behind the earthworks that had been built the night before. It was quiet, too quiet, then suddenly you could hear them. It sounded like rumbling thunder, eight hundred men, munitions and horses just appearing at the top of the hill.

"HERE THEY COME!" One of the younger Puritans excitedly started to prepare his musket and blow on the match cord.

Thomas and John looked out the balustrade and noticed activity at the top of Barker End. Thomas looked at John worriedly, and he felt a wave of fear.

In the distance, they could hear the beat of a drum. They looked out and could see the Royalists coming around the corner, marching down the road. The commanders rode three white horses, followed by several horsemen carrying colourful banners of red and gold. Behind them, there were a thousand men, horsemen, then infantry with their pikes held up high, then musketeers. More horses with cannon being pulled behind them appeared. They halted at the top of the hill out of range, and Thomas could hear yelling and commanders ordering others about. Soldiers were running backwards and forwards along the road, then disappearing into the small laneways.

The Cavalier horsemen got off their horses and moved forward slowly and stealthily crouching and finding cover in the hedges along the road toward the earthworks. The pikemen stayed where they were but placed their pikes on the ground. Other men used horses to move ordinance up and over the top of the hill, which was much higher than the town.

John, a cold shiver running down his back, "Bloody hell, we're gonna be massacred. I didn't sign up for this! Those cannons will smash us ta bits!"

"CALM THYSELF, MEN!" The old Puritan had seen active service in the Bishop Wars and was used to such occasions.

Fearing the panic of his men, he lifted himself and shouted out through the balustrade, "COURAGE OR DIE!"

The men in the steeple and others standing behind the barricade followed suit and yelled the same, "COURAGE OR DIE!" They lifted their fists in a show of defiance.

John looked down towards the barricade. There was a hive of activity; men with muskets loaded them and found positions of advantage. Some men yelled out insults at the men on top of the hill. One man fired his musket at one of the hedges hoping to get the musketeer hiding behind it.

"HOLD YOUR FIRE. SAVE THE POWDER!" Captain Hodgson, who had taken up a position just behind the barricade, yelled out.

The man crouching excitedly began to load his musket again.

The clubmen that had come in from the other villages lined up in rows of four about thirty paces behind the barricade. They each held some type of farming implement, pitchforks, hoes and scythes, and one or two had rusty old swords. Another held an axe, and others had fashioned longish pikes out of sharpened branches. Others with fowling muskets had been ordered to scatter and hide themselves from view around the village.

Thomas heard it, a loud explosion.

"GET DOWN," yelled the old Puritan.

All the men in the church flattened themselves on the dusty floor with urgency, waiting for the shot to hit. There was a loud whistle, the iron ball soaring over the barricade and earthworks, hitting the side of a cottage across the road smashing a hole in the wall. The cottage was empty as the inhabitants had fled days earlier.

There was a pause, silence, then all the men behind the barricade and earthworks cheered, as did the men in the steeple. Thomas peeked over the small wall surrounding the steeple and up the hill. He could see the soldiers moving the cannon closer. He watched them push the rammer down into the muzzle of the cannon, then gunpowder and an iron ball were dropped in and rammed home.

He could see artillerymen using long wooden sticks to reposition the wooden wheels of the cannon to get better aim. Thomas and the other men ducked and held their breath. Another loud explosion and the cannonball flew past the steeple and hit another empty cottage across the road.

Once again, the men cheered and laughed, but the old Puritan was silent. He blew on his match cord and affixed it to the top of the musket, then he opened the pan and steadied to aim. He held his breath, squinted his eye and pulled the trigger. It was a horrific noise, and Thomas and John covered their ears, but it was too late; all they could hear was ringing. The bearded Puritan lifted his head, peered over the wall, and watched one of the Royalist musketeers, who had snuck closer, clutch his chest and fall backward.

The old Puritan smiled, "Got him!"

All the men at the barricade who saw the man fall cheered. Then there was a panic up on the hill, and the horses were used to pull the cannon even closer.

The old Puritan called out, "THEY'RE IN RANGE!"

Thomas looked up to see the Royalist Horse soldiers lined up across Barker End, their steads snorting and biting at the bit. The Horse were supposed to be the best soldiers but had a bad reputation of cruelty. They were a menacing-looking lot with their pistols and swords drawn. The horses readied to charge, the horse commander was out front, and he started trotting his horse and, as they got closer picked up speed.

The enemy musketeers hidden behind the hedges fired off a volley of shots at the church steeple. The barricade then disappeared again to reload.

The Horse were in full gallop now, but rather than riding toward the waiting muskets at the barricade, they rode north of the church and then west to cross the Kirk Gate bridge.

John, Thomas and the other men already lying prostrate on the wooden floor put their hands over their heads as plaster and stone from the volley of musket balls came cascading down on top of them.

When all went quiet, the old, bearded Puritan looked over the steeple wall and yelled, "THE HORSE ARE HEADING INTO THE VILLAGE ALONG KIRK GATE!"

Four of the musketeers picked up their muskets and repositioned themselves on the western side of the steeple. John went with them, Thomas preferring to stay with the old Puritan and reload his musket.

Captain Hodgson, predicting what the Royalists would do, had earlier sent a small group of clubmen and ten men with fowling muskets into the village to take up positions in the lanes and unoccupied houses.

John watched the horsemen ride into town and get off their horses to accost a woman and her husband who were trying to head west out of the village. One Cavalier raised his pistol and shot the husband from point-blank range. They threw their belongings down on the ground, looking for anything of value while others kept watch. Another young man came running out of a laneway but, seeing the Cavaliers, he stopped and turned around. Before he could get back behind cover, one of the Cavaliers had raised his pistol and fired, dropping him instantly.

John felt sick to his stomach, "THEY'RE KILLING INNOCENT CITIZENS THE BASTARDS!"

He watched as suddenly a barrage of clubmen came streaming out of the lanes surrounding the Cavaliers. The Cavaliers pointed their pistols and shot, dropping one man in his tracks. The rest of the clubmen charged, but the horsemen mounted their horse and galloped away along Ive Gate and back to safety.

Meanwhile, back at the top of the hill, the Royalists had continued their bombardment of the town, moving their ordinance closer and closer, this time smashing up several houses along Kirk Gate.

Thomas' ears were ringing from the musket fire, and he was terrified. He tried to keep his head down and load the muskets for the men at the same time with a look of terror on his face.

The wind picked up coming from the west, the temperature plummeted, and it started to snow heavily, sending a cold, windy iciness into the faces of the Royalists up on the hill.

"I can't feel me fingers," yelled Thomas.

John yelled back, "Better to be cold than dead!"

The Roundhead musketeers continued to fire, keeping the Royalists back behind the hedges along the road, firing then darting for cover to reload.

By this time, the Horse had returned, dismounting and joining their comrades on foot and getting closer and closer to the earthworks that Captain Hodgson had ordered to be built.

The old Puritan yelled, "TRY TO HIT THEIR OFFICERS, ONES WITH THE FEATHER IN THEIR HELMET!"

Thomas peeked over the wall to see the artillerymen load and fire the cannon again with a BOOM through a cloud of grey smoke.

"WATCH OUT, HERE IT COMES AGAIN!" Thomas and the men ducked for cover, putting their hands over the backs of their heads.

Other Royalist soldiers were going into houses and lanes along the road, using them as cover to get closer to the barricade. The soldiers behind the barricade shot at them, but they moved closer and closer.

Thomas looked out as others moved further north and west of the church. "THEY'RE TRYING TO SURROUND THE CHURCH!"

Three musketeers crawled over to that side of the steeple and peered over but ducked as an array of shot splintered the stone near them.

Thomas saw a large group of clubmen charge across Sun Bridge toward the Royalists in the hedges. Their musketeers stationed at Kirk Gate fired at them, forcing them back.

One of the Puritans shot then handed the musket to John, "QUICK RELOAD!"

Thomas exchanged muskets with the men on his side of the steeple as fast as he could.

"THEY'RE MOVING THE ORDINANCE," Thomas could see the artillerymen using the horses to manoeuvre the barrel of the cannon toward the church steeple. "THEY'RE AIMING AT US!"

"WATCH OUT, MEN, THEY'RE AIMING AT US!" The old Puritan bellowed.

A few minutes later, Thomas heard the shot fired, but it sailed past the steeple, safely landing in the Kirk Gate area.

Royalist foot soldiers only thirty metres from the church were hiding at the side of some houses, the musketeers trying in vain to hit them. The Royalists began shooting at the church steeple in volleys. Shooting then ducking behind cover to reload.

Terrified, Thomas and John laid prostrate with their hands over their heads, more plaster, wood and stone came raining down on them, then there was silence, and the men slowly raised their heads to take aim and fire back.

"GOT YA! RELOAD!" yelled the old Puritan, passing the smoking musket to Thomas.

The Royalist musketeers hiding in the hedge fired a volley at the barricade. Suddenly all the men that were this side of the barrier charged the Royalist lines. Thomas could see the Royalist musketeers behind the hedges frantically trying to load their muskets, others running back up the hill to the safety of the main Royalist force; others just fled into the fields with clubmen chasing them. The Roundhead musketeers and clubmen from behind the barricade fired, others turning their muskets around to use them as clubs.

Another group of footmen were despatched from the main body of the Royalist force. Still, they were beaten back by clubmen that had appeared from the lanes on the right. They allowed no quarter and ran through those they could, including any officers that were left behind.

The snow started to get heavier, and suddenly there was a loud explosion, louder than usual. The old Puritan looked out, "ONE OF THE CANNONS HAS BLOWN, THEY'RE FLEEING!"

Thomas and the rest of the men in the steeple looked out and watched as the main body of the Royalist force turned and started to move to the rear. The Roundhead musketeers who had now reloaded fired sporadic shots felling several of the retreating army. They climbed over the barricade and continued up the hill in chase, walking and firing, reloading, walking, then firing again.

Fearing a counterattack, Captain Hodgson called out, "WAIT, MEN, COME BACK!"

The musketeers started walking back toward the barricade, swords drawn with several prisoners, some injured, some not, their hands up in surrender.

The Royalists, up the hill at Barker End, mounted their horses and began to assemble. Others assisted the injured, and still others picked up the dead and carried them out of range. Within half an hour, the ordinance had been moved, and the army began to march out of view.

"THE DAY IS OURS!" The old Puritan screamed out to the barricade.

Hearing this, the men in the steeple stood and cheered, as did other musketeers and clubmen who came out of the laneways and houses.

Thomas looked down to see Captain Hodgson surrounded by men congratulating him. His tactics had been successful.

The men in the steeple tried to brush the plaster and dust from their hair and clothes, which by this time had given them a ghost-like appearance. John and Thomas had a sigh of relief, shook hands and congratulated the marksmen. They bid farewell to the Puritans and climbed back down the ladder from the steeple. Picking up their belongings excitedly, they returned to the Sun Inn through the jubilation and congratulatory fervour that was occurring along Kirk Gate.

On the way, they saw Captain Hodgson and walked over to him. They gave him a respectful bow which he returned.

"Congratulations, Captain, but what now?" asked John.

The Captain had already considered his options, "We'll fortify the town more and wait for Lord Fairfax; he will be here in a few days, and you, your plans?"

John looked at Thomas, then back at the captain, "We need to keep looking for our Tommy."

"I would recommend staying here until Fairfax arrives; for all you know, your son could be with him."

"He's right, Thomas and besides, if we go further east, we don't know whose army we'll run into. Better the devil you know than the devil you don't," said John smiling at the captain.

Thomas looked down worriedly, thinking about his son and what mishap may have fallen on him, "I suppose yer right, but I can't help thinking that he needs our help."

"Come on, you two, let's get back to the Sun Inn; supper is on me," said Captain Hodgson, knowing that they probably didn't have coin for a meal.

They walked on together, John and Thomas one step behind the captain as he congratulated and shook hands with men on the way.

CHAPTER EIGHTEEN

Failed Freedom

Robert had told the men that there was a Royalist force close by. They had beaten the Parliamentarians at Piercebridge and were now headed to Tadcaster. Intelligence retrieved by Lord Fairfax reported that Newcastle had split his force, sending some to attack from the east and some to attack from the north side of the town.

On the road to Tadcaster, the corporal yelled, the men straightened, and the drummer started the slow base beat for the march.

"FORWARD!"

The pikemen started their route through to the other side of the town; it was dark, and Tommy felt an uneasiness about the coming days. He thought about how things were going back home in Haworth. The evenings with his family sitting in front of the hearth of the fire. The banter with his father and uncle and playing with his baby son Will. The cold nights in the loft warmed by the closeness of Isabel's body.

As they reached the outskirts of town, the clubmen were still in position, albeit in a lesser number. James looked across, surprised to see Oliver, the man from the farmhouse that they had robbed, standing there putting shillings into the hand of the sergeant who was in possession of his cow. James saw him take ownership of the cow, rope in hand, and as they marched past, he spat in their general direction.

Back at the camp, the fires were already lit, and the earthenware cauldron was bubbling away above the fire. James looked in the cauldron, un-inspired about what was cooking.

"What's fer supper?" asked Tommy.

"Bit of melted snow, pieces of onion and bit a something that looks like meat. We should have kept the cow!" James smiled.

They sat down on the log, warming themselves by the fire quietened by the events of the day. A feeling of foreboding washed over them all now that they were given a chance to sit and take it all in.

"I don't have a good feeling about the comin' days," claimed James, who was usually not one to show his fear.

The corporal, not an experienced soldier, but one that had seen battle, not wanting his men to be frightened off, tried to reassure them. "We'll be alright if we stick together and work as a unit, remember yer training!"

"I heard that most of Newcastle's army is less than half a day's march away; he has 6000 men," exclaimed James worriedly.

Tommy looked up, "How we going to face that and survive?"

"As I said, if we stick together, we'll be okay, besides sergeant told me we're not going to meet them in the field."

"Not meet them in the field? I don't want to meet them anywhere," said James as he smiled, trying to hide his fear.

Tommy agreed, "Aye to that mate!"

James and Tommy looked down at their bowls, stirring the contents trying to find something solid to eat. They had lost their appetite, and their desire to speak as everything about their pending doom started to sink in.

James felt a rumble in his stomach, grabbed his belly and ran off to the latrine leaving the others to ponder the coming days. He returned a few minutes later, grumbling about the soreness and discomfort of various parts of his rear end.

The corporal sat down with the other men, "Tomorrow, we're ta set up rank and file on this side of the bridge as a show of force. Musketeers will defend the earthworks; we'll stand too just in case their Horse breakthrough south-west of the bridge, and we must protect them."

"What if their Horse does breakthrough?" Thomas asked worriedly.

The corporal sounding far from confident looked at Thomas with concern, "We do what we're trained to do."

After the men had finished their broth, they entered the tent tired, filthy and cold. The temperature had dropped, and it had become blustery; the snow began to fall, being twirled around by the wind. Tommy and James took off their boots and laid on their mattresses.

James tucked the blanket under his feet and pulled it over his head to try and get some warmth trapped from his breath. He tried to get some sleep, but it came slowly, and when it did, it was interrupted with panic and worry.

Tommy wished he could sleep and dream of Isabel and home, but his mind was conflicted and in turmoil. He thought about leaving in the night as he heard others had done but thought ill of it, remembering the story of the wooden horse.

He whispered to James, "Are you thinking what I'm thinking?"

"Aye, but don't fancy me arse split from ear hole ta breakfast time on that wooden horse," he whispered his head under the blanket.

"Aye, but only if they catch us," whispered Tommy.

James took a heavy breath, "They got horses; we could never get away far enough."

"We could if we stayed off the roads. Besides, they will be occupied tomorrow preparing for battle," Thomas whispered.

"We'd freeze to death without the fire," lamented James.

Thomas sat up, "Aye, that's what they're counting on, won't expect us to run at night. The farmhouse where we pilfered the food, if we made it there, we could get shelter until the morning."

James laughed, "The old man would draw and quarter us if he found us in his barn."

Thomas thought for a moment, "No, he wouldn't. I lied to the corporal, his family were up in that loft, and I left them one bag of food behind. I'm sure he would show mercy!"

"Are ya now, and what if he does turn out to be a Royalist?"

"Yer well, he won't find us in the barn, will he, rather that than face the Royalist Horse charge. Remember, I didn't sign up for this, nor did you. We'll wait until the corporal comes in and falls asleep." Tommy whispered, then laid back down.

"Okay!!" James whispered, then ducked under his blanket to wait, trying to sleep but on edge and nervously anticipating the return of the corporal.

The other men in the tent heard them whispering but didn't want any part of it and faced away, all the while listening to their scheme.

It was quite a while before the corporal came into the tent, having spent part of the night with the other corporals and the sergeant, who had acquired some rum. He took off his boots and climbed under his blanket, turned over and went to sleep. It wasn't too long before he started quietly snoring.

James shook Tommy quietly in the dark, picked up his boots, and crouched to walk outside. Tommy was still awake and crawled over to untie the ties of the tent flaps.

The corporal stirred but did not wake.

James followed Tommy outside then turned to tie the tent ties back up so as not to be detected by the wandering guard. As James got to the middle one, the pointy end of a sword appeared through the gap between the tent flaps touching James' chest.

"Going somewhere?" The corporal asked in a quiet, sarcastic tone.

"No corporal, just relieving me self said James, you know how it is."

"And yer mate Tommy?" He whispered.

"Same, he's got the runnins' as yer know."

"The runnins', best you untie the tent," commanded the corporal while continuing to hold his backsword to James' chest.

The corporal stood as he went through the tent flap, continuing to hold the tip of his blade at James' chest as he took a step backwards, defensively raising his hands.

A couple of the other men in the tent sat up and looked at each other in the darkness and feared the worst, having seen the agonising pain that their previous tent mate had endured on the wooden horse.

James could smell the odour of rum on the corporal's breath and the sharpness of the tip of his blade on his chest.

Suddenly, Tommy walked out of the darkness from behind the tent holding his stomach and rubbing his behind, "Bloody hell me guts are coming out me arse. Everything all right, Robert, ya seem a bit tense?"

He walked behind the corporal who still had his sword raised at James and ducked his head, going back into the tent. The men already inside slumped back down and covered themselves with their blankets.

Robert turned to look at Tommy curiously as he disappeared inside the tent but said nothing. While the corporal's head was turned, James lifted the blade of his sword away from his chest, took a step to the side and followed Tommy into the tent. The corporal lowered his sword, sheathed it, then stood there for a moment, shaking his head. Once inside, he tied the tent flaps together and climbed back beneath his blanket. He laid there for a moment, looking upward into the darkness before he turned over and pulled the blanket up.

Tommy and James, already under their blankets, faced away from the corporal, their eyes open, looking at the shadows from the fire dancing on the walls of the tent. They felt guilty, and the adrenalin kept them awake. No matter how hard they tried, they wouldn't drift off to sleep and later watched the glow from the early sun lighten the sky.

Robert didn't sleep that night and felt giddy from tiredness as the sun started to come up. He knew that if the two had left the camp, he would have received punishment from the sergeant at the captain's orders. Previously, as a soldier without rank, he'd already received a whipping for being found drunk and disorderly on duty and didn't want a repeat.

"Right, you lot, up and at 'em. Pikes at the ready before the sun gets any higher, lest you get a whipping for being lazy, and I get one for letting you."

The pikemen in the tent groaned and complained because of the disturbance to their sleep through the night, one of them throwing his boot at the inside of the tent.

Tommy and James were up before the other men; two of them had spent half the night on guard duty, it being their turn. They didn't move until the corporal walked inside and kicked out one of the wooden poles holding up the canvas. There were several curses and exclamations with tired, cold men fighting their way out of the canvas. They finally got to the surface, hair standing on end, bags under their eyes and blankets around their shoulders. They swarmed to the fire like moths to the flame fighting for a position closest to the warmth. Tommy stood watching their shenanigans behind the corporal and James.

Robert turned around to whisper, "Tommy, what were you thinking?"

Tommy was embarrassed about their previous night's failed attempt, "Nothing corporal, as James said, just dealing with the runnins'."

"Ya must be thankful I didn't call the sergeant; he would have dealt with the situation far differently," said Robert with a stressed intonation.

"Won't happen again, Corporal," stated James, as he looked at Tommy for support.

Tommy was shocked by James' admission.

"Aye, and see that it doesn't, or else your fate and mine is out of my hands, and I cannot help you," stated the corporal.

Tommy and James took a bowl of pottage, which by now was no

more than melted snow and a few bits of onion after the other men had scooped out the more substantial pieces for themselves.

The corporal, now more suspicious of James and Tommy, yelled out, "RIGHT PACK UP THE TENT AND READY YOURSELVES MEN, WE MARCH BACK TO THE BRIDGE."

After packing up, the pikemen lined up in rank and file for the march back to town.

"READY YER PIKE!"

"SHOULDER PIKE! Now let's get out of here."

Once again, the drummer started a slow rhythmic beat, and they went marching down Tarn Lane toward the river.

The conifers at the side of the road had green branches suffocated with layers of snowfall from the previous night. At times, the white made it difficult to tell the end of the horizon and the beginning of the sky; both engaged in a partnership to fool the eye.

The town was deserted except for a few mangy looking dogs and the musketeers that had shared the guard for most of the night. The pikemen set up on the southwest side of the river, downing pikes and standing easy.

"Now, all we do is wait," called out the corporal.

An hour later, they heard the slow beat of a drum coming from the east; a rider came galloping down Barker End and across the bridge.

"THEY'RE HERE! THEY'RE HERE. MUST BE OVER THREE THOUSAND MEN, CANNON, DRAGOONS AND PIKEMEN!" The horsemen yelled, continuing up High Street to Morely Hall.

"READY YOURSELVES!" The corporal screamed with trepidation in his voice.

Tommy and James lined up with the other men and prepared to lift their pikes.

James saw the colours of the Royalists at the top of Barker End and the sea of men behind them. The musketeers filed in the front and continued towards the earthworks that they had built the previous night. When they got to three hundred paces away, James saw and heard the musketeers this side of the earthworks engage. There was a burst of fire and a flume of smoke that covered the earthworks in a smoky mist.

Having been fired upon, the Royalists stopped and fired themselves, then the first line went to the back to reload and allow the next line to fire. Tommy saw three of the Royalist musketeers reach for their breastplate while propelled backwards by the impact of the lead ball.

The other musketeers just stepped over them to fire again and retreat to the back of the line to reload while the next stepped forward. They started to get closer until a few others fell, prompting the rest to flee. The Royalists tried several times to come forward, but the soldiers behind the earthworks held fast, as did the pikemen.

The musket fire continued for hours with no real gain in territory from either side.

The pikemen ducked but tried to hold their line, "I don't like the looks of this Tommy!" said James as he stood beside him.

Royalist Horse tried to come across the bridge but were beaten back by musket fire. As they retreated, the musketeers on this side of the earthworks were ordered to retreat to the west side of the bridge, and as they did, a cannon fired over the earthworks.

The sergeant galloped up to the corporal, and the men could see him shouting at him with urgency.

"STAY CALM MEN, WE'RE RETREATING," yelled the corporal.

"FULL TURN AND MARCH TO THE DRUM." shouted the corporal excitedly.

The drummer at double time led the company back in the direction of the centre of town. The Parliament musketeers followed closely behind but looked to the rear, firing shots to keep distance between them and the Royalists who were getting closer to the earthworks.

Tommy heard it, a loud thunderous explosion and the whistle of a cannonball close. He heard the loud splat, and looking behind and to the left, was sickened as the head of one of his comrades smashed from its shoulders, the body slowly falling to the ground. The blood splattered on the men marching besides, but they continued to face forward and march. Another dropped being hit by a musket ball which entered the back of his breastplate, part of his internal organs protruding through the hole in the front. As they got to buildings in town, the musketeers broke off and hid among them. The corporal ordered the men to continue marching into the moor. Tommy could hear musket shots being fired by both sides in the distance.

A few moments later, James turned and had a look, the musketeers who were running out of powder caught up to them. Tommy could see the Royalists behind setting up their rank and file to engage; there were thousands of them only three hundred yards away. The clubmen scattered and ran, the sergeant yelling and ordering them to stay in file, which they refused to do and disappeared over the heather. The Royalists followed to the beat of their drummer;

Tommy and his company continued to march south. It was getting dark when suddenly the Royalists stopped advancing,

Robert called out, "HEY, THEY'VE STOPPED ADVANCING!"

The whole company was surprised, especially as they had them on the run. He thought maybe it was because of the approaching darkness. They turned back toward Tadcaster, not wishing to lose men in the moors.

The company continued through the night, fearing the Royalist Horse that would now be on this side of the bridge. They continued to Bramham Moor, where they posted guards and set up a makeshift camp for the night.

Tommy started to feel hot and sweaty, and he could feel his wet undershirt stuck to his back. The rest of the men were tending to the fire, so he spread his thin mattress on the ground and laid down, trying to get some respite from his tiredness and hunger. He took some mouldy bread out of his bag and ate it, then started to scratch his chest. He knew he wasn't right, a wave of feverish nausea overwhelmed him, and he could feel the rumblings in his stomach. As he hadn't eaten, he knew it was only blood and puss that would flow, so he held on and tried not to think about it. He groaned, closed his eyes and took a deep breath as a feeling of exhaustion flowed over his body.

James knew that Tommy had been hit by 'camp fever' as many souls that were no longer with them had. The continual soaking wet snow, cold and lice which like to make their home close to the warm skin, caused fatal consequences. Many of the camps were a breeding ground for cholera, scarlet fever, dysentery and typhus, and many men had been lost in this way.

Tommy was well-liked by his brothers in arms; they had been through a lot together. They followed behind James in support as he walked up to the corporal, "Corporal, young Rushworth, he's in a bad way, sick of the runnin's, thought I might get him to the local alehouse and get some proper grub into him before we continue the march."

Robert was concerned as he had thought the same thing but didn't want to lose another man. Now he felt guilty having lost men previously in the same way. "Aye, he does look a bit grey behind the gills, but be warned, if you take a step in the wrong direction, the sergeant will be after you, and I'll get a whipping for letting" ya go!"

"I hear what ya saying, don't worry, I'll be back," James turned to go and walked in Tommy's direction.

"Wait, take this," the corporal placed several shillings into James' hand. "Pay for the last weeks, eight pence a day."

James walked over and looked at Tommy's face by the light from the fire, it was haggard and drawn, and he shivered yet perspired. James remembered the symptom. Camp fever, they had lost many men to it since the campaign started. "Right, old son, we have to get you some more grub before ya waste away ta nothing!"

James bent down and grabbed Tommy's arm, helping him up, "Come on, old son, let's get you decent grub."

"What about the corporal?" Tommy whispered almost incoherently.

James had a worried look on his face, sensing Tommy's weakness. "Taken care of, told him yer sick with the runnin's and need some decent grub or else you'll be no use to nobody in rank and file. Even gave us coin; I've got yer share."

James pulled the blanket around his shoulders and put one arm around his waist, assisting him to walk. He could feel the hotness of his fever coming through the blanket.

They started walking toward town, James supporting Tommy as they walked. The other men quizzed the corporal about their destination, but he covered for them, telling the other men that they were on a scouting mission in town. Then to appease them, he handed shillings to them that the sergeant had given to him, keeping his share.

"No bloody point in havin' coin if we can't bloody spend it," drawled one of the men.

They walked slowly and gingerly for a while, and James supported Tommy the best he could. They eventually got a lift from a farmer on the back of his horse-drawn cart and found the alehouse in the small village of Bramham. The Swan Inn a small establishment on the main road. They went inside. It was filled with soldiers, their muskets and swords leaning against the wall lined up near the door at the ready.

Tommy and James took off their helmets and warmed themselves near the fire. James listened for any news from the west, but all he heard was the gossip surrounding Newcastle and his large Royalist force nearby.

James plonked Tommy down on a form against the wall, near the hearth, took off his snow-covered square-toed boots and rubbed his toes, "Awwww, that feels good, first time I've felt me toes in days."

The stoutly looking barmaid walked up to the newcomers who by this time were sitting at a table leaning their heads back against the wall, "What'll ya have, gents?"

She was a rather stout lady wide at the hips; her large bosom squeezed behind the tightened laces of her corset. Her greying hair was held back by an off-white piece of cloth to expose her wrinkled forehead. Her arms were full and stretched the sleeves of her dark brown kirtle, the leather stitches straining to keep the sleeve attached at the shoulder. The sleeves of her undershirt pushed up the forearm to expose her thick wrists. Her fingers were dark from the soot of the fire from when she shoved about the embers trying to get the last bit of warmth from the dried branches that she collected from the woods. She had a cranky look, a look that you immediately respected lest be served with a flurry of expletives.

James opened his eyes and focused, "Two ales and two bowls of whatever you've got!"

The barmaid laughed with false hysterics," Okay, roast lamb, spuds, fresh vegetables from the garden coming right up, would you like the Bordeaux with that?" She paused, "No grub, all gone, pilfered by your lot for yer army and the other one before you."

James gestured for her to come closer. He whispered, "You must have something; me mate is sick and needs to put something solid in his guts, we been marchin' fer days."

James stood; he whispered to her, "We have coin."

The barmaid, like most common people, were neutral and bared no allegiance to either Parliament or King and were mainly in their own service to protect their own interests. She knew that she had to acquire as much coin as she could possibly get in when there wasn't much coin about, "How much coin? There's dog fighting out back if yer interested?"

James winked at her, then smiled, "You look like a fine lady, been months since I've had the company of a good woman. Well, get us some grub, and we might make it worth your while. What's yer name?"

"Matilda." The barmaid smiled and was taken back by the stranger's flirtatious ways. Thinking she might get lucky later with a lonely soldier, she winked at him, "Okay, let me see if we have anything left out back."

The barmaid walked toward the kitchen and had to wait as two men at a table got in her way. Their faces were partially covered by the brim of their slouch hats; they picked up their swords and walked toward the door.

James saw them leave, lifted Tommy and slowly guided him to the table. He helped Tommy to sit then sat opposite. Tommy folded his arms and laid his head down on them.

One of the two men opened the door allowing a freezing cold wind to come howling through. Groggily, this caused Tommy to lift his head and open his eyes, but they were blurred and heavy, so he couldn't quite make them out in the dim, smoky light. *They looked familiar!* He thought.

The last one to leave took a side glance at him quickly before he closed the door behind him.

Tommy's speech was laboured and slow, "The...the man that just left... I know him... he..he's from back home. He's the reeve... works for Lord Birkhead... at the manor."

James looked up at the door as it closed, "Does he now? I bet he's come all the way down here just to check on ya. Tommy yer delirious, yer seeing things!"

Tommy's eyes grew wide with life and dismissed his comment, "You're probably right, couldn't be him, my brains not right, seeing things."

Even though he was feeling quite ill, if it was the reeve, he wondered about his purpose here in Tadcaster. He remembered the Haworth troop that the steward had organised on behalf of his lordship and how they had tried to stop the Roundhead horsemen from taking them away. It seemed like years ago now. *The Reeve, he might be on his way back to Haworth; he could take a message to Isabel. I must find him.* Tommy stood and balanced himself, but he felt dizzy and weak.

"What ya doing, lad? Sit down before you fall down," pleaded James.

"I'll be back in a minute," Tommy staggered to the door excitedly and accidentally bumped into the back of a musketeer, spilling half his tankard of ale all over him.

"Aye up, watch out there!" The stranger wiped the residual ale from his buff coat and continued talking to his mate standing beside him.

He reached the door, lifted the latch and staggered out into the street, looking both ways, but the street was empty and dark. It started to snow again, and a wave of sickness overcame him. He felt dreadfully weak because of his exertion and dropped to the snow-covered ground. He knelt in the dark, unable to raise himself.

The door opened, spreading a glow of light around him, and James came out and helped him to his feet, "Come on, let's get you inside, ya not well and lying in the snow ain't helping!"

James could tell that Tommy was delirious, feverish and in an awfully bad way. He lifted him up and threw Tommy's arm around his shoulder to help him inside through the door, "Make way, me mate is sick with fever, make way."

They returned to the table where they had previously sat, and James set him down gently. Tommy leaned his head against the wall and closed his eyes. His hair was wet from sweat, and he had a pale, sickly look about him. James moved his collar; he could see a red, spotty rash on his neck and chest. Tommy groaned from the pain in his stomach. He began to cough uncontrollably, attracting the attention of all in the inn.

James was worried and looked about for Matilda, the barmaid.

Far From Home

The people of Tadcaster started to be overwhelmed with fear of death and the threat of a coming battle. The status of some people was blurred, and those that were once privileged now became threatened. It seemed that pillars of order, morality and righteousness had crumbled. The impact on villages and towns was devastating; homes were being destroyed, livestock seized, and the talk of atrocities being committed by the Royalists made people fearful of what was to come.

The reeve and the steward who had sat there in the tavern could tell that public opinion in the area had swayed in favour of the Parliamentarians. The reeve had noticed Tommy when he and the other Roundhead had walked in. Even though he wanted to stand and greet him, he became fearful of bringing attention to himself. The steward also noticed him and his Roundhead coloured sash and gestured nonchalantly for them to depart.

The reeve noticed Tommy look in his direction as he walked through the door. Once outside, they walked quickly and discreetly down the street and entered a quiet lane out of sight. The reeve peeked back around and watched Tommy come out and fall to the ground. He felt like going back to help, but he knew it was out of the question; they had a more important mission. He saw the other soldier with the orange sash and breastplate lift him and take him back inside.

"He's in with the Roundheads," whispered the reeve.

"Bloody fool," the steward retorted.

The reeve knew Tommy and his family and respected them. After hearing what had happened outside the tavern, he empathised,

"Probably didn't have a choice once they got hold of him and took him away. The Roundheads torture them if they catch them trying to escape."

The steward dismissed his comment, "We'll have to go back to my brother's farmhouse and spend the night, try and make it to Tadcaster early in the morning while there are less people about."

"What about Tommy? He didn't look so well. I saw him when we left the inn; he wasn't in a good state," stated the reeve sympathetically.

The steward grumbled, "None of my concern, besides, can't do much about it now with all these Roundheads about, we'll both end up swinging on the end of a rope."

The reeve paused and thought before saying anything, then whispered, "Begging yer pardon sir, but he's your daughter's husband, your son in law, father of your grandchildren. Do you not want to see him safe, if not for your sake for Isabel and ya grandchildren?"

The steward looked at the reeve sternly in the darkness, "My two daughters and that family were lost to me when they married without my consent, and I'd prefer you to keep out of my business if you would."

The reeve could feel the steward's disdain. He looked down and felt sorry for Tommy and Isabel but knew he was pushing his luck to bring up what he did. He could see the seriousness of the steward's expression in the moonlight.

They walked back to the edge of town along the lanes trying to stay off the main throughway. They rode back to the steward's brother's cottage and stepped inside as the door opened. His brother quickly took the horses out the back and hid them, all the while looking behind to see if anybody had followed.

Once inside the reeve and the steward removed their cloaks and gave them to his brother's wife, who took them and hid them away, "What did you find out?" his brother asked inquisitively.

Sitting down at the fire, the steward took out his pipe and filled it. "There are Roundheads everywhere, makes it even more important to get to Tadcaster and see their fortifications. Saville is on the march, and the Earl will want to know."

The reeve sat opposite the steward on the other side of the hearth, "Roundheads will be slaughtered at Tadcaster; Earl of Newport has over a thousand men and ordinance."

"Newcastle has a further 4000 infantry heading east. They'll be out flanked; this could end the war," claimed the steward positively.

A few minutes later, Oliver's wife poured some spiced wine and plunged a hot poker into the tankards before giving one to each of the men.

Still thinking about Tommy, "Do you think he recognised us?" asked the reeve.

The steward thought for a moment, "Hard to say, he did follow us out the door, there's a chance he did, but in his state probably won't remember in the morning."

"I don't think he was drunk, more like sick the way he was leaning, had a look of the fever about him," said the reeve.

The steward didn't respond and took a thoughtful puff on his pipe, the embers grew red in the barrel, and he blew the smoke toward the fire where it was sucked up into the chimney. He thought about his daughters and the last time he had seen them and felt saddened by the occasion. *It was bad enough that Lucy married into that family, but his younger daughter as well.* It was all too much for him to bear.

Isabel had met Tommy at the wedding of Lucy and William and, although he did not attend, had heard about their meetings and their secret courtship afterwards. He accused her and threatened to disown her if she continued to see Tommy. She being the more stubborn of the two girls, packed a small leather bag and moved in with the Rushworth's without saying a word. It was an incredibly sad day, and he hated William and Tommy Rushworth with all his soul for their transgressions.

Early the following day, the reeve walked up the stairs and woke the steward with a slight touch on the arm. "It's time to go," he whispered.

The steward quickly dressed and walked down the stairs; Oliver's wife had already placed the eggs, bacon and porridge on a plate for him in front of the fire.

The sun was not yet up, and the cock crowed to the lightening blue sky that was slowly starting to reveal itself over the horizon. His brother had already brought the horses around and held them by the reins outside. The steward and the reeve bid their farewells and trotted off into the darkness. Fearing they may need a quick escape, they did not stop and hide the horses as the Roundhead presence in Tadcaster had grown. They continued onto Bramham.

Hold on to Me

The barmaid returned a few minutes later with two tankards of ale, then disappeared, returning with two bowls of steaming pottage and some stale bread. "That'll be sixpence."

James looked up at her, "Six pennies? Yer telling" tales!"

"Times are tough, not much food around, 'cause you lot pilfer it. If ya don't want it, I'll put it back in the pot," Matilda threatened.

James gave her the six pennies and picked up a tankard, "Gew on, get that into ya, Tommy."

He was weak and withdrawn; his skin had lost its colour, and his eyes their sparkle. He could barely lift his tankard, and when he did, his hands shook. The healthy, fresh, plump face had given way to a pale, thin skin covering prominent cheek bones and a frail chin.

Matilda looked at Tommy sympathetically. "Bring him upstairs," she ordered. Matilda had seen it all before, the rash, high fever, nausea, vomiting, delirium and finally, death.

James looked at her, "How many shillings is this gonna cost?"

"Look, if ya want ya mate to get better, bring him upstairs." The barmaid grabbed him around the chest and lifted. He was exhausted and limp, only a shadow of his former self.

James came around and lifted his arm and put it around his neck, "Come on, lad, let's get you upstairs."

They walked him over to the stairs and ushered him up, James still with one arm around his neck and the barmaid slowly guiding and pushing lightly to support and direct them.

One of the soldiers downstairs looked up at them, "I don't think ya can expect much from him, darling."

"Just the way I like it, less effort, more coin," Matilda winked and smiled, then frowned as she went out of sight from those downstairs. She caught up to the two men that had just made it to the top of the stairs and showed them where to go, a room down the end of the landing; she took out a key to unlock the door.

"Bring him in here." She helped James lay him on the bed in the small cold, darkroom.

"He's got the sickness, and he needs to stay here and get well," she said as she dabbed his sweaty forehead with her apron.

She opened his tunic and ripped his undershirt; his body was emaciated and drawn, his ribs protruding through the sickly white skin; pink dots covered his chest, stomach and lower abdomen. He was sweating and started to shiver, and when he opened his eyes, he groaned at the light from the candle.

The barmaid started to undress him, pulling off his tunic, wet undershirt and hose. "Help me," she said while slipping off his boots.

"Stay here with him," she left the room and returned a short time later with a bowl of water. She dipped a linen cloth into the water and gently wiped the sweat from his brow. She rinsed and began to dab the spots on his chest and stomach carefully.

Tommy started to get pains in his stomach and became delirious, ranting and raving, "Isabel, Isabel, WATCH OUT CANNON!"

Tommy arched his back as the fever started to take hold. "Isabel, ya know I love ya, always have. WATCH OUT!" Tommy started to whimper.

"Easy there, lad," James placed his hand on his shoulder caringly and tried to calm him.

She rinsed the cloth and continued to dab the pink sores on his chest and stomach, "Who's Isabel?"

"His wife, I think, he's from the west, Haworth, has family back there," claimed James.

"There were a couple of men in here from out west not two days ago," she answered.

"Is that right? I'll have ta tell Tommy when he wakes," answered James excitedly. "He said he saw somebody he knew; I didn't believe him."

Matilda looked up at James with a serious look on her face, "*If* he wakes, ya mean! I seen it before. Look, the way I see it, if the sweats break in the next couple of days, he'll live, or if they don't, he'll die; he's in God's hands."

James picked up the pile of clothes, "I'll take his clothes outside and bury them in the snow."

Tommy thrashed his head from side to side, then quietened, at one point opening his eyes to look at Matilda, "Isabel, what are you doing here? Who's looking after the bairn?"

Matilda shushed him. "Yer bairn is fine," she rinsed the cloth once again and wiped the droplets of sweat from his brow.

James returned and had a panicked tone to his voice, "I'm going ta have ta run or else the sergeant will be poking about. Me corporal will be tied to the whipping post and me with him."

Matilda wanted more coin for her efforts. "He can stay here; I'll tend ta him as much as I can when I can."

James felt somewhat relieved, "I don't know how to repay you."

Matilda raised her open palm, "How much coin ya got, I want it all! Let's just hope he survives the night," she said sneakily, trying to get the coin.

James rolled his eyes and rummaged around in his belt pouch for their pay, placing it in her hand reluctantly. He gave her all the coin he had, then left Tommy in the room, "Just look after him, will ya!"

Later that night, the reeve and the steward arrived in Bramham and rode quickly through when suddenly, the Steward reined in his horse. He trotted back to the Swan Inn with the reeve following behind, "Wait here a moment," he ordered the reeve.

The steward dismounted and gave the reins to the reeve. He walked up to the front door of the alehouse and banged on the door with a clenched fist. There was no answer, so he became frustrated and did it again. Moments later, he saw candlelight through the mullioned window.

"Orlright, orlright, hold ya horses!" *Who on earth could it be at this time of night?* She thought.

Matilda slowly opened the door just enough and peeked out, "We're closed; what do ya want?"

The steward growled, "The two Roundheads that were here last night, what do you know of them?"

Matilda frowned, "Roundheads, place is full of Roundheads!"

The steward pushed the door open more with his foot, starting to become annoyed.

Matilda took a step backwards, " HEY! You can't be comin' in here at this time of night," she was standing there in her undershirt and sleeping wimple. She lifted the lantern to try to see who it was, but the steward pulled his hat down to disguise his face from the light.

"WOMAN, the two soldiers that you served, breastplates, buff coats...one of them was drunk or sick."

Matilda suddenly realised who he was speaking about. "Oh, those two... upstairs...well one of 'em, the other left last night. One upstairs, he's sick got the pocks or something like it, delirious he is."

The steward lifted his hand toward the barmaid, "Here for his keep and lodging." he dropped six shillings into her open hand.

"Look after him, and there might be more where that came from," he turned away and walked off into the darkness.

Confused, Matilda lowered the candle to see the coinage, then stepped out into the cold and raised the lantern to see where the stranger had gone. She shook her head, turned and closed the door, then smiled. *This is turning out to be quite lucrative,* she thought.

The steward and the reeve continued to Tadcaster. The sun was coming up when they arrived on the outskirts of town. They got off their horses and walked them into town. They talked their way through the roadblock and observed the earthworks on the west side of the river; Parliamentary musketeers were guarding the bridge over the river. "Newcastle can't be too far away; this is where they will make their stand," whispered the steward.

"Best we be off, let's get back to inform the Earl."

The two men mounted their horses and headed out of town west back toward Bramham. They cut across the countryside to miss the Parliamentary roadblocks.

James got back to the camp late and was worried about the consequences.

Suddenly, the sergeant rode up, "Right corporal get yer men on their feet, were withdrawing to Selby."

The corporal walked up to James, "Where is he?" he whispered.

"He's taken ill, extremely sick, back at the inn. I left him there; he was delirious. He's got a fever and red spots all over his body; he's in a bad way. Barmaid at the alehouse reckons he might not make it through the night."

Robert looked at James sadly, "I'll have to inform the sergeant."

CHAPTER TWENTY-ONE

Husband in the Ice

The steward knew that when he died, his land would pass from his daughters to their husbands to do with what they wished. The idea of the Rushworth's having ownership of his land repulsed him. It meant everything to him for them to marry a man of means. A man with his own property and wealth to promote the family forward, not backward.

William looked at Lucy worriedly, "I don't know Lucy, I don't think going against the steward of Haworth Manor is such a bright idea. He could make it exceedingly difficult for me family."

"William, he wouldn't dare, I'd leave him, besides Isabel, I'm the only family he's got left besides a brother."

"Why didn't you tell me you were the steward's daughter?"

"Well, you never asked, would it have made that much of a difference?" it was the first time Lucy had smiled all evening.

"Of course, it would. I would have stayed away!"

Lucy lost her patience, "Well, would you rather me a whore working at the Kings Arms?!"

William became just as angry, "No course not, I'm confused, that's all, dunno whether I'm coming or going with you. One minute you're a barmaid; next, you're not a barmaid, then you're a whore, then you're not a whore! Then ya tell me yer spyin for his lordship. Just tell me the truth!"

Lucy looked at William sadly, "William, you said you loved me!"

"I do love ya, Lucy, but it just seems all too much. Finding out your father is the steward has put me flat on me back. I wish me ma were here; she'd know what to do," William whispered.

Lucy became agitated, "I'm sorry, William, but she's not; we'll just have to work it out ourselves. Besides, I don't know why my father is being so righteous; he comes from humble beginnings himself."

"What do you mean? He's a gentleman, works for his lordship!"

"Yes, now he does, but his father and his father before him were tenants, copyholders for the previous lord. His grandfather was caught fer crimes against persons and property and spent time in the Old Baily. With the coin they had acquired, they bought the farm, and his father sent him and his brother away to become gentlemen. His brother ended up a clerk at court, and he ended up working for Lord Birkhead."

William looked at her astonished, "What? And to think all these years we thought he was a station above, from a family of means when his family are no different to us."

"Yes, well, keep it to yourself," Lucy demanded. "I must be getting back, or else my father will be getting his guts in a garter. Meet me at the oak tree tomorrow at mid-day." Lucy reached up and kissed William on the cheek and ran back toward the farmhouse.

When she got back, her father was sitting in the front room waiting for her. She glanced sideways, their eyes met, and she kept walking past the sitting room and up the stairs.

The steward stood, "Lucy, come here, please!"

Lucy ignored her father and continued up the stairs. He followed her to her room, "LUCY, PLEASE!"

"Father, I've got nothing to say to you," she said dryly as she laid down on her bed and turned her back on him. "I've done your bidding, even worked in that putrid hole, so I can bring in extra coin. Then when somebody does finally come knocking on the door, you send them away."

"You know why Lucy! We would have lost the farm if you hadn't, the land taxes are getting higher and higher, and the price of wheat is getting lower. If it weren't for the wool deals, the rat baiting and the secrets you get, we would have lost everything by now. Do you really think I want you working there?"

"Lucy, your grandfather, God rest his soul, would turn in his grave if he knew you were courting one of the Rushworth's, and that's why I forbid it."

Lucy, still angry, "And what about you and Mother? You weren't so high and mighty when you courted her."

A sadness came over him, and he looked down and became quiet, for it brought back too many bad memories of his wife who had died giving birth to Isabel. "Yes, Lucy, you are correct, but why take the family backwards. You have no idea how hard it was for this family to fight its way out of poverty, working for the lord four days a week, scraping and scratching the dirt to make a living."

Lucy felt guilty bringing up her mother; she paused, "I'm sorry, Father." She stood and watched her father drop his head and slowly walk through the door.

The steward looking forlorn, paused turned and went back downstairs to the sitting room. He stood there in front of the window, looking out sadly. He was hurt, and he tried to dismiss his feelings.

A few minutes later, Lucy appeared at the door, walked up to her father and touched him on the shoulder, "Please forgive me, Father," she whispered.

The steward regretted their argument, "Lucy, I only want the best fer you and Isabel, that's all, do you not see that?"

"I know you do, Father, but I love William." Lucy declared stubbornly.

The steward sat and thought to himself, *there's two ways to skin a cat*. To save the peace, the steward gave in, "Okay Lucy, if you feel so determined, it is your decision but don't come running back to me if it doesn't work out."

Meanwhile, back at the hide, it was starting to get dark. William was walking up the hill towards the cottage, thinking about how he would broach the subject with Thomas and Agnes.

He walked in the door; the English Mastiff was waiting for him and stood waiting for the complimentary scratch behind the ears. He took his cloak and hat off and hung it near the door, looking at Thomas, who glanced at him.

Thomas was sitting by the fire making a basket out of split willow, and Agnes was about to feed wee Tommy.

"Aye up, where ya been William, I needed a hand today," Thomas said with some irritability.

William could sense his brother's annoyance but, after the events of the day, didn't care, "Been in Stanbury."

"Stanbury, what ya go all the way over there for, brother?"

"To see Lucy."

"What the barmaid?" Thomas stopped threading the wicker and looked up.

Agnes looked up at Thomas with a quizzical look on her face but stayed out of it.

William had a confident look on his face, "Yes, and she's not what you think; she's the steward's daughter."

Thomas and Agnes both looked astonished, "The steward's daughter? Noo couldn't be," said Agnes as she continued to feed wee Tommy. "Where did you hear that, somebodies playing tricks with ya."

William walked over to the corner and filled a tankard with ale from the clay jug, "Aye, and there's something else, steward used ta be a copyholder to the lord of the manor."

"Well, I'll be blowed! Noooo yer 'avin us on!" Thomas joined William for an ale.

William touched Thomas' tankard. "Cheers, and there's something else that I've known fer a while, she's not a whore, just works in the alehouse for his lordship ta keep an ear out for him and to make sure the barkeep isn't diddling the taken coin. All the rest is just a ruse to keep the barkeep unaware."

Thomas stood up, "Come ta think of it, I never see her go upstairs with anybody 'cept the baker and the servants from the manor. I thought it was because they were the only ones that had the coin and could afford it."

William sat down at the table and took another swig of his ale, "Not that it matters, steward won't let me court her anyway."

"What do ya mean?" asked Agnes.

"Went round there, I was shocked as theur to find out he was her father, asked him if I could court her and he turned me away. Doesn't think I'm good enough for her, even tried to offer me coin to stay away."

Feeling some sympathy for his brother, "Maybe tis for the best rather than getting mixed up with the likes of him. What are ya gonna do?" Thomas asked.

William had a distressed, melancholy look on his face, "Nowt I can do," he whispered.

The next day, as planned, William met Lucy at the oak tree at the beck. "Lucy!" William called out as he ran towards her.

Lucy went running up to William putting her arms around his neck and he around her waist. "My father has permitted you to court me," she smiled with delight, and she kissed him.

William stood there holding her, frowning, surprised he couldn't get a word out, "Well, how...did...."

"Don't ask, but he'd like you to come fer supper next week. Now

I must go back to the alehouse," she kissed William on the cheek and ran off.

William was left standing there alone, astounded at what had just taken place. He picked up a pebble and threw it along the surface of the water, trying to make it skip. The afternoon had a more peaceful feeling, the beck glimmered, and the trees seemed to take on a more vivid, colourful green. The birds sang, and William's heart was lifted. He slowly strolled back to the hide, a spring in his step and a smile on his face.

Back at the cottage, Agnes was busily preparing the evening meal inside, and Thomas was collecting eggs from the chicken coup. He slapped the cow on the rump as he walked back toward the front door.

Thomas saw William walking up the hill, "Aye up William, you need to take the sheep into the moors for a feed."

"Thomas, she's gonna be me wife and live here with us!"

Agnes appeared at the door. She just shook her head and stayed out of the conversation but felt sorry for William in his predicament. Thomas looked at her, "We haven't got room here for another!"

"Well, we'll 'ave ta make room until I can get a hide of me own, we'll 'ave ta make do because she is going to be me wife," argued William.

Agnes piped in, "William, we have barely enough food fer the rest of us!"

There was a loud knock at the door, "OPEN UP 'TIS THE CONSTABLE!"

"What the bleedin' hell does he want?" whispered Thomas as he walked over and lifted the latch on the door.

Agnes straightened her wimple, and William walked over and stood behind his brother in support.

Thomas opened the door, "Constable, what brings you to these parts?"

The constable stepped forward, "William Rushworth, you are under arrest. Come with me, lad!"

Startled and confused, William stepped backwards from the door.

"What's he done, Constable?" Thomas took a step in front of William protectively as Agnes walked to William's side.

"Step aside, Thomas. Your brother has been seen consorting with a young woman without a chaperone. The witnesses have seen them touching each other inappropriately. I must take him to the lockup until the manor court sits!"

The constable entered the cottage and grabbed William by the arm. Thomas pushed him away, "TAKE YER HANDS OFF HIM!"

Thomas knew that the constable's position was obligatory, unpaid and had been selected by the parish. What he didn't know was that the steward had rewarded him handsomely for his efforts.

The constable took out his sword and pointed it in Thomas' direction, and Thomas took a step backwards.

Agnes screamed and put her arms around him, "NO THOMAS!"

William tried to jostle his way out of his grasp, "I'VE DONE NOWT, THOMAS TELL HIM!"

"Leave him be," yelled Agnes.

"THOMAS THE STEWARD IS BEHIND THIS; HE'S TRYING TO STOP LUCY AND I FROM BEING TOGETHER!"

"Come now lad, don't make it harder on yourself," said the constable as he turned William around and put wrist shackles on him. He pushed William through the door opening.

Wee Tommy woke up with all the commotion and started to cry out, "Maaaaa."

Agnes picked him up, tapping him on the back to soothe him and gently rocked him, so he stopped crying.

Thomas watched as the constable escorted William down the hill; he followed after them, "Is that right, Constable, how much did he pay ya?"

The constable turned and smiled, "It doesn't matter, Rushworth, the law is the law, and the law has been broken by your brother."

Thomas kept up with them, "Where are you takin' him?"

The constable stopped briefly, "He will be interned at the night watchman's lock-up until the manor court tomorrow night, where he will be tried and prosecuted and sent to the prison in York if found guilty."

William started to jostle with the constable, "Leave me be, LET ME GO!"

Thomas called out to William, "DON'T WORRY, WILLIAM WE'LL SORT IT WITH LORD BIRKHEAD TOMORROW!"

Thomas watched the constable walk William off down the hill and into the darkness.

Back in the cottage, Agnes put Wee Tommy back on his mattress and turned, "What now, Thomas?"

"That barmaid, I knew she would be nothing but trouble, now William's gonna end up payin' fer it, I warned him, you know I warned him. GOD DAMMIT!"

"Aye, but not much ya can do if he's smitten," said Agnes quietly.

Thomas thought for a moment, "Not much we can do tonight. I will go to the manor court and try and get him off. I'll talk to the reeve in the morning and see what he says."

Worriedly, Agnes sat down at the table and put her head in her hands. She spoke quietly, "I'll go and see the vicar in the morning see if he can help us."

Thomas walked to his chair and sat, taking out his clay pipe while looking to the hearth. He said nothing, looked nowhere except to the dancing flames and tried to slow his rapidly beating heart. Being the older brother, he had always been the one to bail William out of trouble, but this was different. *He's so stubborn, I told him to leave her be, but he just wouldn't listen. York Castle Prison, if he gets sent there, he'll never see the light of day again.*

The next morning Agnes woke early; she hadn't slept much through the night. Quietly, by the glow of the fading fire, she dressed in the kirtle that she had folded and left neatly at the bottom of the straw mattress. She strapped young Tommy to her back and went about her business, boosting the fire and stirring the pottage before quietly walking out the door.

She left Thomas to tend to the animals walking down the hide and up the hill towards St Michael and All Angels Church. She squinted as she shielded her eyes from the sun and looked up Main Street to see the steeple of the church. As she got closer, people were milling about whispering as she neared the top of the hill. She could sense them looking at her and gossiping about the events of the previous evening. News travelled fast thereabouts, and she felt sorry for poor William who was locked away, his fate in the balance.

Arriving at the church, she walked up the stone steps and along the pathway to the front door. She walked inside. It was only thirty paces from door to altar. It was colder inside than out because of the thick stone walls barring the radiant heat of the sun. The large circular patterns adorning the walls displayed bible scenes, saints, apostles, angels and Christ, all painted in reds, ochres and yellows. The barrel-vaulted ceiling rose to the heavens from the plain, wooden pews below. The chapel entrance was embellished in ornate stone carving with the altar and its wooden cross hidden in semi-darkness crowned by a small opening.

The curate, the vicar's assistant, was dusting the altar and the pewter candlesticks. He turned as he heard her footsteps on the cold stone floor. "Mrs Rushworth, what brings you to All Angels at this hour of the morning?"

"I need to see the vicar," Agnes replied with some urgency.

"The vicar has only just finished his constitutional, barely out of bed. Can you come back later?"

"Tis of utmost importance, I must see him; William has been arrested! I MUST SEE THE VICAR," she yelled.

The curate raised his hands, trying to calm her, "Okay, Agnes, give me a minute; I'll see if he can see you."

The vicar's assistant hurriedly walked out the side door which led to the parsonage. He returned a few moments later and gestured for Agnes to follow. They walked out the side door and up to the parsonage. He lifted the latch and opened the door for Agnes to walk through.

The vicar stood, "Mrs Rushworth, what brings you here at this time of the day? I have barely woken."

Agnes spoke with urgency, "Vicar, it's William. They've taken him to the lock-up. Came and arrested him last night, the constable said something about him having relations with a woman out of wedlock."

"What do you mean relations? Out of wedlock? This is no good, no good at all," the vicar grumbled and thought for a moment.

Agnes had a distraught look on her face, "Constable said that they had been meeting without a chaperone, and he has witnesses saying that they been carrying on inappropriate like."

The vicar frowned, "Agnes, this is terrible, he will be at the mercy of the manor court, and if found guilty, he could end up on the pillory or worse sent to be tried in front of a magistrate."

Agnes was frightened and started to sob, "Vicar is there anything we can do? You know he's a good lad!"

"What do you know of this girl? Have they engaged in premarital relations?"

"Vicar, I don't know. All I know is that he's been seeing her regularly, and he asked the steward if he could court her, but he said no. William said it was the steward's way of keeping them apart."

"Goodness me, this is bad," The vicar paused for a moment. He turned and rubbed his hands together in deep thought.

He looked at Agnes, "The manor court is tonight; it doesn't leave us much time. Agnes go home and return for the manor court; I will find out who this witness is and speak to his lordship."

"Please, vicar, we've got to save our William. He's a good lad, never done harm to anybody," pleaded Agnes.

"Come, Agnes, leave it with me," the vicar slowly ushered her toward the door.

The vicar turned to his assistant, "Go to the manor, tell Lord Birkhead that I must see him straight away, then bring my carriage around to the front of the church. Then, find Lucy Cook and ask her to come and see me immediately!"

The vicar's assistant raced off to do his master's bidding. Going out into the bright light of the morning, he squinted and shaded his eyes as he watched Agnes walk down Main Street toward the lock-up. He ran down the hill the opposite way toward the manor.

The vicar's assistant reached the manor and walked around the back. He noticed the reeve dealing with one of the locals and approached, "Vicar wants to meet with his lordship this morning."

Frustrated, the vicar's assistant turned and ran back toward the church to tell the vicar of the disappointing news.

Meanwhile, Agnes crossed the square and walked up Changegate, turned left on North Street to the lock-up. It was just a small stone box, no shutters and one door. The nightwatchman and his wife lived in a cottage attached to it, so she knocked on the door.

The nightwatchman appeared, "I expect yer here to see young William. Just a tick, I'll get me keys."

The nightwatchman disappeared. A few moments later, he reappeared with a large ring of keys which jingled as he walked. He found the right key put it into the sizeable, rusty lock and turned, lifting it out of the loop and lifting the latch.

"There ya are, misses, now I'll be right out here, so no funny business."

Agnes didn't say a word but stepped into the cold dark room, the walls were smooth and thick, and the wooden ceiling was high. William was curled up on a straw mattress, shivering under a blanket. He heard the door open and quickly stood.

"Agnes," he walked toward her and put his arms around her; she reciprocated.

"William, are yer orl right? I've brought ya some grub." Agnes reached into a market wallet and handed William some bread and cheese.

He grabbed it quickly from her hand and broke it, shoving half of it into his mouth, chewing hungrily, swallowing as fast as he could, "Where's Thomas?" William asked between swallows.

"I left Thomas early to tend to the animals, then he was going to see the reeve. I've been to see the vicar, and he's going to talk to the lord on your behalf."

William looked at Agnes worriedly, "Lord won't do anything; it's his steward that wants to see me gone, doesn't want me near his daughter and will take any means to make sure of it. I didn't do anything, Agnes; you believe me don't ya?"

Agnes put her hand on William's shoulder sympathetically, "Just be patient, William; we're doing everything we can to get you out of here."

"It'll be too late, Agnes, the manor court is tonight, and once I get in there, I'll be done for, the steward will have his way fer sure." William looked down in desperation.

"William, calm thyself lad, we're doing everything we can," Agnes turned to walk toward the door just as the nightwatchman opened it.

A stream of sunlight burst into the room, making William look away to protect his eyes after being in darkness for so long.

As Agnes walked out of the door, a young woman was waiting outside. She looked the young woman up and down and gave her a disdainful glare.

Lucy went to say something, but Agnes didn't wait. She looked down and brushed past her.

The nightwatchman held onto the door, "Right Lucy, I ain't got all day ta be hanging around here, ya got one minute to say your business then I have ta lock him up again."

"Alright, Nathan, two minutes, I beg you!"

The nightwatchman being one of the few besides the constable who knew of Lucy's relationship with the steward, gestured for Lucy to enter. "I don't think yer father would be very pleased if he knew you were here."

He closed the door and sat on the pile of firewood piled up outside against the wall.

"WILLIAM!" Lucy walked in and hurriedly ran and put her arms around him.

"What are ya doin' here, Lucy? I'm in enough trouble already. If somebody sees you in here, it'll make it worse," William tried to escort her to the door.

Lucy tugged her arm away tenaciously, "I don't care, William!"

William whispered, "They think we...."

Lucy was adamant, "I know William, but I'm going to speak to the vicar and tell him that I love you and want to marry you, then I'll speak on your behalf at the manor court. My father won't have any option but to release you, with all those witnesses watching."

William shook his head, "What'll you say? They won't believe you; constable reckons they got witnesses ta say I'm guilty. There's no use!"

"Guilty of what? We haven't done anything," Lucy replied.

William wrapped his arms around her to provide her with some comfort, "Oh Lucy, somebody must have seen us meeting at the beck."

The nightwatchman poked his head in the door and coughed; William and Lucy immediately broke their embrace and took a step backwards.

Lucy kissed William on the lips, "William, I must go, but I will be there tonight and have faith everything will be okay."

William looked down morosely, "That's easy fer you to say,"

He looked up to watch Lucy walk toward the door, then she stopped, turned and ran back to give him another kiss on the mouth, which William wasn't expecting and didn't reciprocate. He stood there, stunned and watched Lucy turn again and run out the door.

The nightwatchman stuck his head in the door, looked at William, shook his head in disbelief and closed the door. William heard him place the lock and turn the key. He sat back down on the straw mattress in the darkness and tried to consider a way out of his predicament.

Thomas had taken the cow and the ox to the common green and tethered them to keep them off the lord's demesne lest he receive a fine. An old woman shovelled manure that had been dropped by the scattered livestock into a wicker basket. Her head was covered with a wimple and held on with a woollen scarf to keep her ears warm. She wore a frayed red, woollen cloak and mittens which rested on the ground before her because of her rounded back and the stoop to which she had become accustomed. She had a phlegmy cough which she hacked out and would not leave her even after Candlemas when it became warm enough to till the fields again.

Thomas dipped his hat as she looked at him, but she said nothing and moved slowly from one pile of manure to another. He continued through the bleak fields; a dog barked in the distance. He walked along Main Street to the manor house then up the pebbled drive.

Walking around the back, he could see the reeve using his pitchfork to take hay out of a cart and put it into a trough for the two oxen to feed. They did so with relish, tugging and twisting their heads to remove bunches of it from the mound, the bottom of their chin moving in a sideways action as they chewed their cud. Their big black, wet, shiny noses snorted as they bit off more hay than they could chew.

The reeve was from a good family, freeholders like Thomas, but as they had held their own lands for longer, had managed to carve out a good living from the entitlement. Furthermore, working as the intermediary between Lord Birkhead and the tenants had its benefits.

Every year at Michaelmas, the reeve was voted in by the inhabitants of the hamlet and adjoining lands. It was his job to keep the peace, delegate the obligatory working parties on the lord's lands and, of course, act as spokesmen for the jury at the manor court.

The reeve saw Thomas as he turned to take more hay out of the cart "Aye up, Thomas, what on earth has young William been up to now?"

Thomas took off his hat, "That's what I've come to talk ta you about."

The reeve looked at him, "Talk to me about, I can do nowt."

Thomas persisted, "But yer on the manor court jury, can you not put in a good word?"

The reeve seeing that Thomas was distressed, stopped what he was doing and leaned on the handle of his pitchfork. "Thomas, ya know I'm only the spokesman; it's the other men you have to convince. What on earth was he doing with the steward's daughter? That was always gonna lead to trouble!"

"Well, that's just it, he didn't know she was the steward's girl, nor did I."

The reeve shook his head, "Yer well, it's not common knowledge, and the steward wanted to keep it that way. Too late now though tis all over the village. He'll end up on the pillory for this or worse."

"Well, that's just it. William thinks the steward is doing all this to get rid of him. Doesn't want him courting his daughter, thinks Williams not good enough for her." Thomas said pleadingly.

"Look, man, me hands are tied, I'll lose me job at the manor if I get involved in the steward's affairs, you know that," said the reeve stubbornly. "I'm sorry, Thomas, there's nowt I can do, just wait for the manor court tonight and see what happens."

"Tonight's too late," stated Thomas as he stormed off angrily toward the front gate.

The lord heard the commotion outside, looked down from the second-floor window and shook his head.

The reeve watched Thomas walk down the drive. *Bloody fool, what was he thinking. Should have known better.* The reeve continued with the feeding of the oxen.

A few minutes later, the vicar and his assistant came riding through the manor gate on a small carriage.

The reeve looked up; *what bloody now?*

The vicar's assistant reined in the horse carriage near the reeve. The vicar called out, "You there, I must see his lordship immediately. Please have somebody inform him I am here and request an audience."

Lord Birkhead watched the vicar arrive from the window upstairs and sent his servant down to speak to him, "Reeve, his lordship says he will speak with the vicar."

CHAPTER TWENTY-TWO ∾

Time of Bride

The steward smiled and stroked his beard, thinking about his daughter and feeling the contempt that he had for William Rushworth. He thought about how he would carry out the charges against him and knew that once his witnesses had said their piece, his fate would be sealed, and he would have his daughter back again. The old couple that had seen William and Lucy together without a chaperone were at the manor court ready to give evidence. *If everything went according to plan, the lad would be gone*, he thought, and it was worth the extra coin paid to the constable for him to play his part.

The steward knew that his daughter's sexuality was his responsibility as her father. If she had been 'tampered with', it was his duty to bring the charges to the authorities. The legal definition of rape was the theft of a woman's virtue, which would be his case before the manor court.

That evening the Kings Arms was even more packed than usual. There was an uneasy, eerie buzz as the patrons waited for the proceedings to start. Some thought of Lucy and how shocked they were to find out the news of her identity after all this time. Others remembered the shenanigans that they had carried on with her, a touch here a flirt there; they hoped the steward wouldn't find out. Others thought of poor William and the retribution that would fall upon him for his indiscretions.

John Pigshells sat in his regular chair at his usual table with his usual mates: Robert Ferguson, Arthur Hart, James Brown and Thomas Weatherborn. The usual joviality was missing as they had all known

William since he was a young lad and feared for his demise. They sat there in silence, tankard in hand, waiting for the manor court.

Robert Ferguson broke the silence, "They'll march him off to York Castle Prison if it's true, you mark my words," he whispered.

John Pigshells was the first to speak, "SHUT YER FACE, Fergie. He wasn't ta know she was the steward's daughter. What about you? I've seen ya ogling her, and what about that time ya pinched her on the arse, ya wanna mention that to the steward?"

"I thought she was just the local whore, can't be blamed fer that," claimed Robert defensively.

John Pigshells, Arthur Hart, James Brown and Thomas Weatherborn just looked at him with indignation shaking their heads.

Fergie, never the brightest of them, looked at all of them confused, "WHAT...what!"

Pigshells heard the door open and looked up.

The steward walked in and immediately held up a scented handkerchief to his nose to cover the smell of the urine and wet manure which covered the infrequently changed straw on the earthen floor.

"There he is, don't look," Pigshells whispered.

The steward could sense the uneasiness in the room, which was layered with the smokiness from the men's pipes and the dark smoke from the burning oil lanterns. Men sitting at the half-cut barrels stopped and turned to look at him. There was a hush, and two men nervously turned their gaze away as he looked around the room. The barkeep had already placed his ale, from the private stock, on the bar top.

The steward turned and lifted the tankard to his lips as men went back to their business whispering and gossiping about the events of the previous day. All except John Pigshells, Arthur Hart, James Brown, Thomas Weatherborn and of course Fergie, who dared not say another thing about the situation.

Pigshells looked at the steward; there was an air of dignity about him. His straight long black hair, dusted with grey, framed his face. A thin grey moustache and a small, triangular nest of facial hair sat below his bottom lip, which brought nobility to his full face. He looked around to see the reeve standing with the twelve jurors that would decide the fate of William Rushworth.

The reeve walked over to the steward, "Your grace, how are you this fine evening?"

The steward ignored his question, "Is everything for the night's court in order?" He asked sternly in a deep serious tone.

"Aye, sir, the night watchman and constable will be bringing him in at eight bells as you requested," replied the reeve. *Although a friend of Rushworth, I must be seen to be impartial,* he thought.

The steward didn't pay his comment any thought, "Well then, best we ready ourselves."

The reeve gestured to the barkeep, who, with the assistance of some of the jurors, set two long trestles to the middle of the room near the fire. Others moved three-legged stools. The jurors took their seats, six on either side of the table with the reeve at the table beside the steward. The new barmaid delivered jugs of ale to the table and then returned a few minutes later with bread and dried mutton, payment for juror responsibilities.

The door opened, and the room went quiet. The nightwatchman and constable came in, leading William, who was shackled at the wrists with weighty iron, rusty shackles. He was intimidated by the situation and had a look of embarrassment as the nightwatchman led him over to sit on a stool in front of the table. All eyes were fixed on him, and there was a low mumble among the crowd, all eager to hear and watch the unfolding events.

William looked exhausted and shivered with an uneasiness trying not to look at the steward. He had a slight look around the room but could not see Thomas, Agnes or Lucy, only sympathetic souls who knew him and his family. He noticed John Pigshells, Arthur Hart, James Brown and Thomas Weatherborn obviously standing on chairs at the back thumbs up, signalling their support.

"He'll get sent to York prison fer sure," cackled one of the local misfits as he jostled for a better vantage point at the front between two sheepmen.

"Shut yer cakehole!" growled one of the men as he took a sideways glimpse at him. If I hear another word out a' ya, I'll rip ya tongue out and shove it up yer arse!"

The local misfit moved to another part of the room.

"HEAR YE, HEAR YE, the Haworth Manor Court is now in session. All who have business on this night come forward and be recognised" called out the deputy.

The steward rose from his chair, an experienced orator, "FOLK OF HAWORTH AND HONOURABLE JURORS. The first case involves this local man who has transgressed upon a young woman, MY

DAUGHTER. She, being a weaker vessel, a creature physically, intellectually, morally and even spiritually inferior to this man, has been taken advantage of and SOILED BY HIS WICKED WAYS!"

The crowd jeered and jostled some at the back even booed, being sure not to be seen in contempt of the steward's court.

"HE'S INNOCENT. LET HIM GO; SHE'S A WHORE!" Robert Ferguson yelled out, trying to save some face in front of his mates. He then crept backwards to the rear of the crowd.

The door opened, and the other deputy walked in, leading Lucy by the arm. The crowd's fervour increased as the steward, shocked by this sight, was for once lost for words. He watched as the deputy led her forward and placed her on a stool beside William. He then walked up to the steward and whispered in his ear. The steward turned his head slowly to look at Lucy.

William was shocked and spoke through clenched teeth, "Lucy, what have ya done?"

Lucy whispered, "Told them we fornicated!"

"YOU WHAT?!" Flabbergasted and frowning, William looked at her, "We've done nothing of the sort. Argh, I'm finished!"

"Aye, but they don't know that," Lucy whispered. "If they're gonna take you, then they can take me as well. Told the vicar we said our I do's in front of witnesses and had relations."

"Lucy, you foolish girl, I'm done for! What have ya done, ya stupid lass."

Lucy smiled and looked into his eyes, "William, my love, trust me!"

The steward looked at Lucy shaking his head, "GOOD FOLK OF HAWORTH, here me, this vile creature, this William Rushworth, this fornicator of innocent women, who without betrothal…."

The door opened again. This time the vicar's assistant came in holding the door open for the vicar, Thomas, Agnes, John and Mrs Hargreaves.

The crowd fell silent and parted to allow the vicar with his assistant following to walk towards the steward and the table of jurors.

"Dear vicar, what brings you to this unholy place?" asked the steward feeling somewhat out of place in his presence, which was usually his place of significance.

The vicar made the sign of the cross. "I have come to inform you that this manor court has now become an ecclesiastical court and, as such, be presided over by the church and as the church's representative, by me!"

The steward became increasingly troubled. "Vicar, respectfully, this is not the church, but the manor court and the manor court has always been presided over by the manor steward and jurors decreed by Lord Birkhead, Lord of Haworth Manor."

Smugly, the vicar handed his assistant a rolled-up piece of parchment paper, who in turn gave it to the steward.

"I think you will find that his lordship's decree provides legitimacy to my claim," appealed the vicar with an air of righteousness and strength in his voice.

The steward unrolled the parchment and slowly read its contents. He looked up puzzled and, not wanting to lose face, politely bowed and stood back to allow the priest to step forward and take his place at the head of the table.

The vicar stood and made the sign of the cross as all present bowed their heads, "HEAR ME PEOPLE OF HAWORTH, who brings accusations against this man and this woman?"

All in the tavern stood quietly except the steward, who stepped forward as the jurors looked at each other for support, "I DO, STEWARD OF THE MANOR!"

"And your grace, what are these accusations?" The vicar asked curiously.

The steward stepped forward confidently and pointed at the old couple standing to the side. "YOUR HOLINESS, it has been witnessed by these two residents of Stanbury that they saw this man, William Rushworth of Hall Green, fraternising with this woman without chaperone and in inappropriate ways. I ALSO ACCUSE HIM OF TAKING THIS WOMAN'S VIRTUE!"

There was a wave of murmuring in the tavern as all mumbled their thoughts on the accusation.

"William wouldn't do something like that; he's a good lad," whispered Pigshells. Arthur, Jimmy and Thomas Weatherborn all nodding their heads in agreeance. Robert Ferguson preferring to bow out of any more comment on the situation.

The steward continued, "THIS WEAKER VESSEL, this woman, a creature physically, intellectually, morally and even spiritually inferior to this man, has been taken advantage of and soiled by his WICKED WAYS!" He paused for effect, "SO CORRUPT IN FACT that she may now not take an honest husband and bare children under the eyes of our LORD IN HEAVEN! WHAT SAY YOU?"

All in the tavern went quiet.

The vicar trying to get the people's support back, stood and, preferring not to take the steward's approach, spoke quietly and solemnly. He looked at the couple and spoke, "What say you, William Rushworth and Lucy Cook?"

The couple looked at each other, at the steward, then back at the vicar, "Aye, we saw him and her touching each other, in public like, without anybody near and no chaperone."

William looked at Lucy forgivingly and whispered so that only she could hear, "I love ya Lucy, always have, whatever happens, know that I love you deeply."

William looked down at his shackled wrists, then stood. The deputy grabbed his arm aggressively, "Your Holiness, she ain't done nowt, let her go, I'm the one that should be damned, let her go!"

The steward smiled and stepped forward again, feeling confident, "YOU SEE, BY HIS OWN ADMISSION, HE ADMITS TO THE WRONGS HE HAS COMMITTED!"

The steward felt as if there should have been a cheer and applause from the patrons after what he thought was an outstanding theatrical display that any playwright would have been proud of.

There was a heightened sense of urgency as the patrons of the tavern started to whisper to each other, gesticulating and voicing their opinions in favour of William.

"HE'S INNOCENT; LET HIM GO!" John Pigshells bellowed while still standing on his chair at the back of the room.

"Yeees, he's done nowt, let him go!"

"What do ya expect, steward!"

Agnes looked at Thomas worriedly, then back at John Hargreaves and his wife who had come in support.

The vicar raised his hands to quieten the crowd, "What say you about these events, William Rushworth?"

The steward smiled and stepped forward, "You see, vicar, the lad has…"

Lucy stood up, "NOOOOO! IT WASN'T HIM; WE SAID OUR I DO'S AND THEN HAD RELATIONS, AND I WAS WILLING!"

All in the tavern laughed and applauded. John Pigshells called out, "GOOD ON YA LUCY!"

The steward leaned in closer to the vicar, "Your holiness, don't listen to her; she is a foolish young woman. CONSTABLE TAKE HER AWAY; we know who the culprit is here."

The steward turned and pointed at William, who looked down,

accepting his fate, knowing that Lucy would be free to go.

"NOOOOOOO," Lucy struggled against the deputy's grasp as he tried to pull her away.

The patrons were on edge, yelling obscenities and castigating the steward. John Pigshells, Arthur Hart, James Brown and Thomas Weatherborn booed from the back.

The vicar yelled, "WAIT, LET US HAVE SOME DECORUM HERE IN THE EYES OF THE LORD, FOR RIGHT NOW THIS IS HIS HOUSE!"

The crowd went silent as the vicar raised his hands and gestured toward Lucy, "PLEASE LET HER BE!"

William had a look of confusion on his face and looked behind at Thomas and Agnes, who smiled discreetly. Thomas winked at his brother.

The jurors looked at each other and were confused by the spectacle that had transpired in front of them and feared speaking against the steward.

The vicar, still standing and in a quiet and gentle voice, smiled, "LUCY, what did you say then?"

The vicar had discussed the issue with Lord Birkhead and told him of the situation, including the steward's part in it. After speaking with the lord, he had already prepared Lucy for her response to the question.

Lucy smiled, "We said our I do's and had willing relations, but William never forced himself on me. He wouldn't do that!"

The vicar raised his eyebrows, "Lucy, can you please say that again so that everybody can hear?"

Lucy tried to look puzzled like everybody else in the room, including the steward.

"WE SAID OUR I DO'S AND HAD WILLING RELATIONS, BUT WILLIAM NEVER FORCED HIMSELF ON ME! HE...WOULDN'T DO THAT! Besides, if he tried, I'd flatten him!"

Those who heard laughed in hysterics, especially those in the tavern who had copped just a little of Lucy's rath previously.

The vicar looked at Lucy and smiled, "Lucy, are you telling me that you and William said to each other I DO?"

William, totally confused by the situation, frowned and was about to stand and say something when the deputy put his hand on his shoulder and pushed him back down on his stool. William was about to retaliate when he noticed the vicar's assistant staring at him and discreetly shook his head, gesturing for him to be quiet.

"Lucy, did anybody witness this conversation?"

"YES, WE DID!" John Hargreaves and his wife Margaret came forward as the crowd parted to allow them through.

"Ahhh, Mr and Mrs Hargreaves, can you tell me exactly what you heard Lucy and William say to each other?"

John Hargreaves stepped forward, "Well, we were at the Rushworth cottage, and they were outside, we heard William turn to the young lass and say, I want ta marry ya, and she said I do, I want to marry you too."

William knew that Lucy had never been to the cottage. He shook his head and held an expression of confusion, wondering and looking at John Hargreaves and wondering what he was up to.

The priest raised his hand, "YES, THEN WHAT HAPPENED?"

John feigned a little embarrassment, "Well, they sort of disappeared down to the beck and came back half an hour later, giggling and carrying on like a couple of dogs in heat."

The patrons laughed out loud, looking at each other and calling out, "Lucky bastard!" All in the tavern knew the voice of John Pigshells and smiled.

The steward, annoyed by the crowd's reaction, stepped forward and raised his voice to quieten the onlookers, "PLEASE YOUR HOLINESS, you can see, these witnesses are contrived. Let this man be put to the pillory then carted to York prison!"

The crowd roared their level of dissatisfaction, and Lucy tried to jostle herself away from the deputy's grasp, "LET ME GO, WILLIAM NOOOOOO!"

The vicar stood again and raised his hands. The crowd went silent, "PEOPLE OF HAWORTH PLEASE, LET ME SPEAK."

The vicar paused and looked about the room, "NO INJUSTICE HAS BEEN COMMITTED HERE; A CLANDESTINE MARRIAGE HAS BEEN WITNESSED. THE COUPLE HAVE SPOKEN THE WORDS 'I DO' IN FRONT OF WITNESSES, SO IN THE EYES OF OUR LORD, THEY ARE MARRIED."

William called out over the noisy, rambunctious murmurings of the crowd, "WHAT DOES IT MEAN LUCY?"

"WILLIAM! WERE MARRIED!" Lucy looked at her father with abhorrence, then turned to William and smiled with satisfaction.

The steward had a look of loathing. He glared at William, frowned and shook his head before storming out into the cold night air alone.

The vicar whispered in the deputy's ear, and then he told Lucy she was free to go. She stood and quickly placed her arms around a still shackled William who stood to meet her embrace. She kissed him on the cheek. William smiled with embarrassment, then looked over at his family, who all had a considerable look of joy on their faces.

The crowd bellowed their satisfaction, and John Pigshells, Arthur Hart, James Brown and Thomas Weatherborn let their feelings be known, "HOORAY! HOORAY! HOORAY!" They clapped their hands, and those close enough patted William on the back.

Agnes smiled and touched Thomas on the arm gently.

Lucy often thought back to those times, *I can never forgive him for what he has done.* She remembered leaving Stanbury for the last time. It was a time of sadness for her because she had grown up in that house, and she would miss her sister Isabel terribly.

A few days later, the vicar had presided over a banns ceremony at the Hargreaves cottage. They had completed the hand-tying, and William had drawn his wobbly X; Lucy's 'Lucy Cook' alongside on the ledger that the curate, the vicar's assistant, so cared for.

Years later, Isabel, fearing her father's wrath wed Tommy in secret to the astonishment of her father. He denounced her as his daughter and demanded her to leave his house after she and Tommy stood in front of him and told him.

Lucy smiled, thinking that it was ironic that her father's only other daughter had also married into the Rushworth family. Now, her father was alone, and she rarely saw him unless she noticed him through the stalls at the market on the way to the manor. Even then, he never acknowledged her or Isabel ever again.

os CHAPTER TWENTY-THREE 80

Shadow of Nobody

The battle of Bradford was a decisive victory for the Parliamentarians, not because of the number of men killed or property won or lost, but because of the morale of the men that fought. Highly outnumbered, facing cannon and calvary, the men of Bradford persevered and won the day.

John looked at the captain tentatively, "We need to keep looking for Tommy."

The captain spoke with a serious tone, "I would recommend staying here until Lord Fairfax arrives because, for all you know, your son Tommy could be with him."

Thomas thought about his son and what mishap may have plagued him, "I'm not sure, suppose you could be right and God willing he is with Lord Fairfax, and he is safe."

The captain spoke calmly and confidently, "Come on, you two, let's get back to the Sun Inn; supper is on me." Captain Hodgson walked on, hoping that the two men would follow.

John looked at Thomas and shrugged his shoulders, then started walking toward the Sun Inn. Thomas, exasperated from the day, took a heavy, slow breath and followed behind them.

Back at the Sun Inn, there was a celebratory mood. Captain Hodgson walked through the door to the sound of merriment, and those who saw him cheered and clapped, shaking his hand as he passed by. Thomas and John stood back, watching the celebrations occur before them.

One of the Bradford clubmen stood and yelled, "THREE CHEERS FOR CAPTAIN HODGSON, HIP, HIP."

"HOORAY!" The soldiers and clubmen lifted their fists and tankards in unison.

"HIP, HIP!"

"HOORAY!"

"HIP, HIP!"

"HOORAY!"

The captain humbly and respectfully nodded, not allowing himself to get too caught up in the revelry, for he knew that even though they had won the day, they had not won the war. Many would die before the King was dethroned. The captain led his two companions to a table against the wall where they sat and discussed the day's events.

Thomas stood there shaking his head, he, also trying to differentiate between dream and reality, then realising the truth which his mind had tried to mask, and yes, he was alive.

"I thought we were done for when those riders started for the bridge," exclaimed John, still coming to terms with the events of the day.

The captain smiled, "Yes, we hoped they would do that, had musketeers hiding in wait for them. They won't be so easily fooled the next time, though. I'm sure they're planning their next attack right now; I hope Fairfax gets here with his forces soon because if he doesn't, we're finished."

After they had eaten their fill and drank their ale, the captain left Thomas and John thanking them for their bravery.

They both stood as did the others, wanting to pay their respects to a man who had done the impossible.

They both walked to the bedroom, but once again, there were no empty beds. Thomas started to undress and climbed into one of the already occupied beds. John peeked under the blankets and tried to see the face of the men asleep, hoping to avoid his previous night's bedmate. Thomas looked at John, who had chosen a bed far away from the door. He dropped his belongings, took off his tunic and stripped to his undershirt. John placed his blanket on the bed, lifted it and climbed underneath. The man beside him grunted and rolled over, taking half of his blanket with him. John tugged part of it back in haste.

Suddenly there was a long reverberating episode of flatulence. Thomas and John both opened their eyes, each hoping that the noise came from one of the other beds. Thomas knew the answer to that mystery when John pulled the blanket up and pulled it tightly around him while silently climbing out of the bed and laying on the floor beside.

Thomas awoke early. He climbed out of his side of the bed, donned his tunic and leggings and walked toward the bedroom door. He stepped over several soldiers that had occupied the spaces between the beds snoring and grunting like wild boars foraging in the mud.

Thomas hadn't slept well that night, still worried about his son. He went outside, it was cold, and ice had formed on the surface of the horse trough. He broke the ice and splashed his face with cold water, which startled him into wakefulness.

There had been a heavy snowfall through the night, and it had settled to sit like a white, undisturbed blanket over the fields and walkways of the town. He could see the steeple of the church rising high above the other cottages. Thomas thought of home and the family, they'd been gone roughly two weeks, and he was sure that Agnes would be worried. He wondered about Tommy and had heard of the battle in Tadcaster and prayed that he was safe and unharmed.

Thomas went back inside and looked for John, who had taken up a position on the floor in front of the fire, which by now was only embers. A soldier had curled up beside him placing his arm around his waist, and had pulled the blanket up to share.

Thomas touched John on the shoulder, and he slowly opened his eyes and sat up shocked and bleary-eyed, "Aye up, ya right Thomas?" He closed his eyes again, trying to get some respite from the light. Opening them slowly, he tried to get his bearings, then looked down at the soldier who had, for lack of a better word, spooned him through the night.

Now that John had raised himself, the soldier had taken advantage and pulled the whole blanket over himself, his face content in front of the dwindling embers of the fire.

John stood and pulled his blanket back forcefully. The soldier tried to hold on but then let go and put his arms to his chest and lifted his knees in defiance of the cold.

"Errgh," John tried to remember the events of the previous night. "After you went to bed, I got up to take a piss. I heard two Dragoons talking about the battle at Tadcaster; there's a good possibility that Tommy was amongst it. They said that the Roundhead army ran out of powder and had to flee. Some were killed."

"I know what ya thinking; Tadcaster is about a day's walk. We could be there by nightfall if we left right now," whispered Thomas,

"Might take a bit longer if we must wait fer your mate to rise."

Thomas dispensed with the trivialities, "Come on, get yer stuff together, let's go," he whispered. John pulled his blanket from the soldier's stubborn grasp, giving him a look of contempt in the process. The soldier reluctantly let go of it, grunted stubbornly and rolled over closer to the fire.

John gathered his things quickly and followed Thomas, stepping quietly over the men lying on the floor.

The room had the smell of stale ale, urine and faeces. The waste bucket was filled to the brim, and there were upturned tankards and spilled ale everywhere. Outside, two men occupied the table, resting their heads on their folded arms; others sat around the bottom of the wall leaning their head back, allowing their chin to drop open and vibrate a glutaral song.

They stepped out into the day; the sky was a light grey and full of the coming snowstorm. They took their first steps crunching through the whiteness, and headed east. The first part of the trip was all uphill, and they laboured under the slippery conditions. Ice had formed under the layer of ankle-deep snow, which made the going slow. They eventually reached the top of the hill and then made their way down the other side towards the township of Farsley.

At times, fearing they would fall into the hands of Cavaliers, they would go off the main road and walk parallel to it using the scrub beside the road to cover their presence and footsteps. There was an eerie silence, all except the crunch of their footsteps. On occasion, they would hear riders in the distance, so they would crouch behind the scrub and wait for them to pass.

They continued to walk in silence, for they feared their voices would carry through the brisk morning air and warn clubmen or soldiers of their approach. It was noon before they stopped and placed their folded blankets on the top of a couple of boulders to rest. Thomas took a piece of bread and a wilted carrot that he had picked up off the table at the alehouse, broke them in half and gave it to John.

"How much further do you think it is?" Enquired Thomas as he started to chew half of the horrid, wilted carrot.

John paused and took a deep breath in, still labouring from the previous night's ale, "I saw a marker back a way; I'd say we're halfway there, if not more. Hopefully, we should get there before nightfall."

"We'll have to be more careful when we get closer; stay off the main thoroughfare," said Thomas worriedly.

John, still struggling and wanting to sleep more than chat, "Aye, well, we been lucky so far. Let's hope it stays that way."

"Last night, I heard the Dragoons saying that the Cavaliers have taken Tadcaster, and the Roundheads are moving south. Hopefully, Tommy will be with them," said Thomas after swallowing his mouthful of pottage.

John stood up and stretched, "Come on, best we be going no point in hanging around here all day."

Thomas picked up his blanket, shook the snow from it and tied it back to his market wallet.

They headed back to the road where the snow was less deep, and they could get better footing.

Suddenly Thomas stopped, "Do you hear that?"

John stopped; they both stood quietly and listened.

"That's an army on foot, Christ, they're coming our way, they're CLOSE," exclaimed John fearfully.

"How far away da ya think?" asked Thomas.

"Dunno, mile maybe mile an' half, we better get off the road," ordered John as he turned toward the scrub.

Thomas followed, "Here, they'll see our footprints."

Thomas quickly broke off a coniferous branch from a tree, walked back to the side of the road and used it to wipe over their tracks as he walked back into the scrub.

John ducked and forced his way through the Red Robin bush at the side of the road, the snow cascading down on him as he disturbed the stark white branches. Thomas followed, turned and bent back the limbs to their original position, lifting and spreading powdered snow allowing it to settle on the leaves as before. John had already begun to dig a trench in the snow parallel to the road for them to hide in. He spread his blanket at the bottom for them to lie on. Once they were in, he pulled most of the spoilt snow back on top of them.

They could hear the monotonous rumble of the march and the closing rattle of sword and sabre, pike and pick; they settled quietly to wait.

When their heads were down, any onlookers who looked would look through the bush right past them. The large Chestnut tree behind them stood as a crowned monarch dwarfing their presence and would hopefully detract from their presence.

The army grew closer. Thomas and John could hear the echo of the horse hooves stamping through the powdered snow to the hard-iced soil below. Their bridles and rein links jingling in the wintery silence; they were only half a mile away now and closing. The chatter of the marching soldiers became more prominent, and John could see the tops of the pike over the scrub as they neared.

Thomas and John slowly ducked below the surface of the snow, hiding their presence but allowing them to have intermittent peeks without being discovered.

"They're Roundheads; Tommy might be with them," said Thomas lowering his head.

John lifted his head and had a peek, "Wait, Thomas do nothing they have ta camp soon, then that's our chance. Let them pass. We'll follow them, and God willing, find Tommy. If we show ourselves and he's not with them, they'll think we're spies."

They laid there in the snow trench, waiting nervously as the Roundhead army marched by.

As night fell, Thomas and John followed the footsteps back toward Bradford. A mile or two down the road, they could see the illumination from the campfires in the night sky. They left their belongings behind a hedge and crept the long way around the back end of the camp. They could see musketeers stationed on guard at various points around the camp, trying to keep warm by their fires. Tents had been set up in regimental rows. Being sure to stay in the shadows provided by the tents, they walked alongside them quietly so as not to attract the attention of the guards.

"You go that way, and I'll go this way," whispered John.

"Alright, I'll meet you back at the hedge where we left our stuff."

"Tommy," Thomas walked along the back end of the tents, quietly calling out.

"Tommy..."

He backed up to turn around and was immediately shocked by the appearance of a soldier standing there in the shadows wielding a sword which he pointed at Thomas' throat.

"What do we have here then, a Cavalier spy?" The soldier gestured for Thomas to walk back toward the fires, his sword held steadily at his back.

Thomas raised his hands in submission and slowly walked toward the illumination. When he rounded the row of tents, he could see the guards looking toward him.

"Found another one," said the soldier.

As Thomas neared the fire, he could already see John Hargreaves bound and gagged, sitting on a log looking disheartened and forlorn. The soldier tied Thomas' wrists and manoeuvred him to the log beside John.

"Couple of Cavalier spies right in our midst, the sergeant will be pleased about this," said the soldier who took off his helmet and laid it on the ground.

"We're not spies," claimed Thomas.

The soldier looked at them menacingly, "Look, if yer out here in the middle of the night and you're not marching with us, then you're spies!"

John was shaking his head backwards and forwards and grunting support for Thomas' claim.

"We're looking for me son, Tommy; he was supposed to be with your army."

Immediately, one of the other guards stood, "Tommy, there was a Tommy. You two are from Haworth!"

"Do you know these men?" The other soldier asked, still brandishing his sword.

"Yes, yes, where is he? Is he here?" Thomas asked excitedly, cutting the corporal off mid-sentence.

"No, don't know them, but remember Tommy telling me about his father and uncle back in Haworth."

James stood. "He was the pikeman, the one that got really sick and died in Bramham if it's the same man, Tommy Rushworth."

John started to excitedly grunt from frustration, his face contorted in emotional pain at the news of his grandson.

"Yes, that's it, wait... sick? Died? Are you sure?" Thomas asked frantically.

Thomas and the still gagged John Hargreaves looked forlorn, "Can you release us, please? We mean no harm to you; we're farmers in Haworth and have no leanings toward you or King."

John grunted in support again, the cloth wrapped around his mouth becoming wet from his ravings.

The corporal stepped in, "Hold on there one-minute old man, how do we know yer not spies come here ta get intelligences for the Earl of Newcastle? We know he's interned east of here."

Thomas pleaded with them, "I swear, let us go, and we'll be out of your way. Please, kind sir, what do you know of Tommy?"

"Just a minute," said the corporal, "not so fast!" He turned to James Fewtrall

"What do you know of this?" He asked while still brandishing his sword in Thomas' direction, becoming increasingly nervous.

James looked at the corporal, "Look, all I know is what Tommy told me that he was from Haworth. Said he had family back there, a father, Thomas I think, said he would look after the family if anything were to happen to him."

"YES, YES, THAT'S ME, I'M THOMAS RUSHWORTH, and this is my father-in-law John Hargreaves, we've been looking for Tommy these past weeks, travelled from the west."

"Orl right calm yerself man," said the corporal who put his sword back in his sheath and, taking his knife out of the scabbard, cut Thomas' bindings and released John.

John stood and opened his mouth and moved his jaw from side to side to loosen the dull ache caused by his gag.

He turned to James, "the last time you saw him, where was he?"

Feeling a bit guilty about leaving him, "Look, the last time I saw him was in the alehouse in Bramham, the Swan Inn, I think it were called. We were fleeing the King's musketeers, but he was just too sick. He had the runnin's real bad, fever, and he was delirious, kept calling out Isabel."

"YES, THAT'S HIS WIFE!" shouted Thomas excitedly.

James went on, "We were friends, marched together and fought together. Anyway, he had the look of death about him, dark around the eyes, sunken like, not like he was when he first came into camp. The barmaid Matilda helped me take him upstairs, and she gave him some grub, but he looked too far gone to me. Had a rash all over his chest; she said he wouldn't make it through the night. That's the last I saw of him. I felt bad about leaving him there, but I had no choice."

John Hargreaves stood, "So you didn't actually see him dead and buried?"

James thought about it, 'No, but as I said, he was delirious, and I've seen what happens to men like him that get the fever; they don't last long. We've lost a lot of men the same way!"

Thomas and John were heartbroken, "Look, we'll stay here the night and head off in the morning; he could still be alive. We can't go home until we know for sure," said Thomas gloomily.

Thomas and John walked back to the hedge in silence to retrieve their blankets and returned to the side of the fire in the camp. They placed tree ferns over the snow and covered themselves with their blankets. They dosed listening to the whispers of the corporal and James but did not sleep.

As the sun rose, Thomas lifted himself and shook the remnants of the previous night's snowfall from his blanket and shook John awake, "Come, let's make way."

They rolled their damp blankets up, grabbed their market wallet and made way easterly toward Bramham. John looked back to see if it was the same men on guard duty, but it wasn't, so he turned and continued after Thomas.

Thomas had not slept and had an urgent, hurried gait about him, fearful of what James had told him about Tommy. They didn't speak for most of the morning and trudged through the new snow that had fallen through the night. They decided to steer clear of Leeds, heading northeast at Farsley to miss the Cavalier roadblocks that the soldiers told them about. Down, down they went.

The Splintered Game

It was more than four days before Tommy broke his fever and another three before he could take what little pottage the barmaid could scrape up from the cauldron. He was frail both physically and mentally, but he had started to sit up in bed and allowed the barmaid to spoon feed him when she wasn't busy with other distractions. The spots had disappeared from his chest, but his eyes were still sunken and dark. He felt washed out and weak from his battle with the fever.

Matilda had washed his clothing and hung them across a line that spanned the room.

Tommy's fever had gone, but he now felt another ailment, one of melancholy. He rarely smiled or spoke, preferring to while away the days looking at the cracked plaster on the wall.

He often thought of Isabel and the baby and wondered if Isabel had lost hope of his return. He thought of the family and how he longed to get back home to them all. He also knew the journey that it would take and worried that he would once again be drafted into the army if they knew he was on the mend.

The barmaid had told him that many had died in the fighting, and he was lucky to be alive. The battle of Tadcaster had been long and bloody, with both Cavaliers and Roundheads losing hundreds of men. Tadcaster was now occupied by the Royalists, she told him, and the war had swung in the King's favour.

Just as the barmaid was about to feed Tommy a spoonful, the door burst open behind her. A drunkard staggered in; he wore the leather apron of a blacksmith worn and peeled of its layers. His long grey beard framed his reddened face burnt by the radiant heat of the fire. His hands were soiled from the iron that he pounded from dawn to dusk. "Come on darlin', ya know we been waitin' fer ya, it's a dry old argument downstairs we need more ale!"

She was startled but put on a brave face, "Where's me brother-in-law, the no good for nothing, lazy son of a bitch."

Her brother-in-law had recently returned from Leeds after his wife, her sister, had died of the pox. She had to take him in because he was the only family she had now, and besides, the extra help came in handy. He was a quiet-spoken man and worked hard to please her. She treated him poorly and often threatened to turf him out if she didn't have her way.

"Who's this then?" the drunkard enquired, slurring his words.

"Never ya mind," Matilda said as she pushed him back towards the door and closed it in his face.

"Go downstairs, and I'll be with ya in a minute," she called out angrily.

There were more Royalists about now since they had taken over Tadcaster. She was worried that somebody would inform on her about the Roundhead that was staying in the tavern. *That would be no good at all, but then again, such information could be quite profitable. No, best to stay quiet for now anyhow,* she thought.

Tommy flipped the blanket back and sat on the side of the bed, ready to stand but felt dizzy and thought better of it.

"Oh no, you don't, lad." The barmaid helped him back under the blanket.

"How long have I been here?" Tommy asked with a croaky voice that he tried to cough away.

"Must be almost a week. You were delirious with the sweats for much of the time. Camp fever, I didn't think you were going to make it back to us."

"I must be getting back home to me family; they will be thinking the worst."

"You wait here a while until you've fully recovered," she said while fluffing the straw pillow behind him. "Besides, the Cavaliers, they're all over the place!"

"I don't know how to thank you for making me well again," said Tommy as he relaxed back against the pillow.

"Don't worry about that. Yer mate has been coming regular ta pay yer way and pay well he does."

"Me mate, ya say, you mean James the soldier that brought me here?"

"No, no, haven't seen him since you came in that fateful night. This is another, been paying yer lodging these past days. Comes every two or three days to check on you, then disappears again into the night. Never says much just gives me coin and leaves. Quite well to do, not dressed like the other folk that come in here."

"Well, what does he look like?" asked Tommy excitedly.

"I dunno, medium height, long greying hair, moustache and little triangular beard under his bottom lip. He doesn't come in or stay long, just asks how you are, pays fer the lodging and disappears into the night. Another usually waits on horse fer him outside. Come now, you try and get some sleep, me lad."

Matilda pushed the blanket up under Tommy's chin, turned and left quickly through the door, closing it quietly behind her.

Tommy could hear the men downstairs complaining and lay there for a while, watching the candlelight flicker against the wall. He was eventually overcome by tiredness and drifted off into a deep sleep.

It wasn't for another four days that Tommy felt strong enough to get out of bed. He donned his undershirt, breeches and tunic and put on his leather boots. Fearing the threat of further military service, he left the leather buff coat, orange sash and helmet that were common to the Parliamentary pikemen under the bed. He picked up his leatherback sack, backsword, dagger and went out the door and down the rickety old stairs.

The tavern was empty, all but the barkeep and the barmaid who went about her business collecting used leather jacks and clay mugs and pouring the leftovers into a small clay jug which would be mixed with the ale in the barrel and re-purposed later.

"Morning to you, good to see you up and about," said Matilda, who was pleased with the extra coin that the lodger had brought in.

Tommy still felt weak and washed out, his eyes were sunken and dark, and he had lost weight. His tunic felt quite loose around his shoulders and his hose baggy around his legs.

Matilda walked quickly and supported Tommy over to the fire, "No love, you sit down, let me get ya something to eat. HENRY, get him an ale, some new ale from the barrel, not the swill you serve out to the others" she demanded.

The barkeep rolled his eyes and turned and poured from the barrel underneath the bar which he kept for himself and the odd favoured patron that frequented the establishment. He brought it over and placed it in front of Tommy, who sat on the bench at the table near the fire.

Matilda spooned some day-old pottage into a wooden bowl and placed it in front of him with bread and cheese, "There ya go, love it's even got a bit of meat in it."

Tommy ate with fervour spilling some of the liquid down his chin and gulping the ale until it was all gone. His hand shook as he placed the empty jack on the table and gestured to the barkeep for some more. He spooned the small pieces of meat and onion into his mouth and topped them off with a chunk of bread.

The wind had begun to pick up outside and whistled through the cracks in the mullioned window. Tommy could feel the draft from underneath the door against the backs of his legs, the front warmed by the embers of the glowing fire not far from his feet. He hadn't seen the alehouse in the light of day before; he could see the sign swinging in the wind out the window, its rusty hinges creaking as it swayed backwards and forwards. There was a grey sky, the wind blowing the dark storm clouds across the white fields and away over the horizon.

The barmaid, the matriarch of the house, went about her business wiping the wooden tables with a wet rag and rinsing it in the accompanying bucket. She barked orders at Henry, who said nothing and continued with his chores wiping the mugs and wooden bowls that were piled high from the previous night's festivities.

Tommy felt a shiver and walked to the door to take hold of the cloak that Henry had lent him. He turned and stood for a moment to look out the window. He looked across the fields, over the dry-stone walls speckled with snow from the previous night's fall. In the distance, he could see the murmuration of a hundred starlings with their dark display of swooping, twisting and turning as they asserted their dominance over the icy landscape. He could hear the melodic song of a robin as it sat on the branch of a tree across the lane. Its orange face and bib a colourful contrast against the white. Placing his newly acquired cloak over his shoulders, he walked back and sat down at the table and watched as the barmaid scraped up the muddy wet straw from the stone floor and replaced it with new.

"Now that yer on the mend, what will you do, lad?" asked the barkeep as he filled Tommy's mug again.

Tommy thought about it for a moment, "My fighting is done; I'll go home. I have a family that needs takin' care of, bairn to feed pray to God, hide to tend."

"And the war?" asked the barkeep.

"It was never my war. My family are simple people and never had fealty to either King or Parliament. I was enlisted into service some weeks ago now; family must think me dead."

The barkeep sat down at the table, "Aye 'tis a terrible business. Thousands have died and more injured. Best you be off to yer moors and stay off the main roads lest ya be put ta more service for Parliament or King, I've heard commanders are not picky."

"My fighting is done; it's time to go home. I'll leave early in the mornin' as the cock crows and travel west."

The barkeep heard his sister walking from the other room, so he stood and walked back behind the bar and feigned being busy lest his sister-in-law berate him and threaten to force him out into the snow.

Tommy continued to look at the fire. It warmed him as he thought about the long journey home and the possible dangers that lay ahead. *I must get home; such a long journey on foot, I'll have to stay off the main roads and go around the roadblocks.*

He could hear the thump-thump of hooves on snow trotting down the road. As they got closer, he stood and looked out the window, thinking it might be the sergeant coming to take him back to camp. The door opened, and two travellers walked through, dipping their heads as they did. They walked to the fire warming themselves, hands held out. Their swords clattered as they walked, and boots clomped on the stone floor muffled by the new straw.

Tommy walked back to the fire and sat back down. He continued to look into the fire, unperturbed by the invasion. However, he felt a quiet uneasiness by the confidence and standing of the men. They had a different accent to what he was used to and assumed they were from down south of the country.

"Barkeep ale for my gentleman friend and myself, from your private stocks if you please."

The barkeep turned and rolled his eyes once again, whispering, "I'll have nowt for meself the way they're…southern tossers!" He shook his head and rolled his eyes sarcastically, which only Tommy noticed. He poured ale into two tankards and took them to the two strangers, placing them on the great oak mantlepiece before them.

The barmaid walked in from her kitchen out the back, "Ahhh, we have gentlemen guests, would ya be wanting some grub yer grace?" she asked.

"No, thank you, kind woman, we must be off to Tadcaster soon. We just stopped to warm ourselves by the flame of your fire."

Tommy stayed quiet, looking down, fearing the worst. One of the men was wearing the red sash of a Cavalier across his chest, curly, brown shoulder-length hair cascaded down his back. A wide-brimmed black hat with a bright orange plumb protruded from his hatband; a flintlock pistol dangled from his waist, and he rested his hand on the hilt of his sword. He wore a brown buff coat with a bright white laced collar folded over the neckline. His brown breeches rested on the top of his downturned leather boots. His friend, similarly dressed, picked up the tankard of ale and took a swig before spitting it out into the fire.

He coughed "ergggh, that's terrible," he exclaimed with his posh southerner's accent.

"Barkeep seems my companion is not a fan of your ale. Bring us wine so that he can rinse the foulness from his mouth."

The barkeep sensing trouble, walked over and took the tankard, "I'm sorry, sir, that is all we have except cider and mead."

Then his companion turned to Tommy, "You there, young man, what do you know of this area? Is there another tavern of a more substantial nature?"

"No, your grace, I know nowt for I am not from hereabouts," said Tommy respectfully.

"Oh, and where are you from, and what do you know of Roundheads in the area?"

Tommy faced his worse fear, "I am just a humble herdsman, Your Grace, returning home to the west after selling my wool at the Leeds market some days ago. I became sick, and this kind tavern-keeper took me in until I could recover."

Sergeant Walker and John Smythe had frowns on their faces, "I see, but Leeds is to the West of here. Why would you travel this far east after selling your wool in Leeds? I believe there is some untruth to your story!"

Tommy stood nervously, "No, Your Grace I...."

Suddenly the barmaid appeared with Tommy's backsword, helmet and orange sash. "Suppose you'll be wanting these then; they must be worth some coin to you."

Henry looked at his sister with ridicule, knowing that she would do anything for coin. He knew what she was like and showed contempt for her betrayal but said nothing.

Both Sergeant Walker and his companion drew their swords, pointing them in Tommy's direction, "JOHN, CHECK THE PLACE, SEE WHO'S UPSTAIRS!"

Sergeant Walker took a step closer to Tommy and placed the tip of his sword on his shoulder, "Now sir, tell me the truth, you are obviously a Parliamentary soldier. Where are the rest of your men?"

A few moments later, the Cavalier reappeared with Tommy's breastplate and buff coat. "A traitor to the King."

Sergeant Walker pulled out his flintlock and pointed it at him.

Tommy raised his hands; he could hear the hooves of other horses and feared the arrival of more Royalist soldiers. A moment later, the door opened, and two more riders walked in. Tommy kept his eyes on the flintlock pistol that was aimed at him.

"WHAT'S GOING ON HERE?" the voice was familiar; the other Cavalier raised his flintlock toward him. Tommy had his back to the door but looked back and couldn't believe his eyes; it was the steward. He turned back to face the flintlock still aimed at him. *Can things get any worse*? He thought.

A moment later, another walked in. Tommy stood there motionless with his hands up in the air staring at the pistol that was still pointed at him. The Cavalier turned and pointed his pistol nervously at the newcomer. "LOWER YOUR PISTOL, SIR," shouted the reeve nervously as he walked through the door.

By this time, both the barkeep and the barmaid had removed themselves to behind the bar and were bent down nervously peeking over it, watching the events unfold before them.

Tommy once again turned and was shocked to see the reeve standing there, pointing his pistol at the Cavalier.

The steward glanced around the room, looked Tommy up and down, then turned to the sergeant.

"IDENTIFY YOURSELF," yelled Smythe.

The steward calmly spoke, an air of superiority in his voice, "We are on the King's service, just returned from Tadcaster on our way to take news to the Earl of Newcastle. Reeve, please show them our papers."

The reeve reached into his tunic to retrieve the King's note which gave them free pass-through Royalist held territory.

Sergeant Walker walked toward him cautiously, taking the note and reading it silently, "It's the King's seal, alright."

Sergeant walker turned his attentions back to Tommy and started pointing his pistol at him again.

The reeve took the paper back and looked toward their prisoner, "Who do we have here then?"

"Traitor to the King, sir," said the woman raising her head from behind the bar.

"QUIET WOMAN," yelled the sergeant.

Henry looked at her; he rolled his eyes and shook his head but kept his eyes at the level of the top of the bar lest the men turn their attention to him.

"We found these upstairs," Smythe pointed to Tommy's breastplate, buff coat and sash.

Tommy turned around and looked at the steward and the reeve but said nothing. The reeve looked at Tommy, shocked to see him looking so thin and frail.

"Earl of Newcastle has garrisoned his army at Pontefract; we will take the prisoner there. Let his prison guards deal with him, might have some worthy intelligence to provide." Sergeant Walker smiled as he lowered his pistol.

Smythe walked behind Tommy, pulled his arms down, and bound his wrists with rope.

The steward looked at Tommy, "Good, he can spend the rest of his days in the dungeon at Pontefract Castle."

The reeve had heard some talk of Pontefract Castle, a terrifying place, a place seeping with cold and damp, a network of dungeons hollowed out of the rock thirty-five feet below the ground. It was said that once a man entered, he never came out. He looked at the steward confused, knowing that the steward had been paying Tommy's lodging here at the inn these past days, he remained silent.

Terrified, Tommy looked at the steward with hatred, thinking that the steward had finally got his way and Isabel and the bairn would never know the truth. A single tear pooled in the bottom of his eyelid, which he quickly wiped away then looked down in despair.

Tommy looked at Sergeant Walker, "Please, I have a wife and bairn back home; I am no threat ta ya!"

"Had a wife," the steward retorted.

The barmaid lifted her head from behind the bar once more, "You would not have known he was a Roundhead unless I told ya, surely worth some coin."

The steward tossed her a shilling it flew and landed on the floor behind the bar, "SHUT YOUR FACE, WOMAN, BEFORE YOU END UP HANGING FROM A TREE!"

Matilda raised her head from behind the bar to get a better look at the men; she looked at the steward, "You, I know you!"

The reeve pulled out his sword and pointed it at the barmaid, "DID YOU NOT HEAR HIS GRACE?"

The barmaid slowly lowered her head behind the bar and went on all fours looking for the coin amongst the straw. Finding it, she peeked over the bar again to watch the proceedings.

"My reeve and I will accompany you as far as Lumby, then turn east toward Selby. The Earl of Newcastle will need to know the state of Fairfax's army. I will give you the parchment to give to him."

"Let us beat the darkness and be off then," ordered Sergeant Walker.

Smythe pushed Tommy toward the door, "Come on, you move."

The reeve opened the door and glanced at Tommy as he looked at him sadly. Tommy looked terrible; his face was gaunt and pale, his eyes were sunken and had dark bags under them. He had lost a lot of weight, and his back was rounded, a shell of the man he once was. The reeve felt guilty that he could not act but knew he couldn't lest he join him on the way to Pontefract Castle dungeon.

Outside, Smythe tied a rope to Tommy's bindings, then mounted his horse and tied the other end to the saddle horn. He walked the horse forward, and his prisoner was awkwardly tugged forward behind him. The steward, reeve and Sergeant Walker mounted their horses and trotted south down Aberford Road toward Lumby. The steward and Sergeant Walker trotted along to lead, but the reeve stayed back behind Tommy, who tripped and lost his balance trying to stay upright when the horse started to trot. He tried to look behind at the reeve but slipped and fell, the horse pulling him along on his front before he managed to right himself and stand again. Tommy increased his pace to get more slack in the rope, which was causing his bindings to dig into his wrists and bleed, but it was hard going, and he fell again and was dragged along behind the horse for a while.

It was about two hours before they reached the tiny village of Aberford, which was marked with a rock boundary marker at the side of the road.

It was wind-swept land, flat and meaningless, the odd cottage spaced here and there could be seen in the distance. A lone beech tree stood its branches bare, a silhouette against the pale grey of the darkening sky. A gate and dry-stone wall curved to the right and headed toward the horizon; clouds retreated to lay bare the wintery night sky.

The snow was getting deeper, making it even more difficult for Tommy to walk. He was exhausted and started to fall more often, now being dragged along face-first through the snow until he could gather enough strength to stand and keep up with the horse's pace. His wrists were bloody from the tightening bindings, and the front of his breeches and tunic were wet, iced and covered in fresh horse droppings from his repeated falls. He couldn't feel his fingers or toes, and his face was grazed and bloodied.

The steward caught up to Sergeant Walker, who rode a couple of horse lengths ahead. "When you get to Pontefract, you must give this to the Earl. It is the intelligences we have sourced; tell him that we now go to Selby and will join him in Pontefract before the week's end."

Smythe looked behind to see his prisoner struggling under the exertion, "We should stop soon or else we won't have a prisoner to take to his lordship."

They turned off the main road into a clearing and headed toward the other side at the base of a woodland.

The steward called out, "Reeve go quickly to the start of that wooded area and set up camp, start a fire for us to rest and warm ourselves."

The reeve trotted by Tommy and had a darting look at his face as he went by; he could tell he didn't have much left in him.

It took the other horses a good ten minutes to get to the wooded area pulling their staggering prisoner behind them. Tommy was pulled along the last fifty feet on his front through the snow. He was barely conscious but still breathing when the horse stopped, even it, breathing heavily under the added dead weight and exertion.

The horses were tied to a low hanging branch, their saddles removed and placed around the fire.

The reeve walked over to Tommy and turned him on his back. He loosened the rope tied to his bindings and dragged him closer to the fire.

The steward dismounted, "Reeve, take the rope and bind him at the base of that tree, be sure that he is bound tightly."

"Sir, he's not in a good way; needs water and food."

The reeve grabbed him under the armpits and dragged Tommy's limp body to the tree about ten paces from the fire and sat him upright facing the fire. Tommy's head was down, and his chin was touching his chest; he groaned as the reeve bound him to the trunk.

The reeve, with his back to the fire, wiped the snow from Tommy's face and tunic. He then took water and held the pewter canister to his lips, "Come on, lad, hang in there," he whispered.

He lifted his chin; Tommy groaned, then as the reeve let go of his chin, it dropped back to his chest. The reeve lifted his chin once again and poured some water into his partly closed mouth. Tommy swallowed then coughed as it caught at the back of his throat. The reeve poured more as Tommy squinted through his almost closed eyelids.

The reeve made sure the bindings were tight as the steward had ordered and walked back over to the fire to join the others as they warmed themselves, "Your Grace, the prisoner is not in a good way."

The steward and the Cavaliers looked up to see the exhausted body bound to the tree with the rope binding him to the trunk around the chest.

"Give him a blanket and bring the wine from my saddle pack," ordered the steward.

The Cavaliers spread blankets and leaned against their saddles; they opened their leather saddle sack to share the bread and mutton that they had saved.

Although exhausted and a little beat up, Tommy kept his eyes closed and could hear his captors whispering.

"Earl of Newcastle has the way to the west cut off from Fairfax he has no way back there, roadblocks and garrisons everywhere. This lot should be finished within a few weeks," the Cavalier gestured toward his captive.

"Aye, it will be nice to get home," said the reeve, who was starting to get tipsy from the imported wine that he was not so used to.

After they had had their fill of wine, the Cavaliers laid down and closed their eyes, tired and comforted by the wine, mutton and bread they had consumed. The reeve and the steward followed suit, but the steward did not sleep; he just laid there with his eyes closed but silently planning his next move.

When the steward was convinced that the others were fast asleep, he stood and started quietly creeping over toward the prisoner. Tommy heard him coming and, fearing the worst started to struggle against his bindings. The steward knelt in front of the prisoner and took his knife out of the sheath.

Tommy had a look of terror on his face and grumbled and grunted, trying to free himself.

Suddenly, the steward put his hand over Tommy's mouth and his finger to his lips to urge him to be quiet. He lowered his knife and started to cut the bindings around his chest. Tommy, looking confused, held out his hands further so the steward could more easily cut the rope around his wrists.

"Take this," the steward whispered and gave Tommy his piece of parchment that held the King's seal.

The steward leaned closer, "Get to my horse and walk him back into the trees. When I lay down, you ride west, stay off the main roads, and if you're stopped, show them the parchment. Take the knife."

The steward pulled the rope from his wrists. Tommy stood and, fearing that it was a trick, didn't move, "You want this, they'll shoot me in the back."

The steward leaned forward once again, whispering, "Release the other horses, Oh, and tell Isabel and Lucy I love them, now go!"

There wasn't much in the hamlet that the steward didn't know about, including the hand-tying and bann signing of Tommy and his daughter. It was a well-kept secret, but the steward managed to find out where the ceremony was going to take place. He watched from behind a tree as his daughter pledged her love for this man.

Tommy, still waiting for the worst, walked back to where the horses were tied and untethered them. His eyes were still partially closed, and his wrists were bloodied and bruised.

The steward crept back toward the fire and was about to lie down when the horse that Tommy untied spooked and rose up on his hind legs.

Smythe and Sergeant Walker were startled awake they could see that the prisoner was not where he should have been and picked up their flintlocks.

"STOP!" The Steward feigned running after him as Tommy tried to get on the unsaddled horse.

"STOP!" yelled Smythe as he raised his pistol at Tommy, who he could barely see through the darkness.

"STOP, OR I'LL SHOOT!" Just as he cocked his pistol and pulled the trigger, the steward ran in-between Smythe and Tommy.

"NO!" screamed the reeve, who realised what the steward was doing.

Tommy heard the shot and a grunt. He looked to see the steward raise his arms and fall forward onto the ground. Tommy kicked the sides of the horse with his heels, and it trotted off into the darkness between the trees.

The reeve ran over to the steward and turned him over; he could see the gaping hole that the lead ball had made, and blood pulsated out of the wound. He placed his hand on it to stop the flow of blood.

Tommy, unused to riding a horse, allowed the beast to use its instinct to meander through the trees, "Come on, boy," he patted him on the neck.

The reeve held a rag to the wound to stem the flow while Smythe ran to the beginning of the wooded area and fired off another shot.

Sergeant Walker walked up to the reeve and placed the barrel of his pistol at his temple, "I thought there wasn't something quite right about you two, Roundhead spies."

The reeve put one of his hands up, "We're not spies, you fool, you saw the parchment, the Kings seal!"

"How did the Roundhead escape then?"

"You saw him running after him, you fool, LOOK IF YOU DON'T LET ME TEND TO THIS MAN, HE'LL DIE; he's lost a lot of blood!"

"Go on then, do what you must but try anything, and you'll join him."

The reeve placed his hand on the steward's chest, waiting for it to rise, but his chest did not rise; he paused, "He's dead...."

He looked at Smythe, who had returned after he had retrieved the horses.

"You've killed an agent of the King; you'll hang for this," said the reeve, looking up at him.

"He ran in the way; it was an accident," said Smythe excitedly.

The reeve stood, "You saw him, he was running after the prisoner, and you shot him in the back!"

Fearing his companion's fate, the sergeant lowered his flintlock, "He's right, he ran in the way. It was an accident!"

The sun was starting to lighten the sky in the east, and the birds began to chatter.

"I must get him home," the reeve retrieved the steward's blanket from the fire and wrapped him in it. He took some rope and bound his body tight, and allowed the cavaliers to assist him in putting the body atop the back of his horse. The reeve said nothing, mounted his horse and walked his horse off toward the sun. His mind was full of sadness; he thought about Isabel and the family and prayed that Tommy would get home safely. It would be too much to bear for a woman to lose both father and husband.

Tommy headed north through the forest, then west, then circled back east just in case the Cavaliers had managed to get their horses back. The sun was low but bright, and a morning shadow crept over the landscape like a cold blanket.

Tommy hadn't ridden a horse that much but started to get the hang of it. He found that if he sat forward and squeezed with his legs, the horse went faster. He held onto the horse's mane and held on for dear life, trying to put his pain to the back of his mind.

For a time, he stayed off the main roads and walked the horse slowly and carefully through the virgin snow. The morning was cold and crisp, but he cherished the freedom it brought, and he longed for the warmth of home.

CHAPTER TWENTY-FIVE

Forgotten Saviour

The land was flat, and mist collected in the low-lying fields giving it a vast ghostly appearance. Thomas and John walked past a large, bare, lone birch tree that stood like a sentry on guard. They conquered the height of the hill with the chilled wind at their backs, helping their momentum forward.

They eventually arrived in Bramham anxiously walking down the main street; they could see the sign of the Swan Inn swinging in the distance. Thomas opened the door and walked inside quickly, John a few steps behind.

The barkeep looked at the men; they were cold and weathered with a look of desperation and anxiousness. Their faces red and wind burnt from their journey, their clothing worn and frayed, hose holed and dirty but wrapped with bits of cut blanket.

James Fewtrall had told them where he had left Tommy. "The Roundhead soldier, where is he?" Implored Thomas as John stood quietly behind him, waiting for an answer.

Henry was shocked by the intrusion and, always suspecting retribution for what his sister-in-law had done, stuttered, "He...he was taken away, by Cavaliers a day ago. He...he was sick...we took care of him."

Matilda heard from the other room and walked in to see what was going on. She was taken aback by the desperate look of the two men.

Somewhat relieved that he was still alive, "Where did they take him?"

"They were headed south with two other Royalists; I heard them say something about Pontefract Castle," claimed Matilda nervously.

"Pontefract Castle that's where the Earl of Newcastle is garrisoned, all the Roundhead prisoners are being held there. If they get him there, we'll never get him out," stated John sadly.

Thomas said nothing but walked to the open fire and, taking off his wool mittens, held his hands up to warm them. A feeling of desperation came over him; he stared into the flames contemplating a possible plan. *If we catch up to them, we could help him escape before they reach the castle.*

John joined him by the fire, "What now?"

"We go on, not much we can do, can't go back home until we know fer sure," mumbled Thomas sadly.

They took off their cloaks and warmed themselves, allowing the iciness on their clothing to melt and steam.

The barmaid brought them ale, and the barkeep went about his business. He went outside to collect wood and returned a few minutes later, arms full. Thomas heard him approach and saw him through the window, so he stood and walked to the door to open it for him.

"Riders are approaching best you make yourself scarce! There's been Roundheads and Cavaliers riding through, and they're always looking for trouble." The barkeep walked to the fire and dropped the wood.

Thomas looked at John, who had picked up their cloaks and walked toward the door.

Henry gestured. "No, not that way, go upstairs no wait, come here hide behind the bar!"

Thomas and John walked over and crouched behind the bar beside the barkeep's legs.

The barkeep started to shine the leather jacks and stack them behind the bar on the shelves, nervously waiting for the riders to enter.

They all heard the horses and men speaking in an urgent, excited fashion. The barkeep saw the hats of the two men pass the window, and then the door was flung open.

"Quickly, man, help me!"

The barkeep turned to see the reeve supporting another man, one arm around his waist the other, holding his wrist around his shoulder. The injured man groaned, and there was blood all over his tunic.

With all the ruckus, Thomas peeked over the bar, it was the reeve, and he was shocked when he saw the steward who was severely injured. He elbowed John and stepped around from the bar.

"Quickly get me hot water and cloth for bandages; he's lost a lot of blood," the reeve and the barkeep set him down on a wooden table. The reeve gently laid him down, then lifted his feet so that he was lying on the top of the table.

The steward had his eyes closed, groaned and clutched his shoulder; blood was dribbling out the wound, down his tunic, and he was sweating and grunting with the pain of movement. Every time he took a breath in, he grunted and clasped hold of the bloodied rag that the reeve had tied there earlier.

The barkeep ran to the kitchen and grabbed a linen sheet that was drying near the fire.

"What's all the ruckus about Henry?" The barmaid asked her brother-in-law as he started to rip the linen sheet.

"Here ya can't be doing that ruining me linen...."

The barkeep interrupted her, "OH QUIET WOMAN and get me some hot water and be quick about it!"

She stood there flabbergasted for a moment but did as she was commanded and poured water from a small cauldron hanging above the kitchen fire.

The barkeep walked back out into the other room. Continuing to rip the sheet, he gave two strips of the linen to the reeve who put them on the wound.

Thomas walked up to the table, "Is there anything I can do?"

The reeve shocked to see him, "THOMAS, what the blazes are you doing here? JOHN HARGREAVES! Quickly hold this against the wound Thomas."

Thomas put his hand on the linen bandage, which by now was coloured red. The steward screamed in pain from the pressure and lifted his head, then he passed out and dropped his head hard back down on the table. The reeve bent down and listened to make sure he was still breathing.

"WHAT HAPPENED?" John asked.

"Long story, quick help me get his tunic off!"

John lifted the steward's limp torso while the reeve undid the leather buttons of his tunic. Thomas helped pull the sleeves off then helped John gently lower him back down on the top of the table.

The reeve ripped the steward's undershirt open at the neck and kept ripping until the wound was revealed, "WHERE'S THAT WATER?"

There was a gaping hole in the front of his shoulder, and the blood flow continued. The skin all around the wound was discoloured and frayed. The reeve took another linen strip from the barkeep and wiped the wound. The edges of the hole made by the lead ball were black and burnt.

The reeve took his knife from the sheath and steadily held it, looking at it and the wound nervously.

Matilda entered the room with a wooden bowl of water; she placed it down beside the reeve, who put two linen strips of bandage into it. He then picked up the wet linen and dangled them over the wound, allowing the water to flush it. The three men looked on nervously. While holding the knife blade like a quill, he proceeded to push the blade into the open wound. He moved the point of the knife backwards and forwards in the wound, and he felt the hardness of the lead ball.

The reeve looked down at the wound, "I can feel it!"

He wiggled the knifepoint backwards and forwards, trying to get the blade behind the lead ball. It was difficult going, and the wound began to bleed profusely. Thomas wiped around the injury with the wet strips of cloth, and watery blood ran down the steward's arm onto the table.

The steward was limp, still unconscious, but his shoulder moved with the movement of the reeve's prodding.

The reeve was having problems getting the knife underneath the lead ball, "John, give me your knife."

The reeve placed the other knife in the wound, cutting into the discoloured piece of skin, he tried to grasp the lead ball, but it was lodged too tightly.

"I can't get it; it's lodged in there too deep," he pulled the knives out and the wound bled further. He took the knife and made a deep incision across the hole that the ball had made.

Thomas wiped the blood with a new piece of linen given to him by the barkeep. The reeve stuck his thumb and forefinger into the wound and grasped the ball, pulling it out for everybody to see.

Thomas wiped the wound and noticed a small piece of bloodied material at the opening of the wound. He picked it out and rewashed the injury.

"Bring me a needle and cotton; I remember seeing me mother doing this."

The barkeep disappeared into the kitchen and returned moments later with Matilda's sewing tin.

Thomas squeezed the discoloured skin together and started stitching; he then placed a clean swab over it and then, with John's help, wrapped a long strip around his shoulder to keep it in place. They then moved the steward up to one of the rooms. The reeve stayed with him for a while, replacing a cold compress on his forehead.

Going downstairs after his shift, the reeve sat at the fire with Thomas and John. "Now, do you want to tell me what the blazes you two are doing here?"

"We been searching for Tommy these past weeks since the Roundheads took him," John said with a disappointed tone.

Thomas looked at the reeve, "We've travelled half the country looking for him and heard from some soldiers that he was sick and possibly died of the fever here in Bramham."

The reeve smiled and laughed, "Have no fear Thomas, your son is alive!"

"What do ya mean, where is he?" asked Thomas excitedly.

"God willing, I'd say by now headed west through Royalist roadblocks on the way back to Haworth," the reeve smiled.

The reeve took out his pipe, "If it weren't fer the steward, it wouldn't be so."

"What do ya mean?" asked John inquisitively.

"He was in a bad way, had the fever and the publican here looked after him until he got well. Steward paid for his lodging came here whenever we passed through to ask how he was doing. He'd lost a lot of weight; they say he almost died. Two Royalist soldiers discovered him; I'm not sure how. Anyway, they took him prisoner and were in the process of taking him to Castle Prison."

The reeve started to recount how he had woken in the darkness to find Tommy released from his bindings. Then he explained how the steward had stepped in the way of the Cavaliers shot. He explained that when he ran over to the steward, he heard him whisper, "Treat me as dead."

The reeve had made such a fuss of his killing that the two Cavaliers didn't even check. He and the steward had tricked the Cavaliers into thinking that he was dead, and they helped him put the steward's bound, limp body on the back of the horse. The steward was still alive, albeit in grave pain from the lead ball lodged in his shoulder. He went on to explain how once down the road out of sight, he untied the steward, bandaged his wound and helped him sit atop the horse. He was in too much pain to gallop, so he walked the horse until we got here.

"The rest of the story, ya know."

"TOMMY'S ALRIGHT, THANK THE LORD!" Thomas grabbed John by the arm and squeezed affectionately.

The reeve smiled, "Yes, a bit worse for wear, but still alive and hopefully on his way west. If he gets past Leeds, he should be okay. The steward has given him a parchment with the King's seal to get through the Royalist roadblocks."

"Now, what of us and of course the steward?" asked John.

"Well, the way I see it, our fighting days are done; once the steward is on the mend, we'll head for home."

Thomas went upstairs to check on the steward. He was still and silent with beads of sweat on his brow. There was a small candle burning on the bedside table beside him and shadows danced on the opposite wall.

Thomas pulled up a stool and sat beside him for a time, "It were a brave thing ya did fer me son, I'll not forget it," he whispered.

The steward was shirtless and turned his head erratically to one side and then the other. His hair was wet with perspiration and stuck to his forehead; the bandage on his shoulder had been changed, but the fever remained. His arms were on the top of the blanket, eyes closed, frowning face, breathing heavily and murmuring words that nobody could understand. Thomas rinsed the linen cloth that was placed on the steward's forehead and put it back.

Thomas stood, touched the steward on the arm and turned around to leave. He opened the door, the light from the fire downstairs flooded the room.

When Thomas went back downstairs, John and the reeve were sitting beside the fire quietly recounting their tales. John spoke of Bradford and their journey east, being sure not to mention any involvement that they had had in the battle. Likewise, the reeve told stories of his and the steward's journey, being sure to leave out the details of their intelligence gathering on behalf of the Royalists.

The barkeep continued to fill up their jacks, but the mood remained solemn and disquieting. They all longed to get on the road home but knew of the dangers that lay ahead. The war was not over, and their trip west when it was time was fraught with peril.

They continued to take turns looking after the steward, dressing his wound with clean bandages and providing water and broth in small amounts when he did manage to wake.

Matilda and Henry had come to an agreement and a liking for each other since his outburst in the kitchen. A liking that they shared with all who could hear on recent nights as the fire started to die down. The barmaid seemed a lot happier as the days went on and would often glance at Henry smiling coyly.

Days passed as the reeve, John Hargreaves, and Thomas waited for the steward to get well or, as they feared, die. The reeve told them the steward's story, how he had been born a tenant copyholder and had been sent away by his father to be a gentleman. How his father had spent time in the Old Baily and how he had married and his wife had died during childbirth. Thomas was shocked to hear such things, but it had confirmed what William had told him of the steward. Thinking of such things made him think of home, and of course, Agnes and the rest of the family who he knew would be worried to death.

Thomas longed for home, the return of the green fields, the beauty of the Haworth moors, the undulating hills and the fields of golden wheat. It wouldn't be long before the melt, he thought to himself. The first rains always caused excitement in the village. The birth of Spring brought with it a renewal, a chance to take stock and prepare for the coming season. Ploughing, seeding, bird scaring and of course, the harvest.

The Truth's Tears

A Cornish Footman slipped and got a fall,
As he was running nigh a garden wall,
Even at that time, that a thick flight of shot,
Came whistling ore his head, he swore by Got,
That he was slain; and panting there he laid,
For Saints and Souls, desiring his comrade
Him there to bury: but to search his wound,
A Surgeon came; behold! None can be found.
They bid him rise, and fight, for nought him ail'd,
But all their words with him nothing prevail'd...

Isabel and Agnes had heard rumours of atrocities, cruelties, humiliation, impromptu executions and the rape of civilians. It was said that the death toll was rising, and many civilians were dying not by powder and musket ball but by an invisible army of disease that didn't take sides.

"It's been almost a month. When do ya think they'll be back, Agnes?" Isabel asked worriedly, forcibly dismissing any thought of Tommy not returning.

"I have no idea. William has gone to the village to hear of any news. Hopefully, we'll find out more when he returns," Agnes concluded.

William opened the door to the Kings Arms; it was almost deserted except for a beggar sitting by the fire and two others sitting at a table playing a card game.

William walked up to the barkeep, "Ave ya heard any news?"

"Only what I told ya yesterday, but that beggar warming himself just came in he's come from the east, reckons the Royalists are taking over."

William turned to look at the beggar who had his back to him and was staring intently into the fire, "Give us two ales; I'll see if I can get some news from him."

The barkeep filled two jacks from the barrel and placed them on the bar. William picked them up and turned to walk toward the beggar. He could see he had been ravaged by the winter, his cloak was worn and frayed, and a raggedy old blanket covered his head, its frayed threads dangling down his back. His posture was curved, and he rested his forearms on his thigh, an empty jack sitting on the stool beside him.

As William got closer, the first thing he noticed was the scars on his wrists and the side of his thin, unshaven face. The beggar was obviously deep in thought as he wasn't disturbed by William's nearing footsteps or his presence. He clutched a torn piece of parchment, holding it so tight the tops of his knuckles were almost white.

"Stranger, barkeep tells me you've come from the east; what news have ya?" William held out the jack toward the stranger.

He did not move, just continued to stare into the fire, so William put the jack down on the stool beside him.

The beggar looked at the jack then looked back at the fire but said nothing.

William was taken back by the beggar's unshaven, haggard face, it was dirty, and there were abrasions and cuts. Still, he could not see his eyes as the hooded blanket shadowed them. He took a closer look at his wrists; they were thin, and the wounds were deep and bloodied. They looked red and painful. His cheekbones were high and pronounced, the skin sagged beneath them, his unwashed beard tried in vain to hide the scurvy caused spots that dotted his face. His expression was one of a destitute man devoid of humanity. What great hardship had this man faced. Was he always a beggar?

"My friend, have ya any news of the goins on out east, what of the war?" William asked frustratedly.

The beggar took the blanket from his head and allowed it to sit on his shoulders. He looked at the jack but said nothing as he took it and, holding it to his thin, thirsty lips, chugged it down in one action coughing some up that had gone down the wrong way.

William watched in awe. The beggar's eyes were closed as he swallowed the ale in one go. His hair was matted and unkempt, but there was something about him, something…that looked familiar. Then he saw it, the scar on his forehead…

"TOMMY?"

Tommy stood and turned to face William; a small tear welled in the bottom of his eyelid.

William held out his arms and embraced him; he could feel the bones of his back and the frailness of his body.

Tommy said nothing and then started to quietly sob.

William continued to embrace him, "Tommy, what are ya doing here all alone? We must get ya home."

Tommy stopped sobbing and sat back down on the stool, putting his face in his hands.

"Tommy, let's get ya home." William helped Tommy up off the stool and put his arm around his shoulder. Tommy staggered to the door, stiff and sore from his long journey; he hadn't eaten in days.

It took William a good hour to help Tommy stagger down Main Street to the bottom of the hide. Often Tommy wouldn't walk at all and just let William carry and drag him, trying when he could to plant his foot down to offer some support.

At the bottom of the hide, Tommy opened his eyes; he could see the cottage up the hill, the smoke billowing out of the chimney against the grey sky. The wet snow over the farrowed fields was starting to dissipate and turn muddy, but they stayed to the side and walked along the small strip of grass beside the dry bap wall.

"Come on, Tommy, we're almost there," William lost his footing but managed to recover, Tommy going down on one knee in the process.

William straightened and helped Tommy up and supported his weight again.

They were close to the cottage, so Tommy put weight on his own feet and began to walk slowly and gingerly toward the cottage door. He took his arm from around William and tried to walk unaided. He staggered and almost tripped but used the last of his strength to steady himself. William walked closely behind him in case he needed to support him. Tommy staggered up to the cottage door and steadied himself. He put his hand on the latch, but he paused for a moment.

He could hear movement inside then the murmurings of a woman, "Isabel, William is back! Hopefully, he has news!"

He tilted his head back and looked up at the sky, and once again, a tear pooled in the bottom of his eye, which he wiped away with the back of his hand.

He lifted the latch, pushed the door open and stood there quietly...

Agnes was facing the other way cutting some onions, "William, where have ya been tis getting late, and the supper is ready. ISABEL, LUCY, WILLIAM IS BACK, AND SUPPER IS READY."

She turned, holding the small bowl of onions and looked up to see a stranger, somebody she didn't recognise standing there motionless and screamed, "ISABEL, LUCY!"

Startled, she dropped the wooden bowl of onions and put her hand up to her mouth, covering her frightened expression.

She sighed in relief as William walked through the door behind the stranger, "WILLIAM!" Agnes was confused.

"Agnes, look who is home!"

Isabel heard Agnes scream and inquisitively looked down from the loft, then started making her way down the ladder, turning to look at William and the stranger.

Puzzled, she walked slowly toward the stranger as Agnes, and the children looked on, unsure what to do.

The two boys, John and Robert, stood there silently in awe of the dirty beggar that William had brought home. They looked at each other, then back at him.

Isabel took another step forward slowly, curiously looking at his dirty, worn clothes and his grazed, soiled face. She then quickened her next step after she recognised the familiar eyes and the scar through the mask of facial hair and dirt.

She opened her arms and threw herself at him, "TOMMY!"

She almost knocked him over in the process and would have if William hadn't braced himself and held onto his nephew.

Isabel began to sob, "OH HEAVENS ABOVE, AGNES IT'S TOMMY!"

She kissed him on the cheek and held him so tight he could barely breathe.

She kissed him on the cheek again and again and kept kissing him, "YER HOME SAFE AND SOUND, MY LOVE, I'VE MISSED YOU SO."

Hearing the commotion, Lucy looked out from the animal quarters.

Agnes walked up and placed her hand gently on Tommy's arm. She could see what state he was in and worriedly suggested that Isabel stop her embrace.

William supported Tommy while he and Agnes walked him to his father's chair near the fire.

Lucy walked up to him and lightly put her arms around him, and gave him a gentle, warm embrace. "Welcome home, Tommy."

Worriedly, Isabel knelt in front of him and looked up into his vacant eyes, "Husband...what have they done ta ya?"

She gently caressed his bearded face looking into his eyes that gazed at her, void of any emotion.

Tommy stared beyond her into the fire.

Isabel leaned closer.

Tommy coughed.

Lucy quickly spooned some pottage from the cauldron into a small wooden bowl giving it to Tommy.

His hands shaking, Tommy reached out, took the bowl and started consuming the contents greedily, some spilling and dripping from the bottom of his hairy chin.

Agnes looked at William questioningly, but he shook his head and looked down at the ground sadly, silently imparting that there was no news of Thomas and John Hargreaves.

Agnes fought back the tears and swallowed the choke in her throat, but then looked up and smiled bravely, "Tommy, we must get these filthy rags off ya." She took the grimy blanket from around his shoulders and undid the dirty, woollen cloak dropping them both to the floor.

"Lucy, heat some water in the cauldron." Agnes undid his ripped tunic, which was frayed, weathered and full of holes and took it off, then pulled his boots off to reveal a bloodied mess. The tops of his toes were black from frostbite, and most of his toenails were missing. The skin on his feet was peeling in rotting layers from the constant wet, and both she and Isabel turned away from the putrid smell.

William helped her pull off his hose, revealing his bruised, bony legs. Agnes and Isabel gasped at the deep cuts, grazes and swollen kneecaps.

William and Agnes helped him up, ensuring that his private parts were still covered by his dirty, grey, ripped undershirt.

"Lucy, hang a blanket over the washing line and bring the animal's water barrel close behind it."

Moments later, Tommy was sitting in the animal's half water barrel naked with Isabel pouring hot water into it. His grazed, bony knees stuck up out of the water. Isabel didn't know the man she loved, he was so skinny and emaciated, but she put on a brave face for his sake. She noticed the deep wounds around his wrists and the red cuts in his knees and chest.

Isabel poured another bucket of hot water into the barrel, then stepped around the other side of the blanket and held her hands to her face, "What's happened to him?"

Lucy walked over to console her while Agnes walked around the other side of the blanket to look at Tommy. She was immediately stunned by the frailty of her son's body. His arms were thin, and his ribs protruded through the skin; then she saw the scars around his wrists and the cuts and bruises all over his chest and knees.

Tommy was oblivious to the conversations on the other side of the curtain. The water stung the abrasions and cuts on his arms and legs, but he sat there looking forward blankly.

Agnes picked the linen cloth out of the water and squeezed the water out of it onto his chest. Then she dunked it into the water again and dribbled it over his head, wetting his hair. He closed his eyes and allowed the warm water to trickle down his face. She did it again and again, trying to wash away the experiences of the last weeks. She looked at his nails; they were black, bloodied and broken. His hands shook as she turned them over to look at the cuts on his palms. She scooped some water with her hands and washed his face, then she stroked the beard on the side of his face softly as a mother would do.

Isabel returned with another bucket of hot water and poured it into the half barrel that by now was grey with dirt, muck and blood. Agnes left them while Isabel took the linen cloth from the water and began to softly dab the cuts and abrasions on his back and chest. Tommy jolted from the pain but said nothing and continued to look forward. Isabel paused; she tried again, this time trying to be gentler. The linen cloth became red with blood, so she rinsed it. She dabbed carefully and more slowly with less pressure. It was soothing, but Tommy said nothing and continued to look forward.

Isabel went back around the curtain and returned with his straight blade; she held clumps of his beard and began to cut into them. Once short enough, she held his chin and slowly scraped away the whiskers. She nicked him a couple of times, but he didn't flinch. She held his face between her hands and turned it toward her. She looked into Tommy's eyes; they were vacant, cold and distant, which upset her deeply.

Isabel helped him to stand in the half barrel. He clutched his man parts while she slowly dabbed him dry, being careful not to touch the abrasions with too much pressure. He stepped out of the half barrel, and she helped him put a clean undershirt on which belonged to Thomas.

William sat near the fire; he watched Tommy walk slowly and carefully over to the ladder. He grabbed the side of the ladder and put one foot on the bottom rung. He gently pulled himself up, and Isabel followed behind and helped him get up to the top of the ladder, then into their bed. The straw in the mattress poked his back, and it hurt, but he was so tired, so very, very tired. Isabel covered him up with the woollen blanket. She pushed the hair from his forehead, and she waited there with him until he drifted off to sleep. She looked at him in the candlelight, then put her head down on the mattress, gently placing her hand over his.

Sky of Ashes

The reeve checked on him during the night and changed the bloodied dressing as often as he could. He wiped the sweat from the steward's forehead and rinsed it in the cold water that sat beside the bed. He often laid out a blanket beside his bed and slept on the wooden floor beside him. It was five more days before the steward's fever broke, and he felt well enough to raise himself from the bed. A further three days before he wanted to remove himself from his room and seek the company of others.

One morning the steward left his room accompanied by the reeve who walked down the stairs looking behind protectively. He walked slowly and gingerly, holding his shoulder where the ball had struck, and he grimaced with pain. The colour of death had faded from his face, and like before, he was beholden to no one.

Still holding his shoulder, he looked around as he reached the bottom of the stairs, "You there, barkeep, fetch ale and the best meat that this establishment has to offer and be quick about it."

Thomas and John stood when they heard him; they were shocked by the steward's manner but knew it was a sign that he was on the mend and intent on hiding his frailties in front of them. They stood taking off their hats as the steward walked to the table in front of the fire.

"What are you looking at? Sit down; you're making me nervous with your fuss," barked the steward.

His shirt and blue tunic had been washed and pressed, but the frayed hole from the ball was still visible even though the woman had tried to mend it. There was a bloodied discolouration around the mend where she had failed to remove all stains of the blood.

The steward took a deep breath and sat carefully and tentatively on the wooden bench, "You, Rushworth, what do you know of the war and the developments in the west?"

"Nothing, Your Grace. I'm sure your intelligences are far better than mine."

"Ohh, and why do you think this is so?" said the steward, testing Thomas' knowledge of his purpose in this area of the country.

Thomas looked at the steward and was going to respond with a recitation of the tales that he heard from the reeve until he was cut short by John Hargreaves.

"Well, what he means to say, Your Grace, is that you being of higher rank, are sure to know much more about the going's on that we are not privy to."

The steward looked at John suspiciously, "Hmmm, you're best to keep to those thoughts and to keep any others to yourself."

John bowed his head slightly and stepped back, as did Thomas to allow the reeve and the steward to discuss matters at hand, which they hoped would involve going home soon.

The reeve looked intently at the steward and whispered, "What shall we do now?"

The steward lifted his tankard, took a swig of ale, then paused for a moment, confused and unsure of what to say, his mind still muddled from his recent convalescence. "I think its time to be getting home ta the moors; our spying days are done," he whispered.

The reeve nodded his head, "While you were out to it, I've heard that the Roundheads have taken up positions of strength near Leeds."

"What if we're stopped by Roundheads? If they open their mouth about our loyalties, we'll hang from the nearest tree." The reeve asked.

The steward looked at Thomas and John, who were on the other side of the room having their own quiet conversation. "We can keep these two with us just in case. We'll bind them and say they are Royalist spies, and we're taking them to York for questioning."

The reeve reached into his tunic," I've still got the parchment with the King's seal that should see us through Royalist lines."

The steward stared at John and Thomas, "To be honest, now that his son is on his way home, I think they want to get home as much as we do, besides we have the parchment, and they need us more than we need them."

The steward stood and called out to John and Thomas, "Right, we leave tomorrow morning before the cock crows, ready your gear and get a good night's sleep."

The steward and reeve sat nervously quiet as three strangers came into the alehouse and were greeted by the barmaid. They stamped their feet on the stone floor to remove the snow from their flat toed boots. They removed their hats; each had a closely cropped haircut and wore the orange sash of the Parliamentarians. They looked suspiciously at the steward, immediately noticing his injured shoulder as he clutched it.

The steward stood and walked toward the stairs; the reeve followed, being sure not to look back. One of the other strangers stood at the bar waiting for his ale and turned to watch the steward and reeve walk up the stairs. He then looked over to the soldier that was also watching suspiciously and raised his eyebrows.

"YOU THERE. WHAT BUSINESS DO YOU HAVE IN THESE PARTS?" The soldier put his hand on his pistol and looked at the reeve and steward suspiciously.

The steward kept walking, but the reeve stopped, "His grace is injured, shot by Royalists on the road from Tadcaster, we prepare for the journey west to home."

"Come, let's talk more of this occurrence and your news of Tadcaster, for that is our destination."

The reeve, sensing trouble, looked at Thomas and John for support and turned on the stairs to come down again, "These are our companions; they were at the battle of Bradford."

"THE BATTLE OF BRADFORD, then there are heroes in our midst," said the Parliamentary soldier loudly.

"Come, sit, tell us of your tales of triumph at Bradford, barkeep ales for all!"

The other two soldiers came closer and stood near the fire as Thomas and John recounted their story of Bradford and how they had helped the musketeers fend off the Cavaliers from the church steeple. They told the story of Captain Hodgson, and the more they spoke, the less suspicious the men became. The dubious mood in the room had turned into one of celebration, and the three soldiers continued to ply the reeve and his companions with as much ale as they could stomach. It was well into the night before they all turned in, Thomas and John preferring to roll out their blankets near the fire, the reeve preferring to share the steward's room.

Thomas awoke to the sound of hard boots on the stone floor, it was still dark, and the fire had all but burnt down, but the Roundheads were up, dressed and armed, leaving quickly on their way to Tadcaster. Thomas wiped his eyes and watched them walk through the door as a burst of cold air rushed in to chill the air. He heard their chatter as they mounted their horses outside and galloped away east.

Thomas looked over at John, who had not stirred and shook his shoulder, but too much ale the previous evening had made him oblivious to the start of the new day. Thomas sat up as Matilda and Henry walked down the wooden stairs. He had noticed that they had begun to share the same room, and their talk had become much more amiable. He watched them as they went about their business tidying up the dirty pewter plates and empty jacks from the previous evening.

John opened his eyes and groaned as his headache reminded him of the copious amounts of ale that he had consumed the night before. He sat up, stood and staggered over to the water bucket, picked it up and poured it over his head. He then growled, closed his eyes and shook his long, wet hair from side to side trying to remove the grogginess from his head. He took a linen cloth that Matilda gave him and dried his face; then joined Thomas, who had already sat at the table eating a bowl of wet oats. The steward and the reeve joined them and greedily consumed what was placed down in front of them.

The steward leaned forward and whispered, "The reeve tells me that if it wasn't for you two, he and I may have been in a spot of trouble last night with those soldiers, so I thank you."

Thomas and John bowed their heads slightly then continued to eat their oats hungrily.

The steward spat an uncooked oat onto the floor and mumbled, "It will be good to get back to the manor and get some decent grub. All this peasant food is not good for my innards."

Still sore from his ordeal, he touched his shoulder, "We'll make haste today before we run into anymore Roundheads on their way to Tadcaster. I've spoken to the woman and purchased an old cart; we'll hitch the horse to it and head west but keep south of Leeds."

"What about all the Royalist roadblocks?" enquired John as he blinked, trying to overcome the pain behind his eyes.

"You let us worry about that," said the reeve who tapped his parchment that was on the inside of his tunic.

Henry opened the door and walked outside, returning sometime later with the reeve's horse bridled and hitched to an old cart. "Yer horse is ready; I've watered and fed him should be right fer a while."

The steward reached into his purse that dangled from his belt and handed the barkeep some coin. He paid more than he had to in appreciation for the service they had provided in his time of convalescence.

The four of them said farewell and stepped out into the icy air. The horse snorted and stomped his hoof, unaccustomed to the extra weight of the cart. His breath billowed out of his nostrils as he tried to become familiar with the bridle once again.

The reeve took hold of the reins and jumped up into the driver's seat while the steward carefully pulled himself up beside him. Thomas and John threw their sacks and rolled blankets into the cart and sat on the edge, their feet dangling below them.

Matilda and Henry came outside to see them off. They waved as the horse and cart meandered down the lane toward Weatherby Road and then east on Thorner Road toward the tiny village of Scarcroft. The reeve kept the horse at a slow trot, but the steward grimaced and clutched his shoulder with each bump in the road.

Thomas closed his eyes and allowed the rising winter sun to shine on his face. *I feel like a weight has been lifted off me shoulders knowing that Tommy is alright.*

It was two hours before they reached the outskirts of Scarcroft, which was nestled amongst a series of farmed ridges and valleys crossed by the east to west flowing Scarcroft beck, which was partly iced over. Old cottages, a church and a village green, sat between a network of lanes and pathways leading to Scarcroft Inn.

They tied up the horse and walked past a Puritan couple with their black cloaks and white ruffles worn around their necks. Thomas heard the man bartering for supper, bed and breakfast for him and his wife. Thomas and John walked in and over to the host's table to eat and pay sixpence for a bowl of pottage and dark bread. Meanwhile, the steward and the reeve rented a chamber at the side and ate alone.

The inn was full of travellers and locals alike in various stages of drunkenness.

There was music playing. One of the musicians held a tabor, another a shawm and another a bagpipe. They played a simple ballad that amused Thomas and John and the rest of the half-drunken souls. Later they switched to a sad English street song that concerned the age-old issue of hopeless love. The patrons stopped what they were doing and listened to an attractive woman with long dark hair sing the sad, deep melody of the 'Lunatic Lover'.

GRIM King of the ghosts, make haste,
And bring hither all your train
See how the pale moon does waste
And just now is in the wane.
Come, you night-hags, with all your charms,
And revelling witches away
And hug me close in your arms;
To you, my respects, I'll pay.

The singer reminded Thomas of Agnes.

Their bellies full, Thomas and John, pulled out their pipes. They began to smoke and watch as three couples began a country dance repeating an execution of a sequence of figures. A pattern that the dancers traced along the floor in longways formation. They held hands aloft and interacted with their partner but then quickly swapped on occasion so that they danced with everyone in the group.

Thomas watched the dancers, but he had other things on his mind, "How long do ya think it will take ta get back, John?"

John looked over in the direction of the steward and reeve, "Suppose it depends on them, but better to ride than walk, besides something tells me they can get through Royalist lines."

It wasn't long before John noticed the reeve and the steward reappear from their private chamber. The reeve stopped and looked behind and, seeing John, gestured for them to follow them as they were leaving. *Best to travel through the night,* he thought.

Going through the great oak door, they were greeted by the cold night air and shrugged, pulling their cloaks tightly around them. The reeve had already retrieved the cart and horse and walked them around. He helped the steward get up on the cart as several horsemen came riding up. They were Cavaliers easily identifiable by their dark curly locks of hair and plumbed hats.

One of the riders halted their horse in front of the cart, "…And who might you be, leaving so soon as the night grows near? The night is a dangerous time; I would recommend you stay."

The other horsemen pulled out their flintlocks and pointed them at the reeve, who by this time had climbed up on the cart and had taken hold of the reins. He looked on nervously, "We are the King's men; his grace was injured in his service."

The reeve reached into his tunic, which brought an immediate reaction from the men holding their flintlocks.

"EASY THERE!" The horseman in front yelled.

The reeve raised one hand and, with the other, gently pulled out the parchment paper with his thumb and finger. He held it toward the horsemen who took off his glove and held it toward the light of the moon.

"The King's seal, tis giving them right of passage."

The horsemen lowered their flintlocks and dismounted, then tied their horses to the horizontal post at the front of the inn.

The horseman gave the reeve back his parchment, "I suggest you steer clear of Leeds. The Roundheads have taken it; we only just escaped. They attacked us from both sides of the river, didn't stand a chance."

The three Royalist horsemen all walked down the cleared path toward the door of the inn. Just as they were about to enter, three musketeers appeared from behind a wall and fired at them. One of the horsemen screamed out, but it was too late. He was hit by the musket ball entering his breastplate, dropping him to the ground. The other two raised their flintlocks and aimed, but they were also dropped in a flurry of shots from behind.

John and Thomas jumped onto the back of the cart and hid down below the wooden side. In all the commotion and smoke from the musket fire, the reeve whipped the horse with the reins and galloped off down the road. Thomas looked back to see the musketeers standing over the limp, lifeless bodies; a pool of red started to spread out over the snow.

One of the soldiers looked up to see the cart race down the road; Thomas noticed a familiar face through the rising smoke; it was Captain Hodgson.

The captain walked out into the middle of the lane and took a few steps toward the fleeing cart trying hard to focus through the dim light on what he thought were familiar faces. He looked down puzzled, then turned back toward the inn to see a crowd gathering around the fallen, his men holding their arms out, trying to keep them back.

The captain walked back towards the dead men, "Take them out the back and give them a good burial. You, there, take three men and bring that cart back!" The captain ordered.

Three parliamentary soldiers disappeared down the lane beside the inn. A moment later, they could be seen galloping down the road in the direction of the fleeing cart.

Thomas could hear the hooves of the horses in the darkness, "QUICKLY THEY'RE GAINING ON US."

The reeve slapped the horse with the reins, but it was at full speed already with the weight of the four men. It wasn't long before the Roundheads caught up to them, calling for them to yield. The reeve pulled up on the reins, and the horse stopped.

The soldiers had their flintlocks out and pointed in the direction of the reeve and the steward. Thomas and John held up their hands.

One of the horsemen demanded, "TURN THE CART AROUND and head back to the inn. Captain Hodgson wants to have a word with ya."

The reeve did as he was ordered and gently pulled the reins to the left to guide the horse back from the direction they had come. They cantered back, one soldier in the front and one on either side of the cart still with their pistols drawn.

When the cart arrived back, the captain was waiting for them at the side of the road, "Would you mind telling me what you are doing here? Gentlemen, you should be more careful with the company you keep; we've been following these two since Tadcaster." The captain turned to look at the reeve and the steward, who had already had their hands bound and were kneeling in the snow.

Thomas looked at the reeve, then back at the captain, "Still trying to get back home, sir."

The captain looked down at his captives, "Take them out to the barn and tie them up, put a guard on them throughout the night."

"You two, take the cart and be on your way; I'll give you papers in case you're stopped by Parliamentary forces on the way home."

Thomas watched as the reeve and steward were escorted out the back out of sight.

"What will happen to those two?" asked Thomas in a way that made it sound as if he didn't care.

"Them, they'll be taken to York Castle Prison for questioning then probably hanged for treason."

The captain gave Thomas a parchment, "Now be on yer way, take the horse and cart before I have you put in uniforms." He smiled, turned and walked toward the door to the inn.

John and Thomas climbed up on the cart; John took hold of the reins and slapped the horse's hindquarters, making a clicking noise as he did. They rode for about twenty minutes, their way lit by the shine of the moon.

They rode for a while, saying nothing, then Thomas grabbed John's arm, "STOP WE HAVE TA GO BACK," yelled Thomas over the noise of the trotting horse.

John pulled on the reins halting the horse, "What da ya mean we have ta go back?"

Thomas spoke honestly and forthrightly, "We can't leave them there; he took a musket ball fer Tommy! I can't face Lucy or Isabel knowing that we left her father behind fer a-hangin', and the reeve he's been good to us over the years."

John rolled his eyes and shrugged his shoulders, then pulled the reins to turn the horse again, "You've done some crazy things in yer life, Thomas Rushworth, but this beats 'em all. We'll be lucky if we don't end up on the end of a rope ourselves, and to be honest, I think we're pushing our luck!"

They made their way back toward the inn, making sure not to take the horse and cart too close, but left it down a deserted lane just on the outskirts of the village. John and Thomas crept up to the side of the inn, and John peeked around. The inn was quiet, the music had stopped, and two Roundhead soldiers could be seen guarding the front door. Their silhouettes could be seen by the small fire that they had lit. John could hear their quiet chatter and complaints about the chill of the night and the length of the march.

John whispered, "Come on!" He turned and crept down the lane towards the barn. The large oak door was slightly ajar, and light emanated from a small fire inside.

John peeked inside the barn and could see the steward and reeve gagged and tied back-to-back to the same post their chins dropped and eyes closed. One Roundhead soldier sat beside the fire on a stool propped up with his back against the wheel of a carriage. His musket and sword were leaning against a spare wheel beside him. His head was leaning back, and his eyes were closed.

Thomas held his breath then looked in quickly then withdrew, "What now?"

John smiled and took a step in front of Thomas; he took his knife from his sheath and was about to creep into the barn.

"No!" Thomas put his hand on John's forearm then crept inside through the door. He paused, took one look back at John, then continued forwards slowly and quietly toward the soldier. On the way, he picked up a small log collected for the fire. He continued to creep toward the soldier slowly and stealthily, one step at a time, trying to limit the rustling of the straw beneath his feet. When he was within distance, he raised the log and brought it down swiftly and directly onto the top of the soldier's head. John, still peeking from behind the door, grimaced as he heard the thud and saw the soldier fall forward to the ground clumsily.

The noise caused the reeve and the steward to raise their heads. The steward who was facing Thomas wriggled to try to free himself from his binding but couldn't. The reeve facing the other way turned his head to see John Hargreaves walking quickly towards them. John took his knife and promptly cut them free, putting his finger up to his lips to warn them. The steward and the reeve rubbed their wrists and followed Thomas out of the barn. John stopped at the corner of the inn and peeked around to see the two soldiers still standing near the fire, chattering, unaware of what had taken place. Thomas gestured for the steward and the reeve to follow him down the road, their presence hidden by the veil of darkness.

Thomas and John jumped up into the driver's seat, and the other two men sat on the back of the cart. Silently and surreptitiously, they walked the horse down the lane. When they were far enough away, John slapped the horse's rear with the reins to speed up, and they continued east along Wetherby Road.

As they drove along the road near Weetwood, they came up over a rise and could see the light of a fire and several men sitting around it. One of the men hearing the horse, stood and picked up his musket. The other four men followed suit, spreading themselves and taking cover behind barrels and piled wooden logs across the road.

Thomas reached down and touched the reeve on the shoulder, "Aye up, we've got trouble, roadblock," he whispered.

The reeve and the steward sat up straight and looked forward perturbed by what they saw.

The steward and the reeve knelt and looked forward from the back of the cart as John slowed the horse to a walk. As they got closer, the soldier with the weapon walked out into the middle of the road and aimed his pistol at John. As the horse and cart got closer, the men behind the barricade started to aim their muskets nervously.

"STOP AND BE RECOGNISED," the soldier yelled. "What might you be doing out here in the middle of the night?"

"I am John Hargreaves, and this is Thomas Rushworth; we are farmers from the hamlet of Haworth returning home after a long journey. Please let us through."

"Aye, and what about the other two? He doesn't wear the clothes of a farmer," he pointed his pistol at the steward.

"I am the steward of Haworth Manor; these are my men, so please step aside and let us through; we mean no harm to you or your men."

"We are friends of Captain Hodgson and were of service to him at the siege of Bradford and have a parchment to prove it," agued Thomas confidently.

John Hargreaves reached into his tunic, which made one of the other soldiers nervous, so he raised his musket and cocked it. All heard it.

"EASY, for all I know, you could be Royalists, so I suggest you don't make any sudden movements or else me men will shoot."

John Hargreaves gently pulled out the parchment that Captain Hodgson had given them and held it up for all to see. One of the soldiers came out from behind his barrel and slowly walked up to the side of the cart. He looked at the reeve, and the steward then looked down to see that the cart was empty. He turned and walked back toward John, who was still holding the parchment aloft. The soldier, his flintlock at the ready, held out his hand and took the parchment. He walked back toward the other soldier and handed it to him.

The other soldier unrolled the parchment and turned the paper so that the light of the fire shone on it, "This is the captain's seal alright, okay, lower yer weapons and let them pass."

The rest of the men stood up from behind the blockade and lowered their arms. Two of them approached the middle of the blockade and started to remove the logs.

The soldier gave the parchment back to John Hargreaves, "Be on yer way and safe journey."

John Hargreaves flipped the reins and slowly guided the horse through the blockade as the other soldiers watched on.

Once through the blockade, Thomas looked back to see the soldiers gather around the fire again, rubbing their hands and stomping their feet to increase the circulation. He turned back around, then thought about the soldier back at the inn and felt a bit guilty, hoping that he hadn't killed him.

Fast Flight

Back at the inn, the soldier on the floor of the barn started to come around. He groaned and held the top of his head. He tried to sit up but was groggy and disorientated. Eventually, sitting up, he looked over to see that the prisoners had escaped. Groggily he stood up and staggered to the entrance of the bar holding the jam to steady himself. He staggered down the alley, using the wall to keep his balance.

Reaching the roadway, he hollered, "THEY'RE GONE, THE PRISONERS, THEY'RE GONE!"

He leaned against the wall holding the top of his head, knowing that he would later get a flogging for falling asleep and allowing them to escape.

Two guards picked up their muskets that were leaning against the wall and ran down the road, then around the corner awkwardly. They ran past the soldier who was still leaning against the wall rubbing his head and looking at the blood on his fingers.

They slowed as they approached the door of the barn and lifted their muskets. They walked into the barn cautiously and then noticed the cut bindings and picked up the bloodied log. "QUICK, WAKE UP THE CAPTAIN!"

One of the soldiers ran back to the door of the inn and ran up the stairs to the captain's room. He banged on the door, "CAPTAIN, CAPTAIN HODGSON, THEY'RE GONE, THE PRISONERS HAVE ESCAPED, CAPTAIN!" He continued to bang on the door until it opened.

"WELL, DON'T JUST STAND THERE, MAN, WAKE UP THE REST OF THE MEN!" The captain closed the door and quickly dressed himself, pulling on his long brown boots and donning his red coat.

He grabbed his sword and flintlock and quickly walked through the door and down the stairs.

The other soldier dropped the bloodied log and stood to attention, looking straight ahead as the captain walked past him. He walked over to the pole where the prisoners had been tied up and picked up the bindings looking at them inquisitively, noticing that they had been cut.

"THEY HAD HELP!" Bellowed Captain Hodgson, "TO HORSES!"

He turned to the soldier who was still standing to attention, "BREAK CAMP, ROUSE THE MEN AND READY THE HORSES!"

The soldier ran out of the barn and up the alley helping the injured soldier across the road to the camp. The troop had already woken and started breaking camp. The horses were bridled and men ready for the forced march just as the sun was starting to come up.

Captain Hodgson walked across the road to the camp; the soldiers stopped what they were doing and stood to attention.

He looked his soldiers up and down, "They can't be more than two or three hours ahead going west. LET US MAKE WAY!"

The captain looked at the soldier who was injured and walked up to him while the medic wrapped a linen bandage around his head. "You there what happened?"

"They got me from behind, sir, didn't see 'em coming."

"If they got you from behind, then why is the wound on the front of your skull? If I find out that you were sleeping, you'll get ten of the best."

"Aye, sir, no, I wasn't sleeping; it's all a blur," he said apologetically.

"SERGEANT PUT THIS SOLDIER ON REPORT; WE'LL DEAL WITH HIM LATER!"

The captain turned and walked away back towards the stairs of the inn; he went upstairs and quickly gathered his belongings, putting them in the leather bag that he lashed to the back of the horse. He ran down the stairs again and out to the horse enclosure, where he saddled his horse and mounted it. By the time he got back around to the front of the inn, his twenty-man troop had already lined up in rows of four and were ready to march. He rode up and positioned himself beside his sergeant, raised his hand and beckoned the troop forward.

The sun was lighting the horizon as the troop marched along Wetherby Road, then turned west on Tarn Lane, heading towards Moor Allerton.

The hedgerows at the side of the road were sprinkled with light powdered snow. The captain could see a farmhouse on the slopes of a small valley partly hidden by a heavy fog. Thick fleeced sheep grazed on wintery grasses that they excavated from the ice and snow.

The captain's horse sauntered on, moving its snout from side to side to readjust the bit. He turned around to look at his men. They were cold and tired, so he held up his fist, which was the signal for them to stop.

The captain turned to his sergeant, "Sergeant, rest the men, give them ten minutes to rest and eat."

The sergeant dismounted his horse, "RIGHT MEN YA HAVE TEN MINUTES."

Captain Hodgson dismounted and allowed his horse to forage for grass at the side of the road. He watched him as he scraped snow away then nibbled at the dormant yellow grass. He thought about the barn and how the prisoners had escaped; they had help. Then he thought about Thomas and John and shook his head, trying to put out of his mind that it may have been them. After all, they were travelling together when they were apprehended. *Could they all be Royalist spies, he thought to himself? No, impossible,* he shook his head and despatched the thought. *They wouldn't be able to get through the roadblock at Weetwood, the parchment that he had given to John Hargreaves, dammit. If they were all in this together, the parchment would allow them passage,* he thought. He became angry at himself, not used to making such errors in judgement.

Looking over the white field, he could see the tracks of a winter fox and thought of home. He hadn't been home to Halifax in so long since being drafted to the regiment of Colonel Forbes. He had been present at the battle of Leeds and Wakefield and now led his troop on the trail of Royalist spies. He was awoken from his thoughts by his sergeant, who yelled orders commanding the men of the troop to get back on their feet and get ready to march.

The captain grabbed the reins and mounted his horse once again; he raised his hand and beckoned the troop forward, then tapped the horse's ribs with his heels. His sergeant was the last to mount his horse then trotted past the troop to take up his position at the side of the captain.

It wasn't too long before they arrived at the roadblock at Weetwood; the soldiers guarding it came out to meet the troop. The captain stopped to talk to the sergeant in charge. "Two men, one dressed well, horse and cart have you seen them?" asked the captain dispensing with usual pleasantries.

The sergeant looked up, "Dressed well, no. Had a few clothiers a few farmers but nobody dressed well, wait." The sergeant walked over to his men and returned quickly, "There was one well dressed, but not two men; there were four. It was dark, but my corporal said this one man had a tunic of blue fabric; the only reason he remembered was that he thought it strange that two farmers were sitting up front and the man of means was sitting in the back of the cart."

"How long?" Asked the captain.

"Just before daybreak, they continued west," answered the sergeant worriedly, thinking he might get a whipping for letting them through.

The captain looked up at the blockade, "LET US PASS!"

The sergeant motioned to his men to move the logs in the blockade, and the troop moved forward.

Thomas and John had swapped places with the reeve and the steward, and they trotted along, keeping a watchful eye out for roadblocks and troops of any kind. The closer they got to home, the happier they felt.

Once on the other side of Headingly, the road became flat, and the reeve could pick up more speed, so he flicked the reins urging the horse to go faster. They arrived at Bingly at mid-day and rested the horse. It wasn't far now, and even though the horse struggled going uphill along Halifax Road, they knew it wouldn't be too long before they reached the Haworth moors. They passed the Fleece Inn and kept going west at Haworth Road past the divided fields and cottages. They passed clothiers transporting pack horses full of woven cloth on their way to the market at Bingly. Up they went, finally reaching Brow Top Road and the village of Flappit Spring. The horse began to labour under the weight of its burden and the steepness of the rise, so the reeve stopped and allowed Thomas and John to get off the cart and walk beside.

At the top of the hill, the reeve reined in the horse to rest a while. The steward stepped down carefully from the cart and walked to the side of the road. He looked over the fields and took a deep breath in, and then exhaled a steamy breath out. He looked down the hill from where they had come and felt a calmness fall over him being so close to home, but he was still troubled.

Thomas walked up quietly behind the steward; he could tell he was in deep thought, "What are we ta do about you and yer daughters?"

The steward heard his footsteps, "Nothing I can do, too much water under the bridge, best to let it go now."

"We have to do something, ain't right all this trouble with you and yer daughters not speaking."

The steward didn't turn to look at Thomas and dismissed his fleeting sentimentality.

"You have grandchildren, do you not want ta see them and young Isabel, her belly's full again. Named the first William."

"I know what their names are. I've seen them, seen them playing ball on yer land," the steward remarked.

"Well, do ya not want to come meet them, talk to them, ya can ya know, come to the cottage."

"No, it's been too long, too much water under the bridge. Lucy knows what I did or what I tried to do to your brother. Something I fully regret now."

"She'll also know what ya did fer Tommy, and for us when we get back, let me smooth the way fer ya."

The steward turned briefly and looked at Thomas but said nothing.

Thomas walked up and stood beside him, looking in the same direction, "You should see ya grandchildren and make peace with ya daughters; neither of us is getting any younger. Don't make the mistake of not healing the hurts before it's too late."

The steward kept looking out, deep in contemplation, "But I don't know how, never been so alone since me wife died and William, he'd never forgive me!"

"Them things are in the past," Thomas put his hand out.

John Hargreaves and the reeve looked on; they saw Thomas standing with his hand out toward the steward.

The steward turned and looked down at his hand, then back up into his eyes, then reached out and shook his hand, "I don't know if this will work, but if there's a chance my daughters will forgive me, then I'll do it."

Thomas shook his hand and smiled and turned to walk away, "besides, we're almost family!"

The steward looked up at him, "small steps Rushworth, small steps."

Thomas started walking back to the cart, a smile on his face.

Suddenly there was a loud blast from a musket, and the steward dropped to the ground clutching his stomach. Thomas looked down the road to see a musketeer reloading his musket just behind a tree in a space between the scrub.

"NOOOO!" Thomas ran back and knelt beside the steward, who held his stomach, blood oozing out between his fingers.

"STEWARD! HELP, QUICK HELP ME!" Thomas looked up to see several men surrounding the cart, flintlocks raised and aimed at the reeve and John Hargreaves, who raised his hands submissively.

One of the soldiers fired at the reeve, who clutched his chest and fell from the driver's seat to the ground with a thud.

"BAAASTARDS!" Thomas put his hand on the steward's hand, trying to stem the flow of blood.

The steward groaned and grimaced through his teeth, "No coming back from this one," he whispered softly.

"Noooo! Steward, we'll get ya home!"

The steward tried to raise his head off the ground, Thomas supported it with his other hand.

With a strained voice, the steward struggled to talk, "Tell Lucy.... and Isabel that I love them,..... always have, tell them I'm sorry, shouldn't have done what I did. Don't let the children...."

The steward went quiet mid-sentence; his head went limp in Thomas' hand, so he gently lowered it to the ground. The steward's eyes were open, but the last sign of life quickly left his body as a pool of blood started to spread across the snow. Thomas paused to look at the man that he had known since childhood and drew his hand down over his eyes to close them.

Just as he was about to stand, a flintlock was pressed against his temple. Thomas raised his hands, "I'm unarmed."

"I know you are." Captain Hodgson paused, then put his flintlock back under his belt, "Stand up, man! I told you to be careful who you associate with. These two escaped, injured one of my men, and I suppose you had nothing to do with it."

Sadly Thomas looked down at the steward, "He was family, me son's wife's father."

The captain looked down at the steward, "He was also a Royalist spy, and he should have known better than to take up arms for the King and betray us. Now, as fer you and your friend, you're lucky my man wasn't injured that badly or else you might be swinging from a rope yourself. I'm taking into consideration your assistance in Bradford, and I'm going to let you go, but you must swear to me that you go straight home."

"Never wanted ta take up arms in the first place," Thomas looked over sadly as John Hargreaves jumped from the cart and knelt beside the reeve who laid there motionless.

"He was a good man the reeve, didn't deserve this end," said Thomas sadly.

"Yes, there have been a lot of good men sent to their resting place in this war. Now give them a good burial and be on yer way," The captain jumped back on his horse that the sergeant had brought over and turned to lead his men who had formed rank and file. He raised his hand and gestured for his men to march. Thomas stood and watched as the troop marched down the hill.

John Hargreaves walked over to Thomas and watched as the captain and his men started marching down Haworth Road toward the Fleece Inn, "Reeve is dead!"

Thomas said nothing but looked at John, who shook his head slowly and then looked at the steward. They picked up the steward by the feet and shoulders and carried him over to the cart, placing him on the back carefully. They picked up the reeve and did the same, then covered them both with their blankets.

John jumped up into the driver's seat, "What are ya gonna say to Lucy and Isabel?"

Thomas jumped up on the cart beside him, "The truth that he died bravely and saved Tommy and was going to make amends for his ways. It's a terrible shame that he couldn't say it himself. He wasn't a bad man; just wanted the best for his family like all of us."

John looked melancholy, then flipped the reins and made a clicking noise to get the horse moving. The horse reared up a little, then moved forward slowly up Brow Top Road. They continued west along Bridgehouse Lane until they reached the manor, then turned south on Sun Street. They were in no rush, nor was the horse who just meandered at its own pace.

They passed the cottages on the right side of the road; some people came out and whispered as they saw the limp feet dangling over the edge of the back of the cart. Thomas and John kept looking forward but felt a little more uneasy as they drew closer to home. Thomas looked down into the valley towards Bridgehouse Beck. John pulled on the reins to halt the horse as they arrived at the bottom of the hide. They could see grey smoke billowing out of the cottage chimney, and the snow had started to melt with the winter sun. Thomas could see William's children, John and Robert, playing ball outside the cottage; they stopped what they were doing as one of them noticed the stationary cart.

Vacant Husband

Tommy would lie there looking up at the timbers and thatch saying nothing. She tried to speak to him, but she could tell there was something wrong as he would not respond. He laid there, arms at his sides, staring upwards.

It was on the third day that William climbed up the ladder and sat down on the edge of the straw mattress beside him. "Tommy, we have to get you up to face the day. It's not good locking everybody out like this."

Tommy continued to look up at the thatch and said nothing.

"Come on, Tommy, let's get ya up," William carefully took hold of his arm and put his hand under his back to lift him up.

William could feel the ribs through the undershirt, and his frozen stare was off-putting.

Tommy cooperated but said nothing and continued to look ahead. William helped him to put on his hose, tied his leggings and helped him raise himself from the bed. Tommy walked to the ladder, turned and slowly descended. Isabel, Lucy and Agnes were busy with the hand-weaving but watched Tommy descend then walk over to his father's chair by the fire. He sat and stared into the flames, and there he stayed. When William came down, he looked at Isabel and shrugged his shoulders, rolling his eyes in confusion.

Sometime later, wee Will came in from playing outside; he walked up to his father, looked up at him and put his hand on his knee. Isabel smiled and waited for Tommy to show him some affection. Tommy looked down at Will, then at his hand on his knee, then returned his gaze to the fire. Annoyed, Isabel walked over and picked him up, embracing him, then putting him down, opening the door and ushering him back outside.

She turned angrily back towards Tommy and took a step toward him with her hands on her hips, "WHAT'S WRONG WITH YA TOMMY? You can't be treatin' yer' son like that, tis bad enough you've been gone all this time and now to treat him like he's not there!"

Tommy slowly looked up at her, said nothing and continued to stare into the flames.

Agnes halted her hand spinning and walked over to Isabel, who continued to look at Tommy in disgust. She put her hand lovingly on Isabel's arm, "Easy pet, he needs time, that's all, just give him some time. Who knows what horrors he's been through?"

Lucy continued her sewing; she watched on then looked at William, who was confused by the whole situation. He walked over to the jug and poured himself and Tommy a jack of ale, walking over and holding it out for him. Tommy ignored his gesture and continued to stare into the flames. William shook his head, skulled his ale and Tommy's, then turned, took out his pipe and walked outside.

Tommy sat there until evening; he said nothing, ate nothing and drank nothing.

Isabel was scaping some leather from the last sheep they had butchered. She stopped what she was doing, looked at Tommy, put her hands to her face and wept; she whispered, "I want my husband back!"

Agnes stood and walked over to her placing her hand on her shoulder, "There, there pet, everything will be alright; look, I'll walk into the village tomorrow and talk to the vicar. He'll know what ta do."

The following day Agnes milked the cow and collected the eggs, then walked to Saint Michael and All Angels. She walked up the path and knocked on the vicarage door. It was a substantial stone building with a grey thatched roof that needed some repair and a large white oak door. After some time, she could hear murmurings inside and then the door opened slightly.

The curate appeared looking somewhat confused and still tired from the night's slumber, "Agnes Rushworth, what brings you here at this time of the day?"

"I need to see the vicar, tis urgent!" Agnes demanded.

The curate looked inside, "His holiness is barely up, hasn't had his constitutional yet."

"As I said, it's very urgent!" Agnes reiterated.

"WHAT IS IT, NATHANIEL? Let the poor women in," said the vicar from inside.

The vicar's assistant opened the door wider and stepped aside to let Agnes through, then closed the door quickly to stop the draught from coming in.

The vicar sat on a high-backed chair near the hearth and rose to greet Agnes, "Mrs Rushworth, what brings you to the rectory on this fine winter's morning? Please sit down."

The vicar gestured for his visitor to be seated on the other chair.

The room was massive in size, with large oak beams running horizontally from one side of the room to the other and an even larger beam running centrally down the middle of the room. The inglenook fireplace was at the centre, which held a large oak lintel. There was a sizable stone chimney and two bread ovens on either side of it. One of the arched openings had sooty traces from the flames and smoke of a previous fire. A wrought iron candle stand held two large church candles in the corner that dripped wax onto the stone floor. The room was simply furnished with a table, two chairs, benches and a stool. All manner of equipment dangled from the walls, including baskets and metal pot covers. A darkened set of worn, thick oak stairs made their way up to the second floor.

Agnes sat at the chair beside the fire, "Vicar, I'm so sorry to disturb you at this time of the day, but it's Tommy; he's not right in the head. He returned some days ago and won't eat, drink or speak, spends his days sittin' by the fire."

"Mmm, is he injured?"

"Well, he's got cuts and bruises, but no serious harm has come to him. William found him at the Kings Arms didn't even want to come home."

"And what of Thomas," The vicar asked.

Agnes dropped her gaze in sadness, "My Thomas and John Hargreaves havn't been seen or heard of these past weeks. We fear for them greatly."

"Agnes, you are to return to Hall Green and wait for me. I will visit thee upon the hour and bless Tommy and once again deliver him unto the Lord."

Agnes stood and looked at the vicar garrulously, "Ah bless yer vicar."

The vicar turned to his assistant, "Nathaniel, get my cloak and prepare the cart; we leave at once."

The vicar's assistant walked Agnes to the door and opened it for her to step outside. She walked down Church Street past the church, then turned right on Main Street and headed for home. It was an icy cold day, so she pulled her cloak around her tightly and walked quickly but steadily, ensuring her balance on the icy road. She thought about Thomas and worried, wishing that he'd never left. *Where could he be?* she thought to herself and tried to dismiss her worries.

An hour later, there was a knock at the door, and they all stood in expectation of the vicar's arrival.

The vicar ducked his head going through the door. He was wearing his black cassock, white gown, and dark tippet draped over his shoulders and holding his King James Bible, "Now, where is this young man that troubles his mother so much?"

Agnes looked at Tommy, who was sitting by the fire still gazing at the flames. He was the only person in the room that didn't turn to look at the visitor.

The vicar walked towards him, but Tommy didn't move. He sat there mesmerised. Agnes, Isabel and Lucy looked on as William brought a chair over for the vicar to be seated opposite Tommy.

As the vicar walked over, he sprinkled holy water in the direction of Tommy, some of it hissing as it landed on the hearth. He opened his bible and started to read while standing over Tommy.

> *"Lord God, whose Son, Jesus Christ,*
> *understood people's fear and pain*
> *before they spoke of them, we pray for*
> *those in need that may have strayed from*
> *your path; surround the frightened*
> *with your tenderness; give strength*
> *to those in pain; hold the weak in your*
> *arms of love, and give hope and patience*
> *to those who are recovering; we ask this*
> *through the same Jesus Christ, our Lord."*

Tommy sat there with disregard staring through the vicar, his face expressionless.

The vicar walked closer and took a bottle of oil from his assistant, who had been standing behind him with his hands clasped as in prayer. The vicar turned the small bottle upside down and poured a small quantity of oil on his finger.

He touched Tommy's forehead with his finger, anointing it with the sign of the cross,

> *"Lord, Holy Father, giver of health*
> *and salvation, as your apostles*
> *anointed those who were sick and*
> *healed them, so continue the ministry*
> *of healing in your Church. Sanctify*
> *this oil, that those who are anointed*
> *with it may be freed from suffering and*
> *distress, find inward peace and know*
> *the joy of your salvation, through your*
> *Son, our Saviour Jesus Christ. Amen."*

Tommy just sat there.

The vicar bent down and whispered, "Tommy, will you accept the love of the Lord in Christ's name?" The vicar said another prayer, but there was still no change in his disposition.

Isabel seeing this put her hands to her face and wept while Agnes and Lucy walked to her and tried to console her by putting their arms around her shoulder, "Lucy, take Isabel outside while I speak to the vicar."

The vicar turned from Tommy to face Agnes, "Mrs Rushworth, I have grave fears for your son; it seems God is punishing him for his sins. He must give his love unto the Lord by observing a strict fast and limit his diet to blessed water, salt, and vegetables and that he abstains from the marital act."

"Vicar, what's wrong with him?" she whispered.

The vicar took off his black biretta and stooped to whisper, "Mrs Rushworth, I'm afraid he is under the devil's control, and he must be cleansed both physically and spiritually to drive out the demon."

The vicar looked at his assistant, who nodded, turned and walked outside to the cart. He returned a short time later with a brown, worn drawstring bound pouch and gave it to the vicar.

The vicar kissed the embellished cross on the front of it, "Mrs Rushworth, we must get Tommy more settled on a mattress on the floor, preferably in front of the fire."

William unrolled the mattress by the wall; Agnes picked it up and placed it on the straw-covered floor near the fire.

William walked over to Tommy and assisted him over to the

mattress, where he laid down on his back and stared up at the thatch, "Come on, nephew, let's get you better."

With no doctor in the village, the vicar was the next best thing, and he was called upon when ailments threatened the health of his parishioners. He thought that the ailment troubling Tommy was sin but also an excess of blood.

While William and Agnes looked on, the vicar took off his white gown and dark tippet and rolled up his sleeves. He then opened the leather pouch and brought out a fleam, a small sharp, pointed blade with a tortoiseshell case. He took a small piece of rope and tied it just above Tommy's elbow. Then he held his arm below and made a small incision in the large vein in the crease of the elbow. It started to bleed profusely, then the assistant placed a small bowl underneath to catch the blood. The vicar began to squeeze his arm to speed up the process. Once the bowl was full, his assistant removed it and replaced it with an empty one from the leather pouch.

Agnes raised her hand to her mouth in astonishment as Tommy just laid there quietly. Ten minutes later, Tommy's eyes closed, so the vicar took a white linen cloth and wiped his arm, then putting pressure on the wound to stem the flow of blood.

"He is weak, so he will sleep now. You and your family members must spend the next days and nights with him, saying prayers and having Godly conversations. This will drive the evil from him and wipe away the sin that troubles him. If he does not return from the devil's abyss by tomorrow, then we must take more drastic measures."

The vicar rolled down his sleeves, and his assistant helped him dress, "May God be with you." The vicar made the sign of the cross. He looked once more at Tommy, then turned toward the door, "I will return tomorrow."

William opened the door for the vicar and his assistant, who followed while Agnes took the bloodied bowls and washed them, pouring cold water from a bucket.

"Aint never seen anything like that before," said William looking down at Tommy's lifeless body.

Agnes walked over and knelt, wiping Tommy's forehead with a wet cloth, a tear formed in the corner of her eye and pooled in her bottom eyelid, then slowly cascaded down the side of her face; she quietly whispered,

*"The Lord is my shepherd;
I shall not want. He maketh me
to lie down in green pastures:
he leadeth me beside the still
waters. He restoreth my soul:
he leadeth me in the paths of
righteousness for His name's
sake. Yea, though I walk through
the valley of the shadow of death,
I will fear no evil: for thou art with
me; thy rod and thy staff they comfort me...."*

William, not quite as pious as his brother's wife, preferred to say his prayers at church. He walked over to the ale jug and poured himself a jack, then returned to the fire and the willow basket that he had started earlier. He looked over at Agnes, who continued her prayer.

*"Thou preparest a table before me
in the presence of mine enemies:
thou anointest my head with oil;
my cup runneth over. Surely
goodness and mercy shall follow
me all the days of my life: and I
will dwell in the house of the
Lord forever. Amen."*

The door opened, and in walked Lucy and Isabel, who, after seeing Agnes praying, thought the worst and started to cry.

"It's alright, pet, he's just sleeping, the vicar has been tending to him, should be right as rain in a few days, so don't ya worry yerself. Tell her William."

"Yer, Agnes is right. The vicar said he'd be right in a few days; he's coming back tomorra."

"We have ta say prayers and have Godly conversations with him while he gets better," demanded Agnes, purposely leaving out the part about driving out the evil.

Isabel walked over and pulled out a stool to sit beside Tommy; she looked down at him, longingly waiting for him to wake. He looked pale, and his breathing was slight and laboured.

Agnes watched her, "It's alright, pet, a couple more days, and he will be back to us."

The following day the vicar returned and spoke to William outside before going in, "Vicar, he hasn't moved."

Worriedly the vicar looked at his assistant, "No change, then we need to resort to more drastic measures. There is only one other way to get rid of this demon that hides in him. Go inside and sit him in a chair."

The vicar whispered to his assistant then went inside. He looked at Agnes and Isabel, who had both been awake all night praying beside him. They both looked weary and fearful.

William and Agnes sat Tommy in a hard-backed wooden chair. The assistant took the vicar's cloak, and once again, he rolled up his black sleeves. The assistant took out some rope from the brown, worn drawstring bound pouch and started to tie Tommy's hands together at the back of the chair. The vicar, meanwhile, took out his bottle of holy oil and made the sign of the cross once again on Tommy's forehead. Tommy stared forwards blankly.

The vicar cleared his throat and looked down, holding out his Bible in front of him.

> *"Our Lord Jesus Christ, present*
> *with us now in his risen power,*
> *enter into your body and spirit,*
> *take from you all that harms and*
> *hinders you and fill you with his*
> *healing and his peace. Christ be*
> *with you: Christ within you; Christ*
> *before you: Christ behind you; Christ*
> *on your right: Christ on your left; Christ*
> *above you: Christ beneath you; Christ*
> *around you: now and ever."*

Holding his Bible in his left hand, the vicar brought his right hand back across his chest and slapped Tommy across his face with the back of his hand.

All in the room were astonished, especially Isabel, who screamed, "NOO TOMMY!"

She was about to walk over to him protectively, but William stopped her by grabbing her around the shoulders, "Let him go, Isabel; it's his only hope!"

Agnes frowned, "Is this really necessary, vicar?"

Tommy's head was smacked to the side, but he said nothing and slowly returned his blank gaze to the front. A small drop of blood started to dribble from his nose.

The vicar looked down at his Bible once again,

> *"Almighty God, heavenly Father,*
> *breathe your Holy Spirit into*
> *the heart of this your servant*
> *Tommy and inspire him with*
> *love for goodness and truth.*
> *May he, fearing only you,*
> *have no other fear; knowing*
> *your compassion, be ever*
> *mindful of your love; and*
> *serving you faithfully unto death,*
> *live eternally with you; through*
> *Jesus Christ, our Lord. Amen."*

Holding his Bible in his left hand, the vicar brought his right hand back across his chest and slapped Tommy across his face with the back of his hand again, shocking all in the room.

Tommy had a look of desperation but said nothing. He slowly returned his blank gaze to the front.

CHAPTER THIRTY
Dying Soul

William's children were playing ball outside the cottage; they stopped what they were doing as John noticed the stationary cart at the bottom of the hill.

Robert also stopped to see what his brother was looking at. He put his hand up to shield his eyes from the sun, then called out, "Da, there's somebody at the bottom of the hide."

William stepped through the doorway of the cottage and shielded his eyes from the sun, trying to focus his eyes on the cart and those sitting atop of it. He called out, "AGNES YOU BETTER COME OUT HERE QUICK!"

Agnes walked out and tried to see what everybody was looking at, 'What's going on?"

John Hargreaves sat atop the cart and looked up to see the Rushworth cottage and the family waiting outside; he waved. "Go on, Thomas, I'll take care of these two."

Thomas jumped from the cart as the horse stepped backwards to readjust to the lightened load. He could see Agnes waiting at the door of the cottage waving.

"I will come to see you tomorrow; I'll take these two to the manor."

"Right, you are John, regards to Mrs Hargreaves," he climbed over the dry bap wall and started walking up the hill toward the cottage.

John flipped the reins and made a clicking noise to get the horse moving. The horse reared up a little then moved slowly forward.

John rode down Sun Street and arrived at the manor. He made his way down the driveway slowly and pulled up at the back of the manor.

Lord Birkhead's new reeve heard the cart and came out of the barn and walked slowly toward it, noticing the feet dangling from the back. He jumped up on the cart and removed the blanket from the faces of the steward and the reeve. Their faces were cold and paste-like, and it saddened him.

The new reeve looked at John then jumped down, "Wait here."

A few minutes later, the reeve returned, Lord Birkhead followed him through the back door. His lordship walked slowly over to the cart with his new steward following closely behind. The three of them looked over the side of the cart at the two bloodied figures in the back.

Lord Birkhead looked up and down at John, who had jumped down from the driver's seat and bowed in front of him. "Welcome back, John Hargreaves. I feel you have much to say and much to tell; now follow me inside, for I would like to hear the stories you have."

Lord Birkhead turned and walked toward the back door, then stopped without turning around, "Reeve have these men taken inside to the chapel, readied for burial and notify the vicar."

"YES, MY LORD," he bowed respectfully.

The reeve climbed up on the back of the cart and, with the help of the stable hand, grabbed the body by the shoulders and hauled it off, setting it as carefully as they could on the ground then replacing the blood-stained blanket, so their faces were covered.

The new steward walked quickly in front of his lordship to open the door for him, and John followed behind. The kitchen maids and the cook stopped what they were doing, turned and solemnly bowed in the lord's presence.

His lordship walked toward the parlour, and once again, the steward walked quickly to open the door for him then ensured he followed him into the room before John.

Lord Birkhead poured two silver goblets of imported wine for himself and John Hargreaves, "STEWARD LEAVE US."

The steward bowed reluctantly and removed himself from the room, closing the door slowly and quietly behind him but being sure to linger a while outside to eavesdrop on the conversation.

Lord Birkhead placed a goblet of wine on the table, "Please, sit John Hargreaves, tell me of your story."

John was seated, "My Lord, you honour me so!"

His lordship sat at the regal-looking, oak carved chair at the end of the table, "John Hargreaves, I have heard of your grandson's plight, and his recent ailments now tell me his story."

John was shocked by his lordship's interest and empathy, "Your lordship, the tales I have ta tell you would shock anybody. My recount is not one from me but from those who lived and fought with him. My grandson is, in fact, a hero having fought at the battle of Tadcaster and being a prisoner of the Royalists who captured him."

John Hargreaves told his story to the lord, and he listened intently, especially to the part the steward played in it.

His lordship finished his wine, "This is a very sad day, and you must be exhausted from your journey, so please go and tend to yourself and your family. My steward will take care of the other matter."

John stood and bowed as his lordship called for the steward who escorted him back through the kitchen.

John jumped up on the cart again and slowly made his way down the drive to Sun Street and Moorhouse Lane and home. While he was riding along, he recounted the last weeks and felt so glad that the journey was at an end.

There was the smell of Spring in the air, and the moors had started to come alive with the return of the curlews and lapwings to breed. The wind was still icy, and the dormant heather tried its best to shed the iciness and remnants of snow, which stubbornly persevered. John was warmed by the "p'weet," p'weet" call of the curlew as if signalling to all that Winter was nearly over. He knew that it wouldn't be long before the hills would be full of young lambs, and of course, the tending to the hide would start all over again.

Mrs Hargreaves walked out the door and around the back of the cottage to get some dried peat. Just before she was about to walk back inside, she lifted her head and noticed the cart and stood silently. She dropped the peat and started walking slowly toward it. Margaret waved and called out to John excitedly, who by this time had jumped off the cart and was slowly leading the horse with its halter.

"JOHN, JOHN MY LOVE," she called out as she quickened her pace.

As they met, John dropped the horse's halter, and they embraced one another. It was a long embrace full of old-time love and devotion.

Margaret, still embracing and with her head against his chest, "Husband, you've been gone so long, I feared the worse!"

"Aye, didn't quite make it ta Sunday prayers like I said I would, but I'm home now that's all that matters," John smiled.

Margaret turned and put her arm in his, "Come on, love, let's get ya inside for some grub; where on earth did ya get the horse and cart from?"

John replied, "It's a long story," he paused then sadly recounted the events that led to the steward and reeve's demise. "Tis the steward and the reeve shot by Roundheads as Cavalier spies. I've taken their bodies to the manor."

Mrs Hargreaves noticed the blood in the cart, "My goodness! Oh no, does Lucy know?"

John and Thomas had agreed not to tell her until the time was right, "The last thing he said to Thomas was, tell Lucy and Isabel I love them."

"Oh, John, that's sa sad," replied Margaret.

Arriving at the cottage, John tied the horse's halter to the tree, and they both walked up to the cottage door and went inside, "By Christ tis good to be home."

"Come, love, you sit down. I'll make ya some grub; you must be starving." Mrs Hargreaves walked over to the cauldron over the fire and ladled some potage into a wooden bowl.

John took off his cloak and hat and sat in his favourite high-backed chair beside the fire, taking out his clay pipe and stuffing it full of tobacco. He picked up a small twig from the hearth and placed the tip into the flame, allowing it to catch alight before raising it to the barrel of his pipe and began slowly drawing on it. He slowly puffed until the tobacco caught, and he was satisfied with the ember. He took the wooden bowl from his wife and, placing his pipe momentarily on the table beside him, put a spoonful of pottage in his mouth. He paused after the first mouthful, "Mmm, been a while since I've had some good home-cooked grub."

Mrs Hargreaves smiled as she placed a tankard of ale on the table beside him then sat in the other chair opposite him, "You must tell me the stories you have, but first, there is some sad news that I must speak of."

John looked at her with concern waiting for her reply…

Margaret had a panicked tone in her voice, "Tis Tommy he's not right in the head, hasn't spoken since he got back."

John placed the bowl and spoon on the table beside him and stood, "I must go to him."

"Well, I'm coming with ya," Mrs Hargreaves took her cloak from the nail beside the door and put it around her shoulders.

John picked up his cloak and did the same; grabbing his felt hat, he lifted the latch on the door and opened it for Mrs Hargreaves to walk through.

He followed quickly behind her as she started walking down the path toward the cart.

CHAPTER THIRTY-ONE

Home

Agnes started walking toward him, picking up speed the closer she got, "THOMAS! THOMAS! You're home," she put her arms out and embraced him as he did her.

Thomas gave her a slight squeeze, as happy to see her as she was to see him, but then realising where they were, dropped his arms, "Come on, love, don't get soppy now."

Agnes smiled, turned to a frown and let go her embrace, "Thomas, you must come quickly, tis Tommy there's something wrong, the vicar...."

On hearing this, Thomas walked past Agnes and quickly up the hill toward William and the cottage. As he neared, he could hear the vicar inside praying and Isabel sobbing. He had a concerned look on his face and walked past William, who tried to explain what was going on.

William tried to interject, "Thomas, the vicar, says he has ta get rid of the evil in him...."

Thomas brushed past him, fearing the worst.

Just as he entered the open door, the vicar let go with another backhander across Tommy's bruised and swollen face, "Be gone demon,

Our Lord Jesus Christ, present
with us now in his risen power,
enter into your body and spirit,
take from you all that harms
and hinders you,
and fill you with his
healing and his peace."

Thomas looked at his son, "WHAT THE BLAZES IS GOING ON?"

The vicar was shocked to see Thomas standing there at the door, "Thomas Rushworth, your back, thank the heavens...... we are trying to save your son's soul and rid his body of the evils that consume him."

"WHAT BY BEATING HIM?" Thomas growled.

He walked over to Tommy and undid his tied hands. He put his arm under his shoulder and around his back and helped him stand, and walked him over to the other high-backed chair by the fire. He gently let him down and turned, "ISABEL get some cold water and tend to these cuts and bruises."

Thomas turned to the vicar with a scowl on his face, his eyes squinting, and his face full of rage, "RIGHT I WANT YOU AND YOUR SERVANT OUT OF HERE AND DON'T COME BACK!"

"Mr Rushworth, we must drive the demon from his body or else he will be lost to Satan forever. Only God's word will cure him. WE MUST PRAY FOR HIS SOUL!"

Thomas turned to look at William, disgusted that he had let this go on, then back at the vicar, "NOW YOU LOOK HERE, THERE'LL BE NO MORE OF THIS SO PICK YERSELF UP AND GET OUT!"

"But Thomas, you don't understand...." The vicar tried to explain but could see the rage in Thomas' face.

"OUT!" Thomas started slowly walking toward the vicar menacingly.

The curate picked up the vicar's cloak and started walking back towards the door.

Just as they reached the open door, Agnes appeared, puffed from the exertion of walking up the hill.

"OUT!" Thomas was still walking slowly toward the vicar, his hands beside him tensed into fists.

"THOMAS! HE'S JUST TRYING TO HELP HIM," Agnes yelled.

Thomas continued to stare at the vicar, "YOU STAY OUT OF THIS WIFE!"

The vicar, feeling threatened, "Mrs Rushworth, will you please talk some sense into your husband?"

"OUT!" Thomas yelled again.

With all the commotion, wee Will started to cry, so Isabel walked over and picked him up. "There, there Will pay no mind." She sat down on one of the stools and gently rocked him back and forth. Isabel undid the leather ties on her bodice and loosened the blouse to reveal a large brown teat which she quickly guided to the infant's mouth. Will moved his head toward it until he latched on and started to feed. Isabel looked down lovingly as he continued to suckle.

The vicar raised his hand and made the sign of the cross in mid-air in front of Thomas, then stepped through the doorway quickly.

Agnes pleaded with him, "Thomas, what 's got into ya?"

Thomas looked at Agnes, "HOW THE BLOODY HELL COULD YOU LET HIM DO THIS TO OUR SON? LOOK AT HIM. HIS FACE IS A MESS!"

Thomas then turned his attention to William, "YOU SHOULD BE BLOODY WELL ASHAMED OF YOURSELF FOR LETTING THIS HAPPEN WILLIAM!"

William looked at Tommy, whose eyes were swollen and closed. Agnes was slowly dabbing his bruised face and wiping the trail of blood that ran down his chin from his nose.

William looked at Thomas and remarked defensively, "WELL HOW WAS I TO KNOW THE WAYS OF THE LORD? IT WAS THE VICAR'S DECISION, NOT MINE!"

Thomas walked over to Tommy and knelt down in front of him, "You all right, son?"

Tommy looked at him blankly through his almost closed and swollen eyes but said nothing.

"William, help me, let's get him up ta bed," Thomas lifted Tommy and slung his arm over his shoulder.

William put his arm around Tommy's waist and helped get Tommy up the loft ladder.

Agnes looked at Lucy, now was comforting John and Robert, who had heard the commotion and had come inside.

"I've never seen him so angry," claimed Lucy.

"Aye, best take the boys ta Mrs Hargreave's until things have quietened down."

"Right ya are then, come on boys," Lucy led the boys outside and started walking down the hill.

William climbed down the ladder; he looked at Agnes then shrugged his shoulders. William walked over to the jug of ale, picked it up, then carried it outside, slamming the heavy oak door behind him.

Thomas sat on the stool beside Tommy and tucked the wool blanket under his chin, "What on earth have they done to you, my son?"

Tommy laid there, his eyes and cheekbones swollen and red. Some of the darkness had gone from under his eyes, but his face still looked gaunt and malnourished. He looked up at the thatch ceiling then a single tear pooled in his eye and dripped across the side of his face.

"Come on, son, we're gonna get ya better," Thomas stood but crouched as he walked to the top of the ladder and called out, "Agnes bring a bowl of pottage."

A few moments later, Agnes' face appeared at the top of the ladder and placed a steaming bowl on the loft floor. Thomas walked over, picked it up and returned to Tommy's side. He put the bowl on the small wooden table beside him that held the candle and lifted Tommy's head up. "Come on, son, let's get some grub in ya. You must eat to get your strength back."

Thomas had heard about the poor harvests and lack of food supplies

He spooned some pottage and carefully lifted it to his cracked lips, slowly pouring it in. Tommy swallowed then coughed, his eyes did not focus, but Thomas could tell he was with him. He took another spoonful, then another and another until the bowl was empty. Then Thomas laid his head back down on the straw pillow and walked to the ladder. Before descending, he took one last look at Tommy's face, his eyes were closed, but he could see him breathing slowly in the light of the candle.

Thomas turned to look at Agnes as he descended the ladder, "Where's William?"

Agnes was annoyed, "Grabbed the jug and left."

"I'll go find him," Thomas replied, feeling a bit guilty about how he had spoken to his brother.

"No, let him be husband you've said and done enough, he's been worried sick about ya, been moping round here fer weeks. I had to do all I could to stop him from leaving and coming to look fer ya! Then when you do get back, you treat him like shite."

Thomas felt even more guilty, "I'm sorry, Agnes, I was just worried about Tommy, that's all!"

"Well, don't ya think we were? That's why we called the vicar. Said Tommy had committed sins, and this was God's punishment, said he had to get the evil out of him. He's been treating him for the past three days doing all sorts. Now I won't be able to face him in church!"

Thomas lowered his voice, "We been following Tommy's trail for the past four weeks, thought he was killed at the battle of Tadcaster until we met up with the steward and the reeve, and they told us he was on his way home."

Agnes stopped what she was doing and looked up, shocked, "Steward and the reeve?"

Thomas shook his head slowly, "Aye, I've got some bad news...

Steward and the reeve...well... they're gone, both dead shot by Roundheads."

"Dead? Oh my, what will we tell Lucy?" Agnes fretted and thought about how they would break the news.

Thomas sat down, "There's something else..., he...the steward... saved Tommy. Cavaliers were taking him to Pontefract Castle prison. He took a musket ball for him. It's so sad, he was going to make up with Lucy and Isabel on his return. We patched him up, and we were travelling together to get home, then we got ambushed by Roundheads who shot both he and the reeve as Royalist spies."

Agnes put her hand to her mouth worriedly, then paused, "We have ta tell Lucy," she whispered sadly. "I don't know how much more sadness she can take; she lost the baby."

Agnes looked at Thomas sympathetically, then explained to him what had happened. "It was a long labour, a breech birth, and the baby were born feet first with the cord wrapped around its neck. I tried to save it, but his face was blue, and it died. William raced to the vicar, but the baby, a boy, died before the vicar could arrive and baptise him. Couldn't give him a Christian burial."

Agnes continued, "She started bleeding and purging and was very weak, could have died herself, but the churching saved her. After that, Isabel and I helped her fight through her melancholy days during her lying in. She didn't eat, drink or say anything for two weeks. The walk to Michael and All Angels every day wasn't easy for her, and William didn't want a part of it; he spent days with his head in the ale jug and often didn't even come home."

Thomas looked down sadly and apologetically, "Wife, I must find William," Thomas grabbed his cloak that he had hurriedly thrown on the form by the door and stepped out.

He knew where William had gone and the smashed clay jug on Main Street had confirmed his suspicions. Walking up the hill, he could see the steeple of Michael and All Angels. He felt glad to be home, but the rift between him and his brother was not going to be easy to repair after his tantrum.

As he ducked his head to go into the door of the Kings Arms, he allowed his eyes to adjust to the dim light then he saw William, standing at the bar with a tankard of ale.

William noticed him come in through the door but ignored him occupying himself by taking the tankard to his lips and guzzling it all down, "Another barkeep!"

Thomas walked over to stand beside him but said nothing and looked at the barkeep, "Make that two."

William kept looking ahead but could sense that Thomas was waiting to say something to him.

Thomas looked forward and took a deep breath, then exhaled and whispered, "Brother, I'm sorry about the baby...and fer what I said back home, it wasn't right! I was dreadfully wrong, brother."

William quickly turned to look at him, angry, "No, it wasn't, I was trying to help him, and I thought the vicar knew what he was doing." William paused, realising how angry he sounded; he paused, "How is he?"

Thomas put his hand on William's shoulder. "Sleeping, he just needs time, that's all, been through a bit our Tommy, almost died of the pocks then got taken captive by Cavaliers. They were taking him to Pontefract Castle prison until the steward stepped in."

William turned quickly, "The steward?"

Thomas conveyed to William what the reeve had told him, "Tommy got the sickness, steward paid for his lodging until he could get better. Took a musket ball in the shoulder for him and helped him escape from the Cavaliers. If it weren't for the steward and the reeve, he wouldn't have made it, I'm sure of it."

Thomas quietly began to recount the stories of atrocities he had heard while on the road, "Twenty-five prisoners slaughtered in cold blood at Hopton Castle, twelve prisoners to whom quarter had been granted, stripped and stabbed to death, some troops quartered in the home of a Berkshire resident took their servant from her bed and raped her. Royalist soldiers assaulted women and forced them into the river, where many drowned."

One of the men sitting close by was trying to eavesdrop on their conversation and then leaned forward and whispered to his mate.

"Well, that's just barbaric. What happened to honour and the rules of war!" William looked ahead again and took a swig from the tankard that the barman had just placed down in front of him. He placed a penny down on the bar for payment.

The barkeep picked it up and handed it back, "No need, those two strangers there, they paid for it."

William and Thomas turned around to look. Two soldiers lifted their tankards to acknowledge them. One of them was wearing a wide-brimmed black hat with a bright orange plumb protruding from his hatband; a flintlock pistol dangled from his waist, and he rested his hand on the hilt of a sword that he held in front of him. He wore a brown buff coat with a bright white laced collar folded over the neckline. His brown breeches rested on the top of his downturned leather riding boots.

William and Thomas returned the gesture and took a swig. William walked over toward them, "My sincerest thanks for your generosity, sir, do I know thee? You are not from parts hereabouts."

"No, my esteemed friend Smythe and I are here on an errand. We look for a friend that was of some service to us back in Bramham," said the stranger with a rather posh southern accent.

William was feeling uneasy in the presence of the two men. He looked at the stranger suspiciously as Thomas walked over and stood behind him, "Everything orl right William?"

William turned to look at Thomas, "Everything's fine; these gentlemen are looking for somebody, a friend they knew from Bramham."

Thomas felt uneasy, "Oh... and what friend might that be? It's obvious yer not from round here, and people hereabouts don't like strangers who ask too many questions, ain't that right barkeep?" Thomas called out purposefully.

The barkeep, an avid member of the lord's clubmen, slowly reached his hand below the level of the bar to place his hand on the hunting flintlock he hid there.

Sergeant Walker and Smythe stood and raised their hands, "Please, gentlemen, we are just weary travellers looking for a friend. There is no need for. ... complications," replied Walker.

With their hands raised, both men took two slow steps toward the door. Smythe turned to look at the barkeep, "Good sir, please take your hand from the weapon, for we depart and bid you a good day. It seems we may have been wrong, and our friend is no longer in these parts."

William and Thomas nervously stood aside and let the two men pass. Before exiting, Sergeant Walker turned his head to take one more look at Thomas before going out into the daylight.

Walker whispered, "He's here, and the older one even looks like him," stated the sergeant.

Smythe kept walking, "Nooo, couldn't be that lucky, it's a long shot."

"I'm telling you, he's the spitting image of him; I bet they're related."

Sergeant Walker smiled, "They're probably all related around here, bloody heathens."

"Hahaha, right you are. Come on, let's get the horses and pay a visit to the lord of the manor. He'll know more."

CHAPTER THIRTY-TWO

Night of the Missing

Sergeant Walker and Smythe were greeted at the back of the manor by the stable hand; he took their horses to be fed and brushed. The steward seeing them arrive, warned Lord Birkhead, who waited for them in the hall. The visitors took off their large-brimmed hats as they walked through the back door.

The kitchen was a hustle and bustle of activity with three servant girls and a cook busily preparing the lord's supper. Large bubbling pots hung underneath a considerable-sized stone chimney that stretched almost the entire width of the room. Steam and smoke from the fire ascended and then disappeared up the chimney.

The steward took them straight through to the great hall; they walked forward, the echo of their footsteps filled the room. His lordship was sitting by the fire and stood from his chair as they approached.

The visitors walked up, took their hats off and dipped their heads, "My Lord, I am Sergeant Walker, and this is my companion Peter Smyth of the King's Cavaliers."

The lord was a heavyset man. He had a dense but neatly trimmed moustache and brown beard, which covered his chin and gave him a regal appearance. His black floppy felt hat with thick golden, crown-like piping was pulled slightly down over his right eyebrow. A maroon felt, and bear hide doublet with golden trim was puffed at the top of the arms. A thick maroon waistcoat edged with clean white lace circled his neck and wrists. He rested his hand on an antique handcrafted staghorn and wood walking stick that had belonged to his father and his father before him.

The sergeant, still bowing, looked up as the lord sat back down in his chair. He took a step forward to present his parchment of service to the King, "My Lord, we are here on the most urgent business, for we believe there is a Roundhead spy is in your midst. We have been on the trail of one for some days now and have tracked him to your lands."

The steward took the parchment and gave it to the lord. He paused, then looked over the paper, then stood again, "Impossible the people here are simple folk, not spies," he said with a deep baritone voice.

Lord Birkhead looked the men up and down to gauge their station in life. They were dirty, and their clothing was weathered and stained. Their riding boots were worn, wet and muddied.

"My lord, a Roundhead soldier, we were taking him to Pontefract Castle to be questioned, and he, with the help of two others, escaped. We shot and killed one of them, but the other got away. They had parchment papers with the King's seal, forgeries, I expect."

"And how did you track them to this village?" Lord Birkhead asked.

"One of the men that helped him escape, sir, he spoke of Haworth when we were interrogating him," the sergeant lied.

His lordship sat down again; he stroked his beard, sensing the sergeant's urgency, "I see, and this fellow can you describe his appearance?"

"Dark hair, deep-set eyes, heavy brow, he'd have scars around his wrists from the bindings. I would definitely know him if I saw him again."

Lord Birkhead always thought before he spoke, "The best way to see the people of the village and local surrounds is at the manor court tonight. My steward here will escort you as the night watchman's bell tolls eight." He signalled to his steward, who leaned over to listen to his whispered instructions.

The steward straightened, stepped back and bowed.

His Lordship stood, "Now, please be my guests. My steward will take you upstairs where you may rest and then join me for wine from my cellar and supper this evening."

The steward took a step backwards and bowed to the lord as did his guests and then turned to walk toward the door. The steward stopped and opened it waiting for the guests to walk through. He then looked over at the lord, nodded, and closed the door behind him. The sergeant and his companion followed the steward up the dark, shiny, worn wooden stairs to the bedrooms.

Lord Birkhead sat quietly pondering the arrival of his visitors. He knew of the Roundhead in his midst, for there wasn't much that happened between Haworth and York that he didn't know about.

John Hargreaves had told him about the return of Tommy Rushworth from the war and the ailments of the mind that troubled him. He had told him of the battle of Bradford and the Cavaliers that had captured Tommy and the part that both the steward and the reeve had played in his escape.

The Rushworths had been copyholders and now freehold tenants on his lands for as long as he could remember, even before his father, the previous lord of the manor. They worked hard and always paid their rents and taxes, and that is why he, on advice from his previous steward, had allowed them to become freemen.

The lord knew that the steward had left to take up arms against Parliament. He had tried to talk him out of it but knew that he had loyalties to King Charles because of his brother Oliver. His politics were his business, and he had no right to stop him. Now the reeve was another point, and he was driven by revenge for the killing of his brother by Roundhead soldiers.

Still in deep thought, he sauntered to the table that stood against the wall and poured himself a goblet of wine. Sniffing the contents, he then returned to his chair in front of the fire. He took a sip of his wine and then placed the goblet on the small, covered table at his side. He stroked his beard and thought about the pending situation. He knew that Tommy was in no state to go to the manor court, but his father, he looked so much like his father, and he knew he would be there or else receive the fine for not attending.

A few moments later, the steward returned and walked across the floor toward his lordship. He stood waiting for Lord Birkhead's instructions.

The lord leaned forward in his chair, his left hand on his walking stick and beckoned the steward to come closer. He whispered, "Get word to the reeve, tell Rushworth not to go to the manor court." The lord sat back in his chair as the steward bowed and walked back across the stone floor and out the door.

That evening when Sergeant Walker and Smythe entered the hall, the servants had already set the large oak polished table. The white linen tablecloth was spread, and six tallow candles stood like sentinels along the middle of the table. The lord sat himself at the foot of the table with his guests on either side halfway down the table.

The kitchen maids brought out the soup, main dishes, side dishes and pastries, which were all placed on the table all at once. A newly slaughtered lamb hind leg was placed in the middle of the table, and fish and accompaniments were placed on the sides and corners. The servant girls served the guests onion and cream soup before pouring some into the lord's pewter bowl. After the soup, a new tablecloth was placed on the table, and the lord's guests were treated to an assortment of fruit tarts and jellies, all washed down with imported wine from Bordeaux.

The guests were offered a small glass of port as they moved their chairs slightly out from the table. Sergeant Walker took a deep breath and burped, "My lord, my sincerest thanks for the meal; the lamb was divine."

"Yes, my cook's speciality, now what news have you from the east?" Lord Birkhead could sense that his guests were at ease, and now was the best time to get information.

"My Lord, Prince Rupert has taken Brentford, and his highness' forces have had victories at Braddock Down and Nantwich."

Lord Birkhead sat back in his chair. He said nothing; he had loyalties but revealed none.

CHAPTER THIRTY-THREE

ℭ CHAPTER THIRTY-THREE ℬ
With Urgency

There was a knock at the door, and Agnes opened it slightly to see the reeve standing there cowering from the windy cold that swept across the moors. "Reeve, what are ya doing here? Come in outa the cold, please," she ushered him in and quickly closed and latched the door behind her.

"Mrs Rushworth, where's Thomas?" The reeve said with urgency while walking toward the fire and holding his hands out toward the flame.

Agnes looked at him curiously, "Thomas, why he's gone to the Kings Arms with John Hargreaves fer the manor court. Why what's happened? What do ya want him fer?"

"Agnes, the reeve paused, the steward sent me to tell him not to go to the manor court."

"Not to go to the court, why in heavens not, he has to pay the steward's fine, and he'll cop another if he doesn't go. Why the urgency, please tell me," pleaded Agnes.

The reeve looked at Agnes worriedly, "Tis Tommy, two Cavaliers, have arrived in the village they've come looking for him, been staying at the manor."

"Tommy, he's harmless, not right in the head since he got back," claimed Agnes becoming distressed.

The reeve looked down at Tommy, who sat there motionless, "Aye, but I heard the Royalists have been rounding up Roundheads and putting them in Pontefract Castle. They know Tommy; he escaped from them."

"Tommy's finished with fighting. Why can't they just leave us alone now?" Agnes lamented while walking over and placing her hand on her son's shoulder. Agnes covered her eyes with her hand and started to sob as Lucy stopped sewing and stood to put her arm around her, "It's okay, Agnes, there, there no more tears."

The reeve, now warmed by the fire, pleaded with Agnes, "We have ta move Tommy, hide him till they're gone!"

Isabel had been listening and walked forward from the animal enclosure, "Hide him, hide him where? Tis freezin' outside."

Agnes wiped the tears from her eyes and focused seriously on their predicament, "We can take him to the Hargreaves. Margaret will look after him and keep him safe until they leave."

Thomas and John Hargreaves walked into the Kings Arms. It was busy as it usually was on manor court nights. All in the village and surrounds were there to pay their fines and have their disputes heard. Thomas' cow had escaped from its tether. She wandered onto the lord's demesne, so he handed a two-penny payment to the clerk who sat at a small table with his ledger. Thomas took the quill and marked the ledger with a wobbly X beside his name where the clerk had written 'Tomas Risheworthe'.

Thomas walked over to the barkeep and purchased two penny ales, then returned to sit beside John, who had taken a seat at one of the forms near the hearth. John could hear the shouting and commotion downstairs and knew it was the rat baiting going on.

Thomas handed John the leather jack of ale, and he accepted with a smile. He raised his drink, "MAY YA BE IN HEAVEN HALF AN HOUR BEFORE THE DEVIL KNOWS YA DEAD."

Thomas laughed at John, who by this time had already had his share of sneaky ales, "Cheers ta ya," Thomas replied as they both lifted their jacks to their lips.

There was a board beside holding a padlock shaped oil lamp. The open flame danced with the draft. Two men sat in deep concentration playing cards, a small mound of coin sitting in the middle.

Suddenly, one of the men stood and attempted to take his knife from its sheath, "YER A CHEATIN' BASTARD!"

As he stood, he nudged the table, causing the coin to scatter and the pewter mugs to fall, spilling their contents over the board and the dirt floor.

The other man more quietly spoke, drew his knife and pointed at him, "What ya on about, just cause I'm winning yer coin."

The barmaid stood between them and put her hand on his wrist to stop him from taking out his knife fully, "Now, now, you two, we don't want any trouble in here. Take it outside."

The dog, a brown and white cocker spaniel, started to bark. The man smiled and scooped up the coin from the middle of the table. Another two men stood between them and ushered the man, who wasn't a local, an outsider to the door. "Let me be; he's a cheating bastard!" Knowing he was outnumbered and in danger, he stepped through the door and walked away.

The local man picked up the rest of his coin and put the knife back in its sheath before walking to the bar and purchasing three ales, one for himself and one each for the boys that ushered the outsider through the door.

The barmaid bent over and picked up the empty pewter mugs and continued to wipe the spilled ale on the table. She then walked up to the bar and stood there with her palm up. The local man smiled and placed a shilling in her hand.

Just as Thomas and John were going to take another swig of ale, the door opened, and the lord's newly appointed reeve walked in. They knew him well, and his family had lived in Haworth for as long as they could remember.

The reeve walked straight up to Thomas and John and leaned down to whisper, "You two have ta get out of here, there's two soldiers, Cavaliers they're looking for Tommy."

"Lookin' fer Tommy, what fer?" asked John.

The reeve had a serious, worried look on his face, "Don't know, but steward and I believe his lordship wants ya gone from here!"

Hearing this, Thomas was concerned, "Come on, John, let's get out of here quick!"

Both men swilled their jacks and walked toward the door and out into the night. They walked hurriedly and nervously toward home, not saying much but breathing quite heavily from their exertions. They reached the door of the cottage,

Agnes heard them approach and opened the door for them. "THOMAS, John, thank the Lord."

Tommy had already been dressed, and his cloak had been put around his shoulders.

"Isabel, come on, we'll get him to our place," said John as he helped Isabel gently lift Tommy to his feet and guide him outside to the waiting horse and cart.

Isabel helped Tommy sit on the back of the cart and sat beside him, placing her hand on top of his. John climbed up and flipped the reins to move the horse along.

As they set off, the final glow from the sun sank below the horizon as they made their way down Marsh Lane towards home.

Back at the Kings Arms, heads turned, and there was a hush as the steward, and the two strangers entered. Sargent Walker and Smythe looked around slowly and purposefully as the patrons looked them up and down, not used to seeing strangers.

"He's not here," said Sergeant Walker.

Smythe spoke up, "What about downstairs?"

The steward turned to him; "Everybody should be here in this room or downstairs as the manor court is about to begin. Anybody not present will be fined for their absence."

Sergeant Walker turned walked to the clerk's table, "Clerk, is there anybody absent this evening?"

The clerk looked at the steward nervously, not knowing what to say, then down at his ledger, "No, all seem to be present either downstairs at the rat baiting or in here."

The sergeant turned to Smythe, "Check downstairs." He walked up to the clerk, "There was a man here on our arrival yesterday, dark greying hair, medium height, had a worn red sheepskin tunic and a brown jerkin on."

"Oh, that sounds like Thomas Rush...," said the clerk as the steward cut him off.

The steward looked at the clerk sternly, "That is not the man you seek, a poor man, peasant family older in years."

Sergeant Walker looked down at the clerk, "Oh, and where is this man? Why is he not here at the manor court?"

The clerk looked at the steward quizzically, wondering what he had done wrong, then back at the sergeant, "Oh, he, he was in earlier but paid his fine and left with John Hargreaves."

"I see," said the sergeant as Smythe arrived back and shook his head, indicating his disappointment.

Sergeant Walker knowing sensing that the clerk was holding something back, pressed him further, "And this Thomas Rushworth, where does he live?"

The steward, still annoyed with the clerk, looked at him, then turned to the sergeant, "Sir, this man, he is not who you seek, too old to be a threat and definitely not a soldier."

Sergeant Walker turned to the steward, "Ah, but you see, we don't look for him; we look for his son, an escaped Roundhead spy if my suspicions are correct. How do I find this man? Where does he live?"

Sergeant Walker and Smythe looked down at the clerk intimidatingly.

The clerk looked at the steward subserviently, knowing that he had done wrong but even more scared of what the soldiers would do to him if he didn't tell them. "He lives at Hall Green about a mile down Main Street from here."

Sergeant Walker sensed the uneasiness of the steward, put his hand on the hilt of his sword and looked him in the eyes menacingly as a warning to not interfere in the King's affairs. "Now, sir, would you kindly show us the way to Hall Green?"

Smythe also placed his hand on the hilt of his sword and slightly raised it from its sheath threateningly.

The steward looked down at Smythe's sword and then back at the sergeant, fearing the worst was about to happen. He paused, weighing up his options, then replied, "Of course, gentlemen come this way."

The steward stepped toward the door, lifted the latch and opened it for the two men to walk through. He followed then quickly into the chill of the night and closed the door behind him. The three of them walked back down the hill to the manor stable and retrieved their horses. The steward preferred to climb on board an open carriage. He flipped the reins of the horse and trotted out the stable door, the two men on horseback trotting behind him. Down Sun Street to Marsh Lane, then up the hill to the Rushworth hide.

The steward hoped that Thomas had left with Tommy, but he could see candlelight through the shutters and was concerned that they were still at home.

Inside, Thomas could hear the approaching horses, so he stood and tried to peek through the gap between the door and the jamb, but it was too dark, and he couldn't see anything.

Thomas whispered, "Agnes, take John and Robert up into the loft and keep them quiet; Lucy, you go with them. William get yer cloak."

Thomas put his cloak on and opened the door; he was immediately taken aback by the face illuminated by the fire. It was Sergeant Walker. He had taken his plumed hat off, brown hair fell at the sides of his face and curled up on the top of the large white-winged triangular collar that spread on either side of his neck. He had a brown moustache and chin beard, which required trimming, and it was evident that he had not shaved for some days.

He had hold of the hilt of his sword and stared into Thomas' eyes menacingly, then looked beyond to see if there was anybody else in the cottage. Thomas didn't move from the door opening.

William stepped out from the side and stood behind him supportively, "What do you two want?"

The sergeant smiled mischievously, "We are looking for someone. Do you not remember our reasons for being in this God-forsaken place? A younger lad looks a bit like you, Thomas Rushworth, your brother, possibly your son? Now show him to me, and this inconvenience will all go away, and you can get back to doing what it is you do!"

Thomas looked down to see the flintlock pistol that the sergeant held at his side, "There's nobody here except me brother and I."

The steward appeared behind him and stepped forward, "Best you let them in Thomas," he said in a low, discouraged tone.

Thomas stared into the sergeant's eyes, then stepped aside slowly and obstinately. William followed suit.

The sergeant, his knife and pistol both drawn, walked into the cottage and his companion and the steward followed. William turned and walked to the bottom of the ladder leading up into the loft.

The sergeant lifted his flintlock, cocked it and aimed it at William; his companion raised his toward the animal enclosure as he crept along the wall, pistol held aloft. As he reached the opening, he peeked around just as the cow lifted its tail and released a hot steamy addition to the growing pile below its hindquarters. He looked again, shook his head at the sergeant, looked at William, then up into the darkness of the loft.

Sergeant Walker raised his flintlock at Thomas, who raised his hands submissively.

The sergeant walked slowly toward Thomas and leaned forward to whisper while holding his flintlock pointed at his stomach, "Who's upstairs?"

Thomas stuttered feeling the pressure of the tip of the barrel, "Children, that's orl, just women and children they're scared."

He looked up at the loft, "Whoever is up there, please come down, and nobody will be hurt. It is not you we seek. If you do not, this man will pay for your stubbornness."

"Please, sir, these are poor, humble people; you do yourself a disservice with your threats, children come down, please," the steward pleaded.

The steward sensing the desperation in the sergeant's voice, walked toward the stairs and looked at William, then tilted his head to call up to the loft. "Please come down, children, do not fear; it is I the steward."

William looked up and could immediately see the back of Lucy's kirtle as she stepped backwards down the ladder, followed by his two sons and Agnes.

As Lucy reached the bottom of the ladder, she helped the children down and stood protectively in front of them, gently holding them behind her. William took a step and stood beside her putting his arm around her waist protectively.

When Agnes got to the bottom of the ladder, she turned to see the sergeant with his flintlock held at her husband's stomach. "Steward ya keepin' the best of company these days," she exclaimed sarcastically.

Thomas looked at her, "BE QUIET WOMAN!" He growled.

Smythe walked toward the ladder, his flintlock pointing to the loft. William and Lucy moved in tandem, their children behind them, backwards toward the wall.

"Please, Sergeant is this necessary?" asked the steward apprehensively.

"There's nobody else up there; this is it, women and children," claimed Agnes defiantly. "Tell me, do the King's men have nothing better ta do than harass innocent people? The stories must be true!"

Annoyed, Thomas looked at his wife but said nothing. Agnes could feel his ire, but his anger soon turned to worry as Smythe climbed the ladder and peeked over the top. He climbed back down and glanced at William, then stared at Lucy for far longer than was polite. William stepped in front of her, their backs to the wall, their children cowering behind them.

"Mummy, John whispered.

"Shoosh, my love," whispered Lucy as she reached behind her to comfort both of her boys.

Thomas was still uneasy. His face went white as the sergeant moved his flintlock from his stomach to the side of his head, "Have you ever seen what a musket ball can do to a man?"

"NOOOO, THOMAS! CAN YOU NOT DO SOMETHING STEWARD?" Agnes yelled.

The sergeant looked at the steward, "Keep her quiet, she's making me nervous, and I'd hate to be suddenly startled while holding this pistol to his head."

Thomas tried to move his head from the tip of the barrel, but the sergeant moved it closer to his temple, cocked it, then whispered, "Where is he?"

"Where's who?" whispered Thomas stubbornly.

"LOOK, THIS CAN BE EASY OR HARD FOR YOU, YOUR CHOICE, SIT HIM DOWN!" Smythe brought one of the footstools toward Thomas. "SIT DOWN!"

The sergeant removed the tip of his pistol barrel from Thomas' temple and took a step backwards, "TIE THEIR HANDS!"

Smythe gestured with his pistol for William to be seated at the table. Lucy tried to cling to him, "WILLIAM...."

He gently touched her on the arm and whispered, "it's all right, wife stay here with the children; all will be fine," he smiled to set her at ease.

William sat down at the table, and Smythe bound his wrists to the table leg.

"This is not necessary. Please release them; they have done nothing," said the steward empathetically.

Sergeant Walker looked at the steward menacingly, took a step, then leaned over to whisper in his ear, "I think it is time for you to depart, my friend and leave the rest of this to the King's men." The sergeant lifted his sword.

The steward looked at Thomas, then at William, a look of apology in his eyes then walked toward the door, took one more look behind, and disappeared into the night.

Sergeant Walker looked down at Thomas and walked behind him, "Where is he?"

Thomas turned his head to try to look at the sergeant but said nothing.

The sergeant looked over at Lucy and smiled, he stroked his beard patiently and spoke in a quiet, eerie tone, "Now, one of you is going to talk. If it's not going to be him, then it will be her."

Smythe started walking over to Lucy as William tried to stand before being pushed back down on the stool by the sergeant,

"LEAVE HER BE. I'LL TELL YOU WHAT YOU WANT TO KNOW!" Called out Thomas worriedly.

The sergeant sheathed his sword, continued to walk toward Lucy and took out his knife.

"LEAVE HER!" Thomas screamed, "Boys go to the loft!" Robert and John were hesitant, not wanting to leave their mother.

Lucy turned to the boys, "Go on do what yer uncle told ya!"

The boys scrambled up the ladder but watched from the loft, scared out of their wits.

Smythe stood behind Lucy, then reached across her chest and held his knife in front of her throat, "Mmmm, such a pretty young thing." He looked at William, "you are a lucky man, Mm… Mm… Mm." He put his face close to her and smelt her hair.

Lucy was breathing heavily; she lifted her chin then moved his hand away from her breast, being careful not to move her neck into the blade.

"Right, where is he? I'd hate for my companion here to slip with his blade across this pretty lady's throat; it would be such a shame, wouldn't it, Smythe?"

"Right, you are Sergeant Walker, but I could think of other ways to get the information we need." He smiled and brought his face closer to hers.

"Ah yes, then there's that," said the sergeant mischievously. "How long has it been since you've had the company of a good woman Smythe?"

Thomas stood quickly, "OKAY, OKAY, HE'S AT A COTTAGE ON MOORHOUSE LANE, NOW LEAVE HER BE!"

The sergeant raised his flintlock and pointed it at Thomas, "There, there, no need to get excited, SIT DOWN!"

Smythe took the knife from Lucy's throat and walked slowly from behind her being sure to linger and look down her top as he did, "Now that wasn't so hard, was it," he drawled.

William frowned and barred his teeth, "YOU SON OF BITCH, IF I WASN'T TIED UP…?!"

"Now, now, there's no need for that," Smythe walked over to William and punched him in the face.

Lucy screamed, "WILLIAM! LEAVE HIM BEEEE!"

William's head was jolted back by the force of his punch, but he shook it off as his cheekbone started to swell and discolour.

"That's enough, Smythe!" Sergeant Walker pointed his sword at Thomas, "You will come with me while my companion stays here and keeps an eye on the pretty lady," then he looked at William and Agnes. "If I don't return with the prisoner within half of one hour, take them outside and kill them all as traitors to the King."

"NOO, PLEASE!" Lucy ran to William placing her arms around his neck.

Smythe pulled Lucy away, "Come on now, why don't you have a seat at the other side of the table, you too, mother, so that I can keep an eye on the three of you."

Agnes and Lucy walked to the table and sat beside each other as Smythe pulled up a chair near the hearth, his flintlock resting on his knee pointing at them.

Sergeant Walker lifted Thomas under the arm, his hands still tied, "Come on you, show me where this traitor is! Moorhouse Lane, you say, lead the way and believe me, try anything, and you'll regret it."

Smythe took a tar-covered branch leaning against the wall near the hearth and dipped it into the fire to ignite it. He handed it to the sergeant, who pushed Thomas through the door and out into the darkness. He followed cocking his flintlock and holding it at waist height and the torch high, which cast a shadow over the whiteness.

Sergeant Walker turned back and looked at his companion, "Remember, if I'm not back in half of one hour, do what you want with the woman and kill the rest! DON'T... FALL... ASLEEP!"

Lucy was frightened. She looked at William, who looked down at the tabletop, then up into Lucy's eyes despairingly, "I'm sorry, Lucy," he whispered, feeling guilty not being able to do more.

"Tis not yer fault son, don't blame yerself," whispered Agnes.

"HEY YOU, NO TALKING!" Smythe pointed his flintlock higher at them.

෬ CHAPTER THIRTY-FOUR ෭
Cavalier's Threat

The steward closed the door behind him as he disappeared into the night; he looked up at the moon that was high and white with mysterious whispers of cloud veiling its face. He used the illuminating light to drive the carriage carefully and hesitantly down the hill to the road.

Once there, he looked left and right, then looked up at the veiled face once more. He took a breath in and blew out, trying to release the pent-up stress and worries as the vapour travelled away with the icy breeze. "*What to do, what to do,*" the steward thought to himself.

He looked upward through the darkness toward the manor, then back toward Marsh Lane and the Hargreaves cottage. He decided to ride back to the manor and speak to Lord Birkhead.

Worriedly, his lordship looked through the lace of the curtain and watched him drive the carriage down the torch-lit driveway and then lost sight of him as he went around to the back of the manor. He sat in his chair by the hearth; *what would his father do?* He thought to himself. Lord Birkhead was more loyal to his freeholder tenants, especially as labour was in such short supply due to the Black Death. The Rushworths were good honest people, always paid their rent and were well respected in the village, and he did not want to lose them.

A few moments later, the large oak door opened, and the steward walked in. He walked over the stone floor toward the lord. He bowed, "Tis the Cavaliers, My Lord, they have accosted the Rushworth family and now approach the Hargreaves cottage where they hid Tommy. All is lost for the poor lad, for they will surely take him away to God knows where."

"I know where they will take him," Lord Birkhead turned and looked into the flame and stroked his beard. "Time is of the essence; you must make haste and go to St Michael's, wake up the vicar and give him this sealed parchment.... Quickly man and go the back way down Dimples Lane, don't let anybody see you!"

"Yes, My Lord," the steward bowed and walked quickly across the stone floor, his head held high and as righteously as he could, out through the large oak door.

The lord took his seat and once again stared into the flames thinking about the Rushworth lad. *It wasn't right what the Roundheads did taking him away; there was no honour in what they did. It seems all honour is lost in this war.*

The steward walked hurriedly toward the door and went through it to the back of the manor and into the kitchen. He screamed at the stable hand, "QUICKLY BOY, MAKE HASTE, WE HAVE AN ERRAND TO RUN FOR HIS LORDSHIP!"

The stable hand was sleeping fully dressed and quickly pulled on his woollen cloak while grabbing the fowl musket that he slept with, used to ward off possible horse thieves through the night. He donned his brown woollen hat and followed the steward out into the frosty darkness, startled by the first freezing breath that he took.

They walked quickly to the stables, and the steward jumped up onto the carriage urgently. The stable hand climbed aboard; the horse was frightened from his slumber and reared up slightly as he was walked out of the stable.

Just as they rode down the driveway, a cart came through the open gate. John Hargreaves reined in the horse and smiled, "Going somewhere?"

Thomas ambled ahead of the sergeant, "Why is he so important ta you? He's just a lad."

"Keep walking," the sergeant pushed Thomas in the middle of the back. "Orders, that's all, just orders we have to round up any traitors to the King, and we know about your boy's loyalty to the traitor Fairfax."

Thomas tried to defend his son, "But he's just a lad, he was absconded into the army, had no choice, Roundheads kidnapped him with the blade of a knife. Forced him to go the bastards!"

"Makes no difference to me. He was in the Roundhead army and now will pay his dues at Pontefract Castle prison with the other traitors to his majesty."

Thomas pleaded, "Please, sir, he's not the same man since he got back, not right in the head."

"Just keep walking," the sergeant pushed Thomas in the middle of the back roughly.

Thomas looked up and started to get more nervous as they continued down Marsh Lane and got closer to Moorhouse Lane and the Hargreaves cottage. He could see the light emanating through the shutters across the hide and tried to think of something he could do. Still, he knew the sergeant had his flintlock aimed at his back, and resistance was futile.

The sergeant grabbed Thomas on the shoulder, "Right, we must be close, no tricks or else you'll feel the lead going through your gut, now where is it?"

Thomas remained quiet for as long as he could until the sergeant pushed his flintlock hard into his back, "Erggh... okay, okay... it's over there across the hide, that cottage... there."

Sergeant Walker followed Thomas and pulled back the hammer on his flintlock, "Now, any tricks and you'll be the first to cop it, just remember what will happen to your family if I am not back in half an hour."

They continued to walk down Moorhouse Lane, Thomas slowing his pace as they got closer to the cottage.

The sergeant's torch went out just as they arrived at the hedge that separated the cottage from the hide, and he whispered, "Remember no tricks."

The sergeant pushed Thomas once again, walked up to the door behind him and spoke quietly, "Call out to them!"

"JOHN HARGREAVES, ARE YOU IN THERE? IT IS I, THOMAS!"

The sergeant whispered to him, "Tell them to open up or else," he pushed the barrel of his flintlock into the small of Thomas' back.

"HARGREAVES, WILL YA NOT OPEN YER DOOR, TIS FREEZING OUT HERE!"

Suddenly, the sergeant grabbed the back of his cloak and pushed Thomas toward the door and impatiently thumped on it, "OPEN UP IN THE NAME OF THE KING, OR ELSE THIS MAN WILL DIE!" He called out threateningly.

The door opened slowly with a creak as Mrs Hargreaves peeked out, trying to adjust her eyes to the darkness, "Who's there?" She asked, terrified by the situation.

The sergeant pushed Thomas forward through the door, and he followed, holding his flintlock up nervously, "MOVE OUT OF THE WAY!"

Mrs Hargreaves took a backward step towards the hearth fearfully. She quickly glanced at John as he appeared from behind the door with a 'shiv', held ready to strike. Sergeant Walker noticing her glance, quickly turned Thomas toward him to take the strike. "GO ON, DO IT!... I'LL PUT AN END TO HIM AS QUICK AS YOU LIKE, THEN YOU!"

"FUCK YOU!" John dropped the knife, raised his hands, and took two steps backwards, looking at Thomas disappointedly.

The sergeant pushed Thomas inside, and he stumbled. He turned his flintlock to John Hargreaves, "YOU, WHERE IS HE, QUICKLY TELL ME FOR MY PATIENCE IS STARTING TO RUN THIN!" The sergeant looked one way, then the other nervously.

Mrs Hargreaves took another step backwards, "Please, there is nobody else here but us."

The sergeant walked around the one-room cottage and stepped up the ladder to the loft, all the while pointing his flintlock at Thomas and John, who were standing behind him. He stepped back down, looked in the animal quarters and poked at the mound of straw with the pitchfork.

Mrs Hargreaves looked at Thomas sadly, then back at the sergeant and back at Thomas, "Tis true we are here alone." She whispered.

Margaret paused and looked melancholy. She walked over to Thomas and embraced him; she pulled his head down and whispered in his ear, "Thomas, I'm sa sorry, but he's gone, weathered away to nothing, died of melancholy and took his own life. I found him hanging out the back," tears started to flood her eyes.

Thomas slowly lowered his gaze, his hands still tied behind his back; he dropped to his knees, tears started to flood his lower eyelids, "MY SON!"

"DO YOU TAKE ME FOR A FOOL?" the sergeant placed the barrel of his flintlock to his temple.

Mrs Hargreaves wiped her eyes and took a step forward sadly, "PLEASE sir, tis true, he was never the same since he returned, wouldn't eat or drink, he died on the battlefield, and his true self never returned. The curate collected his body this afternoon and took him to the church for a Christian burial; you can speak to the vicar himself."

He looked at Mrs Hargreaves suspiciously, then lowered his weapon to his side, "IF I FIND OUT YOU ARE LYING, I WILL BE BACK, AND THE LOT OF YOU WILL HANG!"

"RIGHT, YOU, OUTSIDE!" The sergeant turned to Thomas, lifted him from his knees and pushed him toward the door.

Thomas, tears in his eyes, tried to wipe them with his shoulder and stepped outside. The sergeant stopped and turned and looked at Mrs Hargreaves suspiciously.

Mrs Hargreaves walked towards the door and called out, "MY CONDOLENCES FOR YOUR LOSS THOMAS, I'M SO SORRY!" She followed them for a while, then stopped, walked back to the cottage solemnly and closed the door behind her

Outside, Sergeant Walker pushed Thomas in the back through the gate in the dry-stone wall and up Moorhouse Lane back towards the Rushworth's cottage. Once there, he pushed Thomas toward the cottage door which had been opened by the sergeant's companion after hearing them approach. "Well, was he there?"

Sergeant Walker pushed Thomas toward the door, "NO TOLD ME HE NECKED HIMSELF THIS AFTERNOON, but I'm not convinced, probably lying through their teeth."

Agnes heard the sergeant's claim and refused to believe it until Thomas walked through the door. Agnes could see the dire sadness in Thomas' eyes and started to weep herself, "NO MY BOY!"

Lucy quickly embraced Agnes, and William stood from his chair and looked at Thomas and could tell his heart was broken. Thomas slowly walked over to his chair and placed his face in his bound hands.

"What now, sergeant?" Asked Smythe.

"Let's go; we'll attend tomorrow morning's burial and ensure what they say is true. If not, they will all hang as traitors; we'll seek the lord's favour and the vicars." The sergeant and his companion jumped back on their horses and rode off toward the manor.

Inside, Agnes was beside herself with sadness and wept continually into a linen cloth while Thomas, his face still in his hands, tried hard to control his emotions. William stood and walked over to him and placed his hand on his shoulder, not quite knowing what to do or say. He stood there looking at Lucy, who was busy consoling Agnes and shook his head in disbelief, totally succumbed with grief.

Thomas raised his head skyward and bellowed; all in the village and surrounds heard it "TOMMYYYYYY... WHYYYYYY?"

Sergeant Walker and Smythe, on their way to the manor, heard it also. It sent cold shivers down their back, and Smythe shrugged his shoulders, trembling with foreboding.

Isabel was discreetly walking back to the cottage and halfway home, heard Thomas' wail and started to run. She entered and, seeing his dismay screamed, "NOOOO!" She dropped to the straw-covered floor and began to weep and screamed into the night, "TOMMYYYY!"

The following day, the sergeant and Smythe dressed and went downstairs to breakfast with the lord. On the table sat meat, fish and bread. The meat, poultry and fish were cooked with apples and strawberries, and ale was in abundance.

The lord dropped a chicken bone on the floor, "My steward tells me that the man you seek is dead, took his own life."

Sergeant Walker spat a fish bone on the floor, "I'm not convinced, the family, they could be lying."

Lord Birkhead looked at the sergeant, trying to hide his distaste for the man, "Ohh? My steward tells me that he suffered terribly from melancholy and was never the same on returning from the war; it happens." His lordship grumbled dryly with no sympathy in his voice.

Sergeant Walker leaned forward, putting his elbows on the table. "That may be true, Your Grace, but Smythe and I will visit the church, speak to the vicar, and attend the burial tomorrow morning to ensure what has been said about his demise is the truth."

Lord Birkhead wiped the chicken grease from the corners of his mouth and paused. "I must warn you, I would be careful around here, sergeant, for the people, do not take kindly to strangers interfering in matters of the church. Especially when it involves one of their own."

Sergeant Walker looked at Smythe then back at his lordship. "My Lord, we are under orders to arrest and return the Roundhead to prison, and we will do so unless I see his dead body in a grave. If not, then we will continue to search for the traitor, but before we do, those that have taken part in the charade will hang for treason!"

"Sergeant, there will be no hanging in my jurisdiction, especially if no magistrate is available to try the subjects. The people you speak of are under my protection, and no civilians will be harmed, do you understand? Very well then, I must retire, so I bid you good night, and I wish you safest of travels in the morning," the lord went to stand.

The servant who was standing nearby walked quickly to pull out his chair for him. The lord turned and walked across the stone floor and through the oak door which led to the parlour.

Sergeant Walker watched him walk away from the table, "Somethings not quite right about our host," he whispered.

Smythe nodded his head in agreement, "Wouldn't trust him as far as I could throw him."

The next morning after breakfast, the two men returned to their rooms and packed their saddle packs before bidding farewell. The stable hand had readied their horses and held them by the halter for them to mount. With a slight heel dig into the horse's rib cage, they trotted off in the direction of the church. Arriving outside St Michael and All Angels, they hitched their horses up beside the pillory. They walked up the path to the graveyard at the back.

It was a chilly morning, and snow had fallen through the night and dusted the tombstones with a sprinkling of powder. A lone oak tree, its long bare branches dangling over the graves protectively, hid them from inquisitive eyes. The sergeant and his companion could see a small group of people standing in front of the vicar outside the consecrated church grounds.

"What now?" Smythe asked.

"We wait. When it's over, we'll go over and make sure it's him; if not, then we keep looking." Sergeant Walker continued peeping from behind the tree. He could see the Rushworth family, Thomas and his wife, who was sobbing along with the other pretty lass who was in the cottage that night. He could see the open coffin sitting on two stools facing east-west and many of the men that he recognised from the manor court.

The vicar continued,

"The Lord is my shepherd;
I shall not want. He maketh me to lie down
in green pastures: he leadeth me beside the still
waters. He restoreth my soul: he leadeth
me in the paths of righteousness for
his name's sake. Yea, though I walk
through the valley of the shadow of death,
I will fear no evil: for thou art with me;
thy rod and thy staff they comfort me.
Thou preparest a table before me in the

presence of mine enemies: thou anointest
my head with oil; my cup runneth over.
Surely goodness and mercy shall follow
me all the days of my life: and I will dwell
in the house of the Lord forever, Amen."

The vicar had agreed to the service, but only on the non-consecrated ground at the back of the church. He nodded at Thomas, who then stepped forward, holding his woollen hat in his hands and looked down at Tommy, who had been wrapped tightly in a burial sheet.

Thomas began slowly, "Tommy was a family man who was always there when you needed him. As Tommy grew from a boy into a man, I could see the man that he would become – strong and steadfast as the oak tree. Tommy was loved by his mates and family, and it's a testament to him how many of you are here today to farewell our boy. Not only was he a loving son and nephew, but he was also a kind and giving mate to all in the village. He was a lad who people like to be around. To have lost Tommy in this way is heartbreaking – and tis not right that a father should outlive his son. I know in me heart that he would not want us to grieve fer too long. My lad would want us all to remember the good times. Goodbye, my son. You will live in our hearts forever."

William put his arm around Isabel, who was distraught and continued to weep.

Agnes let out a horrific scream and continued to sob. Lucy held Agnes and tried to comfort her; she shed a tear that slowly ran down her cheek.

The vicar made the sign of the cross as the burial guild lifted Tommy's wrapped body from the coffin and placed it into the pre-dug hole. The sergeant and Smythe started to walk toward the grave as the crowd began to disperse.

Thomas noticed them and stopped, "Go on, Agnes, you go home with Isabel, Lucy and William; I'll catch up in a minute." Thomas watched as the two Cavaliers walked over toward the grave.

Thomas cut them off and stood there defiantly with a furious look on his face, "WILL YA NOT LEAVE US IN PEACE!"

Thomas spat at their feet and looked at them with disgust, "I blame you for this, YOU!"

Smythe walked past Thomas just as the man from the burial guild shovelled the first load of soil into the grave. He walked up and looked in; the body had been wrapped in a winding sheet, but he noticed Tommy's square-toed boots and his orange sash had been placed atop his body.

The grave digger threw another shovel in the grave, "Save you from a haunting if he should look at yer."

He looked up at the grave digger suspiciously, then back down at the body. He turned and walked back to the sergeant, "It's him alright."

"One less Roundhead to worry about. Well then, seems like our work here is done; let's get the horses and be out of this Godforsaken place." The two soldiers walked back down the path and climbed on their horses, satisfied. They trotted off along Church Street then south on Main Street. When they got to Brow Top Road, they started to gallop towards Bradford.

CHAPTER THIRTY-FIVE

Danger Past

The reeve who was peering from behind the church door watched the two Cavaliers ride down Main Street and out of sight. He quickly went outside and went the opposite way toward the manor. Walking down the drive, he looked up and noticed the lace curtains move from behind the mullioned window. He continued around the back of the manor and through the back door into the kitchen. The steward was sitting down at the kitchen table, waiting for him. He walked past the scullery maid, who was busily scrubbing pots and leaned down to whisper in his ear. The steward calmly stood and walked through the great oak door into the main hall, then past the fire and then up to the door that led to the parlour. He knocked on the door thrice.

As he walked through the door, he was met with the radiant warmth from the fire that was ablaze in the large stone chimney. A chandelier holding four bright candles hung from the heavy oak beam on the ceiling. A painting of the former Lord Birkhead sat in an elaborately carved golden frame hung in the middle of the wall above a sideboard cupboard and bookcase. His lordship stood at the side of a large oak table that ran almost the length of the room. It had been covered with a colourful, decorative, locally weaved tablecloth. A pewter candlestick holding a lit candle sat in the middle of the table along with three leather-bound books.

Not used to seeing a stranger in the lord's parlour, the steward looked at Tommy, who was sitting in a high-backed chair at the end of the table, breaking bread and smearing it with strawberry preserve. He looked up at the steward but didn't cease to eat his fill.

The steward walked over to Lord Birkhead and whispered, "They have departed my lord, last seen heading south-east toward Bradford."

"Well then," Lord Birkhead turned toward Tommy, "Seems our little ruse worked, my boy."

Tommy, still shovelling bread and jam into his mouth, spoke while chewing the gluggy morsel far too big for his mouth, "Can I go on home now?"

"Of course, you can, my boy. The steward will see you out, and please take the jar of preserve to share with your family."

"I dunno how I'm going to repay you, Your Grace," Tommy stood and picked up the clay jar of preserve before bowing and walking through the door.

The steward bowed then followed Tommy through the door, lifting the latch and closing it behind him.

Tommy was in awe of the great hall. He stopped and looked up into the roof trusses.

The steward coughed, bringing Tommy back from his wonderment, then walked past him to open the door to the kitchen for him to walk through. "Go quickly to thy mother, for her heart is surely broken, and thy father is probably by now, residing at the bottom of an ale barrel."

Tommy bade farewell to the steward and quickly walked around the manor and down the drive. He thought how strange it was to be hidden by his lordship in the small hidden room in his parlour. A secret room left over from the days of Recusant Catholics and the lord's father who remained loyal to the Catholic Church. It was even more strange to know that the men that were looking for him were asleep in the rooms upstairs or filling their faces in the great hall close by. He could hear them talking through the wall if he put his ear up to the back of the hinged bookcase.

It was the new steward that had helped him recover from his melancholia. There in the parlour when the men were out. By the fire, he had managed to help him come to terms with the war and the terrifying experiences of it. He had helped him confront the fears and nightmares and delivered a spark of happiness telling yarns about his future with Isabel and wee William. It was these thoughts that brought him out, and now he longed to see his family again.

Tommy walked south down Sun Street toward the hide; he wanted to run and longed to feel rational and free back with his family. For the first time in a long while, Tommy smiled. He walked through the gate and up the hill toward the hide. The snow was starting to melt, and it was wet underfoot as he called out for anybody to hear him.

"Mother, Da, William, tis me!"

"The door opened as he approached, MOTHER!"

It was said that spectral figures were often visitors to the world of the living and a variety of beliefs surrounded the process of grieving for a loved one. Agnes stood there in the doorway, took one look at Tommy and went faint. William quickly caught her before she fell to the ground and laid her down gently, "TOMMY, WHY DO YOU HAUNT US SO?"

"No, Grandpa and His Grace planned it all; it was a sham. They hid me away in the manor!" Tommy said excitedly.

William started to gently tap Agnes on the cheek. Shocked, William started to look worried and stuttered, "B...b... but I saw you in the coffin!"

"No William tis me, I ain't dead, and I'm no ghost come to haunt you. It wasn't me in the grave; it was the reeve. They just put my boots on him."

Agnes started to come around, so William picked her up carefully and carried her, placing her down gently on the high-backed chair near the fire. "There, Agnes, you'll be right; I'll get thee some ale."

Tommy walked into the cottage and walked over and knelt in front of her putting his hand on her knee, "Mother, you orl right, tis me fear not."

Agnes slowly opened her eyes and tried to focus on Tommy's face, "TOMMY, YOU'RE NOT DEAD!" She touched him on the face to make sure he wasn't an apparition.

"No, Ma, it was all a ruse to get the Cavaliers to leave the village, Grandpa and Lord Birkhead and the steward planned it all, even hid me in the manor right under their noses."

Agnes took the jack of ale from William, who still wasn't convinced and touched Tommy on the shoulder to see if he was real. She took a sip, took a breath then skulled the rest.

Agnes put her arms around Tommy and squeezed so tightly that he thought that she would never let go, "TOMMY YOUR FATHER AND ISABEL, YOU NEED TO GO TO THEM QUICKLY!"

"Where is he?"

"I think you know the answer to that," exclaimed William.

Isabel had taken wee William to lay fresh flowers on the grave.

Tommy put his arms around his mother and returned her affection, gently kissing her on the cheek before walking toward the door, "COME, WILLIAM, WE MUST HURRY!"

The two men walked down the hill and quickly up Sun Street toward the village. They both walked up the stone path toward the cemetery and stood for a minute behind the Oaktree, watching Isabel lay flowers on the top of the dirt mound.

"I better take care of this before another one faints and ends up on the ground." William stepped out from behind the tree and started walking toward Isabel, who held her hand to her face and wept.

Wee Will saw his uncle approach and tugged on his mother's hand, then pointed.

Isabel wiped the tears from her eyes and waited motionless for William to reach them, "William come ta visit his grave as well," she said gloomily.

William put his hand on her arm, "Isabel, I want you to be strong now for I have something to say to you," William paused, "Well.... It's Tommy; he's not dead."

William turned to look at the oak tree as Tommy stepped out from behind it and smiled.

Isabel looked in disbelief, dropped wee William's hand, then started running toward Tommy. When she got closer, Tommy opened his arms and allowed her to embrace him. Seeing this wee Will ran over to his father awkwardly and grabbed his leg.

Once they had finished embracing, Isabel looked up at him, astonished, "But Tommy how, what...?"

"Tis a long story, and I will tell it, but now I must find me Da, for he does not know the truth. No more tears," Tommy gently wiped the remaining tears from Isabel's face.

Tommy picked up wee Will and hugged him before putting him back down, "Now...you take Will home, I'll find me Da, and we will see you at home shortly."

A few moments later, the latch on the door lifted, and Lucy walked in with the two boys. Agnes had been crying. "Lucy, boys, you must come and sit; I have something to tell ya."

Lucy sat at the form in front of the fire as the boys stood beside her. "What is it, Agnes? Is there more bad news?"

Agnes smiled, "I don't know how to tell you, but Tommy is alive and well."

Lucy frowned with confusion, "What do you mean he's alive and well we buried him this morning!"

"It wasn't him we buried this morning; it was the reeve!" Claimed Agnes.

Lucy looked to the heavens in relief, "CHRIST OUR LORD!"

Agnes stood excitedly thinking about how Thomas would react, "Tommy and William have gone to the Kings Arms. His father doesn't know and will be plying himself full of drink."

William opened the door to the alehouse, and Tommy walked in slowly. All who had been to the funeral were there in various forms of drunkenness. His father was standing in front of the fire, contemplating what had happened. Others had noticed Tommy and stopped talking while the others that they had been talking to turned their head to see what was distracting them.

The room went horribly quiet. Tommy walked past John Hargreaves, who was standing at the bar smiling. Thomas took a swig of his ale then realised that everybody in the alehouse was quiet and staring at him. He looked around quizzically and could sense that someone was standing behind him. He turned and, in disbelief, stood there speechless, looking at Tommy.

John Hargreaves, who had plotted with the lord had convinced them to bury the former reeve's body, stood there beside Thomas and Tommy, smiling mischievously.

"WELL, ARE YOU TWO GONNA STAND THERE GAWKING AT EACH OTHER OR ARE YOU GOING TO SAY SOMETHING?" John called out.

Thomas swallowed the lump in his throat, lifted his arms and grabbed Tommy pulling him toward him. He looked him in the eyes and embraced him tightly, and whispered, "MY SON!"

"Da, yer squashing me!" Tommy pushed away stubbornly, not wanting to show his affections to his father in public.

John Hargreaves walked over and placed his big arms around them both, and the patrons in the alehouse laughed, cheered and celebrated, patting them all on the back.

Thomas looked at John, "John Hargreaves, I get the feeling that you know more about this than yer letting on."

"Aye, Thomas, but that's another story!" John laughed loudly, as did all in the alehouse who were privy to his hoax.

Shawline Publishing Group Pty Ltd

www.shawlinepublishing.com.au

SHAWLINE
PUBLISHING
GROUP

CPSIA information can be obtained
at www.ICGtesting.com
Printed in the USA
BVHW042129100422
633918BV00009B/261

9 781922 701510